HUMAN TIME BOMB!

Lance felt the side of his neck where he had thought he sensed an insect bite. There was nothing he could detect externally, but he still felt uneasy. After all, Hartz and his observant team had missed the implanted device that had killed the hypnotized assassin. Was Lance now carrying around inside him a miniscule bomb that could terminate his life at any second? On the decision of someone he did not know?

Ace Books by Wynne Whiteford

THOR'S HAMMER
BREATHING SPACE ONLY
SAPPHIRE ROAD
THE HYADES CONTACT
LAKE OF THE SUN
THE SPECIALIST

THE
SPECIALIST

WYNNE WHITEFORD

ACE BOOKS, NEW YORK

This book is an Ace original edition,
and has never been previously published.

THE SPECIALIST

An Ace Book / published by arrangement with
the author

PRINTING HISTORY
Ace edition / June 1990

ISBN: 0-441-77789-9

Ace Books are published by The Berkley Publishing Group,
200 Madison Avenue, New York, New York 10016.
The name ''ACE'' and the ''A'' logo
are trademarks belonging to Charter Communications, Inc.

PRINTED IN THE UNITED STATES OF AMERICA

10 9 8 7 6 5 4 3 2 1

To Paul Collins

—*friend and indefatigable publisher of science fiction in Australia during the lean years*

Some of the characters in this novel have appeared in a short story of mine in the anthology *Distant Worlds*, published in 1981 by Cory & Collins, Melbourne, Australia, later reprinted in German and Japanese.

W.W.

chapter
1

LANCE GARRITH OF Solar News found it hard to pinpoint the exact moment when the peaks of Hawaii appeared ahead. He was flying in high from the southwest through a featureless abyss of blue, the ocean only slightly darker than the cloudless sky. The lack of detailed sensory input had an almost hypnotic effect, and after glancing at his instruments he looked up to find he had lost the line of the horizon. When he located it again, he was aware of geometric shapes along the skyline, the vast blunt triangles of the towering volcanoes, only a faintly deeper hue than the background air.

"Stan," he called to his cameraman, who had dozed while checking his equipment in the rear cabin. "We're in sight of it!"

Switching to manual, he eased the nose of the lime-green aircraft down. The change in the whine of the twin hydrogen jets brought Stan Reed to his feet. Stretching like a wakening cat, he moved forward and slid into the copilot's seat.

"How far, mate?" His words were blurred by a yawn.

"Two hundred klicks." Lance pointed. "Those are the main cones of the Big Island dead ahead. Mauna Loa on the right, then Mauna Kea."

Stan leaned forward as if to minimize the distance between his eyes and the far-off mountains. "Gotta be less than two hundred, or we wouldn't see them yet, Len." He had known Len Garrith from boyhood, before he had changed his name to Lance to suit his expanding public image.

Lance shook his head emphatically. "Two hundred kilometers. You're looking through the clearest air in the world, over the middle of the biggest ocean. No industrial haze or turbulence from dense population centers—that's why they built their observatories up there."

Stan yawned, running his fingers through his close-cropped, sandy hair. "That where we're going? Top of Mauna Kea?"

"That's it. Means the White Mountain. Believe it or not, there's snow there some of the time."

"Snow in the tropics? What a hell of a place to work."

"Tynan sounded as if he liked it."

"He's the guy who first found the thing we're covering, isn't he? Is he important?"

"He will be, after our segment hits the air."

Stan leaned back. "Gives us a lot of power, this job, doesn't it?"

Lance grunted, glancing at his altimeter. "Don't let it get out of perspective, sport. Sure, Specialists' Report has been near the top of the world ratings for nine or ten weeks. But remember, this is 2095, with things getting more and more unstable every year. We only stay on top while we work at it in a non-stop frenzy."

The cameraman stretched his arms, grinning. "As long as your charisma and my pictures keep grabbing people, we'll be all right. It'll be a long time before you run out of specialists to interview. Come to think of it, you're about the only guy I know who's *not* a specialist."

Lance didn't reply for a few seconds, and Stan knew him well enough not to interrupt his thoughts. "You know, Stan, I think the world's got too many specialists. Experts in their own compartments, without much grasp of the overall picture. It's as if the human race is evolving into a whole menagerie of sub-species."

"Anyway, we're on a winning streak."

"More to it than that—we're part of a big team, remember?"

After a quick scan of his instruments, Lance pulled a tiny microphone across in front of his mouth, punching an area code and a further string of numbers on a visiphone keyboard at his side. A small hooded screen, popping up just below his line of sight through the windshield, showed the smooth, olive-skinned face of a girl with upswept pink hair.

"University of Hawaii Observatory," she said crisply.

He switched to his broadcasting voice, rich and resonant. "I'm Lance Garrith, Solar News. Could I speak with Dr. Tynan?"

Sudden interest enlivened the girl's face. "Mr. Garrith? I've often watched your program. I'll put you through."

For a few seconds, the screen showed a recorded scene of windblown coconut palms against an azure sky, with surf crashing on white sand. Then it was replaced by the dark, broad face of a man with intense eyes.

"Tynan," he said. "Where are you, Mr. Garrith?"

"I'm landing at Kona Airport in a few minutes."

"Good. I've cleared all the formalities out of the way. I'll meet you there personally." Tynan gave a sudden smile that lifted the corners of his mouth without changing the expression in his eyes. "The fewer people who know about my discovery the better, for the moment."

As the screen blanked out and retracted, Stan laughed. "Millions of people are going to know about it soon, all over the world. What's his worry?"

"I can see his point. He wants to make sure it goes on record as *his*, that's all."

Stan turned in his seat. "What do you think he found, Lance? Just a comet coming in from an unusual angle?"

"Hope we can squeeze more out of it than that, for the sake of the program, Remember when we were kids, the Halley's Comet fizzer of 2062?"

Lance kept reducing altitude steadily, heading in toward Kailua Bay. The great cones towered impressively into the sky ahead, their summits sharp and clear, their lower slopes hazy.

"Bit of mist about," said Stan.

"Vog, they call it here. Volcanic fog. Comes from the crater down to the right."

The peaks of the other islands of the group stretched away to their left in a gigantic, broken rampart—Maui, Lanai, Molokai and Oahu. The farther islands, Kauai and Nihau, were lost in the haze now as the aircraft sank into denser air.

"Came here with my wife, once," mused Lance, almost as if speaking to himself. "We loved the place—but it's changed. There used to be walking trails on those slopes, where all the suburbs are spreading up."

Stan gave him a hesitant smile. "You're always telling me to look ahead, not back, remember?"

Lance gave a short, humorless laugh. When he spoke again, his voice was taut and professional. "Better get an over-the-shoulder shot from here. Take in the coastline and the homes."

"Right." Stan moved back and started his shoulder-held video camera running. "You want sound on this?"

"No. We'll dub it in later."

Stan braced the camera and kept his eye to the viewfinder,

framing the view of the Kona Coast by the windshield and the back of Lance's head and right shoulder. He focused on Lance as he eased the control wheel forward to bring up a vista of boats dotting the emerald shallows shielded from the deeper cobalt water by the long breakwaters of the new marinas.

He zoomed the lens to feature the neo-Brazilian houses swarming up the mountainside, white, yellow, pink and lime in the noon sunshine, their ranks softened by palm, banana and poinciana trees. They had proliferated here and in other attractive regions during the mid-twenty-first century, when so much of the world's population had taken advantage of the new-found chance to live and work where it liked.

Following directions from the Kona tower, Lance swung around to approach the airport from the north, coming down over the flat black area of the nineteenth century lava flow that formed the landing field. Stan kept the camera whirring to show the runway racing to meet them, width and speed exaggerated by his wide-angle lens.

Slowing with the reverse thrust of his jets, Lance swung along a taxiway leading to a marked parking space, passing the open-sided pyramidal buildings of the old airport complex and the new terminal, a late twenty-first century structure with its roof counterfeiting an ancient Polynesian communal house.

"Where are the officials?" asked Stan as Lance maneuvered the aircraft to rest. "This *is* a port of entry, isn't it?"

"Tynan assured me he'd fixed everything for us to land here." Lance opened the door that swung down to give access to the ground by its built-in stairway, and a hot blast of outside air swept into the cabin. "Don't worry," he said as he stepped down, "the local authorities are not going to pass up a chance of publicity. Get a shot of me against this—the jet, the terminal, then pan up the mountain. And sound on."

"Right. Stand near the wing. That's it. Sound on in three, two, one, *now*."

Looking at the camera lens, Lance intensified his expression. "Here we are at Kona airfield. When you look around, you have the feeling of stepping outside of time. Mauna Kea—" he waved his hand toward its slopes, "looked just like that before any man came here, either Polynesian or Haole. . . . Okay, *cut*."

"That'll be good." Stan pointed over Lance's shoulder. "Hey, d'you think this could be Tynan?"

Lance turned as a compact red aircar skimmed down above the

line of parked aircraft. Droning like a monstrous insect, it settled behind the Solar News machine. A dark, stocky man stepped out and walked briskly toward them.

"Mr. Garrith? I'm Dr. Tynan. John Hiroshi Tynan. Have you been up to Mauna Kea before?"

Lance shook his head. "Been here, not up the top. Oh, this is Stan Reed, my cameraman and sound man combined."

As they shook hands, Tynan said, "You'll find it cold up on the summit. We're over four thousand meters, and the wind's often a hundred and fifty kilometers an hour. Freeze the proverbial brass monkey." He gestured toward the terminal building. "Good restaurant here. Want to eat before we go up?"

"I *would* like to put a call through to my office," said Lance. "Get better reception from the ground than from the aircraft."

"No problem. Along here."

Tynan led the way to a visiphone booth, modern enough to have a descrambler slot. After punching out the area code and number for his office, Lance pushed in his private cassette. Within a few seconds Milleen's face appeared on the large hologram screen. She had changed her hair again—but God, with her coloring, why green?

"Anything come in?" he asked.

She looked at him over her half-lensed glasses. "Usual fan mail, a few bills. Oh, there's one bit of originality. Some fellow wants you to drop the story on the probe."

"The *what*?"

"He said the probe, whatever that means. Anything wrong?"

"How—listen, that story was supposed to be alpha-level secret until broadcast. What'd he look like?"

"Couldn't see. Kept his head down, dim light. Important?"

Lance snorted. "Probably some nut. But how the hell did he know about the probe? Never mind—forget it. . . . No, wait! Did you tape his call?"

"Yes, but it's no help. He doesn't show up, even with an image intensifier."

"Suspicious enough to try that, eh? Good girl. Listen, Milleen, don't mention it to anyone yet."

"I did tell Hartz, of security."

"That won't matter. He won't spread it about. Well, I'll catch you again after I've been up to the observatory."

Pulling his descrambler cassette out of the slot, he slipped it in his pocket and went to rejoin Tynan, who was posing for Stan in front of a sculpture representing Pele, the ancient volcano goddess.

"Who else knows about the probe?" Lance asked.

Tynan whirled to face him. "Why?"

"Someone rang my office telling us to kill the story on the probe."

"What? Who?"

"Don't know. Fellow contacted my secretary on the visiphone, didn't give his name, and wouldn't let her have a good look at him."

"Could your secretary have let something slip?"

"Not a chance. She knew nothing about it until this fellow mentioned a probe."

"That's what he called it? A *probe*?"

"That's what Milleen said."

Tynan stared blankly in front of him for several seconds. "Nobody's mentioned the word *probe*," he said. "although the idea crossed my mind. . . . All we've used to describe what we've detected is the word *object*. That's the word we employ to cover any unexplained sighting. We see a point of light moving in relation to the starfield, and it could be a comet, meteor, asteroid, satellite—until we know more about it, it's simply identified as an object."

"You said the idea of the thing being a probe crossed your mind," prompted Lance.

"Did I? I don't want that on record, yet, until we have more data."

"Of course. But why did the idea come to you?"

"Something odd in the path of the object. I found it by sheer accident. I was using our new multiple-mirror telescope, the biggest instrument up there, to photograph an AM Herculis-type system in Centaurus."

"What's that?"

"Oh, it's a close-coupled binary with a white dwarf and a red dwarf drawing gas from each other—but that's beside the point at the moment. I was studying the system by taking a number of successive pictures at regular intervals of time. When I checked them I noticed that a small point of light appeared at different places on each picture. In other words, something much closer than the system I was studying was moving across in front of it. By the time I'd realized this, the Centaurus system was below the horizon."

"This happened last night?"

"Night before last. I alerted other observatories around the world, and we were able to obtain a parallax reading. The object was much closer than I expected—near the orbit of Mars, but obviously far away from the ecliptic."

"Why obviously?"

Tynan gave a slightly superior smile and a strange, one-sided shrug. "Well, obvious to a professional astronomer, perhaps not to a layman. Remember, I was observing in Centaurus. That's mostly forty to sixty degrees away from the ecliptic."

"I see. And the thing doesn't look like an asteroid?"

Tynan shook his head. "Definitely not."

"You said you contacted other observatories. That include the orbiting telescopes?"

"No. They're mainly tied up with long-term observational projects. But I did get a message through to Olympus Mons."

"That's the station on the big mountain on Mars, isn't it?"

"Big mountain's an understatement. The observatory there's practically above the Martian atmosphere. They had trouble locating the object at first, because it was heading almost directly toward them, giving very little apparent angular velocity."

Lance looked at his wristwatch. "Where would you like us to run the interview, Dr. Tynan? Up at the telescope dome?"

Tynan hesitated. "We do most of our work down near sea level, where our brains work better. Up at the summit, you're above sixty per cent of the Earth's air, and you're short of oxygen. The observing's done photographically and electronically, and we study the results down here."

"From our point of view, the summit would give us a more dramatic presentation."

Tynan nodded. "I'd better warn you. The air's very cold up there, as well as thin. You've both had recent blood pressure checks, I hope?"

Lance and Stan exchanged glances, and Lance said, "Solar News makes sure we stay healthy."

Tynan gestured toward his aircar, and they began to walk out to it. "Something puzzles me," he said, looking at Lance's wrists. "Why do you wear two watches?"

"One's set to local time, wherever I am. The other stays on the time in Pacific City, where my program's put together."

Tynan, by now, had reached his aircar. "Come on. I'll take you up the mountain."

* * *

As the aircraft skimmed upward over the rising flank of Mauna Kea, the view was staggering. On the lower slopes, the expanding suburbs were thrusting into a belt of misty rain, the vegetation a sea of vivid, tropical greens, with the red flowers of poincianas and the orange of imported African tulip trees. Then as they rose higher the landscape became drier and more open, with indigenous *keawe* trees.

"Why are those flows of lava different colors?" asked Stan.

"They've come out at different temperatures," said Tynan. "The black stuff, broken into blocks, is *a-a*. The smoother gray material, like asphalt from up here, is *pahoehoe*—that's poured out hotter, around three thousand degrees." He gestured ahead. "I won't fly you directly to the top. There's an astronomers' lodge a couple of thousand meters below it. You'll handle the altitude better if I drive you the rest of the way in a ground vehicle."

The astronomers' lodge was one of a small, isolated group of buildings on the wind-lashed mountainside adjoining a large array of solar units that supplied it with power. The surrounding landscape was bleak, with stunted acacias called *koa* trees and scattered shrubs that Tynan pointed out as *puakeawes*.

He left them for a few minutes outside the lodge, and returned from within it wearing a one-piece suit like an astronaut's. "You'll need warm gear up at the top," he warned.

Stan Reed lifted his duffel bag. "We'll be all right."

The narrow, continuously climbing road twisted in hairpin bends through terrain that grew steadily harsher and more barren, until about 3500 meters it became devoid of any vegetation whatever.

"It's like the Moon," said Stan in an awed voice.

"The nearest approach to a lunar landscape anywhere on Earth," agreed Tynan. He gestured to the lifeless slopes on their right. "This is where the early astronauts tested the first lunar vehicles, more than a hundred years ago."

The road skirted a cinder cone that looked disturbingly recent to Lance, although Tynan assured him that the last volcanic activity here had occurred about 4500 years ago.

"It looks recent because you get practically no erosion up here. It rains only about once in every three years."

Nearing the summit, the road swung around the rim of the crater to link up the dozen astronomical observatories scattered along the ridges. Tynan identified some of the white and silver domes.

"This place was chosen as the world's best site for a ground-based observatory more than a century ago. It's above all the fogs, and most rainclouds. Some of those domes were built in the last two decades of the twentieth century. That's the American infrared, the British infrared, the joint Canadian-French-Hawaiian with the strangely shaped dome. And over here—'' his voice shook with pride, ''—my baby, the big new multiple-mirror.''

He swung his vehicle into a parking space beside the most gigantic of the domes. As they stepped out, a chill wind struck them with appalling ferocity, and Stan's hands trembled as he unzipped the duffel bag. Lance pulled his black leather jacket over his green tracksuit and put on a lumberjack-type cap. Stan's teeth chattered as he worked his shaking arms into the sleeves of a sheepskin jacket.

''I *did* warn you,'' laughed Tynan. ''Keep your breathing shallow. Don't make any fast movements, and don't try to talk too much.''

As they plodded slowly toward the entrance to the great dome, Tynan walked alongside Lance. ''I must admit I've never watched your program,'' he said, ''although I've heard of it, of course. Why is it called 'Specialists' Report'?''

''We go around the world interviewing specialists in different fields. It's one of the highest-rated news commentaries on the worldwide network.''

''And you make it in Pacific City, Australia?''

''We release it live in prime time there, but it's a late night show in California, afternoon in India, early morning in Europe. That's a simultaneous release. Some places run repeats to catch their local evening audiences.''

''You must be under a hell of a lot of pressure,'' said Tynan. Passing through two heavy steel doors forming a wind lock at the base of the dome, they climbed a curving stairway following the arc of the massive concrete wall supporting the dome. Breathing heavily, they emerged from the top of the stairway onto the circular floor under the giant steel hemisphere. Lance leaned back, looking up with undisguised amazement at the complex structure of the multi-mirror telescope.

''I suppose you reporters also become specialists,'' said Tynan.

''In a way,'' said Lance. ''My own specialty has become extraterrestrial life. You know how it is these days. Everyone has to narrow his field down to a tighter and tighter focus. There's a big surge of interest this year in the possibility of life beyond the solar system.''

''Your programs are factual, I hope,'' said Tynan.

"I never distort facts. But sometimes there's a lot of dramatic power in the way you present *possibilities*. That's where the skill comes in."

Tynan's dark eyes never left Lance's face. "Can you elaborate on that?"

"Well, Solar News has an enormous, worldwide computer network. I can call on data stored in hundreds of places, from New York to Nagoya, from Eskodar to the Urabamba."

"What kind of data?"

"Legends. Superstitions. Unexplained facts. It's all raw material to me: stories of strange people who appear and vanish, old tales of flying disks flashing through the sky, reports of ancient footprints in solid rock."

"I thought you said you never distorted facts." Tynan's voice had cooled.

"Look," said Lance, suppressing the burst of enthusiasm that had begun to fire him, "buried in the world's legends are countless thousands of facts that don't fit established thought. They can always be brought to light again, lit from a new angle, combined with other shadowy data to give a new chill to the viewing public."

Lance was walking as he spoke, looking up at the skeletal structure of the telescope as if seeking the most impressive angle to show it. Dr. John Hiroshi Tynan stood watching him, his feet apart, opening his mouth several times before speaking.

"I don't want this broadcast to be a sideshow," he said. "We're carrying out serious research here. I know as well as you do that some of the most spectacular discoveries in this field are being made now with orbiting telescopes, but ground-based instruments still have a respected place."

"I know." Lance walked closer to the astronomer. "Believe me, I'm not going to turn this into a flying saucer story. But you were the first to find this—this object, and I think you should have the acclaim. Publicity never hurt anyone's career, you know, as long as it keeps to verifiable facts."

Tynan seemed to think for nearly half a minute before he spoke, his eyes exploring Lance's face. "Unfortunately, you're right," he said at length. "I sometimes feel the most successful men in my field seem to regard themselves as being in show business."

Lance nodded slowly, as if suddenly brought face-to-face with a truth he had not considered. "That may apply in almost any field."

Tynan tilted his head back, thrusting his jaw forward. "A scientist shouldn't have to be an actor. He should be a pure scientist, not having to worry about performing for, say, grant money to continue his research.''

Lance nodded. ''Perhaps that'd be true in an ideal universe. As it happens, though, we have to deal with the real one.''

''You're right, of course. Unfortunately.''

Stan Reed, waiting off to one side with his camera, made no sound or movement. He kept watching Lance, with an occasional glance at Tynan.

Lance took a few steps toward the base of the telescope, then spun around and looked intently at the astronomer.

''Okay if we go ahead with the interview?''

Tynan nodded, spreading his hands in a gesture of resignation.

Lance Garrith's manner was suddenly that of a brisk professional as he turned to his cameraman.

''Right, Stan. Begin with a shot of Dr. Tynan climbing the steps to the control center of the telescope.''

chapter
2

THEY WORKED ON their editing of the tapes all the way back across the Pacific, and just as Lance had decided he was satisfied with the session, the alarm sounded to warn them that the forward radar had recognized the northeast coastline of Australia.

Lance moved to the controls, switched to manual and eased the wheel slightly forward. The sun was still above the horizon, because their speed westward around the globe had almost equaled that of the terminator between daylight and dark. The reflection of the sun turned the sea to flame, barred by the dark streaks of the Great Barrier Reef.

"How do you think it went?" asked Stan.

"Your part of it, fine," answered Lance.

"It was a photogenic place. The white domes, the dark rock, the clear sky—I could hardly miss."

"Tynan should come over well. Just the right amount of enthusiasm."

Lance switched on his landing lights, heading down the long glide path to the private strip alongside the Solar News tower. He could just see the high buildings of Pacific City now, black against the apricot sky, some of them edged with the fire of the setting sun glancing off smooth metal.

"Want to run through it again in the lab?" asked Stan.

"No. I've seen all I want to see of it. Go through it too many times and I'll lose spontaneity."

Lance lined up with the runway, steadily losing altitude. Below the darkening water was streaked by the white lines of surf on the reefs.

Pacific City had not existed before the middle of the twenty-first century, except as a handful of holiday resorts scattered along the tropical Queensland coast north of Cairns. The growing tendency for people to work where they lived had caused a vast influx of population to the more attractive areas of the Earth's surface.

Lance skimmed in low over the flame-lit shallows, where people were swimming and windsurfing in waters once unsafe for much of the year because of the deadly, now eliminated conefish. As soon as his wheels whistled sharply against the runway, he threw the twin hydrogen jets into reverse thrust, bracing his feet against the deceleration. He looked at his watch. Forty minutes to his segment of "Specialists' Report."

"We're cutting it fine," said Stan, gathering his equipment together.

"Keeps you a hundred per cent alive," said Lance. He steered the six-seater jet into a parking bay near the base of the tower. He had named his aircraft the *Green Flash* on a whim, after a session he had once broadcast on the mystery of the flash of green light sometimes seen at sunrise and sunset over the ocean. The phenomenon had been explained long ago as the first or last rays of the sun refracting through wavetops, but Lance Garrith had ignored any logical explanation and concentrated on the mystery.

His specialty was the arousing of public interest and excitement, rather than the digging out of facts, which often irritated him by confusing his themes.

He stepped into one of the elevators and pressed 59 and 60— the 59th floor for the laboratory where Stan would make the final arrangement of the tapes, and the 60th for the studio where he would be making his telecast in a little more than half an hour.

"Feeling tired?" asked Stan just before he reached his floor.

"No. Still on a high. Being tired comes after the show."

Stan shook his head. "Hope it never catches up with you on camera." He grinned as he stepped out.

Reaching the sixtieth floor, Lance walked along the glassed passage behind the auditorium of Studio One. Not a vacant seat— a live audience of five hundred. He stopped, after another glance at his watch to look at the present segment of "Specialists' Report," the one preceding his.

The speaker was new to him, an attractive-looking girl with dark hair, who seemed to be discussing some historical character. Lance went into the monitor room.

"Hi, Dom. Who is she?"

The man at the bank of monitor screens turned. "She's new. Not doing badly, though, eh? Name's Dorella. That's all she uses."

"What's her specialty?"

"Something about the ideals of Renaissance Man. You know—
the way those boys used to develop the whole man, instead of
trying to specialize. So one guy knew everything."

"Might have worked in Renaissance times." Lance smiled.
"Total knowledge didn't cover such a range then. One guy *might*
have been able to take it all in."

"Maybe. She says the last of these all-rounders died this century. Fellow named Karstrom."

"Karstrom? I seem to remember people talking about him when
I was a kid."

"That'd be him. According to Dorella, he was into all sorts of
things, sixty or more years ago. Genetic engineering. Fiddling
with DNA. Star probes. Radio signals to other star systems—
although he never seemed to get any answers back."

"I wonder."

"Eh?"

"Oh, this probe I'm doing a story on tonight. The astronomer
I've been talking to thought it came from outside the solar system.
Now suppose, Dom—just suppose—it came in answer to a signal
sent out by this Karstrom?"

"I'm not with you. What *is* this probe?"

"Listen to the broadcast. I'm on in eighteen minutes."

"I will. But don't thank me, Lance. I gotta listen to 'em all,
whether I like 'em or not."

While Dorella was bringing her talk to a conclusion, Lance
watched her on the monitor screens. In these days of precise
glandular control, almost every woman looked beautiful—beauty
was a commodity easily bought—but Dorella had added something
to her beauty, a highly individual sense of style. Like most fashion-
addicted girls of her generation, she was slender and as tall as a
man. With the technique of stimulating the growth of selected
long bones, the distal segments of her legs had been elongated to
give height.

By careful timing, Lance passed her on his way into the broadcast area. "Interesting stuff there, Dorella. I'm Lance Garrith.
What you were saying ties in with something I'm just going to
talk about. Maybe we could get together later on some ideas for
a program."

"I want to watch your show, anyway. See you at the end of
it." Her eyes were large—naturally large—and a clear hazel. A

moment later, a warning light sent him hurrying to the broadcast area. As he was entering, a large, blond man with a red, expressionless face moved to intercept him.

"I'm Hartz, Security. We've had a threat about your program."

"I know. Only some nut, isn't it?"

"Think so. Gotta be sure, though. If the lights go out, dive for the floor. Okay?"

"Oh, all right. But why?"

"Few things that don't tie up. Anyway, I've got men all around."

"Thanks." Lance went into the area where his session would be broadcast. The cameras were still off, and he checked the table-top model of the solar system that he had requested. It had just been wheeled into the studio. He looked at the screen where Stan's pictures would appear so that he could indicate points of interest, the rostrum where he would face the cameras, then moved the model slightly. The floor manager, across off-stage, held up five fingers. Lance nodded and moved to the rostrum.

The theme music pervaded the studio, and he looked at the six cameras to see which had the red light above it, then smiled his usual greeting into the lens.

"Tonight," he said, "we have a general theme of history. Dorella has given you an interesting slice of the past, and I have the feeling I may be describing a great historical turning point on the day it's actually happening."

The theme music swelled up and over, and he glanced down quickly at the monitor screen as the commercial ran its half-minute. Then he leaned earnestly forward.

"For two days now, astronomers around the world have been aware of an object approaching the solar system from Beyond." He let the word hang heavily, and his image on the screens in ten million homes receded as the camera zoomed to the model of the solar system on the table. He moved toward the model.

"You will notice that our system of planets lies more or less in one plane, the plane we call the ecliptic. Some of them swing a few degrees above or below, but in general they move at the one level like balls rolling in circles on a table."

He knew this was an over-simplification of the real picture. Some of the asteroids swung well above and below the plane—the orbit of at least one, Hidalgo, intersected the ecliptic at 42 degrees—but that was the sort of awkward fact that he never allowed to interfere with his clear-cut pictures, which he often claimed anyone could understand at a glance.

"This Object from Beyond," he said, giving his key words massive emphasis, "came into our system at an Astounding Angle." He brought his hand up past the model at an angle of 60 or 70 degrees.

"As many of you will know, an object coming into the system from Outside will travel in a parabolic or hyperbolic path, depending on its speed, or if gravitational capture occurs, it will fall into an elliptical orbit around one of the bodies within the system.

"But this object was non-typical. Today, I traveled to the observatory at Mauna Kea, Hawaii, believed to be the best viewing area on the surface of the Earth, to interview Dr. John Tynan of the University of Hawaii, who first discovered this interstellar wanderer two days ago. Here he is, mounting the stairway to the control console of the giant multiple-mirror telescope with which he made the discovery."

He watched the monitor as the taped version of his interview with Tynan ran through. Stan Reed had done an excellent job of capturing Tynan's enthusiasm and carefully repressed excitement at his discovery. Lance had kept a low profile in the actual interview, throwing in only an occasional word or two.

When the red light over a camera showed that the transmission had become "live" again, Lance walked back to the screen where a slide projection showed the orbits of the planets in perspective. Taking a pointer, he indicated a curved line on the screen.

"Now, this object discovered by Dr.Tynan came in here, on a path that would bring it close to the planet Mars . . . that's this one . . . but when it reached *here*, it slowed its speed. Now that's something a normal meteor would never do. In fact, it should have been *increasing* its speed as it drew closer to the center of gravity of the system. But it slowed! And it curved more sharply in its path!

"To me, and to Dr.Tynan, it seems obvious that this indicates intelligent control. The control of an Intelligence from Beyond the solar system." He waved his hand toward the table model. "Of course, you might say the object could be an unmanned probe, pre-programmed to react to masses within our system. That could well be true. But it still leaves us with an unexplained intelligence somewhere Out There!"

Music up and over. Off camera for a few seconds while the screen showed the star-flecked vastness of interstellar space, Lance leaned back, glancing at the monitors showing the studio audience. He had them! He could almost feel the chill in his own blood.

Then, as he watched, he became aware of some kind of commotion in the back corner of the audience. Looking against the lights, he could not see it directly, but a monitor covering the rear of the audience picked the scene up. Three large, efficient men were removing a thin man from the auditorium. One had twisted the captive's right arm up behind his spine, another held a silencing hand over his mouth. They were all out through a side door before Lance could see exactly what was happening, and only ten or twenty of the audience could have noticed the incident.

After his session had ended, Lance went quickly out through the back of the studio. Hartz met him as soon as he was beyond the view of the audience.

"Who was the guy?" Lance asked.

"No name yet," said Hartz. "We're taking him down to the freezer. He seems to be under some kind of dope, or hypnosis, or maybe a combination of both. We'll get more sense out of him after we dry him out."

"Probably nothing to worry about, now that you've got him," mused Lance. "Just an isolated fanatic riding some hobby horse or other."

"Wouldn't take it as lightly as that. He had a very sophisticated weapon. I think someone else did the planning, and programmed this boy the way you program a robot."

Lance sighed. "Well, I hope your fellows can unscramble him."

"We will—given time. Meanwhile—be careful. Okay?"

"Right on. Thanks."

Leaving Hartz, Lance found Dorella waiting for him in the passageway. She brightened as soon as she saw him.

"I thought you'd slipped out some other way," she said. Her voice, off-mike, was deep and faintly husky.

"Look," he said, "there's a restaurant higher up in this tower. Frankly, I'm hungry. Haven't had anything but coffee since I left Hale Pohaku."

"Where on Earth is that?"

"Halfway up Mauna Kea."

She smiled. "As it happens, I wasn't able to eat before my session. Now that it's gone off all right, I'd love something."

He took her arm and steered her toward the small elevators

behind the studios. They did not travel to the ground like the public cars, but merely served the upper floors occupied by the Solar News complex.

He chose a window table with a view eastward over the dark ocean. The rising moon, still low over the horizon, threw a scintillating track of light across the water. Lance pointed to where it was intersected by the dark lines of reefs far out to sea.

He switched the menu onto the screen at the side of their table just beneath the window, and they made their selections and punched them on the numbered keys. Then he turned to her.

"I was interested in your data about this fellow Karstrom. Especially about his sending of signals to other star systems."

She nodded. "Something like that was done a long time ago, back in the twentieth century. They called it Project Ozma. They listened for signals from Epsilon Eridani, Tau Ceti, and a few others of the nearer systems. No joy. But they only gave it a short try, and their equipment was less sensitive than what was available in Karstrom's time."

"What did Karstrom actually do?"

"We're not really sure of it all." She leaned forward across the table in her enthusiasm, her eyes bright, and it suddenly came to Lance that she was half in love with her own mental image of a man who had lived—and probably died—before she was born.

"We know what he planned," she went on. "He sent his signals to a whole range of other systems, some as far as fifty light-years out. He even tried Vega and Arcturus. I think he planned to send unmanned probes to other systems to radio data back, but no one knows now whether he sent any or not."

"Why? Surely some data would have been kept?"

"He ran into trouble with the authorities. Not for his signals, but for his experiments in recombining DNA. I have a whole file on it. They were upset by the way he combined DNA with synthesized stuff. Outcry against tampering with nature, et cetera—you know, it was one of those uptight periods when people seemed to specialize in outcries."

"What happened?"

"He closed his operations down. He was last heard of on Mars."

"Mars?"

She nodded. "He lived in Hellas for a while—the first Martian domes were built there, as you know. Then he moved to the Outlands, and I lost track of him after that. Mars was very sparsely settled at the time. Still is, of course. But most of the people there at that time were prospectors for mining groups, drillers, people like that. You don't get much reliable material on record, except geological.''

Lance looked out thoughtfully through the window at the star patterns above the dark sea.

"Suppose, for a moment—suppose he sent some signals out from Mars. Would that have been possible?''

"Possible, yes, although I've no record of it.''

He brushed the objection aside with a casual wave of his hand. "Let's make out a hypothetical case. He sends out a signal. How long ago?''

She thought for a moment. "Could have been sixty-five, maybe seventy years.''

"Right.'' He gestured out toward the dark sky. "Let's assume that it gets to a planet inhabited by an alien race. They send a probe to see where the signal came from. No, better—they send an *expedition* to the solar system to find out where the signals originated.''

She was smiling. "You use your imagination quite a lot to fill in the gaps, don't you?''

He grinned. "Legitimate. I'm making an entertainment program, remember?''

Their ordered food arrived on the conveyor, and for a few minutes they ate without speaking much, although each of them was thoughtful.

"You know,'' said Dorella, "perhaps I'm too prone to check everything from every angle before I release it.''

"A very good habit for a scientist,'' he said. "At the same time, some of the biggest discoveries have started with someone taking a leap into the unknown, the unverified. There's room for both attitudes.''

"We might make a good team,'' she said, then seemed a little embarrassed by the abruptness of her suggestion, quickly changing the subject. "You know, I'd love to know what Karstrom did after he settled on Mars. Some day, if I ever accumulate enough money, I'd like to go there to find out.''

"I'd give that a lot of thought if I were you, Dorella. It's a long way. About six months on a Hohmann transfer orbit. Most people who go there make it a one-way trip.''

"If I could find some excuse to get someone to finance my trip, I'd go tomorrow. After all, they're advertising for engineers to develop the yttrium mines.''

"I'd forget it, Dorella. It's rough territory. You'd have to live in sealed domes, or use airtight vehicles or suits every time you left the domes."

She smiled wistfully. "You've never been on Mars, I suppose?"

He shook his head. "Nor wish to. I've interviewed men who've been there. It's not my scene."

They finished their meal, and Lance was about to make a date for some future meeting with Dorella when the beeper in his pocket sounded its faint, shrill note. He took it out and thumbed on the four-centimeter vision screen. The head and shoulders of a tense, tired-looking man with narrowed eyes and a long jaw appeared.

"Lance," came his voice. "Where are you?"

Lance brought the unit close to his lips. "At the restaurant on 65."

"Good. Can you get up to my office right away? Something big has just broken. And I mean *really* big."

"You mean about the fellow who tried to break up my session?"

"I said *big*. Can you come right now?"

"On my way."

"Who was that?" asked Dorella, as he sat for a few seconds looking at the beeper before slipping it back in his pocket.

"The Chief," he said. "Mort Channing. Said it was something important." He reached over and touched her hand. "I'll get back to you."

"Sure," she said.

He palm-printed for both their meals, then headed for the elevator shafts. At the door of the restaurant he turned to wave to her, but she was staring out at the night sky.

chapter
3

MORT CHANNING'S OFFICE was on the ninetieth and uppermost floor of the Solar News tower, with windows on two walls looking southward and eastward over Pacific City and the ocean. Channing's desk was set across a corner of the room between the great windows, and as Lance walked toward it from the private elevator, he had to fight a momentary sensation of vertigo as he looked down past the seated figure at the moonlit sea three hundred meters below. A passing aircraft with its lights ablaze, sweeping across the vista below their level, somehow emphasized the impression of space.

"Sit down, Lance." Channing touched something on his desk, and a magnetic-field chair skimmed out and hovered. It sank a few centimeters as Lance sat on it.

A faint buzz sounded in the quiet room, which had sound-deadening carpet and wall hangings. Channing listened for a moment to a voice coming from a hooded screen on his desk.

"All right," he said. "Handle it." He switched off the screen, then turned his full attention to Lance.

"Lance, you're the best expert we have on extra-terrestrial life. You'd agree with that, wouldn't you?"

Lance raised his eyebrows and thrust out his lower lip. "I suppose I'd have to, Chief. Yes."

Channing looked down at some papers and pictures on his desk. "I think something very big has come up in that area, Lance. It's going to need a lot of checking, but it might—it just *might*—be the biggest story that's ever broken. Not just to us. To any news outfit that's existed since they used to carve the news on clay tablets."

He finished speaking and let the silence hang like a thunder-cloud. In spite of himself, Lance felt his pulse speeding up.

"You mean—some definite evidence of ETL?"

Channing looked down at something in his hands. "I'm not a hundred per cent sure, Lance. But I'd like to get your feeling on this."

He put a slide into a projector and touched a control that put out the lights and darkened the polarized windows so that the only light in the room came from the green streaks of luminescence outlining the corners of some of the pieces of furniture.

"This came by tight-beam transmission," said Channing. "Not a good picture, unfortunately. The original was taken in a Martian duststorm by a metals prospector who never claimed to be a photographer. But there! See that?"

"I see it. But what is it?"

"What's it look like to you, Lance?"

"Well, I'd accept that it's a picture taken on Mars. The red, stony desert, the pink dust in the air. I can see something that looks like a small, lime-green tent, with someone—or something—in a space suit standing looking at it."

"You changed from 'someone' to 'something.' Why?"

"Well—if the picture isn't a fake—the thing's not human. The proportions are all wrong. Anyway, it's got six limbs."

"Now look at this." Channing fiddled with the projector for a few seconds, and the picture changed. This one was sharp and clear. It also showed a lime-green tent—not the same one as in the previous picture, because this one appeared brand new, while the other had been stained with prolonged use. This tent also had a figure standing beside it, but in this case it was a slightly plump, fair-haired man. In the background was a sealed roadway with some bulbous-wheeled vehicles parked alongside it, and buildings of concrete or laser-sawn stone under a transparent dome-wall giving a view of a copper-colored Martian sky.

"Who's that?" asked Lance.

"Brad Hagen, our rep at Hellas City. He sent both these pictures to us today. He had the second one taken to give a frame of reference for the first, the one taken by the prospector, a fellow called Jack Darch. The same type of tent—same size—and Brad is 180 centimeters tall, about our height."

"Could I see the first picture again?"

"I can do better than that. I can project the two of them side by side."

Channing switched on a second projector, and the two pictures appeared on the white wall of the office.

"I can zoom them so the tents are the same size. There."

It was obvious now that the six-limbed figure was much larger than the man—about a third taller, and bulkier in proportion. Its helmet was enormous. The figure was standing side-on to the camera, so that the outer metal cowl of the helmet hid the face. The suit was white. Two of the arms it enclosed were gigantic, massive as the arms of a gorilla, while the other pair, set above and in front of them, were slender and wiry in their close-fitting sleeves.

"Look at the feet," said Channing.

"God, yes! They're like a bird's feet, or a bird-footed dinosaur's." Lance turned away from the screen. "It has to be a fake," he said emphatically.

"That's what I said when I first saw it," said Channing, "but now look at this."

The pictures were replaced by a blowup of a detailed map of part of the surface of Mars. Channing switched on a spotlight pointer. "Those yellow areas are plains, the orange cratered, the brown volcanic. The green areas—like these—are what they call chaotic, with broken ridges in random directions. Now just here, where I've made that mark, is where Jack Darch took his picture. It's right in the middle of an area the locals call the Badlands, hundreds of kilometers from any settlement. Now, you notice the point I've marked is near the middle of this oval line that's been drawn in."

"What's that?"

"It defines the area where they think your probe may have landed."

"The one I was checking out with Tynan?"

"That's it. More data came in from Olympus Mons while you were broadcasting."

Lance pointed to the map. "But what could have led the probe there?"

"I don't know. It's what the geologists call karst country. Old underground channels, dating from the time Mars still had surface water. Erosion caves beneath the surface, and gullies where some of the caves have fallen in. No one goes there, except for the odd prospector, like our friend Darch."

"Did he see the thing come down?"

"No. Bad duststorm. They can extend over thousands of kilometers on Mars, sometimes right around the planet. Darch was finding his way back to his tent in his runabout following a radio beep. Got within a hundred meters, and when he saw his tent through the dust, this character with the four arms was standing looking at it as if he'd never seen a tent before.''

"What'd Darch do?''

Channing gave a short laugh. "Nothing heroic. Hid behind a rock until he saw the thing leave. He waited a long time, then dismantled the tent, stowed it in his runabout, and drove all night to get back to the nearest settlement.''

"Then he didn't see the thing again?''

"No. There were big, three-toed footprints leading up to the tent, around it, then back the way they'd come. Darch didn't try to follow them. He went the other way.''

"Don't blame him for that. Could I see the picture of the thing again?''

"Sure.'' The image of the six-limbed figure returned to the wall.

"Did the thing do anything to his equipment?''

"Examined it. Moved it about. Turned things over. Didn't take anything away, as far as we know.'' Channing zoomed the lens until the grotesque figure towered from floor to ceiling. "You'd say that was bigger than life-size, wouldn't you? But look at the tent. That's just life-size now.''

Lance looked up at the bizarre image. "Could be a stunt,'' he said uncertainly. "Trick space suit with a fellow inside it.''

"But why? And how could he be there just after the probe came down?'' Channing flung his arms wide. "Anyway, that still leaves us at square one with the probe. It definitely came from outside the solar system. It's been under negative acceleration since it was first spotted. It lands somewhere in the Badlands, and within an hour or two *this* turns up.''

Lance continued to stare up at the monstrous figure. "I'm damned if I know, Mort.''

"Hell, Lance, how negative can you get? You're our top specialist in extra-terrestrial life, and now that you've got the first really believable evidence we've ever seen, you don't accept it.''

"I'm beginning to.'' Lance shook his head in a gesture of exasperation. "I don't want to, but I can't think of any other logical explanation.'' He continued to look at the projected image, moving closer to the wall so that he could gauge its height. Although he was somewhat above average height himself, his head was below the level of the massive shoulders.

"Nasty character to meet in a dark alley,'' said Channing.

"Just what I was thinking. I wonder how many of them there are?"

"No way of telling. Probably not many—yet. But if it came from another star system, I hardly think it would have come alone. We never did that when we first went to the Moon, and to Mars, and to Titan. We always made the initial exploration with at least three men, even if one of them stayed in orbit while the others went down to the surface. One thing seems odd to me, though."

"What's that?"

"Why Mars? Why not Earth, where they must have been able to detect signs of civilization as soon as they came into the solar system? On Mars, you only have the Hellas settlement, the observatory on Olympus Mons, and a few specialized mining operations. At a distance, you'd write Mars off as an uninhabited planet, even uninhabitable, whereas Earth, blue and white, with oxygen and water, would be the obvious place to look for life."

"Wait a minute. There's another factor we haven't looked at," said Lance.

"What?"

"Suppose the thing came looking for the source of a radio signal?"

"Well, there's a constant barrage of TV and radio signals blasting out from the Earth in all directions, all the time. From Mars, there are only a few tight-beam messages directed mostly to Earth."

"I'm thinking in terms of long-distance beams sent out to other star systems in a deliberate attempt at extra-terrestrial communication. Starting with Project Ozma last century, and Karstrom's experiments early in this one."

"Nothing came of them, though."

"Maybe not until now. Look, there's another thing that supports the idea."

"Like what?"

"There was a lass called Dorella giving a segment before mine. . . ."

"I know. Series on all-round geniuses of the past."

"Right. She was talking about this fellow Karstrom, the man I just mentioned. Did you know he probably sent his last signals from Mars, because he was run off Earth for some reason or other?"

Channing seemed to freeze. "Go on."

"Well, it struck me—suppose some of his signals reached a

planet of some other star where a civilization had developed far enough to have radio and space flight. The signal may have taken ten years to get there, maybe twenty, and they could have decided—"

"I'm with you. That'd lead them to Mars, not Earth. And after a lapse of twenty, thirty years . . . when did Karstrom send out his signals?"

"Dorella thought it would have been sixty-five or seventy years ago. She might be able to pinpoint it better."

"Might give us a clue as to where this thing came from."

"Not very definite, because we don't know how fast their space-craft travel, or how long was the interval between the picking up of the signal and the decision to go searching for its source."

Channing walked across the room and stood gazing up at the projected figure. Suddenly he turned and looked sharply at Lance.

"Tell me, Lance. What's your gut feeling about it? Do you think it could be an elaborate hoax?"

For a long time, Lance did not reply, and Channing did not hurry him. He studied the details of the figure—the strange, divided shoes encasing the three-toed feet, the gloves sheathing the two pairs of hands, one pair slim, supple-looking, the other massively powerful. He looked at the obviously non-standard breathing equipment on the backpack. Finally, he turned and faced Channing.

"I think it's real. I don't think we're being conned. I think the thing's a true extra-terrestrial. No relation to the human race."

"Good. That's the way I read it." Channing walked back to his desk and touched the controls that brought on the overhead lighting and rendered the windows transparent again, bringing back the view of the moonlit sea. He stood for a time staring out at the ocean, and at the lines of headlights of vehicles moving along the esplanade far below. Suddenly he whirled.

"How would you feel about traveling to Mars?"

"*What?*"

"You're free—and you're our greatest expert on extra-terrestrial life—you said so yourself. I'd like to see what you can find out about this thing, before the story leaks."

"But what about 'Specialists' Reports'?"

"This could be the biggest story that's ever broken in the history of the human race! And you'd be first in the field. Solar News controls the news setup at the Martian end, such as it is. Brad Hagen and the other local boys will hold any material until you arrive. I want *you* to cover it. Contact Brad as soon as you get there."

"Can I have a bit of time to think it out?"

"Wait a minute." Channing sat down at his desk and began punching keys, peering into a hooded VDT. Suddenly he looked up at Lance. "There's an yttrium freighter leaving Earth orbit in three days. The last shuttle to reach it leaves Florida the day after tomorrow. I can get you on it."

"How long does it take to get to Mars?"

"A hundred and fifty days, now. Say five months."

"Five months there, five back. That's a year out of my life."

"It's a year that could put you in the greatest story that ever hit us."

"What about quarantine?"

"We can have all that fixed with quick-scan techniques. If you need treatment for anything, there'll be plenty of time to handle it on the freighter."

"Can I let you know tomorrow?"

"Tonight would be better, Lance. I'm going to have *someone* on that freighter. At the moment, I think the best man to cover the story would be you. But if you feel you want to pass the chance up, I'll need as much time as possible to select someone else. Okay?"

Lance nodded. Channing moved closer to him and clapped a hand on his shoulder. "Mars—on an expense account! Think of it, Lance. Lots of men would commit murder for a chance like that."

"I realize that."

"Besides," Channing went on, "speaking of murder, it'll get you away from people like that fellow in your audience tonight."

"What? But he was only a nut."

"I'm not so sure. Neither is Hartz. He called me before you came up here. The gunman claimed to be a member of some pseudo-religious group. Children of something or other. I think they believe all life is confined to the solar system. Either that, or we shouldn't mess with anything outside it."

"But aren't they on a par with the fellows who think the Earth is flat, because it looks flat where they live? Who takes any notice of someone like that?"

"Hartz isn't sure it wasn't a cover, Lance. When his men grabbed the guy, he'd drawn a gun and was sighting it at you. A very sophisticated gun. Solenoid driven, with a battery more powerful for its size than anything Security know about. They've checked every avenue they can to find where it came from, but they've drawn a blank. Silent, lethal, with a telescopic sight. If one of Hartz's boys hadn't knocked his hand up, you'd have been dead in about one second.''

This time, the chill in Lance Garrith's blood was real.

As he made his way down to the Security office in the basement of the tower, Lance felt an unaccustomed sense of uncertainty about several things. A few short hours ago, he had believed in his heart that mankind had a unique position, unrivalled by any creatures of comparable intelligence. He'd accepted theoretically that other such intelligences might inhabit other places far away in the galaxy, but anticipated no communication from them in the foreseeable future.

Now, after seeing Darch's photograph, he found one of his basic areas of certainty violently shaken. Then there was this gunman, who had apparently known about the probe before it had ever been mentioned in the news, and who had an interest in its being kept secret. Where did he fit into the picture?

Hartz and two of his associates were still questioning the man when Lance was let into their outer office. Hartz at once called Lance into an inner room filled with harsh white light.

The thin man was spreadeagled on a metal table with a laminated top. Four pairs of handcuffs secured his wrists and ankles over the edge of the table to its legs, so that he was held flat on his back. He did not show much emotion, his expression dully fatalistic. Wires attached to metal bands around his wrists led to an electrical instrument on which a needle moved against a dial.

''What's that?'' asked Lance, pointing to it.

''Works as a rough lie detector,'' explained Hartz. ''Basically a Wheatstone bridge balancing his body resistance to a small current against a controllable variable resistance.'' He lowered his voice so that the man on the table could not hear what he was saying. ''Actually, it's not an infallible lie detector, but it *does* give an indication of emotional charge. That gives us a clue where to ask questions.''

''Are you getting anywhere?''

''Not yet. He's been hypnotized in some way, but with a sort of hypnotism I've never encountered before. He keeps saying the same things no matter how you approach him. Like a tape recording. In fact, young Joe raised the suggestion earlier on that he might be a robot. But he's human—what's left of him.''

"The Chief said he belongs to some religious sect. Children of something.''

"We thought so at first, but now I think it's a cover. We checked with them, and they've never heard of him. Probably a hypnotic implant, and whoever did it made it stick really tight.''

"Could I try something?'' asked Lance.

"What do you want to try?''

"I'd like to try showing him a picture. See if it sparks any recognition.''

"Okay. Where is it?''

"Haven't got it with me, but I can draw it. Could I have a piece of paper?''

"Sure. Here.''

Lance drew a six-limbed figure in a bulky space suit, with a large helmet, a pair of slender arms above massive, gorilla-like arms, and legs ending in three-toed feet. He had to leave the face blank, as he hadn't seen it.

"Hell,'' said Hartz, "how did you dream that up? Is it some kind of Hindu god?''

Lance shook his head. He held the paper in front of the prostrate man's face. "Ever seen him?'' he asked.

The thin man's dull eyes rested on the paper, and for some seconds there was no response. His irises were the color of weak, milky coffee, with small pupils. Abruptly the pupils dilated, and the eyelids widened, the shallow breathing quickening.

"Hey,'' said Hartz's assistant, who was crouching over the instrument. "We got a surge there! Needle nearly went off the end of the dial.''

Hartz took the paper from Lance's hand and held it closer to the prisoner's face. "Where did you see him?'' he asked in an authoritative voice. But the thin man simply closed his eyes and muttered something incomprehensible.

Hartz persisted for a short time, then gave up. "Mightn't mean much,'' he said. "Could have been the shock of seeing something like a character out of a bad dream.''

"Just a hunch,'' said Lance. "It was worth the try.''

"I'll keep this, if I may.'' Hartz lifted the paper. "After all, it's the only thing that's sparked any response out of him so far.''

"Could I see the weapon he used?''

"Ah, that's really something. Come through here.'' Hartz led the way out along a passage to a small office and opened a steel safe, taking out a weapon that looked at first glance like an automatic pistol. He released a catch and slid a battery out of the butt, placing it carefully on a table. It was not a standard battery. It was black, with cryptic red markings on its sides, and two terminals of a metal that looked like bronze. With the battery out of it, he handed the weapon to Lance, who sighted along it.

What he had taken to be the barrel was actually a telescopic sight, giving a very sharp enlargement of a small section of the wall. He looked through it at figures on a calendar, and found that by moving his thumb against a knurled control on the back of the telescope he could alter its focus. The true barrel, which was very slender, ran along underneath the telescope, most of its length enclosed in a long coil of fine wire.

"Fired iron slugs with a speck of explosive in them," said Hartz. "After we'd checked it for prints we fired it in our test range down below. Didn't realize the little pellets were explosive. Blew one of our targets to pieces. Man, you were lucky."

Lance nodded slowly. "I guess I was. Will you thank the fellow who knocked his hand up?"

"That was young Joe. You can thank him right now, if you like. All part of our service."

As he left Security, Lance thought cynically of his public image. The intrepid gatherer of news, flying to every part of the globe, careless of any risk to life or limb. And now, here at his home base, right in the Solar News Studio One, someone had tried to blow him apart. One of Hartz's aides had taken him down to the subterranean target range and had shown him what the explosive pellet had done to one of their targets—a man-sized figure molded in some kind of foam. The pellet had struck it in the chest region, and the upper half of it had been blown to shreds. They were still digging tiny pieces of iron from the pellet out of the surrounding walls. Whatever the explosive used, it had expanded with inconceivable violence.

As he emerged from the elevator at the main floor, Lance was unable to repress the impulse to glance furtively around. The foyer of the building had a disturbing number of hiding places for a potential assassin that he would never have thought of prior to this—large potted palms, decorative pieces of trellis with vines growing on them. To a marked victim, the place could be a death trap.

He started as someone called his name from one of the alcoves, and spun around to find Dorella rising from a seat. She smiled as she moved toward him.

"It's only me. What's the matter? You looked as if you were expecting someone to shoot you."

"Don't joke," he said, then managed to force a smile. "Our program may slip a bit at times, but it's not *that* bad yet." He took her arm. "I could do with a good, strong coffee. There's a little place across the street. Care to join me?"

As they walked along the broad, almost empty sidewalk, she pressed his arm against her side with her elbow. "Something's wrong. Anything serious?"

"Not really. I'll tell you about it over coffee."

He thought again of that target figure, blown to pieces by a tiny pellet. It was unlikely the assassin had acted alone.

Waiting to cross the street, he scanned the buildings opposite. The city had a thousand places where a marksman could lurk.

chapter
4

THE INDIRECT LIGHTING in the coffee lounge threw a soft golden glow. Lance selected a table near a window that allowed them to look out at the passing scene through one-way glass, an old gimmick recently resurrected in the restaurant milieu.

"Just coffee?" he asked.

She nodded. "For now."

He punched the necessary keys on the table console, and a few seconds later a hatchway opened in the wall below the window, revealing two steaming cups of coffee on a conveyor belt. They lifted them onto the table.

"Now," she said, "what's the trouble?"

"Does it show?"

She nodded. He looked at her for a long time.

"You have beautiful eyes," he said irrelevantly.

"Every girl can have beautiful eyes these days."

"But yours are natural, aren't they? Untouched. Big and lustrous."

"And didn't cost me a cent. I guess I was born lucky." She smiled, then her expression became serious again. "But you're trying to get away from the point. What happened to you between the time you went in to your session and now?"

He looked at the table, and spent a few seconds getting his thoughts in order. "First of all, someone tried to kill me."

"Oh, my God! Where? How?"

"During my session on air. From back of the audience, using a gun." He managed a grin. "It's all right now. The Security boys have got the guy. Probably just a nut."

Her eyes were enormous. "Glad it's all in hand now, but it gives you a nasty feeling, doesn't it?"

He nodded. "That's not the only thing on my mind. Mort Channing wants me to go to Mars."

"To where?"

"Mars."

"That's what I thought you said. But why?"

"You know my story on the probe?"

"Yes. I listened to it with Dom in the monitor room."

"More data came through while I was on air. Apparently it *was* some kind of probe, and it landed in the Martian Outlands. Channing controls the media on Mars, and he's getting them to hold the story from their end until I arrive to do a report."

"Doesn't it take six months to get there?"

"Varies, depending on where both planets are in their orbits. Around now, they've got it down to five months."

"But it'd cost you the national budget, wouldn't it?"

"Solar News is paying, and they're using an yttrium freighter. I think Channing's got a big interest in Martian yttrium. The more the world uses room-temperature semi-conductors, the more yttrium they need, and we get it from Mars. I think some of the ore comes from out in the asteroids, but it's refined on Mars."

Dorella drank some of her coffee. "I wish I could get someone to finance a trip to Mars for me."

"From what I hear, it's a rough place, even now. You breathe canned air all the time."

"I'd still like to go there. I want to follow up more about Noel Karstrom. He had such a fascinating life here, and what we know now is only the first half of it. We don't even know when he died, and we have practically no data on what he did on Mars." She leaned forward across the table, her lips parted slightly. "While you're there, would you see if you can find out anything about him?"

Lance thought for a few seconds. "I'll be doing that anyway. There's a possibility this probe came in answer to a signal sent out by Karstrom. I'd like to find out what kind of message he sent, to see if that explains why he got a response when Project Ozma failed."

"You think it was definitely a probe?" She smiled. "It's not just your tendency to dramatize?"

He shook his head. "It fits together too well. It has to be a directed vehicle of some kind. The change in speed, the course correction."

"But I listened to the recording of your interview with Tynan.

He pointed out that meteors sometimes altered speed and direction when they broke apart. He said if a small part splits off the main body, the direction seems to change."

"I know. But you'll remember he emphasized that was very rare."

"True." She finished her coffee, then punched the console for another. As she lifted it, steaming, off the belt, she said, "I suppose I'm a bit envious, you getting an expenses-paid trip to Mars. It's something I've wanted to do for years. I'll find some way yet. I don't suppose you need a traveling assistant, do you?"

"Costs are so heavy I can't even take my cameraman—and he's been all over the world with me. You know, when the Chief first made the suggestion, I thought about the way 'Specialists' Report' was developing, and I didn't want to go. Now I'm coming round to the idea that this probably *is* the biggest story that's ever broken. Maybe it was the way Mort Channing put it to me. Anyway . . ." He looked at his watch. "Excuse me a minute, Dorella. I'll call him up and let him know I've made up my mind, before he contacts someone else on his list." Taking out his pocket beeper, he punched the code for Channing's office. The Chief's taut, lantern-jawed face appeared on the tiny screen. Lance shifted his position to let the light shine on his face, moving the beeper so that its little wide-angle lens covered him.

"Lance," said Channing, recognizing him before he had time to speak. "Have you made up your mind?"

"I have. You're right, Chief. It looks like the biggest story since Gondwanaland broke up. I'll cover it."

Some of the tension in Channing's face seemed to relax. "I'm glad," he said. "There's a flight leaving for Orlando tomorrow at 1200. I've booked a seat on it. I'll get together any preliminary material you may need."

"Right. Can I get back to you on that later tonight?"

"I'll be here all night."

After he had broken the connection, Lance found Dorella staring at him. "Do you always make decisions as quickly as that?" she asked.

"It only seemed quick. I've been thinking about it for a while."

"Noel Karstrom seems to have been like that," she said. "The more I study him, the more I feel I know him, even though we've never met."

He leaned forward, looking steadily into her eyes, which did not make any attempt to flinch away from his gaze. "Don't get obsessed with him, Dorella. Remember, the guy's dead." He was surprised at the gentleness that had crept into his voice.

"He probably is," she agreed, then a smile twitched the corner of her mouth. "Although one of the things he was working on was the prolonging of human life. He and his team, that is."

"Who were his team?"

"Mostly a lot younger than Noel. You know, he claimed he'd developed some way of increasing human intelligence."

"A lot of people have made claims like that."

"But he had a habit of making unlikely things work. That's why his associates were all loyal to him. When he had to leave Earth to continue his work on Mars, a number of them went with him, although in those days life in the Martian settlements was even more primitive than it is now."

Lance nodded slowly. "Something like the *Mayflower* situation. A group of people who thought differently from their contemporaries forced to try living far away."

"I suppose so." Her eyes looked very large again. "Listen, when will I ever see you?"

"I'll be back in about a year, maybe with the most staggering story that's ever been told."

She passed a deckle-edged business card across the table to him. "I'd like to hear from you while you're there—especially if you come across more information about Karstrom. Keep in touch, anyway. There must be mail brought back on the freighters. And where would I be able to reach you?"

"Solar News, Hellas. You'd better contact me through a fellow called Brad Hagen. He's our rep out there. That'll find me—there isn't a very big population, I understand."

For a time, there was an awkward silence that neither of them could think of a way to end smoothly. Lance felt a sense of frustration building in him. He was strongly attracted to her—her intelligence, her unusual style of beauty, the fact that he felt comfortable with her within minutes of their first being together. He would be leaving Earth, at least for a year, perhaps more. It was not fair to her to begin a close association at this point. He should simply stand up, wish her goodbye, and leave—and that would be the end of it. And yet . . .

After staring out through the one-way window at the stream of passing vehicles and occasional pedestrians, she abruptly turned to face him. "I'm going to miss your program, Lance." She hesitated. "And I'm going to miss you. I'm glad we met."

"So am I." Usually with a turbulent flow of words at his instant command, he felt momentarily almost inarticulate. Was it only fatigue?

"I feel I know you quite well now," she said.

He smiled. "As well as Noel Karstrom?"

He wished at once he hadn't said it. It seemed to shake her a little. She managed an answering smile, yet some of the warmth had gone out of it. When he reached over and touched her hand, it, too, felt cold.

Lance made the flight to Orlando on a commercial hydrogen jet. Although he sat by a window, there was little of interest to see most of the way because of their 30,000-meter altitude that took them almost to the edge of space.

Looking down at the mottled blue and white of the globe below him, he tried to see where the Pacific ended and Mexico began, but a shining carpet of local cloud defeated him.

He smiled to himself as he thought of Mort Channing's skillfully timed maneuvers to get him here. "There's a freighter leaving in three days . . . the greatest story that's ever hit us . . . the best man to cover the story would be you." And then: "If you feel you want to pass the chance up, I'll need as much time as possible to select someone else. Okay? . . ."

And they've often accused *me* of oversimplification, mused Lance. Channing had done just the same thing to him.

From the airport at Orlando, Lance rode a high-speed, projectile-like railcar out along an elevated linear-induction monorail to the spaceport on the coast, the computer-streamlined schedule giving him little time to look about him. However, south along the Atlantic coast he could see the gaunt launching towers remaining as monuments to the era when spacecraft had blasted vertically from water-cooled pads.

He was traveling light, since weight on an interplanetary voyage was horrendously expensive. A pocket video camera, an extremely compact recorder, and a micro-encyclopedia complete with magnifier represented tools of trade pared to a minimum.

Sitting next to him on the railcar was a tall, pale-skinned man whose legs seemed thin in proportion to his somewhat overweight torso. He looked exhausted, as if getting here on time for the takeoff had cost him an immense effort.

"Hi," said Lance, "your first trip to Mars?"

The other man shook his head. "Hell, no. I've worked there ten years. Ten of *our* years, that is—equal to about nineteen of your years here."

"You still think in terms of Martian years?"

"Why not? It's my home. Thought I might come back to retire here, but the place has got a damned sight worse than I remembered it."

There was silence between them for a while as the railcar hummed along with a speed that blurred the nearer scenery.

"By the way, I'm Lance Garrith."

The other man didn't seem to recognize the name. He extended his hand. "I'm Ted Allen. *Your* first time?" He looked at Lance's face keenly. "What'll you be doing out there?"

"I'm a newscaster. Have a session called 'Specialists' Report.' Ever watched it?"

"No. I'm not one for the holos." Allen looked out at the level countryside as the car slowly lost speed. "Nearly there, from the feel of it. I'll be damned glad to get off this lump of dirt. Gravity's enough to kill you, when you haven't been used to it for a while. And the air! How do you stand it?"

"It's all right for me, most places," said Lance.

"Not bad here in Florida. But the big cities! In another fifty years, I reckon it'll be unbreathable."

"Don't you have canned air where we're going?"

"Sure. But it's *clean*. Hasn't been breathed in and out by a million other people before you get it."

Lance felt he had to defend his home world. "They're doing something about it," he said. "Regenerating a lot of the jungle in the Amazon Basin. Getting forests back across Africa. Doing things with marine plankton. There's a long way to go, but I think we've turned the corner."

Allen shook his head. "Better if they got rid of four or five billion people. That's the only way."

"How would they do that?"

"I dunno. Wars, maybe. Or next time there's a big disease outbreak, don't try so hard to stop it for a while." He lay wearily back in his seat, closing his eyes. "Wouldn't matter, much. Lot of bloody sheep, most of 'em, far as I can see."

"How long have you been back here?"

"Thirty days. That's enough. I've outgrown the place."

Lance decided further discussion along these lines would be futile. He enjoyed his life. Allen apparently wanted to return to the womb of safe, enclosed domes with carefully metered air and controlled temperature. Probably Allen had been doing some safe, routine job where he sat in front of a computer all day. He'd let his body grow soft, pallid from lack of adequate sunlight and fresh air. Lance had an impulse to test his judgment.

"What did you work at?" he asked.

"I'm a metals prospector. Had a couple of good finds lately. That's how I was able to finance the trip to Earth. Wish I hadn't, now. Waste of money. Now I'll have to start prospecting again."

The railcar was sliding into its terminal station, and for a time their conversation ended. Out on the runway was the spaceplane that would lift them to the orbiting freighter, a long, needle-nosed craft of gleaming titanium alloy, with stubby, triangular wings upswept at the tips for computer-controlled steering.

"There she is," said Allen, and picking up his small carry-bag he moved out onto the platform, his steps heavy with the gravity in which he had been born, but which now almost overpowered his softened muscles. Lance felt momentarily sorry for him as they joined the short queue of people being processed to board the spaceplane.

"By the way," he said, "while you were prospecting out there, did you ever meet a fellow called Jack Darch?"

"Old Jack?" Allen laughed. "Sure, I know him. Always good for a laugh, old Jack."

Lance looked at him sharply. "Practical joker, was he?"

"You could say that again. Put anything over on you, Jack would, if you gave him half a chance."

They were separated as they went through the cubicles for their final pre-flight medical checks. Lance's examination for blood pressure, respiration rate and other factors took longer than Allen's, since for him it was the first journey to Mars. When he emerged from the cubicle, Allen had already gone out across the tarmac and ascended the escalator to the spaceplane.

Riding up the escalator, Lance took a photograph of the assumed alien from his wallet—a copy of the picture taken by Jack Darch. By Jack Darch, practical joker! Was it too late to call Mort Channing?

Then he thought of the probe, of its change of speed and direction. Darch couldn't have arranged that. He put the photograph away again. There was some story up ahead of him, even though he was uncertain as yet what it was.

Nearing the doorway into the sleek body of the craft, he turned and looked out at the world he was leaving—at the hot Florida sunshine under the hard blue sky. Gulls wheeled in from the nearby sea, and over by the vehicle park grackles swirled above some unseen food source like scraps of black paper in a whirlwind. Earth, with its limitless complexity! Would he ever come back to it?

Almost angrily, he brought his thoughts back on stream and turned again, stepping into the spaceplane, a turmoil of doubt seething within him.

chapter
5

As Lance walked up the narrow aisle in the shuttle's cabin, Ted Allen turned in his seat and indicated a tall, gaunt man on the other side.

"Lance, like you to meet Doc Stein. He's our ship's doctor for the main voyage. Lance Garrith."

The tall man extended his hand. He had rimless glasses and a craggy face of unexpected pallor, his fair hair sleeked back.

"Ted tells me it's your first trip to the Dustbowl." He grinned at Lance's questioning expression. "The Hellas Basin, where they built our city. It's not dusty inside the domes, of course—better air than yours." He waved toward the windows.

"Been on Earth long?" asked Lance.

"Usual thirty days—the standard turnaround time for these ships. Gave me time to take in three medical conferences—Osaka, California, Finland. But God! The gravity! Had to wear electric leg braces to get around."

"Ye-es," said Allen in long-drawn agreement. "The gravity—and the overcrowding! That's another thing I can't take, now. That and all the dirt."

All three of them turned as a newcomer entered the shuttle, a slim, willowy young man with smooth, dark hair that looked as if it had been enameled, and round eyes that seemed continuously surprised. He moved quickly up the aisle, looking from one to another of the seated trio.

"I'm Phil Gray," he said. "Hope I haven't delayed things."

"You couldn't do that," said Stein. "They take off on time, even if there's someone halfway up the steps."

Gray gave a shaky laugh, and sat down on the seat across from Lance's, looking at him keenly. "You're Lance Garrith, aren't you?"

"That's right."

"I watched your program the other night. I suppose you're going to Mars to look for that probe, as you called it?"

"That'd be a long shot, by the time I get there. But I mean to have a look around. Your first time out there?"

"Yes. They're taking me on as a mining engineer. Mainly, we'll be getting yttrium."

"Which outfit?" asked Allen, turning in his seat.

"Crowd called Belastra."

Allen nodded. "Run by J. Borg, right?"

"Yes. After I'd done an entrance exam, I had a visiphone interview with Mr. Borg himself, while he was in orbit." He gestured upward.

Allen smiled. "It's *Ms* Borg, actually. Jocasta Borg."

Gray looked a little shaken. "But the person I spoke to didn't look like a woman on the screen. I saw only the face. Short hair, didn't move the head. I probably called her the wrong thing."

"I wouldn't worry about it, son. She must be over a hundred years old, and as long as I've known her she's been in a cybernetic body. Doesn't matter much whether she started life as a man or a woman. She's mostly machine, except for her head."

"Damn good head, though," said Dr. Stein.

Allen swung around. "Hey, Lance, you play chess? Jocasta will take you on any time at 3D. She's good. The captain plays, too, but he's so bloody good he's unbeatable."

"Handy to know," said Lance, "although I mean to do a lot of work on the way out—research for future programs. That sort of thing."

"Chess might break the monotony," said Allen. "I dodged it on the Earthward trip by letting them freeze me. Not real freezing, something they call molecular stabilization."

"I don't like that," replied Lance. "There's a theory it may kill off some brain cells, and I need all I've got."

Stein, as the expert, evidently felt he had to say something as the others looked at him. "You might lose a few cells—out of billions."

"Didn't seem to hurt me much," said Allen, a little doubtfully. Then he lapsed into thoughtful silence.

The pilot of the shuttle was a lean, dark young man who introduced himself as Alvarez. Takeoff began like that of an ordinary aircraft, the machine gathering speed along the seemingly endless runway, then it lifted, a few meters, and Lance felt the jar of the undercart retracting. For a few seconds, he had an oblique view of an area of green Florida swamp, with lagoons bordered by reeds, and then the nose of the craft tilted sharply upward at an angle that kept him lying on his back in the contoured seat, his feet higher than his head.

There was a few seconds' respite as the jets shut off, then a chilling scream as the oxy-hydrogen rockets took over. Lance tried to estimate the g-force being applied to him, and its duration, but eventually he gave up and simply lay with his eyes closed. At last, the pressure relaxed, and the voice of Alvarez came over the speakers: "Will you all keep your seat belts fastened? I'm reducing acceleration progressively. In three minutes, you'll be experiencing free fall."

When the orbiting freighter finally came within sight through the windows of the spaceplane, Lance was staggered at the sheer scale of the thing. A vast cylinder, at least a kilometer long, it seemed featureless except for a ring of massive rocket motors projecting from one end.

"The surface looks rough," said Gray in surprise.

"Lunar scoria cemented to the hull," explained Stein. "Protection against micro-meteoroids. The radar handles bigger fragments."

The ferry moved slowly closer to the great cylinder, parallel with its axis and midway along its length. Half the immense hull was in brilliant white sunshine, the rest almost as dark as the background of space. Giant, curved doors swung open to reveal a red-lit cavity within the ship, and Alvarez carefullly eased the shuttle closer, until two long, jointed manipulating arms extended from within the bay, seizing the spaceplane with clawlike clamps. They drew it within the metal-walled bay, and the outer doors swung slowly shut, locking home with a booming clang that echoed throughout the ferry.

Somewhere outside the titanium hull of the spaceplane, air was rushing, and metallic clicks punctuated the temperature equalization of the cooling rocket motors and the body of the craft, now that it was shielded from the near-absolute zero of outer space.

Lance glanced impatiently at his watch, reflex action reinforced by long habit. The watch still showed Florida time, which meant nothing now, and in any case, Lance could do nothing to shorten the forthcoming voyage of a hundred and fifty days by as much as a second.

After what seemed to Lance an interminable delay, the neon-red light outside the ferry shut off, leaving an instant of darkness before the metal-walled bay was flooded with white light that showed the various colors of the equipment scattered about. Alvarez emerged from the control cabin, handling the zero gravity with practiced ease, his feet thrust into magnetic overshoes. He opened the exit door by manual controls and swung it out and down.

"You'll find magnetic shoes under your seats," he said. "Slip them on. If you haven't been in zero-g before, don't make any sudden movements."

Without using the steps on the lowered door, he launched himself straight out of the wall of the transfer bay twenty meters away, anchoring himself by gripping one of a network of green ropes festooning the wall. Turning, he called, "Come on out."

Allen followed him, turning easily in the air to end spreadeagled against the net, and both of them looked expectantly at Lance, who had moved to the doorway. Selecting a part of the rope net to hold, he freed his shoes from their magnetic grip of the floor the way the others had done and sprang straight out at his target.

"Good!" said Alvarez and Allen together, and their comment was echoed in the booming voice of a man who had just entered the bay through an inside airlock—a gigantic man in a dark blue jumpsuit, with frizzy red hair and a matching beard. Between the hair and the beard, all Lance could see of his face was a long, sharp nose like a knife, and alert blue eyes. He moved easily forward, using the wall net to hold his position as he watched Gray leap awkwardly across with flailing arms, followed by Stein, who made a restrained, experienced landing.

"I'm Captain Mackay," said the giant. "The *Yttria* is my ship. In other words, for the next hundred and fifty days you'll all be living in an absolute dictatorship. Does that meet with your approval?"

He stood with his feet apart, confident, authoritarian, his gaze challenging his passengers, one after another. No one answered.

"The idea of even a temporary dictatorship may clash with some of your ideologies," he went on, "but once we enter the Hohmann orbit, there's nothing you'll be able to do about it. If you wish to abort your mission, now's the time to say so. You can ride back dirtside with Alvarez."

Still, nobody spoke.

"All accept the conditions, then?" demanded Mackay. "Good!

As long as we understand the picture at the outset . . . Welcome aboard!'' He looked at his watch, then turned to Alvarez. ''Ready to cast off?''

The archaic term jolted Lance for a moment before he realized its nautical origin. Alvarez made a gesture of assent.

''Nothing to go down?'' he asked.

''Nothing,'' boomed Mackay. ''Soon as you leave, we'll be on our way.''

Alvarez wished his passengers well, then returned to his ferry. The door swung up with a sharp finality, shutting off any return to Earth for an indefinite time.

''Through this airlock, everyone,'' ordered Mackay, and led the way to the door through which he had entered the bay. Following him, the others found themselves in an airlock with a similar door at the far end and a window giving a view of the transfer bay. They could see Alvarez in his lighted control cabin.

''What's happening?'' asked Gray.

''Pumping air from the bay,'' said the Captain, ''otherwise we lose a lot of air when we let the ferry out. Power's cheap here, but air isn't.''

They watched, listening to the throb of pumps. At last, the white light in the transfer bay was replaced by the red neon monochrome. Motors whined, and the two great doors forming the curved roof of the bay swung up and apart, showing a strip of dark space. As the gap widened, part of the Earth appeared, a thick crescent of blue and white, ragged along the terminator. Lance suddenly realized that from a terrestrial viewpoint they were all standing upside down. Not that it made any difference—the magnetic shoes supplied an illusion of what was ''down.''

The long, jointed arms lifted the ferry out of the bay, extending telescopically until it was well clear of the ship. The clamps opened, and small puffs of sunlit vapor spurted from the nitrogen peroxide jets as Alvarez maneuvered his craft away from the *Yttria* before using his main rockets. The doors swung slowly shut, cutting off the view of the ferry as it moved away.

Gray drew his breath in sharply. ''That's it. We're committed!''

''You make it sound like a jail sentence.'' Allen clapped his hand on Gray's shoulder. ''You're starting a new life, man! If you're like me, you'll never go back.''

Gray looked round-eyed at Stein, who shrugged. ''Medical conferences are the only things that take me to Earth,'' he said.

Lance looked from one to the other of the older men. Both gave an impression of being sincere in what they said.

The door at the inner end of the airlock opened, and Mackay led the way through.

"I'm going to be involved with the injection of the ship into the Hohmann," he said. "I'll get one of the robots to show you your quarters, set around the periphery of the hull. I'll impart enough spin to the ship to give you 38 centigees—that's Mars-normal gravity."

Gray gave an exclamation of surprise, and Mackay looked at him sharply. "I understood we began with Earth-normal gravity and had it gradually reduced throughout the voyage," said Gray.

"You understood wrong," roared Mackay. "That's an old technique, not mine. It wastes power." He looked aggressively from one to another. "You'll be spending a lot of time in 38 centigees— maybe your whole lives. The sooner you get used to it, the better."

The inner door of the lock gave access to a room with steel floor and walls. In the center of it was a barrel-shaped object of bright metal that appeared to be magnetically suspended above the floor. A pair of skeletal metal arms hung from its sides, ending in caricatures of human hands, and a camera lens stared from the front of it, with the legend *KR 2* painted below it.

"This will be your guide," said Mackay. "Call it Kay. If you let it have each of your given names, it'll store them."

"You know me, Kay," said Stein, "I'm Ralph."

"I know Ralph," came a metallic monotone through a grille below the lens, and the thing turned slightly. "And I know Ted. Welcome back."

It revolved so that the lens faced Lance. "And you are . . . ?" it ended with a rising inflection.

"I'm Lance," he said.

There was a moment's silence, then the strange, hollow voice said, "Lance—do I have it right?"

"That's right, Kay." He felt foolish talking to a piece of machinery, but the thing turned to Gray, who introduced himself as Phil.

"He'll never forget," said Mackay. "Forgets nothing, once he has it in there." He placed his hand on the robot's domed top, which was about level with his chest. "Well, I'll leave you all in Kay's charge. Sayonara."

He walked away through another door, which appeared to open and close for him automatically. Then the robot's voice came from its grille. "Ralph, Ted, Lance, Phil, will you all follow me?"

It led them into what was evidently an elevator, swinging to face them. Lance looked down at it.

"Is it true you forget nothing?" he asked.

"I erase memories no longer needed, Lance," came the uncanny voice. "I never forget data I record in my permanent memory."

There was still no sign of Mackay's promised Mars-normal gravity, and as the elevator moved down they had to rely on the grip of their magnetic soles to keep them in place on its steel floor. They moved slowly down for perhaps a hundred meters before the car slowed to a stop, and the door opened onto a passageway walled with green-painted metal.

"All out, please," came the voice of the robot.

As Lance stepped out, he saw that the passageway swept upward in a curve in each direction, following the circumference of the ship's hull. The robot glided out, pointing with one of its metal arms.

"Ralph, Ted, you have the same rooms. Lance, Phil, follow me."

It glided smoothly along the passageway, its base a few centimeters above the floor, riding a field of magnetic repulsion that must have been tightly controlled. They passed a door with a card fitted into a holder, bearing the name JOCASTA in block letters. The next door had a blank card, and the robot produced a felt-tipped writing implement like a cargo marker from a cavity in its body, to print stiffly and accurately the name PHIL.

"I put you here," came the voice, "because I understand you have business association with Jocasta."

"With Ms. Borg," said Gray.

"One name is all I need," answered the robot. It opened the door of the room, and Gray stepped inside. Lance followed the gliding machine along to the next door, where it lettered his name on the card before admitting him.

"Any other passengers?" Lance asked, looking farther along the annular corridor.

"Few. Freight is our business. Passengers incidental." Although the voice was that of the robot, the phrasing made Lance think of Mackay. It was evident that he had programmed the robot to answer questions as he would have replied to them himself.

The cabin was more spacious than Lance had expected, with its own needle-shower recess, hydrojohn, even a facility for heating coffee. One feature that startled him for a moment was a window that appeared to be looking directly into outside space, but closer examination showed it to be a TV screen apparently hooked in by closed circuit to an external camera. Part of the floor was level, but one side, toward the rear of the ship, was curved up at an angle, with a small chair and table perched there.

"Why the slope?" he asked, wondering as he spoke why he had the impulse to talk to the robot as if it were a sentient being.

"This side when ship spins. That side when rockets drive along axis."

"Thanks." He pointed to the lettering on the front of it.

"KR 2—is that a model number? What's KR stand for?"

The reply was unhesitating. "Karstrom Robots, the firm who made me. Their factory is in Hellas. This will be your room for duration of voyage. Enjoy."

Then it was gone, leaving Lance standing in the room looking at the closed door. Karstrom Robots! That man seemed to have had a hand in everything.

While he was still exploring the details of his cabin, Lance felt the vibration of rocket motors and heard the sound of them echoing through the vast hull. "We're on our way," he said aloud, looking at his watch. After a few seconds, a sensation of weight told him the ship was beginning to spin about its long axis to supply artificial gravity. The needle of a g-meter on the wall began to move slowly, but it was several minutes before he was able to kick off his magnetic shoes and stow them away.

Ultimately, the meter registered 38 centigees. Lance began moving experimentally about, getting the feel of the gravity field in which he would be spending at least the next year.

The TV screen on the wall still showed the same field of stars. He had expected the spin of the ship to send the scene sweeping wildly, but apparently the camera was mounted at one end of the cylindrical hull, isolated from its spin.

After a few minutes of the Martian-style gravity, he ventured out into the passageway. A plan of the living section of the ship on the wall of his cabin indicated that a canteen lay around the curve to his left, and he headed toward it, sliding his feet carefully along the floor, which in spite of its apparent upward curve always felt horizontal beneath him. After passing a number of closed doors, he came to the canteen, identifiable by its laminated tables and molded foam chairs. Inside it, Phil Gray stood talking with another person Lance had not yet seen, and as their eyes met, Gray waved.

"Ah, Lance Garrith! Lance, I'd like you to meet my new boss, Ms Borg."

The woman turned, looking at Lance with a vivid smile. "Call me Jocasta," she said in a deep, smooth voice, and moved toward him.

He remembered Allen's description of this woman: "She's in a cybernetic body, mostly machine, except her head." Prepared as he was, he was inwardly shocked by her appearance. She was tall, and her rather close-cropped blond head and strong-looking face were those of a vigorous woman of perhaps forty, although the skin of her face had a waxy pallor. She was somehow top heavy, her bulky, rounded body in its close-fitting blue leatheroid jacket larger above than below, moving on tapering legs that seemed unnaturally slim. Glancing down, Lance saw that they were telescopic stilts of black metal, shortening and lengthening without bending. They must have been computer controlled, because her balance on them was perfect.

"Lance," she said, as if she had known him for years, "I've wanted to meet you ever since I saw your program the other night." Her lips moved normally as she spoke, but her voice actually came from a small speaker just visible at the neck of her jacket. She extended her hand toward him, a long-fingered hand in a black nylon glove. As he took it, it felt cold and hard inside the glove. Slim metal fingers with pressure-sensors engulfed his hand, holding it firmly. Looking down at her arm in its blue leatheroid sleeve, he saw that it looked flexible throughout its length, like a thick, tapering tentacle. When he raised his eyes again, she was smiling with an expression of amused tolerance.

"There's something I must ask you," she said. "Tell me, what do you really think of that Martian probe?"

"The probe?" Lance shrugged his shoulders. "If it *is* a probe— I have an open mind about it. I simply like to follow up what seems to make an interesting story."

The woman's bright blue eyes studied his face inquisitively. They were the only part of her smooth face that looked old. "But you must have formed some opinion about it," she said.

"Well, I'm fairly certain it was extra-solar in origin."

Her eyebrows lifted. "From some other star system? That's making a big jump in your reasoning, isn't it?"

Lance hesitated. He didn't want to mention the photograph taken by Jack Darch, yet without that piece of evidence his present attitude must appear gullible.

In the interval of his silence, Phil Gray seized the opportunity to rejoin the conversation. "There's a coffee machine over there. Why don't I get us each a cup?"

"Not for me, Phil." The woman curved her flexible arm in a tight arc, and slapped her gloved hand against the front of her body. It made a solid thump as if she had struck a heavy plastic drum. "I don't eat or drink. This has kept me alive for sixty-three Earth years." She ran her hand almost caressingly down the convex curve of her cybernetic body. "Should last me for centuries."

Gray turned to Lance, who said, "Thanks, Phil. I still eat and drink."

Gray went across to the coffee dispenser, and Jocasta waved her hand toward the tables. Lance gestured for her to lead the way, and she walked quickly ahead of him with a strangely doll-like movement, the stilt legs swinging with metronome precision, the bulky trunk in its blue jacket perfectly upright as if balanced by gyroscopes. The thick, flexible arm was not duplicated on the other side. The left arm was smaller, ending in a two-fingered metal clamp.

Lance sat on one of the molded red chairs, while on the other side of the table Jocasta simply shortened her telescopic legs so that her height was reduced, although she kept her head slightly above the level of his.

"You said you'd used that body for sixty-three years," said Lance. "You don't look old enough for that."

An expression of vanity flitted across the pale, plump face. "Thank you. You don't age much in one of these." She patted her hand against the leatheroid-covered barrel of her body.

"What brought you to Earth?" he asked.

"Oh, I didn't go dirtside. Never do. There were a number of business associates I wanted to contact down there. Tight-beam messages from Mars to Earth are expensive, and the delay makes two-way communication tedious. From Earth orbit, I was able to make as many TV contacts with surface people as I liked—with good picture quality and no noticeable delay."

Gray returned with the coffee, joined them at the table, and passed one of the cups across to Lance. Before touching his own coffee, he looked apologetically at Jocasta. "Will you excuse us?" he asked as he sat down.

She gave a soft laugh. "Phil, you don't feel easy with me yet, do you?"

"Of course I do," he protested.

"You must, if we're to work together." To Lance's surprise, with the telescopic legs still retracted, she strutted around the table and stood close beside Gray. The agile, gloved hand reached out, and with a quick movement it took hold of both Gray's hands together. He seemed to make an ineffectual attempt to pull his hands away, but gave it up almost at once. His eyes stared roundly into Jocasta's, and Lance had the feeling the two of them had forgotten his presence. When Jocasta spoke again, her voice was very quiet.

"Phil, you're coming into an environment quite different from anything you've experienced. Now, I've been around four or five times your lifetime. I want you to think of me as a wise elder sister. Can you do that?"

"I guess so, Jocasta."

She gave his hands a little shake, without releasing them. "Good. You called me Jocasta. That's a start."

Lance, finishing his coffee quickly, stood up. "I'll see you both later," he said.

Jocasta rolled her eyes briefly up and sidelong to look at him, her hand still retaining its grip on Gray's. "Yes, Lance, later," she said. Then her attention switched back to Gray.

As Lance took his coffee cup back to the dispenser, they were still looking closely into each other's faces. As he walked out of the room he could hear the subdued murmur of Jocasta's voice, but he couldn't hear what she was saying.

As he walked along the passage, remembering to slide his feet in the reduced gravity, a sudden flash of memory jolted him. The thin man spreadeagled on the table in the security office at the Solar News building. He recalled one of the things Hartz had said: "He's been hypnotized, but with a sort of hypnotism I've never encountered before."

Was it possible the would-be assassin had been hypnotized via a TV contact from orbit? Could it have been done by Jocasta?

He began fitting stray facts together. She had shown an unexpected interest in what he thought of the Martian probe. But if she had hypnotized the gunman, that didn't explain where he'd obtained the weapon. She had not, apparently, gone down to the Earth's surface.

Yet the thought kept nagging at him. Suppose the gunman had

been hypnotized at some previous time, and given the gun to use when needed. Then, just recently, Jocasta could have contacted him from orbit, thrown in a triggering phrase to propel him in the desired direction.

Angrily, he shook his head. He was becoming paranoid! Suspicion of the unknown. Pure xenophobia. The woman looked different from anyone he had known, acted differently, walked differently, so she represented a threat. Ridiculous!

At the same time, back in the studio someone had tried to kill him. There was no way he could ignore that.

Returning to his cabin, he decided to catch up on his overdue rest. The furious pace of the last few days had begun to erode his habitual enthusiasm for life. He lay down on the divan, the light Martian-type gravity making it easy to relax.

He wondered how Mort Channing and Solar News were getting on without him. And "Specialists' Report." Whose sessions was Stan Reed photographing now? Stan had helped greatly in Lance's rapid climb to the apex of the shaky pyramid of world news commentary programs. Who was he helping now? Dorella? Hardly, her style was less visual.

He tried to work out who would have top ratings while he was away, and what would happen on his return, but the whole scene had a fluid complexity that defeated him in his present mood. At some point in his attempted analysis, he fell deeply asleep.

He awoke to the sound of a deep voice booming through the cabin—Captain Mackay's voice. On the TV screen, Mackay's red-haired, red-bearded face looked out at him in sharp 3D, the blue eyes appearing to look straight into his own. Probably the TV in each cabin had been aligned with the head of the divan, but the immediate effect was unnerving until he was fully awake.

"All listen to this," said Mackay. "We're increasing the thrust of the main engines to inject the ship into Hohmann, or more strictly speaking, a hyperbolic transfer orbit which will get us to Mars slightly faster than the ideal Hohmann elliptical section. You may feel movement. The gravity you're experiencing is a resultant of the centrifugal spin and the axial thrust, but our computers will keep it at 38. If you have any questions, we'll be happy to deal with them."

Any questions, thought Lance. He had plenty. He wondered to what extent Mackay's offer to deal with the passengers' questions was just public relations patter.

He walked across to the door of the cabin. Next to the light switch was a push-button with a hand-lettered card above it reading KR 2. The inscription puzzled him for a moment before he realized it must be a call button for the robot that had brought him to his cabin. He pressed it, and a mechanical voice squawked from a speaker on the wall.

"Kay," said Lance, "could you take me to Captain Mackay?"

A moment's silence, then "Why?" grated the metallic voice, "You can reach him through your communicator. Press 'one'."

"I wish to contact him directly. Can you take me there?"

"One moment, please." There was silence for several seconds as the robot enlisted human aid. Then the TV screen flashed into life again, and Mackay's face looked out of it.

"What is it?" he snapped.

"Sorry to disturb you, but there's something important I want to see you about."

Mackay seemed to hesitate for a moment, glancing at his instrument panels. "All right," he said at length. "Kay will bring you here."

Lance went to the door of the cabin and looked along the passageway. After a minute or so the barrel shape of the robot came gliding toward him. It led him along to the elevator, and up to the axis of the ship, where his weight lessened disconcertingly, the "up" direction now toward the end of the ship. A door slid open at their approach.

"Come in," called Mackay's voice, and Lance walked into what was obviously the ship's central control room.

chapter
6

THE WALLS OF the control room were red, and indirect red light flooded the room from neon tubing concealed in recesses. Only the display screens on the walls and the luminous figures on the instrument dials showed any other color.

Mackay sat facing a semicircle of monitor screens that reminded Lance of Dom's array in the mixing room of Studio One, back in Pacific City. But these screens mostly showed views of star patterns on which colored grids were superimposed, while a few bore changing columns of figures and moving line diagrams.

There were two other men in the control room—a stocky, gray-haired man at another console, and a younger man who may have been either Japanese or Korean, who was watching a hologram tank. Mackay didn't introduce them. After the first glance of recognition, he gave no indication that he was aware of Lance's presence for nearly a minute. Then he arose.

"Okay, Stavros, Kenzo. As she goes."

He turned his bleak gaze on Lance, one bushy red eyebrow raised questioningly.

"Could I have a few words with you?" asked Lance.

Mackay led him around a corner into an alcove lined with apparatus on shelving. "Right. The words?"

Lance, swaying in the light gravity of the axial region, steadied himself with a hand on a shelf. "This may be complicated."

Mackay gestured to what appeared to be a view of outside space on one of the screens. "We have a hundred and fifty days before planetfall." He gave an unexpected smile that showed strong teeth. It was a disturbing expression, half a smile and half the snarl of a ferocious animal. With an effort of will, Lance leaned forward toward him.

"Before I left Earth, I made a worldwide broadcast about an unidentified object approaching Mars."

"Yes. I saw a taped replay. Ran it through at twice normal speed, I'm afraid—my time is valuable. It came over rather frantic, hysterical, but understandable."

Lance nodded. "During that telecast, someone in the audience tried to kill me. To shoot me."

Mackay didn't answer for a moment, his eyes fixed on Lance's. Then he shrugged his shoulders. "Primitive planet, primitive people."

Lance shook his head. "There was nothing primitive about the fellow's weapon. We don't know where he got it. And our security men think he'd been hypnotized."

Mackay gestured to the vision screens. "Well, you're away off planet, now, farther every minute. So you should be safe. Safe until you return there, at least."

"I'd like to think that. But I have the feeling something complicated and important is going on, and I'm seeing only small parts of it."

Mackay spread his large hands apart. "Why ask me? I simply haul cargo from one planet to the other—metallic ores from Mars to Earth, specialized equipment the other way."

"And people."

"A few—but that's incidental."

"But I'd imagine your cargo doesn't give you much trouble. The people might."

Mackay's sharp, cold eyes studied Lance intently. "You could say that. But you don't seem to be getting to the point." He glanced at his watch.

"As I said, the man who came into the studio to shoot me seemed to have been hypnotized."

"So?"

"A while ago, I saw one of your passengers using something that looked to me like hypnotism."

"Who?"

"Jocasta Borg. She was talking with young Gray."

"Ah, yes. He's going to work for her. Don't see anything odd in that."

"It's the technique that bothers me, taken with the fact that a hypnotized man tried to shoot me. Jocasta made a number of calls from the ship to people on Earth. Did you keep a record of those?"

"Passengers' calls are all private."

"She's interested in something I talked about on my program."

"The Martian probe, as you called it?"

"Yes, the probe. Now it seems to me that whoever hypnotized that creep who shot at me could have implanted the urge to kill me from on board this ship."

"Why from here, for God's sake?"

"Because almost no one on Earth knew about the probe."

Mackay stretched, a towering figure threatening in its sheer size. "Has Jocasta, or anyone else, tried to hypnotize *you* since you came aboard?"

"No."

Mackay looked down at a desk at one side of the alcove. A number of differently colored pencils were held in spring clips there. He removed one, and with a sudden command, "Catch!" threw it close to Lance, who caught it with his right hand.

"Now this," said Mackay quickly, and threw another of the pencils past Lance's left side. Still holding the first, he caught the second with his left hand. Mackay laughed. "Let's have them back," he said.

Lance wondered whether the responsibility of being master of a kilometer-long ship had eroded Mackay's sanity. He threw the two pencils back to Mackay, one right-handed, the other left-handed, and Mackay laughed again as he returned them to their clips.

"What was that about?" asked Lance.

"Just checking. Wouldn't worry about attempts to hypnotize you. It's very hard to hypnotize anyone who's ambidextrous. Something to do with the two brain hemispheres."

"How did you know I'm ambidextrous?"

Mackay's eyes were steady. "I make it my business to know all I can about people making these voyages. It's not like an international airline flight, over in a few hours. A passenger's on this ship for more than a hundred days, maybe twice that if we have to use a long transfer. I want to know all I can about them."

"You wouldn't have had time to build up a dossier on me, would you? I was booked on the voyage only a couple of days before liftoff."

Mackay nodded. "But you're well known. Plenty of data available on you. I have reliable contacts dirtside."

"What data do you have on Jocasta Borg?"

Mackay's expression hardened. Even though Lance could see little more than his eyes and mouth behind the luxuriant beard, he was aware of the shift in mood. "The data on all passengers is confidential," said Mackay. "But I can tell you this: She's quite stable, reliable. I've known her for years. We use some servo equipment made in one of her factories."

"And how about Dr. Stein?"

"I've known him a long time, too. Solid. Predictable."

"Any passengers on this trip you *haven't* known previously?"

Mackay seemed to consider for a moment before responding. "Only you, young Gray, and the two young girls. Sisters. But it's their first trip to Earth, and they went all over it as tourists. They wouldn't have had time to fit in anything complicated." He made a slight movement as if about to show Lance out.

Lance began to leave. "Well, thanks," he said.

As he neared the door of the control room, Mackay clapped a large hand on his shoulder in a gesture that was almost paternal. "I wouldn't worry about appearances in the relationship between Jocasta and young Gray," he said. "Our civilization is different from yours. Some of us—like Jocasta—have lived a very long time, much longer than an unaided physical body could go on functioning effectively. Longevity brings its own set of responsibilities, its own accumulation of knowledge. People recognize that. You'll get used to it."

Get used to it! Lance smiled to himself as he made the journey back to his cabin, feeling more weight return to him as the elevator carried him farther away from the ship's axis. He felt almost at home now in the Martian gravity. The shower and hydrojohn needed little special adjustment from Earth-normal practice.

His usual optimism began to return, and he actually found himself whistling as he went out along the annular passageway to the canteen.

There were no other passengers there. He selected his food and watched it being warmed behind a glassite door. The canteen was fully automated, and as he poured his coffee he wondered how they managed to supply what appeared to be fresh milk. It was unthinkable that they kept a cow or two somewhere aboard. Then he remembered the molecular stabilization technique. He didn't know how it worked, yet, but if it had kept Ted Allen in stasis on the inward trip to Earth, it would be a simple matter to apply it to a large supply of milk and fresh vegetables taken aboard shortly before leaving Earth orbit. Meat, eggs, cream—the menu printed alongside the cooking console was long and varied.

Halfway through his meal of meat patties, egg and potatoes, he wished he had dialed something more imaginative. Consoling himself that he had the rest of the voyage to experiment, he went ahead and enjoyed it.

He was just finishing his second cup of coffee when Phil Gray came in. "Hi, Lance," he said cheerfully. "Been up long?"

"Had a lot of sleep to catch up on. Feel great now." Lance watched Gray as he crossed to the coffee dispenser. "How did you get on with Jocasta?"

Gray brought his coffee back to Lance's table, his round eyes bright with excitement. "She's an amazing woman, Lance. It's as if she's only thirty or forty years old, but with a century of experience behind her. But say! I just met the most fabulous girls!"

"Where?"

"Just left them up in the library. Their names are Heidi and Joy. They're in cabins just along from ours. Joy's only nineteen, our years. Heidi's a bit older, about thirty, although you wouldn't think it. They look like twins."

Lance grinned. "That might liven up the voyage a bit. Are they easy to get to know?"

"Like I said, fabulous!" Gray sought for a better adjective, failed to find it. "Just fabulous."

"What's the library like?"

"All on micro. Plenty of projection terminals. Encyclopedias, everything you're likely to need."

"I must have a look at that. I'll check it out now."

Gray grinned as he finished his coffee. "I'll take you up and show you," he said.

His terminology was still Earth-oriented. When he had said "up" to the library he was influenced by the apparent upward curve of the passage that ran around the circumference of the ship, so that you always had the visual illusion of walking upward, yet the tactile sensation of moving along a horizontal plane. About a third of the way around the ship, Gray led Lance through a door marked LIBRARY.

All the books were on microdisk, and it probably took some time to become familiar with the indexing system. Lance didn't try—there was plenty of time to master it, and he was mainly interested in the two girls sitting in front of display screens feeding books through. Both turned as Gray called their names. "Heidi, Joy—I'd like you to meet Lance Garrith. He's the man who presents those programs called 'Specialists' Report.'"

The two girls stood up. Both were striking blondes, and Lance could see why Gray had been stuck with the repeated adjective "fabulous." They were—he sought for a word for some seconds in his mind before he found it—simply fabulous.

With the exception of the cybernetic-bodied Jocasta, they were the first Martian-born women he had seen. Tall, slender, supple, they had a deeper chest development than most Earth girls, bringing their breasts forward and upward. They stood very erect, heads back, looking at him with friendly smiles. They wore close-fitting garments like swimsuits, leaving their limbs completely bare, with brief skirts added apparently to supply pockets. They looked at first glance like twin sisters, their figures almost identical, but he could see the difference in their ages by the subtle contrast in their facial expressions. Joy had the wide-eyed look of a girl to whom everything is a fascinating new experience. Heidi's eyes, the same brilliant blue as her sister's, gave the impression of having seen far more.

"We watched your program last night," she said. "A taped version." She spoke English with a trace of some mixed accent—with hints of Japanese, Russian, Italian?—Lance was unable to analyze it. He knew that the Martian settlements had drawn specialized people from a number of countries, and apparently the original North American English tongue had been contaminated—or enriched—by nuances from the others.

"What did you think of it?" he asked, a question he rarely put to anyone directly.

"We often watch 'Specialists' Report' back home," said Heidi. "Usually, it's half a year after you've made it, because the disks are shipped out. Theoretically, Solar News controls the dissemination of Earth news all over Mars, but in practice any really 'hot' story gets out as soon as it happens."

Lance wondered what Mort Channing would have said if he'd heard that. Perhaps it would be better for all if he never knew that his absolute power over his empire didn't extend as far as he thought.

"By the way," broke in Joy, "what do you think that thing that came toward Mars really was?"

Lance looked at her. "That's funny. Jocasta Borg asked me the same question."

It was Heidi who answered him. "Naturally. Jocasta saw the program with us. We were all talking about it."

Something seemed familiar about the two girls, and suddenly

Lance realized what it was. The smooth oval faces, the blond hair, the shape of the eyebrows.

"By the way," he said, "she's not your mother, is she?"

The girls exchanged glances, then Heidi burst into sudden laughter. "How old do you think she is?"

"Sorry, I didn't stop to think. She told me she'd been in that body for sixty-odd years, so I guess it's impossible."

"I suppose a lot of us *do* resemble each other. The gene pool on Mars wouldn't be as extensive yet as it is on Earth."

Joy turned abruptly to Gray, who had been standing by in silence. "Phil," she said, "I've finished what I was doing here. Would you like to see that video I promised to show you?"

"Sure," said Gray eagerly.

"Will you excuse us?" Joy took Gray by the arm and led him out of the library. Heidi flashed a sudden smile at Lance.

"The joys of the young," she said.

"You don't look much older than your sister," objected Lance.

"I'm sixteen, she's eleven." Heidi smiled at his expression of disbelief. "*Our* years, of course."

He made a rapid calculation. Sixteen Martian years multiplied by one-point-eight-eight would make her about thirty terrestrial years old—a little older than she looked, but he had heard the light Martian gravity was less aging than Earth's.

The hundred and fifty days of the voyage had been looming as a long, dull gap in his busy life. Now, however, the prospect was becoming more tolerable.

But then he recalled that someone had tried to kill him, perhaps masterminded by one of the people on this voyage. And if some determined person on board wanted him dead, there was no place he could hide for five months.

Was he developing paranoia? Or was he simply being realistic?

As the voyage went on without any perceptible threat directed toward Lance's well-being, he began to feel a little more relaxed. Shipboard routine was quite flexible for the passengers, without any external rhythm of day and night to govern their schedules. Lance spent a considerable proportion of his time in the library, running through disks showing all aspects of Martian life.

The disks built up for him a picture of an unexpectedly complex civilization. He had the impression of a culture in some ways less civilized than Earth's, yet technologically more advanced, more vigorous. Logical, when he came to consider it, because its original immigrants had been largely composed of scientists and engineers who had found Earth organizations restrictive—men like Noel Karstrom, and others who had followed his example, perhaps using him as a role model.

Another person who spent a large amount of time in the library was Heidi, although she used it to make a study of the culture and history of Earth, while he was gathering data on Mars. They soon fell into the habit of exchanging information about their respective homes, and a friendship rapidly deepened between them.

Heidi's thirty-day visit to Earth had been a prominent highlight in her life. She had obviously planned it in meticulous detail for a long time before the voyage, and had landed with a long list of places and things she felt it essential to see. It was not quite the list Lance would have expected, although on reflection it made sense to him.

She had been fascinated by Earth's abundant water—by the oceans, rivers, the glaciers of high latitudes, and seaports. Tropical vegetation had thrilled her, too, and equatorial jungles and coral reefs had featured high on her list. On the other hand, mountains and deserts did not seem to have impressed her. Her own planet abounded with these, and she had apparently toured over many parts of it, in sealed ground vehicles or in the local type of aircraft called rotojets, a sort of helicopter with large rotating wings driven by compact jet motors mounted on the actual wings, an old, relatively unsuccessful terrestrial idea from the middle of the twentieth century adapted to deal with the extremely thin atmosphere of Mars.

Lance was intrigued by an ornamental headband she always wore, with a blue jewel in the center of her forehead, like a large sapphire in an intricately carved setting. Once, he touched it lightly with his finger.

"You and your sister both wear these," he said, "all the time."

She made no comment, apart from a brief nod.

"May I have a closer look at it?"

He took a small folding magnifier from his pocket. As he looked at the jewel closely, she remained perfectly still, without any change in her expression.

"Is that a tiny lens in the center of the jewel?" he asked.

She hesitated, then nodded. "It's a little TV camera. Do you mind?"

He tried to lift it away from her forehead, but it seemed to be stuck to her skin, and she gave a little murmur of protest.

"Can't you take it off?"

"Not easily. Does it bother you?"

"Yes, damn it, it does! Who's at the other end of the line?"

She laughed. "Only a recorder. These paid for our trips to Earth—both Joy's and mine."

"How, for God's sake?"

Perhaps for the first time, she looked furtively away from him while speaking. "I suppose I'd better explain. A—a group of people wanted to make an in-depth study of lifestyles. We simply volunteered to have these fitted and went about our everyday business of living, and everything we looked at or listened to was automatically recorded."

"*All* of it? In something *that* size?"

"Relayed, of course, to more bulky equipment. But all of it." She looked back at him, her eyes wide and candid. "An enormous amount of data for someone to sift through, some day. But don't worry about it—Joy and I have nothing to hide, nothing we wouldn't want the observers to see."

"What sort of observers? God, what sort of voyeurs would spend their time eavesdropping on you?" He took hold of her slim shoulder. "You traveled all over Earth with these things, didn't you?"

She forced a smile. "If you're thinking of espionage, don't worry. Most of us know more about your world than ninety-nine per cent of your own people." A heightening of color in her normally pallid cheeks warned him not to pursue the subject any farther for the moment.

He took his hand off her shoulder, and she gently caressed the place he had held with her other hand. He could understand her motivation in wearing the camera. The lure of a journey to the Home Planet, by-passing the massive cost involved, would have been a powerful incentive.

Apart from this one clash over her recording camera, there seemed to be no taboo subjects between them. As long as he kept away from this one topic, they felt easy in each other's company. In a way, she reminded him of Dorella.

Dorella! He remembered her individual sense of style, her vivid enthusiasms. But it would be a year before he would be able to see her again.

And this girl was here!

* * *

As the voyage went on, taking the *Yttria* farther and farther away
from the Earth and the Sun, Lance and Heidi drifted into the habit
of spending more and more time together. From Lance's point of
view, she was the only logical companion.

Captain Mackay, and his assistants Stavros and Kenzo, were
too busy with their obsessive supervision of the almost completely
automated running of the ship—or at least that was the public
image they presented. At the other end of the scale, Phil Gray
and Joy seemed to have formed a close social system of their own,
isolated from the other passengers by a generation gulf.

Dr. Stein spent most of his time in his cabin, reviewing the
recent medical data he had accumulated on his visit to Earth, and
Ted Allen was making practically the whole voyage in stasis, so
that after the first few hours in space no one saw him.

Lance did, at least, have a few games of 3D chess with Jocasta
Borg after staggering through a few tentative games with Heidi.
Neither he nor Heidi had played the game before. It was played
by keyboards, the pieces appearing in a hologram cube with 512
small cubes within it, eight files across, eight ranks deep, and
eight levels high, like eight old-style chessboards piled one above
the other. The translucent cubes were alternately clear yellow and
green, and the projected white and red images of the pieces flicked
from cube to cube in any direction on commands from the keyboards.

Lance, though quite a competent player of the old-style two-
dimensional chess, was unused to the idea of pieces that could
attack vertically, or up and down a forty-five degree slope, and
the knight's move in three dimensions was something he felt he
would never be able to master.

His games with Jocasta taught him something about the game,
but as she had played it for many years, there was no real contest
between them. Lance found her a disconcerting opponent. He had
always been good at reading an adversary's body language, but
Jocasta's was nonexistent. The cybernetic body was as motionless
as a plastic barrel in the uncreased blue leatheroid jacket, except
for the occasional darting movement of the black-gloved hand as
she made a move. She kept her facial expression under complete
control. Heidi, watching the game from the side, seemed to sense
his irritation.

"It's not fair, Lance. She can alter her glandular secretions any
way she likes. Can't you, Jocasta?"

"If necessary," said Jocasta.

"How do you do that?" asked Lance.

The pale blue eyes looked up at him, and suddenly they darkened as the pupils seemed to expand to almost cover the irises, while the rest of her face blanched. She made a sudden movement with her left arm, the small one ending in the two-fingered clamp. "This doesn't need all the nerve channels that used to control my left hand. Now, some of them directly control my hormone balance from inside my body—if I need more adrenaline, more thyroxine, more pituitary stimulation of one kind or another, I can program myself, be any sort of person I wish, and no one can see me make the change." Her gloved hand whipped forward to the keyboard. "Check! From the far upper corner."

Lance stared at the hologram cube. "I didn't see it. And the next move's mate, isn't it?"

"Not quite." Jocasta's hand danced over the keyboard, and the pieces moved in response. "You could go there, but I'd get you from down here."

Heidi came to Lance's defense. "He's used to having sixty-four squares to watch. Now he has to keep his eye on five-hundred-odd."

Jocasta lengthened her telescopic legs, rising to look down on the hologram cube before flicking off its switch. "If you'll excuse me, youngsters, I have work to do." Turning, she strode away with her firm, stiff-legged walk.

Lance began another game with Heidi. They were better matched, although once or twice he had the feeling she purposely didn't take advantage of early mistakes on his part.

There were a few things that still puzzled him about Heidi. Neither she nor her sister ever spoke of their family. Although he thought this odd, Lance didn't pursue any inquiries lest he unearth some family secret traumatic to both girls.

Heidi didn't mention any previous male friends, but on the other hand, she never asked him about his relationship with his wife or about any other alliance he might have formed. She simply didn't appear curious about any past chapters in his life.

Lance, who had lived at high pressure for a long time, found her company relaxing. They seemed to slip into each other's lives as if they had known each other for years.

They had most of their meals together and spent some time in the observation room, where wall screens gave the illusion of sitting on an open veranda in the middle of interplanetary space.

The Earth and the Moon were far distant now, just a pair of bright stars, the larger noticeably blue, and on another screen Mars looked hardly any closer than when they had first seen it from space.

"Lance," she said after one of their long intervals of mutual silence, "have you ever made love to a girl in 38 centigees?"

He hesitated a long time before he replied. "Listen, Heidi, I can see the next question, but have you thought it through?"

"What d'you mean?"

"This: You come from a disease-free environment, what amounts to a planet-size cleanroom. I come from Earth, and I wander all over it. To your people, it's a planet jumping with every conceivable variety of disease germ and virus, a thousand things against which I've built up resistance, but you haven't."

"Do you think I'm stupid?" Her voice took on a hard edge. "I know the examinations they must have given you before you were allowed to travel on this ship."

He put his hands on her shoulders, and her eyes looked directly into his. With the back of his fingers, he gently stroked her cheek, the angle of her jawbone, the side of her neck. Suddenly she put her arms around him, pulling him against her. Her perfume was subtle, evocative, stirring something within him.

Almost unwillingly, at first, he brought his lips against hers.

Although Heidi had never mentioned any previous association, when she made love to him it became obvious from her originality and variety that a considerable reservoir of experience lay in her past.

But once, when he was lying alongside her, a strange thing happened. An impulse made him throw his arm around her and draw her tightly against him, his cheek against hers.

"I can hear the beating of your heart," he murmured. And then, with his ear close against hers, he had the odd feeling that he could hear a voice at the very threshold of his hearing, like a whisper within her skull. He did not catch what it said, but he had the impression it stopped immediately as though its originator had abruptly become aware that he had heard it.

"What's the matter, darling?" asked Heidi.

"Nothing. I thought I heard someone speaking. Must have been noises in my head."

She stirred slightly, but did not reply for a few seconds. "Perhaps it was the voice of your conscience," she said lightly.

"That never speaks to me now," he said.

"Maybe you've offended it."

He rolled into a half-sitting position, resting on his elbow and keeping very still.

"What is it now?" she asked.

"Just listening. Someone in one of the other cabins must have been playing a radio or something. I could have sworn I heard a voice."

"I heard nothing. Wouldn't have been a radio out here, though. Must have been a recorder, something like that."

He was silent for a few seconds. "Yes, something like that," he agreed.

But he still felt an uneasy tension. He was not quite certain he had really heard the voice, but that one flicker of doubt remained to give him a haunting feeling of insecurity.

Heidi swung her legs off the divan and stood up in a single fluid motion. Watching her, Lance smiled. If he had tried to stand up like that in this gravity, he would have ducked his head to avoid ramming it against the ceiling, but a lifetime of Martian gravity had enabled Heidi to coordinate her movements perfectly. She glided across to the dressing table and began spraying perfume on her body from a bottle with a little pressure bulb. Against the white of her breasts, her areolae were lilac.

"Here," she said. "Roll face-down, honey, and tell me how this feels."

She began rubbing some liquid onto his bare back.

"Good," he murmured, his eyes closed.

"Relax," she said, and her hands moved up and down the length of his spine, fingers working each side of his vertebrae.

"Better?"

"Uh-huh. Great."

The massage continued. "Not worried about hearing voices anymore?"

"No. But, you know, I *did* hear something, whatever it was."

She said nothing for a minute or two, continuing her skillful pressure with her fingers. Then she stopped and he heard bottles or jars clink. Suddenly, something cold sprayed on the skin of his back. "That feel good?" she asked.

"Cold. Feels funny. It seems to go right into my skin—like benzol."

"It's supposed to. It'll make you feel good."

He remained lying face-down, enjoying the brisk pressure of

her hands. He thought vaguely of Dorella. He wouldn't have thought she'd have this expertise—like a chiropractor. Then, abruptly, his mind sharpened. This wasn't Dorella—it was Heidi.

But the moment of sharp focus was brief. Dorella—Heidi—perfume—cold stuff on his back—it all seemed to run together in a blur. He made an effort to roll over and sit up.

But something had gone wrong with his coordination. And with his sight. One instant, the room about him seemed vast, like an enormous hall, with a blurred, gigantic figure towering above him. Next, its walls seemed to crowd together, within touching distance . . . Then everything began to dissolve in a roaring vortex . . .

chapter
7

HE AWOKE LYING on his back under harsh white light. The ceiling above him looked like white plastic, curving smoothly into walls of the same material. It reminded him of something he couldn't place for a while, as the mist cleared slowly from his mind.

He had the back view of a tall man in a white coverall, standing at a table. When he tried to say something to attract his attention, his voice squawked like a rusty hinge.

The man turned, and Lance recognized Dr. Stein. He moved closer to Lance and stood looking down at him.

"How are you feeling?"

"What happened?"

"You passed out. Common enough phenomenon in someone who's just made a major change in gravitational field."

"It's got nothing to do with gravity. I was doped."

Stein looked down at him for a long time, then slowly shook his head. "Couldn't find any symptoms of doping. No sign of an injection. No—"

"No injection," said Lance. "It was skin absorption. Something she sprayed on my back. Went into the skin like benzol."

Stein half-turned away. "She said she rubbed your back with a preparation. Common enough stuff—trade name Glissade. It's possible you may be allergic to it. Often you find a substance that's innocuous to nine hundred and ninety-nine people out of a thousand, and the thousandth comes down with an allergy from the slightest contact with it. Happens with foods—"

"This was no allergy. How long have I been out?"

"Well, you've been lying there for almost an hour, since Jocasta and the girls brought you to me."

"Jocasta? But I wasn't with her."

"No. You were with Heidi. When you passed out, she didn't

know what to do. She called her sister, then Jocasta. Apparently they spent some time trying to revive you, then brought you along here. By the way, they brought your clothes. They're here.''

"And this is—" Lance looked around the white-walled room.

"We call it the ship's hospital," said Stein. "Compact, but quite well equipped."

"Have you a medical reference library here?"

Stein glanced at a side door. "What did you want to know?"

"Have you a list of known drugs and their effects?"

"Fairly up to date, yes. Of course, new compounds come out every few days, both on Earth and on Mars. You'd need an enormous facility to keep up with all the work that's going on.''

"Could I see what you have?"

"You're welcome, any time. What did you want to look for?"

"Drugs that can be administered through the human skin."

"Aren't you—well, overreacting about this?" Stein made a dismissive movement with his hand. "As I said, most likely an allergy problem. Happens all the time."

Lance sat up on the table and swung his feet to the floor. He hesitated before standing, and Stein said sharply, "What is it?"

"Dizzy, that's all. It'll pass." Lance stood up, swaying slightly. He put his hand up to the back of his neck, feeling a spot just behind and below his right ear. "That's funny."

"What is?"

"Slight itch—just there. Feels like an insect bite."

"Couldn't be. Not here. But let's have a look." Stein moved behind him "Can't see anything. No, wait a minute." He went to his desk and returned with a powerful magnifier with a built-in light. "Hold still a second."

Lance waited while Stein examined the spot he had indicated. He heard Stein exhale.

"There *is* something there. Does look like a small insect bite."

"How the hell could an insect get aboard this ship?"

"It *has* happened. Things come up on the shuttles, sometimes in cargo. Get loose inside the ship. Wouldn't worry about it. The thing will die soon enough."

"Probably a mosquito, or a flea, if it lives on blood."

"Neither of those. The bite's so small I can hardly see it without the glass." Stein put his magnifier away. "If it gives you trouble, come and see me. Better see me anyway. I'm under contract to keep all the passengers healthy." He gave what was intended to sound like a cheerful laugh.

Lance dressed, then walked slowly about the room, testing his balance and timing. Whatever had caused the loss of consciousness, there seemed to be no lasting effects. Stein watched him without comment, except for a brief "see you later," as he went out into the passageway.

By the time he reached his cabin, he felt normal, as if nothing unusual had happened. But when he checked the time, and remembered looking at the clock before Heidi had begun massaging his spine, he realized that there was a bigger gap in his consciousness than he had thought—as nearly as he could calculate, between ninety and a hundred minutes.

He could recall nothing of that period, yet several people had been with him—Heidi, Jocasta, Joy, Stein, at least.

He made himself a cup of coffee, drinking it slowly and thoughtfully. Then, with a sudden resolve, he went out and followed the passageway to the library. At the moment, there was no one else there. He found the indexing system and looked up the microdisks for medical data.

The sheer volume of the material defeated his purpose. He didn't have enough specialized knowledge to know what to look for, and after a time he abandoned his search. He browsed through a number of unconnected subjects, then selected some disks on microminiaturization. He was astounded at some of the strides that had been made quite recently, with circuits containing parts only a few molecules thick. He was particularly astonished at some of the research and development carried out on Mars using some of the formerly rare metals now mined out in the asteroids.

While he was studying the data, a two-way TV unit at the end of the room came to life, its screen showing Captain Mackay's red-bearded face, startling against the background of a green wall, while the movable camera below the screen swung to focus on Lance.

"Ah, there you are," boomed Mackay's voice. "I've received a message for you from—" he glanced at something in his hand, "from Mort Channing of Solar News. Person-to-person message. If you come up to the control room, I'll run it through for you."

Mackay met him at the door of the red-lit room and led him into a small adjoining space where a TV screen faced a table and seats. "Think you'll find this interesting, in view of some of the things you told me." He started the cassette running. A series of figures lit up on the screen, and then Lance found himself looking at a fairly sharp image of Mort Channing.

"Personal call to Lance Garrith," said Channing. "We can't two-way with this because of the distance, Lance, but I want you to call me back as soon as you've heard it. There's a delay of fifteen seconds each way, as you're four and a half million k's out." It was obviously night where Channing was transmitting— the window behind him showed dark except for a few scattered points of light. His expression was serious.

"Lance, when you get to Hellas, be careful! I don't know what we've stumbled on, but someone doesn't like what we're digging up. You know the fellow who pulled a gun in your segment of 'Specialists' Report'? He's dead. While he was being held for questioning, something implanted inside him exploded, apparently by radio detonation. Only tiny—Hartz and his boys missed it— tiny, but placed so that it killed him. Now, I don't like that. Very sophisticated technique.

"Something bad's linked with this thing, Lance, and I haven't a clue what it is. So be damn careful! And keep in touch. Call me back when you've heard this, and get back to me as soon as you've contacted Brad Hagen. Good luck. I'll see you."

Mackay snapped off the seat as the screen went blank. "You want to reply to him?" he asked.

"Yes. Can I have a copy of that?"

"Sure." Mackay touched the ejector and handed the cassette to Lance. "You can tape a reply here, if you like. I'll send it right away."

He went back into the red-lit control room, and Lance fitted a blank cassette into a recorder on the table. He thought for a while before beginning.

"Personal call to Mort Channing, Solar News Building, Lagoon Boulevard, Pacific City." He held down the pause button while he recalled the zip code, added it, then paused again. At last, he made up his mind how he would handle this.

"Mort, I received your warning. I'll be careful *if* I ever make it to Hellas. I think someone may have tried something already, here on the ship. If I don't arrive in good condition, you might have a check run on some of the passengers. I think Captain Mackay's okay, but there are a couple of others. A girl called Heidi, Mars-born, about thirty, may have slipped me an updated version of the old Mickey Finn. Skin-penetrating spray. I was out for about an hour and a half after it. Then there's a woman called Jocasta Borg. Cybernetic body, claims to be about a hundred years old, runs a firm called Belastra. Then there's the doctor on this ship, Ralph Stein. They were all around me while I was unconscious—look, Chief, if anything happens to me, I leave it to you to follow up. Be in touch later. I'll call you just before planetfall, if I can do that.''

He took the cassette in to Mackay, who accepted it with a nod. Crossing the room, he placed it in a recorder. "Have to listen to it before I transmit it—Line rules,'' he explained.

Lance, unprepared for this, said nothing, but he watched Mackay as he listened to the tape. He smirked slightly when Lance's voice said: "I think Captain Mackay's okay,'' but when he mentioned the other passengers his expression grew stony. Before the cassette had finished, he stabbed his finger at the rewind button, ran it back to the start, then pressed erase. As the tape whirred across the heads, he looked coldly at Lance.

"I can't transmit a thing like that,'' he said. "If Earth's media got hold of it, there'd be all hell breaking loose. All I can let you send from here is a straight acceptance of Channing's message. Oh, you can say you'll contact him when you reach Mars, if you like. Now, try again.'' He handed Lance the now blank cassette.

Lance tried again. This time, the message satisfied Mackay, but it must have told Mort Channing practically nothing.

Returning to his cabin, Lance felt the side of his neck where he had thought he sensed an insect bite. There was nothing he could detect externally, but he still felt uneasy. After all, Hartz and his observant team had missed the implanted device that had killed the hypnotized assassin.

Was Lance now carrying around inside him a miniscule bomb that could terminate his life at any second? On the decision of someone he did not know?

Fear was an emotion Lance Garrith rarely felt. In almost every situation in which he had found himself in the past, his natural optimism and his faith in his own survival ability had precluded any long-term experience of fear. True, like anyone else, he had felt moments of fear, as when a vehicle he was driving skidded on a slippery road, but within a fraction of a second this had always been swamped by the vigorous animal reactions of self-preservation, the burst of adrenaline flooding his bloodstream.

But here was a situation different from anything he had encountered. No rapid animal reflexes could handle it. He was quite convinced, on further thought, that some miniature device had been implanted close to the base of his skull. Moreover, the person who had implanted it was still here with him on the ship. One touch on a switch, somewhere, might blow his head off.

Sweat began to trickle down his body as he had a vivid memory of that polystyrene foam dummy in Security's basement shooting range back at Solar News, the top of it blown to shreds by a tiny pellet of explosive smaller than a pin's head. That gave him a measure of the power of the explosives these people used.

Yet that amount of destruction would be unnecessary. A still smaller charge of the same material against the base of his skull, could kill him instantly without any externally obvious damage.

But who had actually implanted the thing? Jocasta? Mackay? Stein? Even Heidi?

The thought of Heidi was particularly painful. He had trusted her completely, and he felt an enormous sense of betrayal. Whether she had implanted the device or not, it was she who had sprayed him with the skin-penetrating drug that had wiped out his consciousness for an hour and a half, making the secret implant possible.

He would still be on the ship for nearly five months, and there was no way he could escape from it. He could send out no messages that would reveal his plight—Mackay would see to that. As to escape, the chances were zero. From an aircraft in atmosphere, from a seaborne ship, he might have had a chance. But from the *Yttria*, surrounded by cold, boundless, utterly hostile vacuum, there was no way out.

He spent a few hours lurking in his cabin and in the library avoiding other passengers. Slowly, however, the first chilling paralysis of fear began to dissipate.

There was no need for anyone to kill him right now. He tried to work out what he would do if the positions were reversed.

Why kill the victim immediately? Far better to wait until he left the ship. Suppose, after he landed, someone followed him, carrying the radio device that would trigger the explosion? They could wait until he began driving a vehicle, or walking across a busy street, then press the switch. His death would be written off as simply another accident.

After the next meal period, during which he ate without much enjoyment, he went to see Dr. Stein.

"You told me to come back to you," he said.

"Ah, yes. Has anything changed?"

"Only that I'm quite convinced now that someone implanted something at the base of my skull. Just here."

Stein tilted his head back and looked at Lance through his rimless glasses, his large teeth showing in a cheerful grin. "And you think it might have been me—is that it?"

Lance shook his head. "Pointless coming here if I suspected that, don't you think? Look, I want you to give me a microscan through the neck, at whatever angle you think best."

Stein looked away, rubbing his lean fingers across his long jaw. "I don't know about that."

"Have you the equipment here?"

"I have it, yes. But I've heard about these implants before. Sometimes they're made so a scan triggers the explosion. Could be dangerous. Not to me, of course, because I'd see to it that I wasn't too close. But quite a small explosion there would do you no good at all."

Lance stood up angrily, forgetting the light gravity, and quickly thrust his hand against the ceiling to halt his upward movement.

"Careful!" warned Stein.

Lance gave a sardonic smile. "Don't want an explosion in here, eh?"

Stein shrugged, and pointed to Lance's neck. "Doesn't have to be a bomb, of course. People often implant things for other purposes than destruction. But you'd better play it safe."

"How do I do that?"

Stein thought for a while. "Well, if we assume it *is* an explosive, someone must have the idea you're likely to say something or do something that might be dangerous to them. All you need to do is figure out what you're not supposed to say, or do. Then make sure you don't do it—or better, convince them that you're not going to do it."

"But that's ridiculous. I don't even know who I'm dealing with, or what's their problem."

Stein shook his head with a maddening smile. "It's not *me* you have to convince of that."

Lance went back to his cabin. Perhaps, he thought, all these people were in a conspiracy together—Mackay, Jocasta, Stein, Heidi— or was that the kind of thinking leading to paranoia? "They're all out to get me!" He had encountered that reaction in other people and had always found it mildly amusing. Now, it didn't seem funny.

It occurred to him that he would gain nothing by trying to avoid everyone for the rest of the voyage. It was one of those situations where attack might be the best form of defense.

If it was a conspiracy between these four people, the weakest link in the chain was probably Heidi, the youngest and least experienced. But how would he approach the subject? A straight accusation that she had doped him would meet with a vigorous denial, making further communication between them unworkable.

Perhaps the best line of approach would be a casual meeting with her, pretending he had forgotten the incident. But where? She had not appeared in the library since the time when he had been doped, which in itself was enough to fuel his suspicion of her.

By leaving his cabin door open, he was able to hear any activity along the passageway, and when he heard the voices of Heidi and her sister, he was able to slip out and follow them along to the cafeteria, arriving as if by accident. He went up to Heidi as she was pouring herself a cup of coffee. She turned—a little too suddenly, he thought—as she sensed him near her.

"Lance! Are you feeling better now?"

"Sure. Must have been what Doc Stein said, the sudden change in gravity. He told me it happens to a lot of people." He began pouring his own coffee while Heidi stood by with hers, and as soon as he had finished, she nodded toward a table. Her sister was already sitting at another table, watching a video screen with apparent absorption.

"You know," said Heidi, "I feel responsible for what happened to you, somehow."

"Why?"

"That spray I used on your skin. I can't help feeling someone may have put something into it."

"Where did you get it?"

She hesitated. "The ship's store, I think. Might have been there from a previous voyage. Afterward, I took the container along to Doc Stein and let him have a look at it. Funny, it seemed to me it felt different. Lighter. I wondered then if someone had switched the containers."

A neat escape route, thought Lance. Had she planned this way out from the beginning? The blue eyes looked utterly candid and guileless as they stared into his. The eyes of an innocent girl, or a confidence woman? Take your pick.

"Who do you think might have done it?" he asked.

She shook her head. "I can't think of anyone. Can you?"

He changed direction. "What *was* the stuff you sprayed on me?"

"Only Glissade—a sort of lubricant for rubbing tired muscles. It penetrates a bit, has a slightly anaesthetic effect inside muscles when they're aching. Perhaps you're allergic to it, as Ralph suggested."

"Ralph?"

"Doctor Stein."

"Ah, yes."

She nodded at the motionless form of her sister. "She's rapt. She's a video freak. Let's go along to my cabin." She kept her voice down to an almost inaudible whisper. Close to him, she had a scent like frangipani, and the pulse in his ears was like a drumbeat.

In her cabin, he lay beside her on the divan, and they both watched the screen that gave a view of outside space.

"It was good when you were making love to me," she murmured. "You're different from anyone else I've known. So strong, with your Earth-gravity muscles. Gentle, but you can feel the strength there. On Mars, you'll be like one of those mythical supermen." She smiled, running her slim fingers around the curves of his deltoids. "You ought to wear a leotard with your initial on your chest, and a red cape. And maybe a helmet with horns like the Vikings wore into battle—or was it the Samurai?"

Lance grinned. "That's probably an old fallacy. I doubt whether anyone, Viking or Samurai, went into battle wearing a helmet with horns. Nobody would be such a damn fool. The other guy could use one of the horns as a handle."

She thrust out her lower lip. "There goes one of my romantic dreams."

"Sorry. I'm a realist."

"All Earth history and mythology seem romantic to us. There's so much of it. But I suppose most of us aren't sure which is history and which is myth."

"A lot of people on Earth are hazy about that."

"Really?"

"Since photography and recording and TV came into use, history has been easy to check. Before that—" He spread his hands.

For a few seconds, they were both silent. He caressed her, then kissed her, bringing his ear close against hers. He held his breath, listening for any whisper from that voice he had heard, but this time he detected nothing. Either he had imagined the whole thing, or—

The alternative was something he didn't want to confront. Not yet, anyway. He put his arms around her and held her tightly. They lay like that for a minute or two, then suddenly she jerked her head back from him with a convulsive movement so that she could look into his face.

"Not still listening for voices in my head?"

He hesitated a moment, then laughed. "No. I've given that up. I think they hear me coming."

It was her turn to hesitate. Obviously, that was not the kind of answer she expected. "You still think you might have heard it?" she said in a small voice. "Tinnitus, perhaps?"

"I thought I heard something, from somewhere nearby. But let's forget it."

But it was clear to him that she had not forgotten the incident. The unanswered question seemed to hang between them like a thundercloud.

Alone again, Lance found himself comparing Heidi with Dorella. In appearance, general bearing, there was little to choose between them—both tall, slim, supple. Certainly, one was blond, the other dark, but to him that was an unimportant difference. Heidi seemed more sure of herself, at least on the surface, although he had known Dorella when she was under a certain amount of tension— her first night before the cameras of a worldwide television program.

Heidi had seemed more skilled at making him enjoy her company, yet there was something about Dorella's electric enthusiasm for whatever held her interest that resonated with a similar kind of enthusiasm within him.

But he would not see Dorella for another year. On the other hand, her image kept getting between him and Heidi.

Irritated by a feeling of indecision, he went to the library to work on his preliminary study of conditions on the planet toward which they were moving. It seems odd to him that the external viewing screens showed little change in the apparent distance of Mars, although the *Yttria* was moving through space faster than Lance had ever traveled in his life.

He had been unprepared for this five-month hiatus in his swift-flowing career. Probably it would not have been so traumatic for a person less obsessed with time. He still looked frequently at his watch, although the arbitrary ship time meant little out here. At least, he had begun leaving off his second watch, the one set to Pacific City time. When they were nearer Mars, he would adjust his watch to Hellas time. Then he realized he would need a new watch on arrival. The Martian sol of 24 hours, 37 minutes was beyond the reach of adjustment on his existing watches.

Looking through the histories of Martian settlement, he found that for the first few years settlers had used standard hours and minutes, beginning their day at midnight, and tacking the odd thirty-seven minutes onto the end of the day. Then they had adopted Martian Time, dividing their day, or sol, again into twenty-four equal Martian hours, each longer than a terrestrial hour by a minute and fifty-four seconds. Each minute was stretched by nearly two seconds, the difference masked by the alien tempo of movements generated in the lighter gravity.

To get Dorella and Heidi out of his mind, he forced himself to concentrate on his reason for being here. He was, after all, on his way to investigate the extra-solar probe that had landed on Mars. He still carried Jack Darch's photograph of the six-limbed alien in his wallet, and once again he took it out and placed it on the library table in front of him. After hearing Ted Allen's evaluation of Darch as a practical joker, he had begun to wonder whether the picture might not have been a hoax, like some of the flying saucer pictures of the last century, or earlier stories of dragons and basilisks. Yet now, when he looked at it, the stark, unearthly reality of the thing chilled his blood.

He took out his magnifier and studied it again in detail. He was so absorbed in it that he did not hear anyone else come into the library until a crisp female voice said, "What have you there?"

Startled, he looked up to find Jocasta standing in the doorway. She was wearing a different jacket, this time of bright yellow leatheroid, uncreased and new-looking on the rigid mechanical trunk. She stilted forward on the telescopic legs until she was right alongside him. It was too late for him to hide the picture, and he showed it to her with a short laugh.

"Just a fake picture done by someone back home," he said. "Good for a laugh at parties, sometimes."

She looked at it without smiling, taking it in her gloved hand. "Quite well done, isn't it?" she said. "You'd swear it was real, if it wasn't so impossible."

He put the photograph back in his wallet as she returned it to him. Standing close by his left side, she shortened her legs, keeping them parallel and vertical, tiny motors whining almost inaudibly as the legs retracted to about half their length, bringing her body down level with his.

"How are you feeling now?" she asked.

He looked directly into her eyes. They were as clear and candid as Heidi's. In the back of his neck, behind the right ear, he felt a strange, localized numbness. Something like an electric shock seemed to strike across to his cervical vertebrae, and the strength seemed to evaporate from his limbs. He felt as if he had taken a heavy blow across the back of the neck, a "rabbit punch."

He kept watching Jocasta, but she made no movement. With a gigantic effort of will, he stood up, and she immediately lengthened her legs to keep her face level with his.

"You look unsteady on your feet," she said. "Lean against me."

He leaned involuntarily against her. Inside the smooth jacket, the mechanical body was a solid, unyielding barrel, and she put the strange, flexible arm around him like a fat tentacle.

"I'll help you to your cabin," she said, the voice coming from the little speaker in front of her neck, or, rather, where her neck should have been, had her head not been set directly on her body.

"I'll be all right," he said, and with an intense burst of energy he slipped out from the encircling arm and went off through the door and along the passageway, lurching as if drunk. Halfway to his cabin he looked back and saw Jocasta standing just outside the library door, watching him. She lifted her hand and gave him a little wave, her expression unreadable. Above the robot-like body, her blond, plump-cheeked head looked grotesquely, vitally alive.

Back in his cabin, with the door closed, he lay down on the divan. His heart was beating unnaturally fast. The numbness had gone, but his muscular strength was returning only slowly.

What had happened? Clearly, whatever was implanted in his neck had the power to interfere with the nerve messages running from his brain down his spinal column, causing partial, temporary paralysis. Whoever controlled it could use it to kill him just as surely as if a bomb had been implanted in him. They had only to wait until he was hurrying across a street in front of oncoming traffic, or coming down a long stairway—any one of a thousand situations where correct coordination was essential.

Was it controlled by Jocasta?

He had watched her when the numbness first struck him, and she had not made the slightest movement. He had especially watched her hand—the long, metal-fingered hand in the black glove. It had not twitched a finger. Then he thought of the smaller arm on her left side, ending in the two-fingered clamp. He recalled what she had said when he had played chess with her: "This doesn't need all the nerve channels I used for my left hand. Now some of them directly control my hormone balance." That, and what else? Did some unseen nerve impulse and its relay inside the barrel body control the device implanted against his skull?

Or was the control in the hands of someone else on the ship, with Jocasta simply acting as observer?

One thing gave him limited satisfaction. There had been an attempt to control him, but to some extent, at least, *it had failed!*

He set his jaw, staring up at the ceiling. Whatever organization he had antagonized, it was not invincible!

chapter
8

THE REST OF the voyage was a mixture of boredom and nagging tension for Lance, until they decelerated to enter the final phase—insertion into a low elliptical orbit around Mars. At one point all spin-induced gravity was cut off for a limited time, while Mackay used his maneuvering jets to swing the great length of the *Yttria* end for end, so that the main rockets pointed forward.

Most of the passengers found the experience of free fall exciting, giving them the feeling of "really being in space" as Heidi put it to Lance. Free fall! This was the way the frontiers of the solar system had been opened up.

As they neared Mars, swinging down toward periapsis over the Hellas Basin, the viewing room became a popular venue. Hour by hour, the image of the planet grew on the screens, and Lance was appalled by its overall barrenness.

"Home!" said Heidi to her sister as they stood side by side, looking at the wild, orange-tinted landscape. From space, they could see the arid surface far more clearly than they had been able to see the landscapes of Earth from a similar distance out. A telescopic view on one of the screens scanned a strip of the surface as the ship moved around the globe, showing the vast shield volcanoes of the Tharsis Ridge, the almost Lunar craters and monstrous canyons, and the dry, ancient watercourses winding down northeastward toward the windlashed deserts that covered half the planet.

"Hellas City!" said Joy, pointing. "You can see the new high-way running out toward Argyre. They're still working on it."

Before he had left Pacific City, Lance had made a copy of the map on which Channing had sketched the area where the probe had landed. He took it out of his pocket now and studied it, but the area was hard to identify on the screens. Much of the region east of the Tharsis Ridge was chaotic, with jumbled arroyos and gullies. This was the wilderness in which Jack Darch had spent much of his life searching for valuable minerals, apparently without conspicuous success. The telescopic magnification of the vista unrolling across the screen showed a harsh, varied strip of terrain.

"Does anyone ever go out in those areas?" asked Lance, pointing.

"A few rare-metals prospectors and ice miners," said Heidi. "Most of our development is scheduled for the old impact basins. Hellas, which we've just passed over, Isidis, up that way in the northern hemisphere, and Argyre. It'll take time, of course, but we have plenty of time."

"You mean plenty of time as a race? Or as individuals?"

"Both. For a start, most of us tend to live longer in the light gravity and controlled atmosphere in our domes. Then there's another thing: Most of us have the ambition to succeed well enough to be able to afford life-extension systems when we're older."

"You mean like Jocasta?"

"Yes. Better, perhaps, by the time I need extending. They're making them better all the time."

Lance looked at her thoughtfully. "But what happens when your population becomes cluttered up with people who don't die? With heads and brains kept alive indefinitely by cybernetics?"

"There'll always be young ones coming up."

"But a planet gets filled up with people, eventually. Look at Earth! We're in a hell of a lot of trouble already trying to replace the tropical jungle areas that used to maintain our atmosphere balance."

Heidi laughed, and gestured to the screens. "We'll always have room to expand. There are other worlds. Even other stars. There's a whole galaxy out there."

Lance shook his head. "It mightn't be as easy as that."

Her expression became more serious. "Why? We're evolving new techniques all the time. Trouble is, you have a dirtside mentality, Lance. No, I shouldn't say that—but there's a tendency there. You've been contaminated by contact with all the billions of losers on your planet."

He was about to snap at her: "We're not a race of losers!" But the knee-jerk slickness of his retort stopped him before he uttered it. Instead, he silently looked down at the wind-eroded Martian surface rolling across the screens.

Billions of losers. Ridiculous? Yet he couldn't dismiss the idea as easily as he would have liked. "I think you're being a bit unfair to us," he said in a carefully controlled voice.

Heidi turned. "Let's ask Jocasta."

Jocasta Borg had just come into the viewing room, a bright splash of color in her yellow leatheroid jacket, her hand resting casually in its pocket. He realized now why her jacket always looked new, as if it had just come out of a showroom. The metal and plastic body didn't make the innumerable small movements of a living, organic body. It always stayed serenely upright on its black metal stilts, electronically balanced.

"What did you want to ask me, Heidi?"

"I've been telling Lance his optimism has been contaminated because he comes from a planet of billions of losers."

Jocasta turned to face Lance. With her head cushioned on the rigid trunk without a flexible neck, she turned her whole body with an almost dancing movement on the tapering legs.

"I don't think that's fair, Heidi. Lance comes from a world where losers tend to accumulate as the techniques of living advance. But that's been going on since the beginning of life. It happened when the first few species crawled out of the sea. Their descendants went on and up on the dry land, while the majority were left behind. That's a trend that'll go on forever."

Lance had to exert conscious control to stop his voice from rising. "I don't think it's quite like that. People's lives are always more complicated than they appear on the surface. I should know—I've interviewed people everywhere. A person who looks like a loser may be a success in some field you haven't thought of."

Jocasta turned to the screen, her hand pointing to the red landscape unrolling below. "I'm talking about winning and losing in a statistical sense, not looking at individuals. The living standards down here are much higher than the average levels in any part of the Earth. To me, that means our branch of the human race has moved another rung or two upward on the evolutionary ladder."

Her eyes looked straight into his, their expression supremely confident. Her face looked plump when she smiled. The thought came to him that she must have exceptional physical courage. He could have reached out and touched her unprotected face and head, motionless on its cushioned collar, yet she showed no fear of him. Then he remembered the implant at the base of his skull that had temporarily paralyzed him. If Jocasta indeed controlled it from within her cybernetic torso, she could at any instant deliver that rabbit-punch shock that could stun him. Her eyes were confident, yes, but watchful. Her hand rested in her pocket, and on the other side the smaller arm with its shining claw hung motionless. No visible movement in any part of her.

Heidi laughed suddenly. "Don't feel bad about it, Lance. Nobody wins an argument with Jocasta. She's seen all the gambits a thousand times."

"I don't doubt it," said Lance.

Jocasta gestured toward the screens. "We're swinging farther out. I'll come back to watch the next peri." Lance watched the back of her top-heavy, erect body as she stilted out with long, precise strides.

Heidi touched Lance's arm. "Quite a lady, isn't she?"

"A very complicated lady."

"Complicated—how?"

"It must do something to a woman's personality—to her ego—when she lives as a head on top of a machine."

Heidi laughed. "She gets by better than you'd think. I've known her for a long time. When I was a young girl—pre-puberty—I stayed with her while she was getting used to a new arm. She found the flexible one was better than one with an elbow, but she was awkward with it for a little while. Not long. I was soon superfluous."

"I can't imagine you ever being superfluous."

As she smiled at him, he was sharply aware of the jewel in her headband with its tiny lens. The micro-miniature TV camera within it was probably working right now, and somewhere a device was recording everything within the field of the minute fish-eye lens. He drew back. He had seen extreme close-ups taken with a fisheye lens, and the idea brought an uncharacteristic wave of reserve over him.

When the *Yttria* was halfway around its first Mars orbit, past the point they called apoastris, Lance was alone in the viewing room. He was glad of the temporary solitude, as it gave him a chance to review the strange succession of events that had happened to him.

He tried to build up a mental picture of the red planet on which he would soon be landing. He knew from photographs what it *looked* like, but what of its social structure? He thought of Jocasta's description of Earth as a world where losers multiplied as living techniques advanced—a process, she had pointed out, that had been going on since the beginning of time. Could he really say she was wrong?

He was jarred out of his reverie as Dr. Stein came in, his arm around the shoulders of Ted Allen.

"Here's Ted," he announced. "I brought him back to watch his homecoming."

"Hi!" said Allen, waving to Lance in a gesture of vague goodwill. Lance looked at him keenly. He was the first person he'd seen who had just been brought out of stasis. Allen looked slightly confused, an effect he tried to cover by a comedian's patter of stale jokes. He became more integrated when Lance drew his attention to the screens.

"We call that the Badlands," said Allen, pointing out the broken ground east of the Tharsis Shield. "Like the stuff your geologists call karst country in eroded limestone areas. No limestone down there, but the principle's the same."

"How?"

"Mars used to be wetter on the surface. Old watercourses have gone underground, and you've got what you'd call tunnel erosion on a hell of a scale. When everything dried out thousands of years ago, some of the tunnels fell in, and you get those steep-sided gullies. See?" He pointed to the screen.

Lance, who had by now learned the controls of the screens, brought the magnification up. "What's that?"

"What?" Allen moved closer to the screen.

"That thing with the long shadow. It looks artificial."

"Oh, that? It's one of the old launching towers Karstrom and his team used for their rockets. There's another, see? Farther along the same ridge."

"What rockets were those?"

"Oh, I believe they were sending satellites into space to beam signals to other star systems. Don't know whether they ever got any response. The towers haven't been used for years—you can see the way the steel's oxidized to the same color as the rocks. We've got a very rusty planet down there."

Stein broke into the conversation. "They're doing something about that. They're replicating a lot of the atmosphere generators they were experimenting with last year. Atmogens, they call them—get oxygen out of the rocks and start building the atmosphere."

"They reckon it'll take a hundred years," said Allen scornfully. "Who's going to wait for that?"

"Some people can," said Stein.

"You mean the immortals, as they call 'em?" Allen looked sour. "Why should *they* live as long as they like, just because they can afford it?"

"Don't kid yourself, Ted," retorted Stein. "You'd have been one of them if you'd struck paydirt down there."

"Don't think I'd bother, now. Different if I'd been able to extend while I was younger. But the way I feel now—jeez, why go on forever this way?"

Stein turned to Lance, winking. "We'll see what song he sings if he really strikes a bonanza. No one turns down an offer to live forever if it's put within his reach."

Lance looked at him thoughtfully. "How does that alter your society? People who don't die off."

Stein showed his large teeth in a grin. "It's good for it, in the long run. Look, most of our big decisions are made by people who are going to live for hundreds of years. They don't mind spending money and time on projects that aren't going to pay off until next century. That's good. We get long-range planning, which you never get to the same extent on Earth. All of your governments, whatever their political shade, are made up of men and women who know they'll only be in power for a decade or two at the most."

"That's an over-simplification," protested Lance.

"Course it is," broke in Allen. "Any political comment is—jevver think of that? And Ralph here's an over-simplifier from way back."

Stein shook his head, jerking his thumb at Allen. "Bring a fellow out of stasis, squirt the breath of life back into his frozen hulk, and he wakes up and insults you."

After some verbal horseplay that Stein was probably using to stimulate Allen, Lance said, "I'd better get a message down to my contact."

He made his way to the red-lit control room, where Mackay met him at the door, glancing pointedly at his watch.

"I want to send a message down to Solar News, Hellas. Want to tell them I'm arriving, and that I'd like to be met."

"Fair enough." Mackay handed Lance a micro-disk and indicated a recorder. Lance inserted the disk, took from his pocket his note of Hagen's address, and began recording:

"This is Lance Garrith, Solar News. To Brad Hagen, 1501 Viking Building, Octagon Plaza, Hellas Central 1000.

"Brad, arriving *Yttria* as scheduled. Hope to see you at the terminal. Lance."

That should be innocuous enough, he thought. Mackay's face was noncommittal as he ran the disk through his preliminary inspection. Then he gave it a second test on a slow-running machine, watching a cathode screen where a voice print danced in jagged peaks.

"Why all this?" asked Lance.

"I have to check. Line rules. Some people hide a compressed blip in a normal message. This is okay." He sounded slightly disappointed and sent the message out on the radio channel. "You'll get a reply back straight away," he said. "You may as well wait for it."

Lance waited. After a minute or so, a high-pitched voice came from a speaker on the wall. "The number you have called is not answering." The sentence was repeated.

Mackay looked at Lance and shrugged. Lance checked his note, but he had given the right number.

"They might be on their way to meet you," suggested Mackay.

"Wait. I have a backup number here." Mackay punched it out as Lance read it. After a delay, a woman's voice came over the speaker.

"Rita Mori here."

Mackay looked at Lance. "Know her?" When Lance shook his head, Mackay spoke into the mike. "Message from Lance Garrith for Brad Hagen."

"I'll take it," said the woman. Mackay ran the disk through, and as it finished the woman said, "Tell him he'll be met at the terminal."

Mackay switched off the transmitter and moved back to the control room. "We'll have to leave it at that. I'll be busy now for a while."

"Of course," said Lance. "Thanks."

As he rode the elevator down to the zone of Mars-normal gravity, the thought came to him that he was in the greatest danger when alone, as he was now. He began to imagine he could feel the implant at the base of his skull.

As he stepped out into the annular corridor, Captain Mackay's voice boomed through the public address system: "This is your captain here. I'm killing the ship's axial spin in a few minutes to allow the spaceplane from Hellas to dock with us. This means your gravity will fall to zero. I suggest you fit magnetic shoes now.''

By the time Lance had returned to his cabin to slip on his magnetic overshoes, the gravity was already noticeably reduced, and the hollow whistle of the jets controlling the spin of the ship echoed throughout the hull.

A few minutes later, all the passengers had assembled in the viewing room. The only persons on board not present were Mackay and his crew, and Dr. Stein. Lance, standing at the back of the group, watched the others keenly, but all of them had their attention on the screens. Allen was pointing out to Gray features of the landscape sweeping past below. Joy was standing alongside Jocasta, who had her thick, flexible arm around the girl's shoulders. Jocasta was the only one not wearing the magnetic shoes supplied to the passengers, and Lance realized that the round, padded feet at the ends of the stilt legs were themselves magnetic, accounting for her sure-footed movement. Her head was now protected by a tough-looking glassite bubble helmet that seemed to be fitted directly to the top of her cybernetic trunk.

The screen showed the Martian spaceplane coming up for its rendezvous. It was differently proportioned from the one in which Alvarez had brought them up from Florida to Earth orbit, lighter-built, with enormous wings designed for the thin Martian atmosphere. They were segmented and apparently folding, like the wings of a monstrous bat. As the craft neared the *Yttria*'s transfer bay, its wings folded in, and the nitrogen peroxide maneuvering jets nudged it toward the yawning doors of the bay, from which the ship's manipulating arms reached out with their giant claws.

Internally, the spaceplane was little different from the Florida-based machine. As he entered it, Lance took out his compact video camera.

''Best view on the left,'' said Allen, and Lance took one of the left-hand seats, Allen sitting in the one in front of him. He fastened his seat belt, watching the others do the same, except Jocasta Borg, who stood in front of a folded seat, legs retracted, holding herself upright. Lance waited for the thrust of the rockets to slam him back in his seat, but the start was more gentle than he had anticipated. Escape velocity on Earth was more than 11 kilometers per second, whereas on Mars it was barely five. This craft was lighter, frailer, with less atmospheric violence to contend with.

The transfer bay doors of the *Yttria* swung slowly shut. Lance almost expected to hear the clang of the metal, forgetting he was separated from the big ship now by vacuum. Soundless, the ship that had been his home for the past five months became already one dimension less real.

As the spaceplane picked up speed for its downward flight, he knew he had passed another point from which there was no turning back.

As they slanted down between the vast shields of Avonis Mons and Ascraeus Mons, still well above almost all of the Martian atmosphere, he started his camera running.

"Looks a hell of a place from here," he said to Allen during the quiet interval in the rocket firing.

Allen turned his head. "I like it. You feel you're *building* something, out here."

The thin, high shriek of the atmosphere against the titanium hull intensified gradually until speech became impractical. The broad wings, now fully extended, vibrated in the upper-air turbulence, and the leading edges began to glow with friction. They were traveling east-southeast as they lost altitude, swinging down from the Tharsis highlands over the jumbled arroyos of the area Allen had called the Badlands. In the vast wilderness ahead, a flat, orange-tinted circular area like a dry seabed opened out. This was the Hellas impact basin, two thousand kilometers across, named by Earthbound astronomers long before anyone had reached Mars. It was the lowest part of the surface of this planet.

Hyperlift flaps slowed their descent into the tenuous atmosphere. Even at the bottom of the sunken basin, the air was thinner than on the top of Earth's Mount Everest. The pilot swung the craft in a sinuous path to lose altitude and speed.

As they skimmed down on their approach to the landing field, Lance kept his camera rolling on Hellas City, ten or twelve kilometers to the north. It had begun with a great central dome of inflated plastic, sprayed with something like fiberglass to give it rigidity. From the dome radiated eight huge, barrel-vaulted galleries of uneven length, like the tentacles of a monstrous starfish, linked here and there by connecting passages.

The landing was almost an anti-climax, little different from the touchdown of any large aircraft. The runway was smooth, but the same color as the arid surrounding plain, as if a strip of the stony ground had been rolled and vitrified. The machine came to rest in the green-tinted shade of a structure like a giant carport. Lance peered again in the direction of the city, but it was now hidden by the enormous cloud of fine dust thrown up by their landing. Gradually, the material dispersed, deepening the pink of the sky to a coppery tint.

"Here they come!" said Joy excitedly, pointing.

Lance saw a denser cloud of dust boiling up from the flat orange horizon in the direction of the still hidden city. Against it was the sharply defined shape of a bulbous vehicle coming toward them, a metal and glassite shell on a number of fat wheels. It seemed to have two decks, like an old-fashioned double-deck bus. In fact, it reminded Lance of a child's toy plastic bus inflated so that it bulged.

It maneuvered alongside the spaceplane and extended a transfer tube that linked with the plane's airlock. Lance heard the positive click of clamps, then the brief hiss of equalizing air pressures. He released his belt and stood carefully up, hand against the low ceiling to avoid striking his head.

The airlock opened, and two people in orange and black uniforms came through the transfer tube into the cabin, a man and a woman. Like Heidi and Joy, they were taller than the average Earthborn person, but lighter in build. Whereas the two sisters had exercised vigorously for a long time in preparation for their trip to Earth, these people had not. Although Lance had seen pictures of Martian people, he found he was still unprepared for the modifications to the human body effected by life in a sealed city, under little more than a third of Earth's gravity and barely a third of its atmospheric pressure. They had long, slim legs and almost globular trunks, shoulders lifted as if they had just taken deep breaths.

"Welcome to Hellas City," said the man in a high-pitched voice. "How many of you first time on Mars?"

"I am," said Lance, and noticed that his own voice came out higher in pitch than he had expected.

"Me, too." Gray's voice was almost a squeak.

The uniformed man looked from one to the other. "One thing I must emphasize—we have absolute ban on smoking, not only in vehicles, but everywhere in the city. We have sealed, almost pure oxygen atmosphere, fire easily ignited, highly dangerous. Have you any smoking materials?"

Lance and Gray shook their heads.

"Wait there a minute," the man said, and turned to the other passengers.

"You know me, of course." Jocasta Borg moved forward. The

uniformed man and woman bowed simultaneously, moving aside to let her stalk through into the transfer tube.

The woman in orange and black came forward, holding her clipboard so that she could see it. "Name?" she asked, looking at Lance.

"Lance Garrith, Solar News."

"Is one I want. Come." She turned and strode into the transfer tube. Still careful of the light gravity, Lance copied her gliding walk, sliding his feet as if moving on ice.

The tube led into the upper deck of the wheeled vehicle, which had its own airlock. A stair ran down to the lower level, which appeared to be devoted to cargo, while the upper floor had seats like those of a bus. The section was deserted except for the motionless figure of Jocasta Borg, who stood right at the front on retracted legs, gripping the back of one of the seats. She did not turn.

The woman with the clipboard indicated a seat to Lance, and sat facing him.

"I am Glaya, Department of Immigration." Her voice was thin and metallic. Standing, she had been very tall, a few centimeters taller than Lance, but now that they were seated he found he was looking slightly down at her. "Normally," she said, "you would take some time to go through immigration processing. Most people come to settle permanently. Since you won't be staying long, Solar News has arranged to speed you through."

"Thanks. I intend to return to Earth quite soon."

She frowned slightly, making a mark on her clipboard. "Seems odd, to come halfway around orbit, not stay."

"Time's valuable to me."

"Not much of a compliment to our planet, is it?"

"I didn't come here to do a travel story, much as I'd like to."

"Then what?" Her voice had a tinge of hostility.

"I'd rather keep the story a surprise. Increases news value. Adds impact."

"I see. Has to do with probe, yes?"

"Could be."

She mimicked him. "Could be." A deep vertical crease formed between her sandy brows. "Many Earth people who come here expect us to be stupid. Statistically, we have a higher average intelligence than the population of Earth."

"Naturally," he said. She looked at him sharply, and he spread his hands. "Obvious, isn't it? Nobody's going to send idiots all this way."

Surprisingly, her frown cleared, and one corner of her mouth curved in a half-smile. "You'll get on well on Mars," she said. She spoke into a wrist radio, then looked at the tiny visual display on it. "As soon as the others come through, we'll be away. Solar News representative will meet you at Spaceport Road Airlock."

Glaya stood up. When Lance did the same, he found she was nearly half a head taller than him. He had forgotten the great length of her slender legs.

"You have enormous shoulders," she said. "You must have immense physical strength."

"Normal in an Earthman," he said, but she shook her head.

"Not at all. I've seen many." She took a card from her pocket and handed it to him. "You have any trouble, contact me, at Department of Immigration. Ask for Glaya."

"Thanks," he said.

He watched her stride out through the airlock and the transfer tube, back to the spaceplane. He went up the aisle to the front of the vehicle, where he could get a better view through the huge bubble windshield. Jocasta, with her back toward him, looked like a grotesque piece of sculpture, motionless, her hand in the pocket of her jacket. Looking at the curve of the flexible arm, he tried to work out the mechanics of it. Evidently made of some strong, tough plastic, it was probably curved or straightened by a changing balance of hydraulic pressures within it. While he was trying to visualize the chain of control from mind to metal hand, she brought the hand out of her pocket, holding what appeared to be a small radio. She lifted it to the speaker mounted in front of her neck, and he was near enough to hear her speak.

"Ren? Jocasta. Bring my car to the Spaceport Road Airlock." A pause, while someone apparently answered her, then she laughed. "You boys worry too much. What could happen to an indestructible lady like me? See you at the lock."

The other passengers came into the vehicle one by one, and when the last was aboard it began to move with a thin whine of motors. Allen came forward and sat next to Lance. "Good to be back home, isn't it?" he called to Jocasta.

The boulder-like body turned. "For me, home is wherever I am." She slapped her hand against the front of her body. Glancing at Lance, Allen pointed to her mechanical hand.

"You know," he said, "she had to kill a fellow with that once."
His voice held admiration.

"That was years ago," said the woman. "And it was self-defense."

"Sure," said Allen. "Everyone agreed on that." He turned back to Lance. "It was out in the asteroids. Used to be a wild place, out there."

"Let's look ahead, not back," said Jocasta, turning to face forward.

"Yeah," said Allen, and lapsed into silence.

Lance had not realized the vastness of the domed city until the vehicle had traveled ten or twelve kilometers toward it. The nearest dome, at the end of the southward gallery, rose against the salmon-pink sky to eclipse the others, dusty enough to be opaque for the first fifty meters up from the ground. Above that, the faceted surface was clear enough to show buildings within, some of them high and graceful.

Outside the end of the dome was an area of hard, vitrified sand, beyond which a row of airlocks jutted from the curving wall. Their vehicle rolled in through an open door of one of them and came to rest. Red lights glowed around the walls as air was transferred. Heidi examined her reflection in a small mirror, adjusting her hair. When the lights changed to green, the inner door of the lock opened dramatically, and Lance found himself looking down a long, tree-lined avenue alive with a vigorous flow of traffic—mostly small, open cars and trucks that seemed to be electric. A few were enclosed, like plastic bubbles. Behind the trees rose tall, fragile buildings with the delicacy of light gravity construction.

To the right was a two-level staging, its upper floor dotted with people waiting for the vehicle to dock. Most had the characteristic Martian physique, some looked as if they had come from Earth, and a few seemed different again, sometimes grotesque, defying Lance's attempts to classify them.

They filed out of the machine, and at the door Lance found Glaya waiting for him. She pointed at the staging.

"Solar News rep," she said. "Dark man in green."

"Thanks," said Lance. As if on an afterthought, he said, "By the way, what do you know about a man called Noel Karstrom?"

"Nothing." The answer was lightning-fast. She pointed to the man in green. "Ask him." Then she was gone.

As Lance stepped out onto the staging, the large, dark man

glided closer to him. "Lance Garrith?" he asked in a resonant voice.

"That's right."

"I'm Pango Mori, Solar News, Hellas." Mori extended a large brown hand, teeth showing in a spontaneous smile. "You want to eat somewhere?"

"Not now, thanks. I'd like to go straight to the office, as soon as I've collected my gear."

"That comes out at bottom level. Come."

Mori led the way with long, gliding strides to an escalator. As they rode down, Lance said, "I'm supposed to contact a fellow called Brad Hagen."

"That'd be a bit hard," said Mori over his shoulder. "He's dead."

chapter
9

LANCE NEARLY STUMBLED as he stepped off the escalator. "Brad Hagen? Dead? When?"

"Couple of months ago. Tell you about it later."

Lance picked out his two bags by their distinctive yellow and red markings. Mori lifted one with astonishing ease, and Lance was impressed for a moment until he picked up his other bag, which seemed almost weightless in the Martian gravity.

Mori led the way to a small, open car, and they stowed the bags in the back of it. A few seconds later, they were out on the wide avenue. The trees lining it were terrestrial palms and eucalyptus, lemons and guavas. The buildings behind them looked mainly residential.

Mori kept glancing in his rearview mirror. "Just making sure we're not followed," he said. "After Brad Hagen went, I don't feel easy." He flashed a quick, sidelong glance. "By the way, I've replaced him. I was his assistant."

"What happened to him?"

"Never found out. Inquisitive guy, Brad. Persistent. He went into the outlands to follow something up. You've seen the pictures we sent Channing, I suppose? Well, we never saw Brad again. No trace. Him or his roto."

Lance looked at his wrist, where he would normally have worn his watch. "What time is it?"

"Fourteen thirty-five. We go by Hellas time all over Mars, since there are not enough people elsewhere to need local time. Not yet, that is." Mori gestured ahead. "Better get one of the local watches. They're reliable—all our locally made things work well."

"This car seems to move along fine. How long do your batteries last?"

"They're rechargeable—part of the Council's service. We always park over spring contacts that come up underneath and charge the batteries while the car's not moving."

"Where do you generate your power?"

"Outside. Nuclear, a safe distance from the city."

Lance was looking at the people they passed. "You don't look like these people. You from Earth?"

"No, born here. But I play a lot of sport, exercise, things like that. Like to keep my muscles developed, the way they'd be in primitive conditions. I guess some of us are a bit fanatical about that."

Lance smiled to himself as he thought of Mori's description of Earth environment as primitive. The men and women he saw about him moved as if the whole scene was part of some gigantic ballet. Plump, sometimes almost spherical bodies glided smoothly on thin, elongated limbs. They gave an inescapable effect of moving in slow motion, body rhythms adjusted to a gravity in which a falling object took three times as long to drop as on Earth. He thought of Glaya's comment: "You have enormous shoulders. You must have immense physical strength." And earlier, Heidi's suggestion that in Martian conditions he would be like one of those mythical supermen popular in fiction the previous century.

The barrel vault of the gallery was far above, its translucent material letting through the weird light of the Martian sky. Some of the trees seemed to grow unnaturally tall for their species, *citriodora* eucalypts towering seventy or eighty meters. He pointed them out to Mori, who apparently accepted them as normal.

"They give 'em plenty of water."

"I thought water was short on Mars."

"Not here." Mori pointed downward. "We mine it from the permafrost. Even run fountains, now."

Ahead, the gallery ran into the great central dome. Here stood the city's highest buildings, some rising perhaps two hundred meters. Mori drove around the octagonal central plaza, pointing out the City Hall, a squat old building of laser-cut rock. Most of the other structures around the plaza were high, flimsy-looking boxes of metal and glass, and he drove the car into the entrance of one of these, spiralling expertly up a seemingly endless ramp in the core of the building. He parked, then led Lance through a door in the wall marked SOLAR NEWS HELLAS.

The office was small, with two of its three rooms overlooking the plaza with its ant-files of moving vehicles, fifty meters below. Mori waved to a drink dispenser.

"Have anything you like. Beer, coffee, kava, you name it."

"I'll stick to coffee for a while. Does it cost much to import?"

"Import? They grow it in annexes off the East Gallery." Mori was riffling through files in a metal cabinet. "Ah, here's what you'll want. This is the original of the picture we line-scanned to Earth."

The print of the strange figure standing near the lime-green tent in the duststorm was smaller than the copy Mort Channing had shown Lance, but sharper. Mori handed him a magnifier, and he examined the picture carefully.

"You think there's no possibility of a fake?" asked Lance.

"Doesn't look like it to me. Anyway, whythehell anyone go to that trouble?"

"True. But what have you got on the prospector who took the picture?"

"Jack Darch? Been trying to contact him for days. Forty years old—that's our years, about seventy-five of yours—he's spent more than half of that on Mars. A week ago, he moved from a small dump in the Southwest Gallery to a more up-market place out west. Place called the Star of the Outlands. He evidently thought this deal would bring him more money. Anyway, I haven't been able to reach him. He's probably nudging the acid. Try now, if you like—the number's on the pad."

Lance punched out the number and looked at the screen. It remained glowingly blank for nearly half a minute, then showed a thin, bored-looking man with receding hair plastered to his scalp like streaks of oil.

"Star of the Outlands," he said.

"Could I speak to Jack Darch?"

The man looked at something to one side of the field of view for a few seconds. "He doesn't answer," he said. "Come to think, I haven't seen him since the day he checked in."

"When was that?"

"Six, seven days ago." The thin man shrugged. "They come, they go. It's the way life is, right?"

Lance looked across at Pango Mori, who spread his arms as the man at the Star of the Outlands broke the connection.

"Not very helpful, are they? I tried myself a few times over the past few days."

Lance looked at his wrist and swore briefly. "I'll have to get a watch! I'm lost when I don't know the time."

"We'll get you one." Mori looked at his own watch. "It's fifteen ten."

"When can I contact Earth?"

"Better do it soon. After sunset it has to bounce from an extra satellite. You can send your message from here, but you have to wait about eight minutes for the signal to go both ways."

"What time is it in Pacific City?"

Mori tapped some figures on a keyboard, looking at a display screen. "Around nine o'clock in the evening. That okay?"

"Right."

Mori explained how they could get the connection through a huge dish antenna on a distant peak. "Keep it short," he warned. "It costs the national income."

Lance worked out a concise personal call to Mort Channing: "Arrived okay. Contacted Pango Mori. Hagen dead. Have not reached Darch yet. Lance. Over."

Mori put the call through to the beam transmitter, then set a timer for eight minutes. Lance sent another call, this time to Dorella: "Arrived Hellas. Investigating K. Lance."

The time lag was irritating, even though the two planets were still roughly on the same side of the Sun. You said something, then had several minutes to think about whether you had said it as you intended while the signal went on its way at 300,000k's per second. A few seconds after Mori's timer pinged, the bell of the video chimed.

Channing's image was barely distorted, in spite of the vast distance the signal had to travel, and his voice was clear: "Can't see you very well, Lance. Listen, be careful! We ran into a dead end investigating the fellow who tried to kill you on your program, but we're sure he didn't act alone. Something bad's linked with this thing, and I haven't a clue what it is. So be damn careful, and keep in touch."

Lance looked across at Mori as the image flickered out. Mori was not smiling now. His eyes were wide as they met Lance's.

"What was that about someone trying to kill you on your program?"

Lance told him about the assassin caught by Hartz and his team. Mori seemed particularly horrified when he heard of the manner of the man's death.

"I don't like that," he said. "Not that way. The fellow deserved to die, sure. But like that?'' He shook his head. ''A shot, a knife-thrust—these things could be sudden anger. But to bury something inside a man so you can detonate it when somebody's likely to make him talk—that's cold, brother. Really cold.''

''Looks as if there's some group, some organization, that wants to keep this probe out of the news.''

''The way I read the message, there might be something in that. And I was the guy who sent the first pictures of the alien to Earth.'' He looked at Lance steadily. ''You married?''

''Was. Not now.''

Mori nodded. ''I've got a wife and two kids. I think this could get savage.''

Lance waited another half-hour for the return call from Dorella, but apparently she was unavailable. Mori later took him to a small restaurant high in the tower, looking westward through the relatively clear top of the dome toward the last traces of the fantastic Martian sunset, with its high ice-crystal clouds painted in bizarre streaks of crimson and violet.

''Who's this Dorella?'' asked Mori suddenly.

''Just a friend. She's done a session on 'The Specialists,' giving a history of Noel Karstrom, as far as she was able to dig it out.''

''Karstrom,'' mused Mori. ''He was a big name here. Started a lot of things.''

''I promised Dorella I'd see if I could dig out more material about him at this end.''

''Bit late, now. Secretive, Karstrom's people. Been in trouble with the authorities, here as well as on Earth. They don't trust anyone, especially the media.'' He seemed to think for a while, then snapped his fingers. ''Tell you who might be able to fill you in on Karstrom—the Ambon twins. You can check if you go over to the Star of the Outlands looking for Darch. The Ambons run the place, and they used to work for Karstrom, years ago.''

''Thanks. The Ambon twins. I'll remember that.'' Lance made a movement to look at a nonexistent watch, and Mori laughed with him.

''Let's get you the time,'' he said. ''Otherwise you'll go nuts—or drive *me* nuts. There's a shop down the Octagon.''

They rode the elevator down to the ground level and went out through the foyer of the Viking Building to the street.

''Why Viking?'' asked Lance, indicating the name.

''Historic. First unmanned spaceprobe to travel from the Earth to Mars. Landed away back, now. There's a replica in the museum." Mori led the way along the sidewalk until they reached a brightly lit shop containing electronic equipment. Lance selected a wristwatch of local make, set it, and strapped it on his wrist. Mori paid for it with a credit card. "I'll charge it to the company," he said, grinning. "If they can afford to send you to Mars, they can stand the price of a watch."

As they emerged from the shop, Lance heard his name called. Looking around in surprise, he saw Heidi coming along the sidewalk. He didn't recognize her for the moment, as she was wearing the type of clothing that seemed fashionable now among Martian girls—a brief, sleeveless shirt that made her bare legs seem abnormally long. She still wore the headband with its miniscule TV camera.

"Where are you staying, Lance?" she asked.

"Oh, Heidi! I'd like you to meet Pango Mori, of Solar News. Heidi was one of the passengers on the *Yttria*," he explained to Mori. "By the way, you haven't found me a place to stay yet, have you?" Looking straight at Mori, he gave a minute headshake.

Mori was fast on the uptake. "Not yet—I'm working on it."

"And you?" Lance turned back to Heidi. "Where can I contact you?"

She flashed a smile. "Not sure where I'll be for a while. I can get in touch with you through Solar News."

She walked away along the Octagon, Mori looking after her appreciatively. "Nice girl," he commented. "I think I used to see her around."

"Something odd, though," said Lance. "She comes from Hellas, and she's only been away less than a year, yet she doesn't know where she'll be staying. Would you believe that?"

"Maybe. People here often stay with friends for a while, keep moving about. Don't you trust her?"

"Not certain. After someone took a shot at me, I might have started to go a bit paranoid."

"Hell, if someone took a shot at me, I think I'd head for the Outlands. But listen. If you're worried about someone making another attempt, let's do it this way. I've registered you into the Mangala, next door to the Viking Building, Room 803. Stay registered there, but stop a few nights at my place. It's well out of the central district, I've got plenty of room, and no one would find you there."

"Thanks—if you're sure it won't endanger you." Lance looked

at his newly acquired watch. "Now, do you have any maps of the area where the probe went down?"

"Better. A stereo view of the whole area."

They rode the elevator back up to the fifteenth floor. The sky above was dark now, and most of the light from the windows of the office came up from the street below. Mori took a number of large aerial photographs from a set of drawers and assembled a system of lenses that gave a startlingly real stereoscopic view. Lance had the illusion of looking straight down on the Martian landscape from a height.

The best of the country looked like the stony deserts of Arizona or Central Australia, and from there any change was for the worse. As photo followed photo, moving at intervals of ten kilometers across the tangled ridges of the Badlands, Lance began to wonder what he was really looking for.

"We flew over some of this country on the way down, Pango," he said. "There were a couple of old steel launching towers."

Mori said "Ah!" and began sorting through a stack of photos. He grunted and placed one under the lenses. "That the thing you saw?"

"Could be. The angle's different, but that must be one of them. Where is that, exactly?"

"Here." Mori spread a multicolored map of part of Mars on a desk. He checked the coordinates printed on the margin of the photograph, then carefully examined the map. "There you are— it's along that ridge. There, and there." Bringing the photo across to compare it with the map, he made two pencil marks. "That what you wanted?"

"Exactly what I wanted." Lance looked up. "These old towers are right in the middle of the area marked as enclosing the landing point of the probe."

"So?"

"So I was right. Look, Pango, I've thought for quite a time this extra-solar probe must have come in answer to a signal sent by Karstrom."

Mori studied him for several seconds. "You're tired, man. You're not thinking straight. Those towers just launched rockets. The rockets put satellites in orbit. The signals would have been sent from *them*. Okay? That wouldn't lead the probe to the Badlands, would it?"

Lance stood for a few seconds in silence. "You're right, of course. But couldn't he have sent signals from a dish on the ground? With the thin atmosphere, a satellite wouldn't gain much.''

"He might have had dishes. Let's have a close look around the same area.''

They looked at picture after picture, but apart from the corroded towers they saw no sign of human handiwork in the barren landscape.

"Of course,'' said Mori. "It was a long time ago. Dishes could have been taken down, recycled, parts used elsewhere. But the towers wouldn't have been worth salvaging.''

Mori spun around at the sudden chime of a bell. "Must be a beam message coming in.'' He went to the console and opened a channel, and a man's face appeared on the screen.

"Is there a Lance Garrith there?'' he asked.

Lance moved forward into the field of the camera. "I'm Lance Garrith.''

"I have a call from a Ms Dorella.''

"Right. I'll take it.''

The screen flickered, and then, unbelievably, the face of Dorella looked out at him. He shouted her name before he remembered the delay dictated by distance. She began speaking.

"Lance!'' She seemed taut with controlled excitement. "You'll never believe this. I'm aboard the freighter *Iridia*! I'll be with you in about forty days. A lot of people want to know more about Karstrom, and after my broadcast a foundation paid my fare to follow up my research on Mars. The *Iridia*'s the same line as your *Yttria*, following it forty days behind. Over.''

Lance looked at Mori. "Can I send a reply?''

"We can try. Not like sending a signal to Earth—they'd be aiming at a spaceship, remember—a single amoeba in an ocean. But they're pretty good. Let's try it.''

Lance left Mori make the arrangements for the transmission. He looked sharply at Lance. "This on your expense account?''

"I could try it.''

"Keep it short. Very short.''

"Okay.'' Lance stepped in front of the TV camera and pressed the START key. He spoke quickly.

"Dorella! This is tremendous news! Meet you at the terminal when the *Iridia* arrives. Over.''

The message sent, there was nothing more to do about it. He was glad for Dorella—this had been an all-consuming ambition of hers, to come to Mars and follow up her research on the history of the man of whom she had built up a mental image that obsessed her. He hoped the reality of Karstrom's life didn't let her dreams down.

"Okay?" asked Mori suddenly.

"Sure. Just thinking."

"Another very nice girl. Man, I reckon you've got some trouble coming up."

"I've got forty days to sort it out." Lance didn't voice his unspoken addition: *If I live another forty days.*

A sobering thing had happened to him since the voyage. He had lost his natural young man's illusion that he was going to live forever, an illusion never brought to full consciousness and examined, yet always there.

But now it had gone. He felt with his fingers the spot on his neck where the implant had been inserted. Now all he could do was take life day by day. He looked at his watch.

"Don't suppose she'll call back. Say, where's the Star of the Outlands?"

"Hey, you're not going out there tonight?"

"I always try to be a jump ahead."

"Ahead of who, for Maui's sake?"

Lance grinned. "I don't know, in this case. Just ahead."

Mori looked at him for a few seconds, then shrugged. "As you wish. I've got a spare car you can use, but always make sure you park it on the lines. That puts you over the charging contacts." He went to a desk and took out a folded map. "Here's the layout of the city. Starfish with eight arms, see? We're here, where someone's put that red spot. That's the west gallery over there— mostly industrial, factories, storage, depots, a few offices. Out near the airlocks at the end you've got the Star of the Outlands. Old hotel. Lots of prospectors and ice-miners stay there, when their money's in good enough supply. Be careful, though. It's not like the Central Plaza down there."

"In what way?"

Mori grimaced. He held out his hand horizontally and rocked it from side to side to give an effect of instability. "Lot of fellows out that way haven't been too lucky. Makes 'em harder to get on with. Losers, you'd call 'em. But you should be okay. I was forgetting, you come from a world with billions of losers, right?"

"That seems to be a popular belief around here. It's not true." Lance thought for a moment. "Well, not *completely* true."

Mori grinned as he took a key from a wall cabinet. "Anyway, take the green car outside. And be careful."

Lance flung up his arms. "You and Mort Channing! That's all I get, lately: Be careful!"

Mori did not smile. "Don't know about Channing, man. But I'm not kidding."

All the cars in the park reminded Lance of the little electric vehicles in an amusement park, compact, open at the top. He slid into the green one and turned the key. The controls were simple—steering wheel, lever to select forward or reverse, speed pedal, brake. The car had individual wheel motors. With a wave to Mori, Lance drove around to the down-running spiral ramp and on downward in an endless curve until he finally nosed the car out into the traffic flow of Central Plaza.

Frail-looking, neon-lit buildings soared high into the dome on all sides of him. Before coming to Mars, he had expected to find an enclosed city stifling, but now he had to admit to himself that the air here was better than in most of the cities he'd known on Earth, perhaps because of stricter controls here on such things as the burning of fuels or waste.

He drove around to a sign indicating the West Gallery and turned into a long avenue under a high, barrel-vaulted roof that extended so far he couldn't see the end of it. The nearer part was brightly lit, but as it reached out farther from the central dome it grew progressively darker.

Factories loomed on either side of the avenue, with only an occasional lighted window where someone was working late. The few cars he saw were parked near the buildings showing lights.

Somewhere along the avenue, he began to have the feeling that a car behind him was following him. It was the only other moving vehicle in sight, a long car with a darkly opaque bubble top. There seemed to be three figures inside it, but he couldn't see them clearly. When he pulled up in front of a lighted office, the car stopped a hundred meters behind him.

He sat motionless for a while, his heart pounding, acutely aware that this was not his environment. The lighting here was dim. Two men emerged from the long car and began walking toward him. Lance watched them in his mirror until they were within ten meters of him, then drove off at his car's unimpressive top speed.

At least he had separated them—one in the car, two in the street—and by the time the driver stopped to pick up the other two men, Lance was three hundred meters away. He passed a brightly lit area that appeared to be focused on some kind of power-house, with a number of small cars parked in a side street. He swung off, parked in a gap in a row of stationary cars, switched off his lights, and crouched down.

The dark car went on down the avenue. About five minutes later it came slowly back, disappearing in the direction of the Central Plaza. Irritably, Lance waited another quarter of an hour, and then he drove cautiously back to the corner of the avenue.

There was no sign of the dark car now. After he had made sure it had gone, he drove on toward the end of the gallery, which terminated in a dome like a small version of the central one. There was an airlock system, less elaborate than the one at Spaceport Road, and on one side, overlooking a scrubby park, stood an extraordinary building of laser-cut stone and glass, the stone looking like volcanic pumice.

Four stories high, it looked as if it had been brought here from some Earth town built during a nineteenth century gold rush. Only a few lights showed in its windows, which gave the impression it had a large number of small rooms.

Lance steered the little car carefully into a lined parking area. He heard the metal contacts rise to recharge its batteries, obviously a free public service operating all over the city.

There was no sign of the car that had followed him. He walked up to the main entrance of the building, over which a black-on-yellow sign read STAR OF THE OUTLANDS, Props: B. & M. AMBON. He went to the reception desk where the same tired-looking man he had seen on the visi still sat. He recognized Lance, but did not smile.

"Still looking for Jack Darch," said Lance. "Is he back?"

The receptionist shook his head.

"While I'm here," Lance went on, "I want to see the Ambon twins."

"Did you have an appointment?"

"No. Can you contact them?"

"Yes, but I don't think—"

"Tell them it's Lance Garrith, of Solar News, from Earth. Say I want to see them about something involving the Karstrom Foundation."

The man's expression was unreadable. "Just a minute." He spoke quietly into a hooded video terminal, then looked up. "They'll see you." He sounded surprised. "Through that door into the courtyard, and wait."

* * *

The courtyard filled a large hollow square in the center of the building and was planted with vegetation kept green by intermittent overhead sprays. On all sides, the building rose four floors, with railed balconies running around each floor facing the courtyard.

In the far right-hand corner, the lights of an elevator moved down from the top floor. It reached ground level, and a figure— or was it two figures?—came out and strode toward him across the courtyard. He didn't know what he was looking at until the figure came under a central cluster of lights.

Then he realized the Ambon twins were some kind of siamese pair. They were tall, heavily built women whose trunks seemed to be fused together side by side. The inner legs were united from the hip down to the foot, so that they walked as if on three legs. The heads were those of women in their forties, with a twin-like similarity of features but a curious difference in expression. The right head looked stern and hard, with a straight mouth, creased brows and rimless glasses, while the one on the left looked sensuous, sullen and bored.

They walked straight toward Lance with a regular, almost military stride, with practiced control of the central leg, the other legs moving in precise synchronization. The right head spoke as they halted in front of him.

"Lance Garrith?" she snapped.

"Yes," he said, "and you—"

"The Ambon sisters. I'm Belle."

"I'm Maya," cut in the left head with a sudden livening of expression, looking Lance boldly up and down. Both heads appeared extremely intelligent and observant.

"I'm gathering data on a man called Noel Karstrom," he said. "I understand you ladies worked for him at one time."

"Long ago," said Belle. "He died nearly twenty years ago."

Lance looked from one large, smooth face to the other, and Maya smiled. "We don't look our age," she said.

"What do you know about Karstrom?" asked Belle. One of the women began speaking the instant the other finished, and Lance had the feeling that he might soon find their conversation overwhelming.

"I came here from Pacific City, Earth, to do a story on an extra-system probe that apparently landed in the Badlands about 150 days ago."

The two heads exchanged a quick, sidelong glance. It was the first time they had taken their bright gray eyes off Lance's.

"What's that to do with Karstrom?" Belle's eyes flashed behind her glasses.

"I'm not sure, but I feel there's a connection."

A low-voiced, incredibly rapid exchange passed between the two women. It sounded like fragments of words elided together, played on a tape at too high a speed, and Lance understood none of it. With their scrutiny withdrawn from him for a moment, he was able to glance down at their huge double body.

They wore a knee-length, wraparound dress of some gleaming gray material, enclosing the fused side-by-side torsos together, fitting smoothly over their four large breasts, which rose and fell in unison in a slow, regular rhythm. Below were three glossy black boots, the central one monstrously wide to enclose their double foot. They were as tall as Lance, their double body grotesquely broad. Their bare arms had an impressive thickness of muscle that did not seem to belong in the light Martian gravity.

Quickly, both faces turned to Lance again. "We'd better discuss this up in our apartment," said Belle.

They turned, pivoting on their central foot, and Maya slipped her arm through Lance's. He was surprised at its strength, as he found himself drawn along, automatically falling into step with the sisters. Their three legs swung in metronome precision, their central boot making a hollow thump like a drumbeat, which they seemed to use to synchronize their movements.

Crossing the courtyard to the far corner, they opened the door of a small elevator and sidled into its bright cubicle, standing with their backs against one side of it and half filling it. Lance, moving in, found himself standing facing them, their two pairs of gray eyes scanning his face, one pair with glasses, the other with tinted eyeshadow. He tried to divide his attention between the two faces, with their quite dissimilar expressions, as the elevator moved slowly upward.

Close to the sisters, he realized for the first time that they shared an arm as well as a leg, but the arm was a stubby, dwarfed vestige protruding from their joined shoulders, with two little brachydactyl hands fused at their outer edges. He became aware of it when they lifted it briefly to look at a watch strapped to its plump wrist. They thrust it back into a pocket in the front of their dress, and when he raised his eyes again, for the first time he saw their faces with a matched expression.

Both were looking at him with suppressed anger.

The elevator reached the top level, and the sisters opened the door and moved out with carefully controlled sideways steps. They opened the door of an apartment at the corner of the balcony and gestured Lance to enter.

"After you," he said, but Belle took him firmly by the arm and moved him into the open doorway.

"Don't let's waste time," she said irritably.

chapter
10

THE ROOM WAS large and almost circular, occupying the top of one of the round towers that formed the corners of the building. Other rooms opened off it, and a curved wall of glassite looked down over the park and the airlocks. The furniture was varied and seemed expensive.

"Nice place you have here," said Lance.

"Naturally," answered Maya. "We own the building, so we have the best rooms in it."

"You must be good businesswomen."

"We make a good team," said Belle. "Sit down." She indicated one of a set of molded foam chairs, and Lance lowered himself into it carefully, still unaccustomed to accepting the strength of flimsy-looking materials to support his weight in the light gravity.

"Cafeno?" asked Maya, and when he nodded the women moved across to a dispenser against one wall. *Now* who's trying to gain time, he thought to himself. They coordinated their movements well as they operated the dispenser, although each controlled one of the large, efficient hands.

"How did you come to start this?" asked Lance.

"Noel Karstrom started us up in it, after we left off working for him," said Belle without turning. Their hair was pulled back in two dark ponytails.

"Generous of him," said Lance.

"He felt he had a responsibility," answered Maya. They poured three long glasses of ice-cold cafeno and brought them back on a tray to place them on a small table near Lance.

"A responsibility? How was that?"

The women sat on a sofa after moving it so that it faced Lance's chair. He took one of the glasses, and they each did the same.

"If you've done any research on Noel Karstrom," said Belle, "you'll know by now he was using recombinant DNA with synthetic genetic material to evolve a superior human being. He had more failures than successes at first, and most of those disappeared. Maya and I didn't develop as he planned, but we were very bright, and we worked with him. When the powers in command stopped our research, Noel set us up in this place out of gratitude for our support."

"Did he ever succeed in producing a superior being?" asked Lance.

"Us," said Maya promptly, with the flicker of a smile.

"Yes, us," agreed Belle. "However, it was while we were still growing up that the authorities stopped that line of his research, and he switched over to concentrate on interstellar signals."

"That's what I want to look into. I think one of his signals may have got an answer."

"What d'you mean?" demanded Belle.

"I think this probe from outside the solar system may have been sent by an alien civilization to see where Karstrom's messages originated."

Again, the women exchanged an almost inaudible, high-speed flow of fragments of words, like a verbal shorthand. Then Belle answered him.

"Possible. What do you want to do about it?"

"I'd like to have a look at the place where it's supposed to have come down."

"But that's sixteen hundred kilometers away," said Maya.

Belle turned her head sharply to look at her sister's profile. To Lance, the effect was bizarre.

"So somebody said," added Maya. "I forget who it was."

Lance suddenly realized he'd run into a dead end. Both the women were loyal to Karstrom and whatever organization had survived him. He finished his glass of cafeno, then stood up. "Well, ladies, thank you for your help."

They stood up, their eyes on a level with his. "It's been interesting talking with you," said Belle. "You must call back some time and tell us anything else you've found out about Noel. And we may think of something else."

"Thank you. I'll remember that."

"We mean it," said Maya, and once again a blur of telescoped words ricocheted between the sisters. The massive left arm suddenly pulled him against them, and Maya's large hand took hold of the back of his neck, maneuvering his lips against hers. She laughed as he drew back, shocked at the suddenness of her movement, the intensity of her feeling.

"You'll have to excuse my sister," said Belle in a level voice. "She's emotional."

"That's all right," said Lance, recovering some of his poise as he stepped back. "I like spontaneity." He moved toward the door, the women beside him. "By the way," he added, "for people living in light gravity, you're very strong."

Belle slid open a wide inner door opening off the round room, and Lance saw in the room beyond a set of exercise equipment: a climbing machine, rowing machine, sets of weightlifter's bars and weights on a rack. "You may need to keep your muscle tone up from time to time," said Belle. "You're welcome to our gymnasium."

"Any time," added Maya.

Lance nodded. "I'll bear that in mind," he said. At the door, he turned. "Sixteen hundred kilometers, you said?"

"What?" asked Maya.

"Where the probe landed. You said sixteen hundred kilometers away?"

"So someone said," answered Belle quickly.

He nodded. "I might rent an aircraft and take a look out there."

The sisters exchanged glances. "You might find it hard to rent an aircraft here," said Belle.

"I have an international flying license."

"That's for Earth. Conditions are different here. They won't even let Maya and I have a flying license. Something about a possible conflict between our two brains interfering with our reflex actions. The fools! They don't know how we operate." Belle sounded as if smoldering anger were about to erupt.

"We'll see you to your car," said Maya suddenly.

"No need."

But they ignored his protest and rode down with him in the elevator. As they crossed the courtyard, Maya slipped her arm through his, holding it against her body. He found he was able to walk in step with them, as if in a military march. At the reception desk, Belle spoke to the man with the thinning hair about something connected with the ordering of food for a restaurant incorporated in the building. Then they went out with him to his car, waiting while he started it.

As he reversed out of the parking slot, they lifted their hands to wave at him. He had a lasting mental picture of their three black boots gleaming in a row, the middle one absurdly wide. As he drove away, he glanced in his mirror and saw their broad, fantastic figure moving swiftly back to the front doorway. Their energy was almost athletic.

He was halfway back along the dim avenue to the Central Plaza when he realized the dark-topped, enclosed car was again behind him, steadily gaining. He increased his speed to its limit, but the other machine continued to draw closer.

The bright lights of the plaza were very far away. The other car drew level with him, then half a length in front, matching his speed, and then it slowly bore inward, forcing him nearer the curb.

Acting by reflex alone, he swung the little car into a narrow lane between two buildings. Thirty meters onward, his way was blocked by a parked truck.

The dark car stopped at the entrance to the lane, and its bubble top swung open. Three men sprang out. Something covered their faces, but he saw light flash on the blade of a knife.

Jumping out of the small car, he ran past the parked truck. Fifty meters beyond, the land ended, a cul de sac between dark factory-type buildings. He could hear the sounds of pursuit behind him.

Suddenly, it occurred to him to make use of the fact that he had grown up against gravity nearly three times that of Mars. One of the buildings enclosing the lane was only three meters high. He flexed his legs, and without much effort he gained the roof in a standing jump, turning to look down at his pursuers. They stopped, then ran back to the parked truck, while Lance ran lightly along the roof in the same direction.

The first man leaped from the tray of the truck to the top of its cabin, then reached for the edge of the roof. His head was hidden by a black fabric bag with eye slits.

With a sudden feeling of cold resolve, Lance sat on the roof, his knees drawn up. As the masked head came over the edge, he lashed out with his heel.

Lance himself was astounded at the result. The masked man somersaulted as if in slow motion to crash against the wall of the building on the opposite side of the lane, then dropped in an inert heap on the ground. The second man, holding the knife, paused on the top of the cabin, and Lance swung himself across the edge of the roof and lashed out with both feet.

Then it was practically over. As the second man slammed into

the wall, the third began running back to his car. Lance sprang
lightly to the ground, hardly feeling the jar of the three-meter
drop, and raced after him with giant strides, overtaking him just
as he reached the car and opened the top.

Lance did not use his fist. He stayed where he knew he had the
advantage, leaping shoulder-high and kicking with the flat of his
foot. The other man crashed into the car, sprawling across the
seat. Lance lifted his legs and swung them aboard, then slammed
the top down.

With a grim smile, he bent his knees and gripped the bottom
edge of the car's body with both hands. Then, with a straight lift
with his legs against the weak gravity, he rolled the machine onto
its side, then pushed it over on its top. The man inside it was now
effectively imprisoned there.

Lance looked about him. No one seemed to have heard the
commotion, or if they had, they'd decided not to become involved.
Walking back along the lane, he picked up the fallen knife—a
switchblade—and slipped it in his pocket. He reversed the green
car out of the lane, leaving the inert men where they lay, drove
around the overturned vehicle and headed along the avenue toward
the bright lights of the plaza.

He drove back to the Octagon and the Viking Building without
incident, and mounted the spiral ramp to the fifteenth floor. Pango
Mori was still in the Solar News office and opened the door as
soon as Lance reached it.

"Any trace of Darch?" he asked, handing Lance a drink.

"No. They claim at the Star of the Outlands they haven't seen
him since the day he checked in."

"What's your feeling about that?"

"I don't like it. I think he stumbled onto something big, and
someone's made sure he disappeared."

"People don't often disappear in a sealed city like this. It's a
closed system. They keep a record of everyone going in or out
through the airlocks, in case someone's lost outside."

"So there's no way you could smuggle a body out?"

Mori frowned. "There was a case of a fellow's body being
dumped out in a truckload of waste, so it *can* happen. Rare,
though."

"I think that nearly happened to me tonight. Three goons in a
car ran me into a lane and had a go at me with this." Mori's eyes
widened as Lance showed him the switchblade.

"What happened?"

Lance finished his drink. "They hadn't allowed for me growing up in Earth's gravity. I kicked them unconscious and overturned their car."

"Overturned it? Just using your hands?"

"With one of them inside it. No way he could get the lid open with it upside down."

Mori threw back his head and laughed. Then his laughter chopped off short. "I'd watch it, though, Lance. That mightn't be the end of it. They underestimated you this time, but they could try something else."

Lance walked across to the window and looked down over the plaza. A thin trickle of traffic was still moving around the Octagon, but the sidewalks were almost deserted. The blazing overall level of light had waned, and the great dome above was completely dark, like an overcast night sky on Earth.

"Pango," said Lance, "suppose some alien race has already landed here? Got control of a few key people?"

Mori frowned thoughtfully at his glass. "Like the boy in Darch's picture? No way, man. They'd be spotted."

"Suppose you're right. Imagine one of us trying to infiltrate a world where they were all about three meters high and had six limbs." Lance walked back to Mori. "But suppose the thing Darch saw was only the first of two or three. I don't suppose the probe would have held more."

"Are you sure it's the first probe?"

They looked at each other for a while, and Lance shrugged. "Hell, no. We're not really sure of anything, are we? Still, I may know more about it tomorrow."

"What's happening then?"

"I'm going to try to fly out where the probe's supposed to have landed, if I can rent an aircraft. The Ambon women out at the Star told me no one here will rent an aircraft to someone from Earth, though—is that right?"

"They may be right. It's all different here. The air outside's only about a hundredth the pressure you have on Earth. You have to fly in a spacesuit, and the aircraft are different from anything you'd have flown. They're scared someone will prang an aircraft into a city dome—explosive decompression's our number one nightmare."

"Well, I'd better try."

"What's the hurry?"

"I'm beginning to think there are a lot of people who don't

want me to dig into this thing. The sooner I act, the better chance I have of taking them by surprise.''

Mori went over to the window, looking down. ''I think you'd be a sitting pigeon in that hotel next door,'' he said. ''I called Rita a while ago. She'll be quite happy for you to stay the night out at our place.''

Lance looked at him in surprise. ''You're sure it won't put you and your family at any risk?''

Mori spread out his hands. ''Minimal, I'd say.'' He went to a desk and took a key out of a drawer, holding it out to Lance.

''What's this?''

''Room 803, the room I booked for you at the Mangala next door. Eighth floor. I dropped your two bags in there while you were out looking for Jack Darch. Better do it this way: Leave your bags in the hotel room, bring whatever you need for the night back here, and you can lie down in the back of my car as I drive out. Anyone watching the building won't see you leave.''

Lance rode the elevator down and walked out onto the sidewalk. There were a number of people still around, and he felt particularly uneasy about some on seats on the plaza opposite. Any of them could have been watching the entrances of both the Viking Building and the Mangala.

As he was walking into the foyer of the hotel, a voice from the reception desk challenged him with an authoritative ''Just a minute, friend.''

He turned. The receptionist was a large, bloated-looking man with fair hair. ''I try to memorize all the guests staying here, but I can't quite—'' He left the sentence unfinished.

Lance walked over to the desk. ''My name is Garrith. My room was booked by my associate, Pango Mori, next door. Room 803.''

The man consulted something on his desk. ''Ah, yes. Lance Garrith, Solar News. Requiring breakfast?''

''No, thanks.''

Lance rode an elevator to the eighth floor and went along a passageway lined with numbered doors of what looked like green fiberglass. He found 803, opened it with the key, and saw that his two yellow and red bags had been placed on the floor against one wall. He opened one, took out his pyjamas and razor, and slipped them into a small plastic bag. Relocking the large bag, he glanced around the room. Neat, clean, bare—the word that immediately came to his mind was ''Spartan.'' As he was turning to leave, the visiphone rang.

He hesitated a few seconds as it went on ringing. Then it occurred to him that it might be Mori trying to reach him, and he went across and opened the channel.

Unbelievably, it was Heidi's face looking out at him from the screen.

"How did you find me?" he gasped in genuine astonishment.

She gave a secretive smile, and adopted an unnatural stage accent. "We have ways," she said.

That headband, with its jewel containing the tiny video camera, was focused on him from the screen.

Lance sat on a chair facing the screen, with the light from above falling directly on his face. He saw a minute movement of the camera below the screen as Heidi glanced down to make some adjustment to the controls of her set. The hooded lens turned straight at him.

"I don't understand this," he said obstinately, "I only arrived today, and this hotel room was booked by someone else. This is the first time I've been here."

"I know. I've been calling you."

"But how the devil did you know where I was?"

Her expression simulated weariness. "Don't put me down, Lance. That may work with your giggling Earth girls, but it turns us right off. Figure it out for yourself: You're attached to Solar News—you told me that. I had only to look up their Hellas address—the Viking Building—and come past to have a look at it. The Mangala, with plenty of accommodation, is right next door to it, so—"

He held up his hand. "Okay. So I underestimated your initiative. Sorry." He managed a smile. "Hope I haven't permanently turned you off, as you put it."

She thrust her lower lip forward. "Not really. I realize I have to make allowances. You've been used to being surrounded by stupid women."

"Not me," he protested. "Most of the women I've known have been well above average."

"No doubt. But your Earth average is so low, isn't it?" She smiled more broadly. "No reference to present company, darling."

He remembered Glaya's reaction during her interview with him on his arrival. Apparently these Mars-born girls were touchy about the differences between themselves and their counterparts on the home planet.

"I'm sorry," he said. "I suppose I wasn't allowing for the effect of the processes of selection. All of you are descended from above-average people. Another rung up the evolutionary ladder."

It had worked with Glaya, and now it worked with Heidi. At once, she looked more relaxed, a trifle self-satisfied.

"As long as you keep that in mind, Lance, we'll get on fine together," she said.

"Where are you right now?"

"I'm in a public visi booth not far away from you at the moment. I'm staying the night with Jocasta Borg—she has an office in one of the buildings just off the Octagon. I didn't want to ring from there, because she's on the visi every minute to someone or other since she came back. Besides, I feel happier talking with you privately."

"Good," he said, trying to think of something to add.

"I was wondering if we could get together somewhere." Her eyes looked wide and somehow vulnerable, but he was unable to ignore that headband jewel, with its miniature camera watching him like a third eye. Who else saw what it recorded?

"That'd be nice, Heidi, but I feel washed out right now. I've had to see a few people today, and I need rest. Maybe tomorrow night, you could show me some of the local life."

She seemed to brighten. "Tomorrow night, then. Say at nineteen hundred?"

"Nineteen hundred will be fine. Where can I pick you up?"

"Don't come here. I'll see you in the foyer of the Mangala."

After the screen blanked out, Lance stood up, and it seemed to him the camera moved slightly. He stepped sideways, but this time it didn't follow him. He frowned. He could not be certain. . . .

Picking up the small plastic bag with his overnight needs, he went out, locking the door. As he walked out through the lobby, the receptionist didn't challenge him, and he simply strode out along the sidewalk and reentered the Viking Building.

"What happened?" asked Mori as he went into the office. "Did you try the bed out and fall asleep?"

"Nothing as simple. I had a visi call."

"But how? No one knew the room number except us."

"One of my late shipmates found it out. Girl called Heidi. You saw her at the terminal. Girl with the headband."

"But I told no one that number except you."

"She added a few numbers together and came up with your address, found the Mangala was next door, and so on."

"I don't like people that bright," said Mori.

"At least she's not boring."

"Suppose not. Listen, you ready to move out of here? Sooner we go, the safer."

"Any time you like."

Mori led the way out to the circular car park, locking the office behind him. He went along to a red car parked beside the green one Lance had used.

"Lay your seat back until we're clear of the Octagon," he said. "Anyone'll assume I'm on my own."

A minute or two later, they were out on the Octagon, Mori driving around to the Northeast Gallery. Soon, Lance was able to sit up, bringing his seat to the upright position. The great barrel-vaulted gallery stretched into the distance ahead, like the one in which he had driven toward the west. As in the first, they passed through a brightly lit residential zone at first, then into a darker area. But this region was not occupied by factories—it passed transverse galleries filled with orchards of fruit trees, hydroponics tanks of close-growing vegetables, and crops growing under different colored floodlighting.

Mori pointed out galleries filled with growing wheat and corn, one with twenty-meter bamboo, another with ten-meter-high sugar cane.

"How does it grow to that height?" asked Lance, remembering the canefields in Hawaii.

"Several factors: the low gravity, plenty of water mined from the permafrost, and the work some of the boys are doing with DNA."

"Why are those galleries closed off with what look like airtight doors?"

"Fireproof, as well as airtight. Before they harvest that cane they burn the top of it. Seals the juice in, or something. Can't risk using the oxygen out here. Spectacular sight, when they fire it. You can see it from my place, just along here."

Mori swung the car into a transverse gallery enclosing a high structure like an elongated step pyramid, with row above row of apartments, each with its own small open garden or courtyard. He drove up ramps to one of the upper levels, giving a view through two translucent domes to the sugarcane and wheat plantations they had passed. Slowing, he swung the car into an open-topped carport.

"We're home," he said as he stepped out of the car. "No one will find you here."

Lance didn't reply. Remembering how easily Heidi had located his room at the Mangala, he wasn't so sure.

chapter
11

MORI LED THE way through an entry green with potted ferns and palms. "Rita," he called, and a tall woman came out to meet them.

Tall? Lance checked his initial mental description. By terrestrial standards nearly all these women were tall. Rita was about the same height as Mori and Lance, but with the typical Martian-born physique—long, slender limbs and an almost globular torso. Her dark eyes looked Asian, and her head gave the impression of having been pushed down into her body with hardly any neck visible. She wore a wrap-around short overall of vivid cyclamen color.

Mori introduced her with his arm around her. "Where are the kids?" he asked.

"Both in bed," she said. "You know what time it is?"

"I kept us late," said Lance. "I had a few calls to make."

As Rita walked ahead of them into the apartment, Lance looked down at her thin legs, so long from the knee downward, and wondered why these women didn't wear long skirts or trousers. Then he reflected that most races seemed to dress to emphasize their national peculiarities. In this milieu, long, thin legs and plump bodies were "in." Perhaps Heidi and her sister wore trouser suits to hide the unacceptable muscular development of their legs, exercised in preparation for Earth's gravity.

"Have you eaten?" Rita called over her shoulder.

"Not for hours," answered Mori.

"Both of you sit down. I'll put something in the micro."

Seated at the table, Lance looked around the room, while Rita moved into the kitchen area. The slow-motion movements of her legs and torso contrasted strangely with the rapid dexterity of her hands and arms. Lance's attention was caught by an oil painting on the wall facing him—an Earth scene, with palm trees and white coral sand bordering a turquoise lagoon, evidently somewhere in the Pacific.

"Painted by my grandfather," said Mori. "I've never been there myself."

"I've seen a lot of islands that look just like that," said Lance. "He's even caught the change in color of the water as you get beyond the reef."

"He painted a number of those. I think he was homesick for years after he came here."

Rita had come back into the room. "Pango's grandparents were the people who laid out that public garden at the corner of the avenue—little lakes, palm trees, sand, the lot."

"Except that the sand is orange," added Mori. "That's all he could get around here."

The meal was warm and very welcome to Lance. "This meat is delicious," he said to Rita. "What is it?"

"Comes from the Southeast Gallery. They grow muscle tissue in vats. It's chemically the same as real beef, but the texture is different. The potatoes and onions come from hydroponics tanks."

Rita suddenly looked at a door behind Lance's shoulder. "I thought you two were supposed to be asleep!"

Lance turned his head. A boy about ten Earth years old and a girl a couple of years younger were peering at him through the open door. They wore toweling garments like Japanese hapi coats, and both were dark-skinned, dark-eyed, and quivering with curiosity.

"All right." Mori looked meaningfully at his watch. "You can stay up for another ten minutes."

"Are you from Earth?" asked the boy, looking round-eyed at Lance.

"Just arrived from there."

"Is it true Earth people are three times as strong as Mars people?"

Lance looked at him in the eyes as if he were an adult. "It's half true. Compare me with your dad. His arms would be as strong as mine, but my legs would be stronger, because I'm used to walking around in heavier gravity."

The little girl chimed in. "Like a man carrying two other men on his back wherever he went."

"That's not a bad description."

"I don't think I'd want to go to Earth," said the boy. "I'd be like some of the zeegee people when they come here.''

"Zeegee people?''

Rita explained the term. "He means people who've grown up in the asteroid settlements where they have almost no gravity at all. When they're old enough, they send them here for school.''

"One of my friends—'' began the little girl.

Rita stopped her. "Time you were in bed. Don't you have tests coming up in a few days?''

Obediently, the children went back through the door.

"Bright kids,'' said Lance.

"They have a good educational system here,'' said Mori. "Keep stretching them to reach farther, do better all the time.''

"What about the kids not bright enough to stand the pressure?''

"You can't pace your program by the losers.''

Lance thought for a while. "On Earth, we tend to look after our losers.''

"And look where it's got you.'' A slight edge of contempt seemed to enter Mori's voice.

"Well,'' retorted Lance, "we can't sort out the philosophies of two planetary governments in one night. Let's focus on the job in front of us. How do I go about tracing Darch, and for that matter Brad Hagen?''

Mori shook his head. "Tracing Brad is a dead loss—I've been trying for forty or fifty days. But Darch—I'd try the Department of the Coordinator of Personnel, at the City Hall. I'll drop you there tomorrow morning. For the moment, let's sleep.''

The City Hall of Hellas was an anachronism, a copy of a classic Earth building of perhaps the late nineteenth century, which in its turn had architectural roots going back to Periclean Greece. It was built of volcanic pumice sawn by laser into precisely fitting blocks, with fluted columns supporting a massive-looking portico.

Directed to the third floor, Lance stepped off the escalator to see the Department of the Coordinator of Personnel clearly marked. The choice of the word seemed odd to him. *Personnel*— it was as if they thought of the whole city as a single integrated organization. Perhaps it was, to a far greater degree than a similar sized city on Earth. Here, with airlocks leading to a lifeless outside world, there was more justification for control.

At an inquiry desk, he was directed to a large office where a number of people sat at desks loaded with advanced-looking electronic equipment. An albino woman with tinted glasses motioned him to join her at her desk, and he produced the two photographs Mori had copied for him, one of Brad Hagen and the other of Jack Darch.

"How long have they been missing?" asked the woman, blinking through her glasses.

"Hagen, about sixty days."

She tapped her keyboard, looking at her terminal. "Yes, we have a note of his disappearance. Last seen sixty-one days ago. Nothing further has come in—no report of his body being found. And the other one?"

"Jack Darch, metals prospector. He's been missing eight days."

The woman shook back her snowy hair and tilted her head back, looking at him through her glasses. "A prospector, missing eight days? Hardly time to get your viscera in a knot, is it? Those people wander about the Outlands for a hundred days at a time."

"This fellow disappeared from the Star of the Outlands, West Gallery, and I believe there's no record of him leaving through any of the airlocks."

"Just a minute. I'll check that."

He waited as she pounded her keyboard, looking at her terminal with a frown of concentration. "You're right," she said after a while. "There's no record of him going Outside."

"I think something bad may have happened to him. I believe he'd stumbled onto something that some group of people want to be kept quiet."

"If there *is* a case to investigate, I'll get one of our people put on it."

"There's some urgency about this. Could I wait and see the person covering it? It might save time."

"As you wish." She spoke into an interoffice phone, then directed Lance to a passageway leading toward the rear of the building.

The investigator met him in the passage, introducing himself simply as Magill. He was a wiry man whose age Lance found it hard to estimate, with a long, hooked nose and a tight mouth. He led the way to a small office with a window looking out of the back of the building to the dusty curve of the great dome.

Lance handed him the photo of Jack Darch. He punched out some data on his keyboard, studying the terminal on his desk.

"Where did he disappear?"

"The Star of the Outlands."

Unexpectedly, Magill stood up. "Let's start there."

He led the way down a back escalator to a car park, and a minute later they were driving along the West Gallery in a gray, bubble-topped car. The morning sunshine slanted in over their right shoulders. They passed the lane where the three men had tried to attack Lance the previous night, and Magill jerked his thumb toward it.

"Had an incident there last night."

Lance feigned mild surprise. "Yes?"

"Two men knocked unconscious, another trapped in an overturned car. Some inter-gang trouble, I think. Two of the victims were wearing masks, and the man in the car had a mask in his possession."

"Had they been shot?"

"No. Overpowered by someone very strong." Magill gave a sidelong glance at Lance. "I'd say someone from Earth. The fellow turned a large car over by just gripping the bottom edge of the car body."

"Might have been more than one man lifting it."

"No. One set of hand marks. Too blurred for prints."

"Any motive?"

"Not yet. We're not worried much. We know two of the men who were knocked out. On dope—they'd do anything for money. Haven't any record of the third man yet. But we'll sort it out."

There was a different receptionist on duty at the Star of the Outlands, as bored-looking as the first. The only difference was that this one looked like a bored Asian.

Magill went straight to the point. "I'm trying to trace a man called Jack Darch. This is a recent photo of him."

The receptionist studied the print. "Oh, him? Haven't seen him for a few days." He punched a number on the internal phone after checking a list on his terminal. "No answer," he said after a while.

"Could I see his room?"

"Just a minute." The receptionist touched another switch, and after some delay spoke into a mike. "Belle? There's an investigator here called Magill—yes, he showed me a badge. Wants to see room 38." He listened to some response. "That's right . . . the prospector fellow . . . No . . . All right. I'll take him through."

He took a key from a board and led the way through the doorway into the square courtyard. It looked less sinister than it had appeared the previous night.

Darch's room was bare, Spartan. A bed, a small table, a wardrobe, a telephone. Magill stood in the doorway for about a minute, his eyes moving unhurriedly to scan every part of the room. His gaze sharpened as he looked at the rear window that was set high up.

"When was that window replaced?"

"I don't know," said the receptionist. "Looks new, doesn't it? Must have been done some time when I wasn't on duty."

Magill grunted. He went over to the wardrobe and threw its flimsy doors open. "Did he take all his clothes with him?"

"I don't know."

Magill made a sweeping gesture with his hand. "The whole floor looks as if it's been scrubbed."

"Might have been."

Magill zipped open a bag he had been carrying and took out a device that looked like an electric hair dryer with a small cathode tube mounted on the back of it. He switched it on, sweeping it across the pillow on the bed, watching the little screen, on which Lance could see a sharply peaked line flickering.

"What's that?" he asked.

"We call it a sniffer. Analyzes traces of scent. This can pick up things a bloodhound would miss. Each individual's scent leaves its own pattern. See?" He swept the nozzle of the device across the back of his hand, and the zigzag line on the screen changed its pattern. He returned it to the pillow and swept it carefully, the tiny fan motor whining.

"That would have been changed," said the receptionist.

"There's a trace here from underneath the cover," said Magill. "Enough for me." He strode over to the window. "Come here."

Lance went across to him, the receptionist following reluctantly. Magill's lean forefinger pointed to a smeared mark on the bottom edge of the window frame. "I'd say that was blood." He took a large magnifying glass from his bag and inspected the smear. Then he scraped some of the stain with a knife and put it in a small container like a test tube, labeling it and stowing it in his bag.

Lance heard a heavy, measured step coming along the veranda on the courtyard side of the rooms, a double footstep alternating with a heavier single thump. The receptionist moved to the door, and a moment later Belle and Maya Ambon appeared. Their hair was worn up this morning, and they were dressed in a gray business suit adapted to their physique, the huge jacket enclosing their double torso, while below it three tightly fitting stretch trouser legs were tucked into three black, knee-high boots.

"Hi, Lance," said Maya as soon as she saw him.

"What have you found?" demanded Belle, looking at the investigator. "It's Magill, isn't it?"

"That's right. You have a good memory for names."

"You came here to look into a theft a couple of years ago," said Belle. "But what do you think happened here?"

"I think there was a struggle here, and a man was abducted through that window. Did you find it broken?" Belle nodded, and Magill went on. "Someone broke the glass, reached in, opened the window, came in, overpowered Darch. Or perhaps they came in when he wasn't here and waited beside the door or in that wardrobe." He looked from one to the other of the women's faces.

"The window was broken," admitted Belle after a short hesitation. "We had it replaced soon after the room girl reported it."

"And who ordered the scrubbing of the floor?"

"We did. There was broken glass under the window, and we had the whole floor cleaned."

Magill pointed to the empty wardrobe. "Has that been cleaned out?"

"Yesterday," said Belle. "We took Darch's things out and stored them for him. We might have a chance to let the room again."

"Could I see his belongings?"

"Come this way." The women stepped back, coordinating their movements smoothly as they pivoted on the central leg. Belle glanced at the receptionist. "You'd better get back to the desk," she said.

"I'll do that." He hurried off across the courtyard.

Lance and Magill followed the Ambon sisters along the veranda. Lance was surprised at how quickly they moved. They walked with the rhythm of a one-legged person using two crutches, their broad double body bouncing as they swung the thick central leg forward. Stopping in front of a plain green door, they opened it with a key, showing their first sign of awkwardness as they edged sideways into the room.

It was a storeroom with suitcases and other objects stowed on two levels. Belle pointed to two worn cases. "There's Darch's stuff—all of it. Not much to show for a life of prospecting, is it?"

"He was looking in the wrong places," said Maya.

Magill silently went through the two bags, after opening them skillfully with a bunch of skeleton keys. Articles of clothing, a flashlight, which he tested, a few small hand tools. With a sharp exclamation, he took out a handful of maps held together by a rubber band. He took them over to a table in the corner and spread them out, studying them intently.

While Magill was absorbed in the maps, the women stood in silence on the motionless tripod of their legs, and Lance wandered casually around the storeroom. He noticed that Maya gave him all her attention, while Belle kept an undeviating focus on Magill. As he moved farther around the room, his attention was caught by the sections of an extraordinary spacesuit, the lower part with three legs, the upper enormously bulky, with provision for two helmets side by side. He looked at Maya in surprise.

"You go into space?"

"Sometimes," she said.

At that moment, Magill found something of interest in the maps. "I'll take these, if I may," he said in a tone that suggested his politeness was a mere formality, and that any protest would be instantly overruled. "And now I'll have a look around the outside of the building."

"There's a door here," said Belle, and the sisters moved suddenly, striding across to the door indicated and opening it.

A short flight of steps led down to the reddish ground. Magill went quickly down, followed by Lance, and they walked along toward the room that had been Darch's, Magill looking for the replaced window. Nearing it, he held out his hand to stop Lance from walking too close to it.

"One advantage in the soil under these domes," he said. "With no wind, it holds footprints for a long time."

There were a number of prints around the area, concentrated on the space immediately below the window, where a few shards of broken glass still glittered on the ground. Magill brought out his "sniffer" and switched it on, waving it across the footprints. Catching a movement from the corner of his eye, Lance saw the Ambon sisters coming toward them in a curious, skipping run. They came quite close before they halted, breathing heavily, and looking with interest at Magill's detector.

"He was dragged away," said Magill emphatically. "Here's his scent trace, see? And here's the memory of the pattern I took inside. Weak, but unmistakably the same peaks and dips."

"Why did you say 'dragged'?" asked Belle.

"Heel marks—see? Two men dragged him between them, with his heels trailing. I'd say he was unconscious."

He followed the scent like a dog, holding the detector on an extended handle so that the fan intake was close to the ground. "They were heading for that small airlock. Wait a minute." He took a few steps, then said again, "Wait a minute." Then, "*My god!*"

Lance and the Ambon women moved alongside him. Suddenly Maya gave an uncharacteristic cry, almost a shriek, pointing to the ground. Lance, following the direction of her pointing finger and Magill's concentrated gaze, felt a taste like metal in his mouth.

On the ground was a footprint like nothing human. A large, three-toed footprint, like that of a gigantic bird or some long-extinct dinosaur. And like something else he had seen.

He took a copy of the photo sent by Jack Darch out of his pocket, looked at it, then again at the footprint. Meanwhile, Magill had found another of the prints.

"God," he said. "Look at the length of the stride! What made it?"

Lance showed him the photograph. "Could it have been something like this?"

chapter
12

MAGILL KEPT LOOKING from the photograph to the footprint, then back again.

"Where did you get this?"

"Jack Darch took it, sent it to us on Earth. That's what brought me all the way here. We magnified the original, and we didn't think it was faked."

The Ambon sisters moved closer to Magill, so that they could see the photo. "It has to be a fake!" Belle asserted. "These crazy footprints could have been made by a fellow with things strapped to his feet. Remember Bigfoot?"

"Bigfoot?"

"A legend back on Earth in the last century, in Canada, I think. Some old man finally admitted that when he was young he'd made huge apelike footprints with carved wooden slabs."

"No," said Magill decisively. "The stride's too long for a man to fake with things on his feet. And look at the depth of the prints. This fellow was carrying a lot of weight—probably Darch's plus his own, and that must have been two or three times an ordinary man's."

"What sort of scent do you get from those prints?" asked Lance.

Magill swept his instrument across the three-toed prints, watching the cathode screen. He breathed out audibly. "Like nothing I've ever seen. Look." He let Lance look at the zigzag on the screen, but it meant little to him, apart from looking very different in pattern from Darch's, Magill's or his own.

"They're not bare feet," said Magill. "Soles of something like synthetic rubber. But it's the shape! No human feet could have fitted into them, yet you can see from their flexibility and load distribution that there were *some* living feet inside the things. And they seem to match this photo."

They followed the prints across to a small airlock, losing them as they reached the paved area near the inner door of the lock. Magill, with a patient thoroughness that fascinated Lance, moved slowly around the periphery of the paved area with his detector, making sure that whatever had made the prints had not stepped off in a different direction.

"No," he said emphatically. "It went out through the lock, whatever it was."

"No use trying to follow prints outside," said Belle Ambon. "The winds out there would wipe them out in a few hours."

"Nevertheless, I'll try," said Magill. "It looks as if this thing is bigger than any of us thought. I'll get a suit sent down from HQ." He took a radio from his bag, making no attempt to use his small wrist radio, punched out a call sign, and spoke with his mouth close to the mike. "Snowy? Magill. Can you get back to me right away with a list of all personnel who went out through—" he looked at the number painted above the airlock, "—Airlock WG3. . . . That's right, one of the little ones. . . . Right, I'll hold."

Both the Ambon women seemed shaken by the sight of the footprints, disturbed in different ways. Belle seemed to be struggling against disbelief, while Maya looked definitely frightened. As they turned back toward the Star of the Outlands, Lance noticed a breakdown in the tightly drilled cooperation between them. They almost stumbled as they turned, and they staggered for a few steps before they regained their synchronization.

Magill, waiting for his return call, gave Lance a wintry smile. "They may say that two heads are better than one, but anything unexpected seems to rock those ladies."

Lance walked back and looked at the deeper prints of the three-toed feet, where they crossed an area where the ground had been moistened by some outflow from the building. The texture of the soles looked scaly, with a regularity that suggested a non-slip pattern molded into a tough, flexible material. He took close-up shots with his small pocket camera.

He felt a coldness throughout his body, the beginning of a threatened cramp in his clenched jaws. He recalled the feeling that had assailed him when Mort Channing had first shown him Darch's photograph. The unreasoned fear of the unknown had receded when he had heard Darch described as a practical joker, but perhaps that was because he had listened to what he wanted to believe.

Now, the specter of the extra-terrestrial was back. The thing had been *here*, treading the very stretch of ground on which he now stood.

He was jerked out of his reverie by Magill almost shouting into the mike of his radio: "What? . . . But they keep lists of *all* people coming in and out. . . . What? . . . For the whole four hours? . . . Well, there's not much we can do about it. But one other thing, Snowy. Can you get Ari to run my spacesuit down to me? I'm going Outside. Probably won't learn much, but I have to try. I can suit up in a room near the lock. I'll wait here. Out!"

He put the radio back in his bag. "Never struck that before," he said.

"What happened?" asked Lance.

"There's an automatic videotape taken of everyone who goes in and out of these locks—all of them. They're computer co-ordinated for the whole city. See? There's one of the cameras up there. Yet for four hours, eight nights ago, from 1:00 through to 5:00, the tapes on this lock are blank. The technical boys think they've been erased magnetically by some kind of beam. See, the tape stays in the camera for about four hours. A strong magnetic field—whoosh!" He made a gesture of wiping his hands together.

"Then this was well planned," said Lance.

"You can say that again. And by someone with a lot of technical expertise available. Whoever snatched this guy Darch really wanted him out of the way." He held up the photograph. "May I keep this?"

"I don't think that'd be wise." Lance held out his hand. "We don't know yet if it's genuine, and if we gave it early publicity it might cause a general panic."

Magill turned the photograph over and looked at the back of it. "This was copied here in Hellas," he said. "So you have other copies. Think I'd better hold on to it. It's up to the boys upstairs to make a decision on this one."

"Okay. But remember it was Solar News who put you on to it."

"I won't forget that. I knew Brad Hagen—got on well with him. I want to find out what happened to him as much as you do—and I think this Darch snatch connects with it."

After his spacesuit had been brought to him, Magill put it on, tested it, then went out through the airlock. Lance waited, but as he had expected Magill found nothing of value. The wind outside the domes had driven away any scent that his detector could have picked up and obliterated any footprints.

"Dead loss," he said on his return, after he had removed his suit. "Except that it gave me time to think about what we've found to date." From his pocket, he took the picture. "This thing obviously isn't human. We've no idea where it came from, or what its motives might be. It might belong to a race that sees humanity as a competitor to be eliminated. And it might be capable of doing it."

"One of them on its own?"

"Possible. Disease germs, things like that."

"But listen! If they aimed to exterminate us, why did they need to grab Jack Darch in the middle of the night?"

"Don't know. But the stakes are too high for us to take any chances."

Lance nodded. "Something bothers me: The thing just arrived here recently, apparently from an alien planet. Right? Doesn't speak our language. Now, how the hell did it find where Darch was hiding in a city this size? It must have had inside help. Like the three—"

Magill's eyes seemed to bore into his. "What were you going to say? Like the three men who attacked you last night in the West Gallery?"

"I didn't say that was me."

"I can't prove it was. But between us, it's okay with me. Two of those thugs were permanent losers, and I imagine the third was a boyo who'd do anything for money, although we haven't any file on him."

"D'you want to do anything about that?"

"Not as long as we're cooperating on the main problem." Again, Magill tapped his finger on the photograph.

"I'll go along with that." Lance reached out his hand, and after a second's hesitation Magill gripped it.

On the way back to City Hall, Magill drove in silence for most of the way. Then Lance said, "I appreciate you keeping this quiet for a while."

Magill gave a short laugh. "I'm not doing that for *you*. I'm carrying out an investigation into a simple disappearance that's blown up into something that could rock our whole system. I don't want the scenario fouled up by hundreds of scene stealers you'd get forcing their way on camera with descriptions of imagined aliens. It'd be like the old twentieth century epidemics of flying saucer sightings. You'd never know where the hell you were."

"Has anyone ever come up with a report of anything that looked like the figure in that picture?"

"Never heard of it. It looks as if Darch was the only one who saw it. Whether he told someone, and it got back to the alien — well, I don't know."

"The thing *must* have had a human accomplice."

"We know that. Two of 'em—the boyos who snatched Darch from his room. There was no trace of the alien in the room— probably too big to get in the window."

"Then how did he communicate with the two? Could he have had them hypnotized?"

"Listen, don't let's get too far ahead with unsupported speculation," said Magill. "I've been thinking of the craziest things, like mental telepathy leading the thing to single out Darch among all the thousands in the city. But for God's sake, let's walk before we fly on this thing."

"Have you any way of tracing the two men who actually got into the room?"

"I've got their scent prints recorded. If we pick them up, I can identify them, but we might have trouble finding them in the first place."

Back at the Solar News office, Lance took an atlas of Mars from the reference library. One thing the Ambon sisters had said had lodged firmly in his mind. When he had suggested flying out to where the probe had landed, Maya had said at once, "But that's sixteen hundred kilometers from here."

He had the feeling that they knew more about the location of the probe than had been generally revealed. Perhaps Mort Channing's attempt to withhold information about it had been applied too late, or from too far off, to be effective. Belle Ambon had tried to deflect his interest from what her sister had said, but had inadvertently had the effect of fixing it indelibly.

He took photocopies of the maps of the areas around sixteen hundred kilometers away, west, northwest and north of the airlock dome of the West Gallery. He fixed them edge to edge on a large table, then, with a cord pinned at the location corresponding to the dome, he drew an arc scaled to sixteen hundred kilometers radius across the maps with a red felt-tipped pen.

The red arc ran through a surprising variety of land types,

beginning with the heavily cratered plains west of the Hellespontis Mountains, then swinging north and east through country described on the legends of the maps as labyrinthine—a chaotic jumble of gullies running in random directions, sloping down to finish in the open plains that covered half the planet.

Somewhere along that arc, Tynan's mysterious object had landed. Pango Mori was out of the office this morning covering a dispute in the Southwest Gallery between management and employees of a plant that treated metallic ores brought in from the asteroids. Lance decided to wait for Mori's return to see if he could use his local knowledge to rent an aircraft to explore the areas he had marked on the maps.

It was nearly midday when a visiphone call came through. Lance opened the channel and found Magill's thin, sour face looking out at him.

"Could I see you?" asked the investigator.

"Right away, if you like. I'll come around."

Lance put the maps in a desk lent to him by Mori and took the elevator down to the Octagon, where streams of pedestrians were moving in their Martian slow-motion walk between offices and restaurants. He went along to the City Hall and rode the escalators to the third floor. The albino woman, who was obviously expecting him, directed him along to Magill's office.

Magill closed the door of his office after Lance entered. "We've picked up the three fellows whose car you overturned last night," he said.

"*I* overturned?"

"Well, let's say a person unknown, probably recently arrived from Earth, who could have been mistaken for you."

"Yes?"

"The two men left in the lane were known to us—just local adrenohype-heads who needed money for a fix. The third man, though, was something else altogether. He has an off-planet record. They're looking for him on Ceres."

"What'd he do out there?"

"Something they take very seriously in the 'roids. He tried to extort money from a mining company by threatening to bomb a hole in one of the domes enclosing a big ore-processing complex. Easy to do, with something like a rocket bomb, or explosive in a remote-controlled surface vehicle."

"Yes, I can see that. Did he collect the money?"

"Not according to the company threatened, but that may not

be true. They may think that if word got around that they paid him, others might try it.''

"How did he get here, if he didn't collect the money?"

"We think he sneaked off Ceres in an ore freighter. His extortion attempt happened about three hundred days ago, so there was plenty of time for him to come here—or be brought here by someone who wanted to use him. I'm inclined to think someone in Hellas had him brought here and kept in cold storage until they needed something done they wouldn't want to be involved in themselves. Probably gave him an implant so they could blow him away any time he didn't do what they told him.''

"What's happened to him?" Mention of the implant chilled Lance.

"He *is* carrying an implant—a type than enables a monitor to hear everything he hears, everything he says.''

"Did you get it out?"

"Couldn't risk that. We put him in a cell filled with random noise—a lot of disks played fast simultaneously, some in reverse, so that no one would be able to make any sense of anything he heard.''

"God, did he go mad?"

"Not yet. We shot him full of heavy tranquilizers. When he comes out he won't know whether he's in the moons of Jupiter or next New Year. That's if *they* let him come out. They might get tired of listening to the recorded gibberish and terminate him. That's why we didn't question him about who pointed him in your direction. If he'd started to tell us anything, they'd have blown his fuse.''

"Doesn't give him much future, does it?"

"He doesn't deserve any." Magill's face looked as hard as rock. "Any animal who gets money by threatening to blow a dome— if I had my way, I'd throw him to the vacuum without a suit. That's what he was willing to do to a lot of other people.''

Lance reflected for a while in silence on the savagery of justice in this world where people had to contend with a violent environment. He decided to change the subject.

"How can I get out to the area they call the Badlands?"

Magill looked at him in surprise. "Why?"

"I might find out what all this is about."

"That's what Brad Hagen thought. I think *they* found *him*."

Lance nodded. "Are there any astronomers here who'd know anything about the probe?"

"There could be."

"Can you put me in touch with one of them? I've interviewed John Tynan in Hawaii, the astronomer who first found the thing. I understand he was in touch with an astronomer at Olympus Mons."

Magill shook his head. "The observatory up there is automated. Sticks up almost out of the atmosphere. They run their telescopes by remote control from the astronomical section of the University up in the North Gallery."

"Who do I contact there?"

Magill tapped more keys, eyes on the screen. "You'd do best to find a Dr. Des Segal. He's big in the Astronomy Division. Came here from Earth eleven years ago. He might know the man you interviewed in Hawaii."

"Tynan."

"Whatever." Magill pointed to a large wall map. "Drive around here, then up the North Gallery. The University's halfway up, both sides of the avenue, mostly red laser-cut buildings. The astronomy complex is on your left—no telescopes—they're all somewhere else."

"Thanks. You've been a big help."

Magill gave his sour smile. "Great, what an ulterior motive can do."

Dr. Segal was a tall, lean man with a smooth Shakespearean forehead above a sharp, triangular face, rimless glasses and a ragged mustache that did not seem to belong with the rest of his features. He took Lance into his office.

"John Tynan," he said as soon as Lance mentioned him. "Yes, I knew him well. Ironical that he should have been the man to make this discovery. We each had the opportunity to come here, and he chose to remain in Hawaii." He showed irregular teeth in a sudden smile. "Here am I, practically on the spot, and I knew nothing about it until he reported it from the next planet."

"I believe the object came down about sixteen hundred kilometers northwest of here."

"No. I don't think that's right. Where did you hear that?"

"Just indirect gossip. I don't know where it originated."

"It's wrong, anyway. It was twice as far away as that. Say thirty-three hundred k's, give or take a hundred."

So, thought Lance, so much for Maya Ambon and her sixteen hundred kilometers, and Belle's quick correction, which had fixed the figure in his mind. Perhaps the two sisters had worked together more subtly than he had realized to give him a wrong steer. But why?

Or—was it Segal who was giving him the wrong steer?

Was this the road to paranoia?

"Did anyone fly out to investigate the place where the object landed?"

"We tried. Found nothing. Dreadful terrain to search for anything. A jumble of ridges and little valleys running in every direction. People have been lost out there—run out of air before they could be found. No place for an amateur."

Lance looked steadily at Segal. "What's *your* theory about the object?"

"Well, I've seen a tape of your telecast. Rather dramatic, but quite good. But as to what I think of the probe, as you termed it—I simply don't know. I'm supposed to be an expert, but any expert's opinions are only as good as the data supplied to him, and, frankly, I've found no trustworthy data about this object."

"Do you have the feeling some people are hiding something?"

Segal glanced around. "Lance—may I call you Lance?—I've been here twenty Earth years—that's eleven Martian years—and I'm still learning about the local scene. What you have here are a number of highly skilled and intelligent elites. Not just one elite, giving you classical haves and have-nots, nothing as simple as that. We have a number of competing elites, with various groups within them sometimes cooperating with others. It'd drive you mad, trying to get inside the local political setup. I don't try, now. I just get on with my work."

Lance handed him Darch's photo of the being in the duststorm. "What do you think of this?"

Unexpectedly, Segal showed little surprise. "Yes, I've seen a copy of this picture. My feeling was that it might be a still from a science fiction program."

"I don't think so. I've seen actual footprints that looked as if they were made by the thing in that picture."

"Where?"

Lance told him about Jack Darch, the broken window in his room at the Star of the Outlands, Magill's tracing of his abduction with his scent detector, and the footprints in the soft ground near the airlock. Segal went to his desk, sat down, took a magnifying glass from a drawer and spent some time scanning the picture.

"You don't think the footprints could have been faked?"

"No. They were very deep, as if made by something quite heavy, and the stride was too long for a human stride. I don't know what the thing was, but I've never met anything like it. Frankly, I don't want to."

Segal put his magnifying glass away and sat looking at the picture, leaving it propped against a telephone index. "If this thing is an alien," he said slowly, "it looks to me as if it didn't come from any planet in the solar system. From a gravitational point of view, Earth would come closest to suiting it, but there's been nothing on Earth with feet like that for over sixty million years. As to the four arms, there's been nothing remotely like that, ever."

"Except—" Lance hesitated, while Segal looked at him with an eyebrow cocked. "Except there was an idea someone put forward when he saw this. It looks like some of the old Hindu gods. Suppose something like this came to Earth long ago?"

Segal frowned thoughtfully, shaking his head. "Where would that get us? There have been Hindu gods with multiple arms, sure. But there have been others with elephant heads, bull heads—or was that Minoan?—all chimeras built up out of someone's imagination. But *this*—" he gestured at the photograph, "this looks real."

"It *is* real. Real as you are. Remember, I saw its footprints only a few days after they'd been made. Put my own alongside them for comparison. They were much deeper, and farther apart."

"But how did it get right into the city, kidnap a man, and get out again without anyone seeing it?"

"It was night. Not much nightlife out near the end of the West Gallery. There's no operator on the airlocks there at night — they're left on manual control by the persons using them, with surveillance cameras. This thing, when it went out, apparently blanked out four hours of the recording on a camera."

"Then it must have had human help. An alien being who'd just arrived on the planet wouldn't know enough to do that."

"He had help, sure. The two other goons who actually broke into Darch's room and dragged him out."

Segal seemed absorbed in his own thoughts. "But from *where*? Obviously from somewhere with a gravity field much stronger than Mars', probably stronger than Earth's. What do we have in the solar system with gravity higher than Earth's? Only Jupiter, Saturn, and the other two gas giants. Couldn't have come from there—and that leaves us the nearer star systems. Alpha Centauri,

Barnard's Star in Ophiuchus—there are planets there—Bessel's Star, or what we call 61 Cygni, with a known planet, Tau Ceti, Epsilon Eridani—but they're a hell of a long way for anyone to come.''

"Especially if he came on his own."

"That's unbelievable. But wait! Suppose there's a mothership somewhere, orbiting the Sun farther out, where we haven't looked for it? The thing doesn't have to be near the ecliptic—it could be in any direction."

"This probe came in at a steep angle, didn't it?"

"Yes. As I say, I watched your program. You made that part of it very—convincing, shall I say?"

"Did you find it factually okay?"

"Reasonably. I realize you have to overdramatize for a media audience, but you used a certain amount of restraint. One thing puzzles me, though."

"What's that?"

Segal held up the picture of the alien. "Why didn't you use this?"

"It only arrived while I was on air. Incidentally, you mentioned you'd seen a copy. Where was that?"

"Brad Hagen showed me one like it. He came here about sixty days ago, wanted to know what I thought of it."

Segal's jaw clenched, and tendons stood out like wire cables down the sides of his neck. Something warned Lance to remain silent.

"I liked Brad," said Segal. "But it might have been better if he'd never known me. I was the one who suggested he go into the Outlands where I'd figured the object had landed. I never thought that'd be the last I'd see of him."

"You knew him well?" asked Lance quietly.

"We both came from Earth about the same time, and we used to see a lot of each other. Came out here thinking that by this time we'd be running Mars." Segal gave a bitter smile. "Don't make the mistake we did. The local competition can be very tough, very quick, and very deadly."

chapter
13

THE DAY THE *Iridia* arrived in Mars orbit, Lance took one of the Solar News cars out to the terminal at the South Gallery Airlock. From the radio room at the terminal, he was able to put through a call to Dorella as the ship passed over on its penultimate circuit before the spaceplane made its rendezvous.

When Dorella's face appeared on the screen, it was obvious that she was in free fall, her hair a dark cloud around her head. Her face looked pale, yet as intensely alive as when he had last seen her.

"Lance!" she said. "It's wonderful to see you again! Did you find what you came looking for?"

"Not yet, but I'm on the track of it. How was your trip out?"

"I've had wonderful luck. Met three people who actually knew Noel Karstrom. Captain Matsuoka was one, and I'll introduce you to the others when we come down."

"When's that?"

"On the first shuttle. Next orbit."

"I'll meet you at the terminal building. I've fixed accommodation for you—place called the Mangala, right next to the building where Solar News has its office."

Her face changed expression. "Oh, sorry, Lance. I've been invited to stay with one of the people I was talking about. Woman called Thyra. She *knew* Noel Karstrom, so it's a wonderful opportunity . . . Do you mind?"

"Of course not. By the way, I found out a bit more about old Noel, but that can wait until you're down here."

"Right." She glanced briefly aside. "I'm talking too long, Lance. Looking forward to seeing you. Bye."

Then the screen was blank.

Now Lance had nothing to do but wait. He wandered aimlessly

about the concourse for a few minutes, then went to a visi booth and cancelled the extra room he had booked at the Mangala. Then he looked down at the vehicles beginning to occupy the terminal park below, most of them trucks, a few enclosed, more of the flat-tray type used for carrying the ubiquitous containers. A few men were already climbing into powerful exoskeletons that could amplify their physical strength many times over.

Later, he saw the spaceplane moving out on its strip to take off, again surprised at the enormous span of its batlike wings, even though he had seen it when it had brought him down from the *Yttria*. He watched it rise slowly into the pink, dusty sky, following the starlike points of fire of its rockets as it climbed toward its coupling with the *Iridia*, somewhere above the shield volcanoes of the Tharsis group.

When it returned, Lance watched its slow, graceful landing, with its great wings fully extended, their lift in the meager air augmented by vertical rocket blasts that threw up a veil of dust. The bulbous transfer vehicle was already rolling out to meet it, with a number of tray-bodied trucks lumbering after it.

Impatiently, Lance kept staring along the strip until the glassy bubble body of the transfer vehicle reappeared from the dust.

"Not thinking of leaving us, Mr. Garrith?" He turned to find Glaya standing behind him in her orange and black uniform, her clipboard resting on her arm. It seemed a permanent fixture, and he had a momentary mental picture of her sleeping with it.

"Not yet, Glaya. I'm getting to like your planet better as I know it more."

"That happens to many people," she said. "Meeting someone?"

"Yes. A Ms Dorella Wade."

She scanned her clipboard. "Ah, Dorella Wade. Booked by Solar News and the Techno-Historical Society." She lifted her eyes to look into Lance's. "Who are they?"

"Techno-Historical? Never heard of them."

"No matter. She's aboard. Know her well?"

"Yes. We've worked on the same TV station."

Glaya glanced around. "You may as well go through the transfer lock. She'll feel better meeting someone she knows."

"Thanks, Glaya. That's thoughtful."

Her smile betrayed a hint of self-consciousness. "We're not all machines in Immigration."

She opened a gate in a barrier, and they stood near the passageway leading out from the lock. Glaya smiled at Lance appraisingly, glanced through a window to estimate the distance of the approaching vehicle, and put her clipboard down on a table. Still with a half-suppressed smile, she moved over to Lance and stood directly in front of him.

"Those enormous shoulders!" she said, and ran her fingers over the curves of his deltoids, biceps and triceps. Her eyes looked sexually aroused. "Your strength must give you a great feeling of confidence."

"Not with attractive women," he said, and as he said it he realized that Glaya did seem attractive now, whereas on first meeting her he had thought she seemed not quite human. Was he getting used to the look of Martian women? Or were his tastes simply broadening?

The sound of motors heralded the approach of the transfer bus, and a red light glowed above the airlock door. Glaya stepped back, picked up her clipboard and immediately reverted to her role of impersonal immigration officer. Her associate, the man in orange and black who had been with her when Lance had first arrived here, came along and stood beside her.

"Settling in?" he asked, looking across at Lance. He was even taller than Glaya by a few centimeters. Winking unexpectedly at Lance, he jerked his head toward Glaya.

"Want to watch her. She gets turned on by strong men." He seemed, like Glaya, to have dropped his hard, official attitude now that he considered Lance as someone other than a passing visitor.

The red light went out, and the door slid open, and Glaya and her partner became briskly efficient again. A tall man in gray stepped out confidently.

"Brendan Shang," he said.

"I know. Welcome home."

As Glaya made a check mark on her board, Lance studied Shang. He had the Martian physique, apparently strengthened by exercise to deal with Earth's gravity, then allowed to soften on the voyage home. He was obviously of Chinese ancestry. He produced some papers, but the Immigration man waved them aside.

"Pleasant voyage?" he asked.

"Extremely interesting," said Shang noncommittally, and he strode out through the barrier with the air of a man who owned the whole terminal building. A moment later, Lance's interest in the man was deflected as Dorella came out through the airlock.

"Name?" Glaya caught her attention immediately, so that she did not see Lance standing on the other side of the doorway.

"Dorella Wade."

Glaya made a check on her board. Lance had taken a second or two to recognize Dorella. For one thing, she didn't seem quite as tall as he remembered her, perhaps because she was overtopped by Glaya's height of a shade over two meters. Her hair looked different, too, still extended in the dark cloud he had seen when she was in free fall, and some of her tan had faded during the voyage, leaving her with a creamy pallor.

Seeing Lance, she rushed across to him and flung her arms around him.

"Lance! Wonderful to see you again."

He hugged her. She was wearing a sleek green leotard that clung to the contours of her body, with a ridiculous little cape of the same color. Her perfume brought back to him that night in Pacific City.

"You're looking magnificent!" he said, and moved his lips close to her ear. "I've been surrounded by Martian women ever since I came here. I'd forgotten what a girl's neck looks like."

"Are they all—" Dorella hunched her shoulders up almost level with her ears, "all tall?"

"Most of them. It's the light gravity."

"Could I have her back for a moment?" called Glaya. As Dorella walked back to her, followed by Lance, she asked, "Where will you be staying?"

"For a time, with one of the other passengers—Thyra."

Glaya looked at her board. "At her permanent address? On Lake Circle, up in the Northeast Dome? You said for a time?"

"A few days?"

"And then?"

Lance broke in. "Later, you can reach her through me, at Solar News."

Glaya nodded. "Is all I need. Enjoy your stay here."

Lance slipped his arm through Dorella's. "Come on. I'll show you where to get your baggage."

"Wait, darling. I want to help Thyra."

"Help her?"

"She's blind."

"How did she get about on Earth?"

"She finds her way around with a radar torch, and she has other equipment that amplifies her hearing and sense of smell. She's rather incredible—ah, here she is."

A tall woman in a hooded white coat came striding out from the airlock, her hood pulled forward so that it covered most of her face, leaving only the firm mouth and chin visible. She walked with her left hand inside a white plastic tube that extended in front of her for half a meter, sweeping it from side to side in rhythm with her steps. She halted in front of Glaya and turned to face her, scanning her with transverse movements of the tube. "It's Glaya, isn't it? You know me, of course. Where's Dorella?"

"Over there." Glaya took hold of the white tube and pointed it at Dorella. At once, the blind woman crossed over to her in three or four long strides, making them all the same length.

"Thyra, this is Lance Garrith," said Dorella.

The tube pointed up at Lance's face, and he saw a little aerial and parabolic reflector inside its oval end, alongside a grille covering a tiny intake fan like the one on Magill's scent detector.

"Describe him to me, Dorella," said the woman, and as she spoke she lifted her right hand and threw back her hood. The upper part of her face was covered by a skin-colored plastic mask that came right down where her eyes and nose would have been— there was no projecting nose, just a finely perforated grille on the flattened front of her face. An insulated wire ran up to a thing like a hearing aid in her left ear, and another wire came over the ear and across to the nose-grille.

"Well," said Dorella. "You can sense his general shape. Darkish hair, blue eyes, strong jaw. Looks quite handsome, and when I say it he's not even blushing, so I suppose you could say he has a big ego."

Thyra reached forward with her right hand, its long fingers outspread. "Would you mind if I touched your face?" she asked. "No."

Her fingertips slid delicately over the planes of his face—forehead, cheekbones, jaw. Her mouth lifted its corners slightly. "Thank you," she said. "I used to be sighted. I like to be able to picture the person I'm talking to."

"How did you like Earth?" asked Lance.

"Terribly crowded in the cities. I loved the seashores, with the waves thundering in. And the wind through the trees, and the aromatic gardens. Come on, Dorella."

Brendan Shang met them on the concourse with their baggage piled on a trolley. "I'll take you up home," he said.

Dorella introduced him to Lance. "Brendan and Thyra have a research facility specializing in neuron-electron interchanges. They make the trip to Earth at regular intervals to exchange ideas with research people there."

They headed out to the vehicle park, Shang wheeling the baggage trolley, which seemed to be electrically propelled, and Thyra walking beside him with her long, measured stride, her radar sensor swinging from side to side in rhythm with her steps. She had pulled the hood forward over her face again.

"You're sure Dorella won't be in your way?" called Lance. "I had a room already booked for her."

"My family is expecting her," answered Thyra.

They reached Shang's car, and he loaded the baggage aboard, sending the trolley back on automatic to the holding area. Thyra climbed in beside him in the front seat, and Dorella took the seat in the rear. "I'll see you soon, Lance," she said. "And thanks for coming to meet me."

"We'll look after her," said Thyra.

Lance followed Shang's car at a distance after they left the car park. Its color, sky blue, seemed rare among the vehicles here, and he was able to keep it in view without moving too close to it. As he expected, Shang drove straight up the avenue to Central Plaza, then turned right around the Octagon. He passed two intersections, then turned right into Northeast Avenue.

This was in the gallery where Pango Mori lived, and for the first part it was familiar, looking much the same in daytime as at night, as the lighting systems were mostly left on to supplement the weak sunlight filtering through the dusty, barrel-vaulted roof of the gallery.

They went past the region of orchards, vegetable tanks, and plantations of wheat, corn, sugar cane, bamboo, on past the pyramidal building where Mori and his family lived. They continued on past citrus orchards and other tight-packed zones of ordered vegetation until they reached a large dome at the end of the gallery, where the road ran in a circle around a park with an artificial lake, with impressive houses lining the road on the outer side of its circle, their facades overlooking the lake.

Slowing to a stop where the avenue reached the circle, Lance waited as if making up his mind which way to turn. The sky-blue car was traveling to the right, and he watched it move about a third of the way around the circle. The two women got out, and both walked up to the front door of a blue three-storied house, Thyra using her sensor, while Shang remained near his car, looking over the park and the lake. A minute later, a silvery robot like that used on the *Yttria* by Mackay glided out to the car, picked up the baggage with effortless power, and followed them into the house, while Shang stepped back into the car and drove off farther around the circle.

Lance swung onto the circular road, and drove slowly around to have a closer look at the three-storied house. It seemed to be built of laser-cut pumice, with broad windows facing the park, some shielded from excessive light by old-style Venetian blinds. Next door to it was a similar house, colored yellow where this one was blue. There were no gates in front of any of the houses, but the one Dorella had entered had an ornamental gateway bearing the name ISMENIA. Lance repeated it silently to himself. It seemed to ring a bell somewhere in his memory, but the exact association eluded him.

As he drove past, the Venetian-type blind on one of the windows of the uppermost floor changed position, as if someone had abruptly closed it. Then two of the slats of the blind separated a little, as though fingers had been thrust between them to allow someone to look out without being seen from outside. Lance drove on at the same even speed. At least he knew where Dorella was staying.

He drove back to the Viking Building and walked into the Solar News office. Fran, Mori's girl assistant, looked up from her desk as he entered.

"Hi!" she said. "I have a message for you."

She put a disk into a slot and pressed a key. Lance peered at the screen as the machine began rolling. Magill's unhappy face confronted him.

"We have a new development," he said. "Contact me as soon as you're able."

Lance put a call through to Magill's department, where the albino woman asked him to wait while she located Magill. After a minute or so, he appeared on the screen.

"I'd like you to get around here," he said. "We have one of the men who kidnapped Darch. Not the thing with the dinosaur's feet, but one of its human helpers."

"How did you get hold of him? Through your scent print?"

"No. It was easier than that. He came to us."

"What made him do that?"

"Fear. His friend who helped him in the kidnapping is dead. He thinks he was murdered."

Lance looked at his watch. "I'll be there in a few minutes."

When Lance stepped off the escalator on the third floor of the City Hall, the albino woman directed him straight along to Magill's office. "He's expecting you. Go straight in."

Magill was sitting behind his desk, with an array of electronic equipment in front of him. A thin man with wild-looking, dark-shadowed eyes sat in a chair by the end of the desk, with wires running from contacts on his wrists and other parts of his body to a device in front of Magill that was evidently a species of lie detector.

"Come in." Magill waved Lance to another chair without using his name. "This is one of the men who abducted Jack Darch from his room at the Star of the Outlands." He switched his attention back to the man he was questioning. "Would you explain again what happened?"

The thin man's eyes brightened momentarily in frustrated anger. "I've told you already. Jeese, you've got it all on record."

"Tell me again. I want to make sure you haven't overlooked something."

"There's not much to tell. Like I said, a bloke contacted Willy and me down at Rudy's place in the West Gallery."

"Who was he, this bloke?"

"He only called himself Ben. That probably doesn't mean anything. Way things turned out, I reckon he wouldn't have given us his real name. Willy and I were both on adrenohype, you know. It's getting bloody expensive. This Ben bloke gave us some money, told us he'd add ten times as much after we'd snatched Darch. He reckoned Darch put one over involving a mining claim, or something."

"What did he look like, this Ben?"

"Nothing special. Average height, build. He said he'd introduce us to his principal, as he called him, the night we picked up Darch."

"Where did this meeting take place?"

"I've told you. Back of the Star of the Outlands."

"And the principal?"

"God! I'll dream about him as long as I live."

"Describe him."

"You'll reckon I was hyped."

"Describe him, I said."

"Well, he had a sort of huge black cloak, with a hood that covered his head. I think he was wearing a spacesuit under it. And his feet—that was all of him I could see—were like big bird's feet in spacesuit shoes made to fit them. But the thing was, he was *big*. About twice my height."

Magill glanced at the ceiling. "Then he couldn't have stood upright in this room?"

"Eh?" The thin man looked at the ceiling. "Well, maybe. I suppose he wasn't *twice* my height, but he looked like it out there."

"What did he do?"

"After we got Darch out of the room, he carried him away, out through the airlock. Ben went with him as far as the lock and operated the doors for him."

"What did Ben do then?"

"He went over to the camera with a thing the stranger must have given him. He pointed it at the camera for a few seconds, and a noise came from it, a sort of buzz, like a transformer interrupter. Then he said everything in the camera would come out blank."

"Then?"

"He gave us the rest of our money, divided into two equal packs, and left. We went home to our pad. Willy had a bad attack of nerves. I went out to get some adrenohype, and when I got back, Willy was dead."

"Tell me about that again."

"He was lying on the bed, with blood all over the place. Looked as if someone had come in and hit him with a hammer, or something like that. Just here." He put his finger to the left side of his head, behind the temple.

"Any sign of a struggle?"

"No. That's what I don't get. I don't see how the bloke got close enough to Willy without him sitting up, or trying to put up some sort of a fight. The door was locked when I came back."

"Had you locked it when you went out?"

"Thought I had, but I couldn't be sure. You know how it is. If I left it open, whoever killed Willy could have tripped the lock when he went out, pulled the door shut."

Magill stood up, signalling with a movement of his head for Lance to do likewise, and walked across to the open window of his office, Lance joining him. Magill, standing so that he could still see the man in the chair, lowered his voice as he spoke to Lance: "My boys found no weapons when they examined the room, and no sign of forced entry. There was a window open, but the room was on the seventh floor of a tenement building, and there was no way anyone could have climbed to the window. People in the building said they heard the sound of a shot, but we couldn't understand that, because we found no bullet. The victim's parietal bone was shattered—inward."

"Inward? So it wasn't an explosive implant?"

"Looked like a bullet wound—with no bullet. We have a couple of theories how it might have been done. There was a thing called a captive-bolt pistol used on Earth to kill livestock, and another suggestion was a gun firing a bullet made of solid CO_2—dry ice—but that's tricky, and it'd need equipment hard to hide."

Abruptly, Lance jerked his head back as an insect flew in through the open window from the garden below. "What's that?"

Magill didn't reply. The insect droned around the room, metallic blue, with wings blurred by their rapidity of motion. It was the first insect Lance had seen on Mars—probably something that had lived in the sugar cane. It suddenly swooped toward the man Magill was interrogating. It landed on the left side of his head, just behind the temple, and he lifted his hand to brush it away.

What followed was a scene out of a nightmare.

A flash of light so brilliant that it left Lance and Magill blinded for some seconds coincided with a sharp crack like the shot from a small caliber pistol. The bright spot of aftervision danced wherever they looked, first vividly blue, then yellow as the spot expanded and faded. When they could see again, the man who had been questioned was toppling slowly from the chair, to sprawl on his side on the floor, obviously dead.

Footsteps pounded along the corridor, and several people came crowding in through the doorway, including the albino receptionist.

"What happened?" "Who shot him?" Eyes swept from Magill to Lance, then back again.

"I don't know what happened yet," admitted Magill, and he and Lance both stooped over the lifeless body.

"Something hit the desk—about here," said Lance, pointing.

Magill looked at the spot indicated with his magnifying glass. He grunted, then squatted down and began examining the floor. Breathing out heavily, he took a pair of tweezers from his pocket and picked up something small.

"It wasn't a shot," he announced. "Look at this."

The thing he held in the tweezers was an extremely thin piece of blue metal, so thin that when he turned it edge-on Lance was unable to see it at all.

"That thing was no insect," he said. "It was a miniature flying bomb. That's what killed Willy. The boys were wasting their time looking for a weapon like a hammer. They should have looked for the microscopic parts of something that landed on his head and exploded."

"But how did it find him?"

"A television camera can be made very small, these days." Magill gestured at the open window. "Someone flew the thing by remote control, watching a screen that gave a view from its camera, which wouldn't have been much bigger than a sugar grain."

"Who makes things like that?"

"Micro-equipment? Could have been made by any one of a number of firms." He reeled off a long list of organizations, a list he must have committed to memory and used many times, walking across to the window as he spoke and looking down. The dusty curve of the great dome was not far away from the building, and below was a luxuriant stretch of garden, with palm trees and melaleucas glistening from a spray of artificial rain. There was no one in sight below.

"Could have been controlled from a thousand meters away," said Magill, and with a sudden movement he reached up and closed the window. "But one is enough for the present."

Lance said nothing, musing over the list of names Magill had recited. Most meant nothing to him, but three were names already in his memory. Belastra, Shang, and the Karstrom Foundation.

As he walked back around the Octagon to the Viking Building, Lance felt a paralyzing sense of insecurity, like a man walking across a frozen lake without knowing the thickness of the ice beneath his feet. Back home on Earth, he had felt competent to handle any eventuality that appeared, but here he was threatened by an array of technical tricks of a different order of magnitude from anything in his experience.

As he neared his destination, he heard his name called, and turned to see Phil Gray hurrying to overtake him, dressed in an obviously new suit of a style worn by local people who liked to keep up with trends.

"How are you settling in at Belastra?" asked Lance.

Gray gave a nervously spasmodic grin, retaining his expression of almost permanent surprise. "Still learning. I'm at Head Office for the present." The way he said "Head Office" emphasized the capital letters. "Later, when I've absorbed the Company methods, I'll have a spell out in the 'roids."

"What'll you be doing there?"

"We have a lot of automated mining operations out there. We get a number of what you'd call rare metals, refine them on the asteroids, and ship the finished product back here. The metals go mostly into micro-equipment."

"Belastra makes some of that, doesn't it?"

"Some, yes. A lot of firms here specialize on certain things—temperature control units, little TV cameras, things like that."

"Implants?"

"How was that?"

"Implants? Things for putting inside people to control them?"

"I wouldn't know about that. Possible, I suppose, judging from some of the other things they make."

Lance looked at Gray closely. "You didn't wear a hearing aid on the ship, did you?"

"Oh, this? It's not really a hearing aid. Just a communication device. Like a beeper crossed with a midget radio telephone. Works by bone conduction." He removed the arc of soft, skin-colored plastic from behind his ear and showed it to Lance, who examined it with interest.

Lance pointed to the two tiny grilles of close-set holes. "Looks as if it can hear as well as talk to you." He handed the device back to Gray. "So someone can listen in to any person you meet? Hear what you say to them, and what they reply?"

"Yes, but that's not primarily what it's for."

Lance didn't reply to that. In his present mood, he doubted it. They walked along together, automatically falling into step, their strides shorter and faster than those of the gracefully moving local people.

"Seen any of the other passengers on the *Yttria* since you arrived?" asked Lance. "Apart from Jocasta Borg, of course."

"I haven't seen much of her, actually, although she often gets in touch with me through this." Gray touched the communication device behind his ear. "I've seen Joy a few times. How's Heidi, by the way?"

"Fine, when I saw her the other night."

"By the way," said Gray, "Joy's having lunch with me in a

little while. Place called the Casemi—no, Cassini.'' Lance wondered at the correction. Had Gray misheard an auditory prompt? He felt almost certain, at the moment, that Joy had access to the channel through which Belastra transmitted its instructions to Gray. ''Why don't you join us? It's close to here.''

''I'll have to take a rain check on that, Phil. That's if they have rain checks here where it never rains. But I have to call in at our office. Remember me to Joy.''

''Will do. Bye.''

As Lance walked on alone after Gray entered the building containing the Cassini, his pocket beeper shrilled faintly. He flicked it on, and Pango Mori's dark face appeared on the tiny screen.

''Hi, man. You far away?''

''No.''

''Just had a call from guess who—Mort Channing. Think you'd better get here right away. This is a big one.''

chapter
14

BACK IN THE inner office of Solar News, Mori switched on the tape from Mort Channing. The window behind Channing's tired face showed darkness, so for him it was evidently late night or early morning. Lance glanced at his wrist before remembering that he had stopped carrying the extra watch set on Pacific City time.

"Hi, Lance," came Channing's voice. "What's happening about the probe? We've a new development at this end. John Tynan, in Hawaii—remember him?—just got in touch with me. He's found what looks like *another* probe—I'll give you the relevant bit of his tape."

He looked aside, and the broad, dark, enthusiastic face of John Hiroshi Tynan replaced his on the screen. Tynan was already talking: ". . . still covering the AM Herculis-type system in Centaurus. Tonight, another unexplained object showed up, like the one that appeared nearly six months ago. Same direction as the earlier object, same right ascension, declination, same path—too much for coincidence. . . ."

Tynan's face was replaced by Channing's. "Well, there you are. If you can get a fix on where the first probe came down, try to get as near as possible to the same point on the surface of Mars before the next one arrives." He gave one of his rare smiles. "Don't get *too* close. I don't want the thing to flatten you. But good luck, and get back to me."

Lance looked at Mori. "Sounds bad, doesn't it? So far we've only had tangible evidence of *one* of these things with the four arms and the three-toed feet, and I'm damn glad I didn't meet up with it. Now, it looks as if there are more on the way."

Mori's eyes showed a lot of white around the irises. "The first of their boys was very competent for something that had just arrived on the planet, wasn't he?"

"If he *was* the first—unbelievably, by our standards."

"You going out there to wait for the second landing?"

"I have to, or I wouldn't be game to go back to the Chief."

Mori looked thoughtful. "The first one might be there to welcome it in. Did that occur to you?"

"No, but it's in the cards, isn't it? Can I have a copy of Tynan's part of that tape? I'd better play it to Segal. I'll see him before I send a message back to the Chief. Haven't much positive to give him yet, except a kidnapping and a few unbelievable footprints."

"If I were you, I'd contact the Chief now. He might have some other suggestion before you see Segal."

"Perhaps you're right. Can you set it up for me?"

On Mori's signal, Lance stepped into the floodlight and began to speak: "Hi, Chief. I'll be there waiting for this one, if the first bogey doesn't get me. I'll show Tynan's tape to Segal at this end. Okay? Remember me to Milleen and Stan. Contact you later. Out."

Lance waited long enough in the office for Channing to have received his message and sent a reply, a matter of twenty minutes or more with the planets in their present configuration, then he put through a call to Dr. Segal.

When he told him of the fresh data from Tynan, the astronomer agreed to see him right away. He drove up to the University and found Segal waiting for him in the foyer of his building.

"What's John come up with now?" Segal asked as they walked along the passage to his office. "A more accurate fix on the probe?"

"Better than that. He's found another probe."

The tall astronomer missed a step and stood with his feet apart in the middle of the passage. "Where? When?"

"It hasn't arrived yet, but it's coming in on the same trajectory as the first one."

"When's he expect it to arrive?"

"He didn't say. He says it's approaching from the direction of Centaurus."

Segal continued walking, silent until he reached his office. He held the door open and motioned Lance inside. "That would suggest a planet orbiting one of the suns of Alpha Centauri, or possibly Proxima. Or would it?"

"I would have thought so. They're the nearest, aren't they?"

"Yes, but think it through. Distances between stars are enormous. Perhaps these probes passed close to other stars on their way here, wherever they came from, in case they had to make an emergency stop. Remember the first flight across the Atlantic Ocean?"

"You mean Lindbergh's?"

"No. That was the first solo flight. I'm going back to 1919, the flight by Reed and his team in the NC4 flying boat—they didn't fly across in one hop. They went from America to Bermuda, then Bermuda to the Azores, finally from the Azores to Lisbon. If the people in Lisbon hadn't known they were coming, they might have assumed they came from the Azores, not America. See what I mean?"

"So Alpha or Proxima Centauri might have been their second-last port of call, as it were? What's beyond them?"

"Well, you're looking in the general direction of the Galactic Hub. Alpha Centauri's about 1.3 parsecs from here. Then you have Barnard's Star, with the Van de Kamp planets, at less than two parsecs, Bessel's Star in Cygnus and Ross 154 at three and a half." Segal, sitting behind his desk, spread his arms expansively. "Then, when you get about five parsecs out, you have a whole swarm of systems on the same side of the sky—Altair, 36 and 70 Ophiuchi, Sigma Draconis, Delta Pavonis. Then out to Vega and Zeta Herculis, still only seven parsecs away."

"So these things could have come from any of those systems?"

Segal took off his rimless glasses and polished them with a piece of cloth from his desk drawer. "Picking systems where the sun is close to the color and temperature of ours, I'd bet on Alpha Centauri, Sigma Draconis, maybe the companion of Vega. On the other hand, I suppose their sun doesn't have to be like ours. Judging from that photo and the footprints, we're just making wild guesses about the sort of world these things came from."

"What would you say to traveling out and trying to intercept the next probe?"

"I'd say it'd be bloody dangerous, but maybe the reward could be more than worth the risk."

"Could you organize transport?"

"I could do that. Yes."

"There's one point Pango Mori brought up. The thing that kidnapped Jack Darch might go out to meet the incoming probe.

It might find us before we found it. Are you willing to take a chance on that?''

Segal's eyes shone behind his glasses. "This could be our very first contact with extra-terrene life. Not only that, but extra-terrene *intelligence*. That would more than make up for my marking time here for eleven Martian years. I could arrange for use of an aircraft tomorrow.''

"With a local person to fly it?''

Segal shook his head. "No need. I have a local license. The ban on off-planet people flying came in only a few years ago, after a crash near a dome. I'd got my license before that happened. We have a roto belonging to our department. But meanwhile, I'll see if I can get some time on one of the smaller telescopes on the Olympus summit. If I can track this thing myself—from here, of course—I might get a better idea of what it is and when it will reach here.''

He picked up a phone on his desk and spent some time talking cryptically with someone whose image Lance was unable to see. Putting the phone down at last, he swung his swivel chair around and began punching a keyboard in front of a large screen. A false color image appeared, shifting as he operated the keys.

"Should be in this area,'' said Segal over his shoulder. "This is the scene at present, this is the same two hours ago. I'll alternate them. *There!* See it?''

One point of light was moving back and forth with the time change. Segal pointed to it in triumph. "The others are all background stars, parsecs away. But this is in our own system, and close! Notice there's not much change in position, but a big variation in brightness. That suggests it's heading almost straight toward us.''

"Can you estimate how long before it arrives?''

"Need a radar fix for that. But it shouldn't be here before tomorrow, and by then we'll be waiting for it out in the Badlands.'' Segal's eyes blazed fanatically. "Within a day or two, we should be contacting an extra-terrestrial intelligence!''

Lance nodded. "Remember, though, the thing looks like a cross between a dinosaur and a Hindu god. From what I've put together, it's very bright, quick, and utterly ruthless.''

"On the other hand, we're prepared for it, and we're on our home ground.'' Something had happened to Segal since their last meeting. Then, all the enthusiasm, the drive, the enterprise had resided in Lance. Now, the dynamism lay mainly with the astronomer. His pale, triangular face looked suddenly much younger as he put his hand on Lance's shoulder. "Will you come with me?"

"Any time you're ready to leave."

Segal looked at his watch. "Say in two hours? I can get you a spacesuit. By the way, we'll need to get out to the Badlands before sunset. We have good heating in our rotos—and believe me, we'll need it."

Lance went back to the Solar News office, where Pango Mori was still working on editing a forthcoming program.

"Pango, I'm going out with Segal to try to intercept this new probe. But don't tell anyone about it—not even Fran. Have you got a set of those radios we can tune in to a coded scrambler?"

"Sure."

"We'll need three. Two for Segal and I to communicate with each other, and one for you."

"I get it. So I can monitor and keep track of where you go."

"And let us know if anything new comes up. If anything happens to us out there, someone in Hellas has to know, and I guess you're the guy."

Mori gave an elaborate bow. "Thank you." He took three little radios from a cabinet and adjusted the code dials of their built-in scramblers. Lance packed two of them into a carry-bag, and added a compact camera, while Mori watched with a concerned expression. "Be damn careful, man. We don't know what we're getting into, do we?"

"Not really, Pango. But nobody ever achieved anything much without taking some sort of chance."

"I'd be happier if the odds were loaded more our way."

By the time Lance got back to Dr. Segal, the astronomer had arranged spacesuits, the rotojet, and two telescopes mounted on tripods with circular scales of the type used in fire-spotting triangulation. He drove Lance to the airlock of the North Gallery, where they suited up for the outside near vacuum. Then he drove through the airlock and out across the reddish plain for several kilometers to a small airport, where a number of hangar buildings sheltered aircraft from the periodic winds that lashed the impact basin. On the way, Segal explained his intended project.

"Here's a map of the area where we think the previous object landed. Now, I'll fly you to this high point, here, and we set up one of the telescopes. Then I fly to this point, here, and I place the other, giving us a baseline of about a hundred kilometers. We'll keep in radio contact, and sight the exact direction of the object as it comes in. That way, we can pick its landing point within a few meters.''

"What happens then?''

"If there's anything living aboard, it will wait some time for the outside of its craft to cool off before it comes out. That should give us time to get as close to it as we feel safe. I'll set up a number of automatic TV cameras to cover it from various angles. That way, we'll be able to observe anything that comes out from a safe distance.''

"Don't you think this thing could be too big for us to handle on our own?''

"Before any being emerges, I'll contact the university and arrange for them to pick up the pictures from the cameras. I've already set up the necessary gear back at the Astronomy Division. For the rest of human history, the first contact between human and interstellar alien belongs to us!''

Lance permitted himself a half smile. And they accuse *me* of having a big ego, he thought.

There were a few men in spacesuits moving about the hangars, and one of them used a small tractor to haul Segal's roto out into the open. He climbed aboard, Lance following to take the copilot's seat. Segal started the jets running and let them warm up for a few minutes, the huge, frail rotating wings swinging above the delicate hull.

"We'll head toward the base in Mariner Valley until we're out of range of the Hellas ground radar,'' said Segal. "Then I'll swing to the right, over toward the Margaritifer Sinus. Before we reach it, we'll strike the two high points where we can set up our telescopes.''

He fed more fuel to the jets, and a spinning ring of fire traced their orbit as the machine slowly lifted into the rarefied air, vibrations humming and buzzing through its ultralight airframe.

It was not a ride Lance enjoyed, despite the closeup view of the Martian terrain. He had the feeling the machine was operating at the extreme limit of its power, and he had the uncomfortable feeling that it needed only one of the four wing-jets to lose thrust for them to finish their flight, and possibly their lives, on the boulder-strewn slopes rising to the western rim of the great impact basin. By the time they had lifted over the rim, zigzagging to use a lower rate of climb, the city of Hellas was out of sight across the arid plain.

Beyond the basin was a chaotic wilderness of snarling fangs of rock that seemed to reach up at the aircraft to seize it. Segal flew endlessly onward, occasionally finding a few more ounces of power to clear some of the higher ridges, until Lance wondered if they would ever find their way back.

The sun was already low in the west when Segal landed the aircraft on the crest of a ridge. They both got out and set up one of the triangulating telescopes on its tripod, sighting carefully on a distant volcano summit for orientation, as the magnetic field on Mars was so weak and unreliable that a compass was useless.

"Here's one of the maps," said Segal over the suit radio. "You're here." His gloved finger indicated a spot on the map that he marked with a red pencil. "I'll be here—" he made another mark to the north, a hundred kilometers away by the scale—"and we'll get a simultaneous fix on the object as it touches down. We'll confer by radio. It's essential the two observations are made at the same instant."

Lance watched the rotojet leave, following the ridge to the north until it was a speck in the distance, vanishing against the blurred, dusty skyline. He realized that at this moment he was probably more alone than he had ever been in his life. The only sounds were the rasping of his breath inside his helmet and faint noises from the life-support system in his backpack.

"Why the hell am I doing this?" he asked himself aloud, forgetting his suit radio was still on.

"I've been asking myself that for the past ten years," came Segal's voice. "But now, after all this time. I think it's going to pay off."

"You guys okay?" came a third voice, faint with distance.

"We're fine, Pango," replied Lance. "But nothing's happened yet."

"The observatory says Centaurus is rising," continued Mori. "I just checked. This baby should land while the direction it's coming from is above the horizon, right?"

"Thanks, Pango. We'll let you know if anything happens here."

Lance settled down to a long, boring wait.

It was within an hour of sunset when something happened. It was not the expected approach of a rocket flame, but a strangely localized cloud of dust, dense and compact, with the sunlight behind it, rising above the purple horizon away to the northwest. As he watched, it rose and spread laterally.

"Des," he called into his radio, "There's a cloud of dust—"

"I see it," came Segal's voice. "Can you get a fix on the center of it before it diffuses too much?"

Lance aligned the telescope on what he took to be the center of the cloud that was expanding visibly as he looked. He locked the telescope and peered at the circular scale.

"I make it a bearing of 310."

"I get 230 from here. Let's see." Segal was silent as he scaled the directions on his map. "That'd put the middle of the cloud about a hundred kilometers off. It's come from below the horizon."

"Wait a minute. There's a second cloud starting to the south of the first one."

"You're right. And look! There's another to the north of it. They must be fifteen or twenty k's apart."

"Do the duststorms here normally start like that?"

"Never. I think the clouds have been stirred up artificially. Not hard on Mars. You've seen the way vehicles throw up clouds that hang in the air for a long time."

"Does this remind you of something?" asked Lance.

"What?"

"When Jack Darch saw that first alien, he was in a duststorm, remember? Yet no one else reported one. Aren't duststorms on Mars usually planetwide?"

"Planetwide, and of long duration—the dust stops up in the air for weeks. That's what made us suspicious of Darch's report of a storm. But this looks as if he was right. This dust has been deliberately stirred up."

"Could it be a sort of smokescreen—or dustscreen—to enable the thing to land unseen? But that would imply help from the ground. After all, the first alien got help to kidnap Darch."

"There's another way it could have been done," said Segal. "Explosive missiles fired ahead of the main ship, along the same trajectory. They throw up dust, it follows, and— Hey! What's this?"

The change in Segal's voice was dramatic. A second later, Lance realized why. Slanting down the sky from the northwest was a sparkling point of fire, brilliant as an electric arc.

"I see it!" he shouted.

"Get a fix on it when I say," said Segal. "I'll give you a countdown."

Lance hastily turned the telescope on the fiery spot, having trouble at first getting it into the field. "Right," he said.

Segal began to count, while Lance kept his telescope centered on the spot of flame. "Five, four, three, two, one, *now!*"

Lance locked his telescope and read the figures from the dial. "I get 313 degrees," he said.

Segal repeated the number. "I have 235. Let's try it again."

But the flame vanished in the clouds of dust before they could get another reading.

"Never mind," said Segal. "It's hitting dirt a bit over a hundred kilometers west of where you are. Wait there. I'll pick you up."

Wait here, thought Lance. Where the hell does he think I'm likely to go? But he said nothing.

The sun intersected the ragged horizon in a blaze of alien color combinations, with tinges of violet that would never have touched an earthly sunset. Lance turned up the heating unit in his backpack when he felt a sudden shiver pass through his body, as the chill of the Martian night came upon him like the spring of an animal. Even in the impact basins, there was under one per cent of Earth's surface atmosphere, and up here on this ridge there would not have been half that, so heat radiated away quickly. However, his suit maintained his small private bubble of atmosphere intact—they had been making spacesuits for so long now that they had reached practically a hundred per cent reliability.

It was quite dark when his external suit microphones picked up the pulsing scream of Segal's roto. Segal was flying without lights, running at reduced speed so that the flaming ring of his jets did not appear, and Lance was unable to locate the machine until its dark shadow was almost upon him.

The roto landed, and Segal emerged and walked over to Lance, who had already dismantled the telescope and folded its tripod. Together, they looked westward, where the faint, blurred cone of the zodiacal light slanted above the point where the sun had set. The last rays of the sunset still caught the top of the pink dust cloud. Segal pointed at it.

"All right," he said. "Let's go."

Together, they climbed aboard the roto.

Flying without lights, Segal used the rotojet's ATRAN to scan the broken terrain in the darkness below them—an uncomfortably short distance below, it seemed to Lance. A few of the higher ridges were still faintly visible in the afterglow of the fast Martian sunset, but he could see nothing in the black, contorted gullies between them.

"Will you try to fly above the dust?" he asked, pointing ahead. With the fading of the sunset, the color of the dust had deepened to an ominous red.

"Have to go through it. It must go up two or three thousand meters. We'd never get up that high in this air. We're near our absolute ceiling now."

Before long, they were flying through the suspended dust in featureless darkness, their visibility cut down to a few meters at the most.

"We'll never see anything in this," said Lance. "Is there any point in going on?"

As if to answer him, a pale blur of light glowed through the dust far ahead, somewhat to the left. Segal grunted and changed course slightly to head directly to the light, although it vanished within a few seconds.

"Looked the wrong color for a rocket flame," said Lance.

"How do we know what fuel they use? Anyway, it switched on and off too suddenly for a rocket. Looked more like a high-powered searchlight."

"Listen, I think I'd better get Pango Mori to record anything we say, just in case anything goes wrong. That okay with you?"

"Sure. I'm going to contact the Astronomy Division soon, anyway."

Lance raised his voice. "Can you still hear us, Pango?"

The reply was faint. "Still getting you, but the sound of your jets nearly drowns you out."

"Can you record all this?"

"Already doing it. Got the lot taped since you first took off. But be careful! Where you going now?"

"Saw a light through the dust. Investigating it."

"Rather you than me, man."

Segal reached for a plug on the instrument panel, pulled it out against the resistance of a spring-loaded reel, and plugged it into his spacesuit.

"I'll contact the division on the standard radio," he said, and opened the channel to the Astronomical Division back at Hellas University. "Segal on AD 2, calling Division HO."

"HO here. Where are you?" came a voice from the speaker above the control panel.

"We were on our way to Mariner Valley base, when we saw what appeared to be a meteor descending to the north. We flew north to investigate. I believe it to be an alien probe or spacecraft, using its retro-rockets in its descent."

"Wait. I'll put you through to the director."

The dust outside the aircraft was thickening and darkening. Segal held the same course.

"Bergsen here," came a new voice from the speaker. "Describe what you saw, Des."

Segal described the dustclouds and the landing.

"Did the dust come after the landing?" asked Bergsen.

"No. The dust came first. Then the object landed in it."

There was silence for a while. "Keep the same course, Des. I'll get back to you in a couple of minutes."

There was no further sign of light in the dust ahead. Lance felt turbulence as they passed over some unseen irregularity in the ground. Abruptly, the speaker crackled to life again.

"Des. This is Bergsen again. Leave that area alone. Return to Hellas, or if you haven't enough fuel, go straight to Mariner Valley base."

Segal sat immobile for a few seconds, then pulled the plug of his radio partly out of its socket and pushed it in again a few times. "Something interfering with transmission," he said. "Can't hear you properly. Will you repeat that?"

Bergsen's voice thundered from the speaker. "Return to Hellas. Repeat, return to Hellas. If insufficient fuel, go to Mariner Valley. Repeat, Mariner Valley."

Segal spoke with one hand on the plug, moving it so that only an intermittent connection was made. "Can't hear you. Sorry. I'll be in touch later." He withdrew the plug enough to make it arc in its socket, so that the sound at the other end would have been a meaningless crash and crackle. Finally, he switched off the radio altogether.

Lance smiled at him. "I didn't think you had that in you," he said.

Segal made an impatient gesture. "This is the biggest thing that's ever happened to our division! Perhaps the biggest thing that's ever happened to the human race! Bergsen wants the spotlight himself—but we'll see about that."

For a minute or so, he flew on in silence, leaning forward as if to get a better view of the darkness.

"Eleven years I've been in this damn place. As far as career is concerned, I'm no farther forward. The boys at the top stick together here. But this'll change everything!"

An unexpected bump warned of an uptrend from some ridge of rock that must have been very close below them. "Hey!" said Lance. "Did that hit the undercart?"

It was an exaggeration, but it had its effect. Segal snapped a few switches, setting his screen to pick up infrared and turning on an IR searchlight. The screen showed a ragged, hostile landscape a frighteningly short distance below them. It also showed something else.

"What's that light?" asked Lance.

"Someone else with an infrared searchlight—and I think they've picked us up. Wait!" Segal swung the aircraft to one side. The beam, which was narrowly focused, moved to keep them covered. "Yes. They're on to us."

"What the hell is *that*?" Lance jabbed his finger at the screen.

Against the glow of the infrared searchlight, a sinister silhouette was rising to meet them. At first, Lance had no idea how large the thing was, or how far away. But as Segal swung around in a 180-degree turn to the left, the thing kept pace with them, sweeping around on a larger radius and maintaining an unvarying position abeam from them. Lance began photographing it.

When Lance looked directly out the window, he could barely see it against the reddish gloom. But the infrared screen showed strange details. The thing was quite small, perhaps only a meter or two in length, with no parts large enough to contain a human pilot, but there were several projections that might have been cameras or weapons. He couldn't decide what power source it used. There was no jet flare, but it had things like venturi tubes running full length, open at either end. Shorter tubes pierced its wings vertically.

"What is it?" shouted Segal, his voice an octave higher.

"Some kind of automatic device. It's not moving to attack us yet, but I think it's a good time to blow the scene. May as well use your lights, now they know we're here."

"I'll keep using the IR for a while. They mightn't have figured out we know they're there yet—might have thought we'd turned around without seeing—*that*."

"Fat chance of that. But if we keep on flying straight away from them, they might leave us alone."

For a couple of minutes, neither of them spoke. Then Segal said, "Is it still there?"

"Hard to see without the lights on it. Yes, it's still there. No closer. Want to try to shake it off?"

"Wouldn't be a chance of that. The thing's more maneuverable than we are."

"It looks as if it flies by sucking air into one end of its tubes and squirting it out the other. Not like a ramjet. I can see a blue electrical discharge like a small St. Elmo's fire."

Pango Mori's voice cut in. "What's happening out there?"

"We're being chased by a thing like a flying spider."

"Can you outfly it?"

"No. Don't know what happens if it follows us all the way home."

"How big is it?"

"Only about the size of some of those model aircraft kids play with. But sophisticated, and sinister. Doesn't seem to be going to attack us, though—it's had plenty of chances."

"Perhaps it wants to get you away from its territory so if it prangs you, the wreck won't lead rescuers to where its people are."

Lance felt a chill seeping into him. He hadn't thought of that, but Mori was probably right. He remembered the minute flying device they had mistaken for an insect in Magill's office, the device that had killed the man Magill was interrogating. If this thing used a similar explosive, it could have enough power to blow their aircraft to fragments.

They flew on through the night, directly toward Hellas. Eventually, they passed beyond the slowly dispersing clouds of dust, and the sky above them showed stars. Lance looked for the shadowing flier.

"It's gone!"

"Are you sure? It might be right under our tail, where we can't see it."

But a circling maneuver revealed no sign of their pursuer.

"Whoever controlled it might have thought we just happened to be in the area," suggested Lance.

"True. People *do* go out into the Badlands to make aerial surveys."

"At night?"

It was still dark when they reached the North Airfield. They went through the airlock into the North Gallery and climbed out of their spacesuits. Then Segal drove Lance back to the university. There were still a few lights on in the Astronomy Division, and when they reached Segal's office, they found Bergsen waiting there, sitting behind Segal's desk.

"What happened?" he asked as they entered.

Segal made a quick introduction. Bergsen was heavily built, pale-eyed, with a short, blond beard. Segal outlined an edited version of their experiences.

"I want you to drop it for the moment, Des," said Bergsen.

"Drop it? But I believe it's an extra-solar contact!"

"Yes, but we haven't enough data yet to go rushing out there. We could risk bringing disease of unknown type back here, or alternatively, infecting some other life form with our micro-life."

Segal stared at Bergsen stonily. "You've been got at, haven't you?"

Bergsen's pale eyes seemed to become a shade paler. "Would you care to elaborate on that remark?"

"One of the main purposes behind astronomy is to find evidence of extra-solar life. Now we have *it* coming to *us*. And you want to drop it."

"Not drop it—just proceed carefully. But what did you mean by somebody getting to me?"

Segal shrugged. "You've always seemed full of enthusiasm for the job. Now, you're acting out of character. It suggested someone else's influence—that's all."

Bergsen stood up. "You're tired, Des. You've had a heavy night. So have I. I suggest we talk about this after we've both had some rest."

Segal saw Lance out to his car. "You know," said Lance as he was slipping into the driving seat, "I've never met Bergsen before, but I've known a lot of people. I'd say someone *has* got to him."

"Glad you feel that way," said Segal. "Trouble is, I don't know who—or why." He gestured vaguely. "Well, thanks for your help."

"And thank you for a very interesting day." Lance started the car and drove off. As he went, he looked back at Segal in his mirror. Somehow, the astronomer looked older.

* * *

When Lance returned to the Solar News office, he found the lights on and two people waiting for him. One, as he expected, was Pango Mori. The other, surprising him, was Dorella.

"Great to see you, man!" said Mori exultantly, gripping his hand. "You had us worried."

"I'm glad you're back, too," said Dorella. She was wearing a Martian-style suit that must have been selected for her by some local woman. It seemed to minimize the differences in proportions between her physique and that of a Mars-born woman, with frilly Filipino-style sleeves that made her shoulders seem higher, and loose, flowing trousers that hid her muscular legs.

"You look nice in that gear," said Lance, making a conscious effort to inject sincerity into his voice.

"It's not *me*. But never mind about this. What happened when that thing was chasing you?"

"It gave up halfway here."

"Do you think they're really extra-solar?" asked Mori.

Lance nodded. "I can't think of any other explanation. What we saw wasn't faked, I'm certain of that. Darch's photo just could have been a fake, taking into account what I've heard about Darch, but the things we saw out there were on far too big a scale for anyone to have faked them."

"Definitely a spaceship coming in, was it?" asked Mori. "What was it like?"

"I was too far away to see anything but the flame of its retro-rockets. But the thing that flew alongside us as we came away was different in style from anything I've seen. And then there was the deliberately contrived duststorm that hid the landing."

"How'd they do that?"

"I don't know. But they did it. It's the wrong time of the year for duststorms, and they don't have localized ones like that."

Dorella suddenly moved forward and put her arms around him, hugging him fiercely. He returned her embrace, and she tightened her grip about him, tilting her head back to look into his face. "Try to find a Martian girl who can squeeze you like that," she said. Then she brought her face forward again and kissed him. "I was terribly worried. I wanted to talk to you, but Pango wouldn't let me. Said he'd promised you there were only three people linked up on your radios."

"That's right. Segal, Pango and me."

"At least he let me listen. He's taped it all, and he's promised to let me copy the tape later, if it's okay with you."

Lance stood still for a moment. "You mean you would have used it on a program if I hadn't come back?"

"Hey! I didn't think of it like that! I made the arrangement with Pango before we started to cut the tape." She didn't look at him for a few seconds, then gave him a small extra hug. "I suppose a bit of paranoia's natural when you've had someone try to kill you. Anyway, you're *alive*! That's the main thing."

"That sums it up," said Mori. "You're alive. A few hours ago, I wouldn't have bet on it."

Lance looked at him somberly. "Frankly, neither would I."

"Want to put a report through to Channing?" asked Mori.

"Suppose I'd better. Might find it hard getting support from Segal, though. His boss—a fellow called Bergsen—doesn't want him to follow it up. I get the impression someone or some group—is leaning on Bergsen."

"Could be," agreed Mori. "You know something? I think there may be some group of people here collaborating with the aliens. They knew when to start the duststorms to hide the landing—easy enough with a few jet engines thrusting into windblown dunes."

"Of course, they had one ally already here—the thing that kidnapped Darch. The one in the photo."

"You think *he* might have gone out there and started the dust storms?"

"But he looked so weird," protested Dorella. "How did he get about without anybody seeing him?"

Lance gave a short laugh. "Judging from what happened to the fellow Magill picked up, and his mate, it's not healthy to see him. You tend to finish up dead."

"They're not interested in making a good first impression, are they?" said Mori. "Anyone gets in their way—*wham*!" He drove his fist into his palm.

"And this was the first one they sent," mused Dorella. "Perhaps they picked the most diplomatic. They might get worse from here on."

"Well, I'd better send that report to Channing," said Lance. "I'll just give him the straight facts as I observed them, warn him about the Bergsen and Segal clash, and let him take it from there. You can send it by satellite right away, can you?"

"Can do. Coffee while you're putting it together?"

Lance made a rough tape first, edited it, then gave the succinct version to Mori. "That should do him," he said.

While Mori was transmitting the report, Dorella came close to Lance. "Tired?"

"Hungry rather than tired. You don't tire much in this gravity, I've found."

"That may be temporary. I'm hungry, too. Been here all night. Know anywhere to eat around here?"

"Eh? Yes, there's a place called the Cassini."

"Let's go."

They called their goodnights to Mori. On the way down in the elevator, Dorella said, "I want to tell you about something I stumbled on, Lance."

"Something else about Noel Karstrom?"

She shook her head. "I've discovered something about your girlfriend Heidi," she said with a Mona Lisa smile.

He felt a twinge of anger. Why was she digging into his personal affairs? "Oh, yes?"

Dorella looked at him, her large eyes widening. "Lance—did you know she's a clone?"

chapter
15

"A CLONE?"

When they were seated at a two-place table at one of the front windows of the Cassini, Lance looked at Dorella with an expression that must have conveyed stupefaction, because she frowned slightly. "You know what a clone is—"

"Of course I know what a clone is. But whose tissue was she cloned from?"

"I don't know yet. But she and her sister Joy are both clones from the same source, generated ten years apart."

"So that's why they look so much alike."

"Yes, but there's more. There's at least one older woman called Kalli, about ten years older than Heidi. There's a small girl, about five. Then there's Thyra, the blind woman you met at the space terminal—she's older again, but she's not the original." She smiled. "Kalli's quite a nice woman. If you're really interested in a relationship with Heidi, I can introduce you to Kalli and give you a preview of what Heidi will be like in ten years' time."

Lance digested the news in silence that masked a turmoil of thought. At this point he welcomed a diversion, the arrival of their food, steaming and aromatic. They lifted their dishes off the conveyor, but without beginning to eat, Lance looked across at Dorella.

"It sounds as if some woman has been having clones of herself made every ten years or so. But why? And who?"

Dorella shrugged. "Haven't figured that yet. We'll have to look for someone like the others, but with the stiff joints and a dowager's hump."

"How did you find out about this?"

"Two things. One was in tracing all the records of Noel Karstrom's work. He was into all sorts of things—but I'll tell you about that side of it later. The other was that Thyra invited me to stay with her so she could fill me in on Karstrom.''

"Go on.''

"It turned out they have three adjoining houses up on Lake Circle where a whole team of them live, all clones from the same tissue preserved by molecular stabilization. In the house next to Thyra's live Heidi, Joy, Kalli, and young Elli, who's still at what would correspond to primary school. She's the brightest little kid I've seen—like a tiny version of the others.''

"Good God, where does it finish?'' Lance ate some of his meal, chewing absent-mindedly. "A race of identical women, going on forever.''

Dorella smiled mischievously. "And I think you've started to fall for one of them. It'd have some advantages. When she gets too old, you could try another one of the same pattern.''

He did not reply, covering his shock by eating. Dorella went on.

"From what I've seen, they think alike as well as look alike. They're not just like sisters. Normally, a girl gets half her genes from her mother, half from her father, and in different siblings you get a different mix from the two genetic streams. But these all get their genes from the original woman, so they're more like duplicated copies. Different stages of development, that's all.''

"If they're as identical as that, there might be a form of telepathy between them.''

"I've seen something like that at work, although it's not real telepathy. While I was visiting Kalli, Joy was there. Kalli and I were talking in their lounge room, with a big window looking out over the park, the one around the lake. Little Elli was playing there. A little boy came along on an electric bicycle—he would have been about six, a year older than Elli. The kids knew each other, and he was offering Elli a ride on his bike. Kalli broke off what she was saying to me, and said to Joy, 'Come and handle this.' ''

"What happened?''

"Joy took one look from the window, then took a thing like a small radio out of her pocket. She made an adjustment, spoke into it. She said, 'Elli, no! Tell him nicely you have to come inside in a minute.' I saw Elli say something to the little boy and point to the house. Then he rode off on his bike and Elli trotted toward the house.''

Lance sat thunderstruck. Fragments of memory and speculation whirled into place.

"You think they talk to each other through something implanted inside them?"

"Obviously, they do. One of their associated firms specializes in micro-miniaturization. Tiny parts made with monomolecular films, things like that. If they grow up with a built-in direct line to their big sister—or someone closer than any sister, closer than a mother—you can imagine how much advice gets passed along the chain. I saw little Elli, aged five, advised how to handle a six-year-old nuisance. Years later, she'll be getting advice about business deals, personal relationships, all kinds of data, and no one will ever realize it."

"It's like a group mind," said Lance.

"And a new individual's added every few years. It's frightening, isn't it?"

Lance thought back to the time he had been surprised at the smoothness and variety of Heidi's sexual techniques. But *whose* techniques? Accumulated in how many relationships, with how many identical women's minds listening in? He felt heat on his face and neck, then a coldness down the length of his spine.

"You made love to Heidi, didn't you?" said Dorella, watching him.

"Yes." He looked about him. *They* knew this place. Joy had been here with Phil Gray. He finished his meal without speaking much, then picked up a paper napkin and wrote on it with his pen: *Think I've been bugged for sound, the same way.* He handed it to Dorella, watched her eyes widen as she read it. He pointed behind his right ear, and made the motion of injecting something. He handed Dorella the pen, and she wrote: *Do you think they might hear us talk?*

He nodded. She began writing again: *What range these units?*

He took the pen and paper. *Pickup with a booster could amplify the signal. Then distance would mean nothing.*

Dorella frowned, then wrote: *Let's go someplace where they wouldn't have planted a booster.*

Paying for their meals, they left the Cassini without saying anything. He directed her by hand movements—down the elevator, along to the Viking Building, up to the car park, into the green car. He drove down the spiral ramp to the Octagon, and on impulse headed down the Southwest Gallery, perhaps because it was farthest from the Northeast, where the clones lived, and partly because his map showed it devoted to heavy industry. It was like a different planet Southwest. They passed huge rolling mills, furnaces with complex equipment to recover waste products from the exhaust, sealed-off buildings where molten metal glared on its way to casting. Eventually, he swung off the main avenue into a small park between factories.

"We should be safe here," he said.

"What was this about you being bugged?"

"It happened on the ship coming here. I was unconscious for an hour and a half. I think something was implanted against the base of my skull—here. The ship's doctor wouldn't touch it. Said he'd heard of units like that exploding when they were micro-scanned."

"But who would have done it?"

"I think it was done by a woman called Jocasta Borg."

"Jocasta Borg? The people I'm staying with know her. What's she like?"

"Cybernetic body. Says she's a hundred years old. Her head looks as if it belongs to a woman of about forty, but all the rest of her is machine."

Dorella shivered slightly. "Some of this is starting to make sense, isn't it?"

"How do you mean?"

"I've been wondering who'd want to have clones of herself made every ten years or so. This Jocasta Borg woman would be just the sort of person who'd do it. She's probably fantastically wealthy by now, and she's going to live practically forever. The only thing she hasn't had is a child. Cloning from her own cells is a way of getting herself a family, all identical to herself and growing up from a child like she was to girls, women, a race of similar women at different stages."

"And all in continuous contact with each other. Once, when I was very close to Heidi, I heard a voice I'm certain came from within her head, at least from against her skull."

Dorella nodded. "Someone advising her, the way Joy advised little Elli. My God! They could go on like that forever! It's horrible."

He was silent for a long time. "Not horrible from their viewpoint, Dorella. They probably feel they've hit on a very satisfying lifestyle."

"Safe, I suppose," said Dorella. "Some accident must have happened to the blind one, Thyra, though. Her main ambition is to get an eye transplant from some accident victim, she told me. Hope they don't arrange an accident some time.''

"Now who's getting paranoid?"

"How did you get on with Jocasta Borg on the ship?"

"Okay, except for the suspicion she had something to do with the implant someone put into me.''

She gave a long sigh. "Lance, do you get the feeling we're out of our league in this place?"

"In some ways, yes. But I think we're both bright enough to learn.'' He put his arm around her shoulders. "Look at it this way, Dorella. It's a challenge. The parents and grandparents of these people who have settled Mars were all highly selected. You'd have some of the most progressive people from America, Japan, Brazil, India or wherever—coming into this planet's gene pool. So it's only taken a few generations to evolve systems a long way ahead of anything back home.''

"Ahead?"

"Well, maybe that's a value judgment. Let's say a series of systems more variable from an evolutionary standpoint.''

"You think they're a step up the ladder that leads from a chimpanzee through us to a theoretical superman?"

"Someone once said the goal of evolution was heightened awareness. And you have to admit most of these people are big on awareness, with their micro-implants, flying TV cameras that look like insects, things like that.''

For a while, she did not speak. It seemed to him as if she had almost forgotten he was there. He waited.

"You know," she said at last, "I think I'll put together a program on Martian ways of life. I suggested it to the girls up at Lake Circle, and they're willing to help me on it, at least help in the assembly of data.''

"Are you going to drop your research on Karstrom?"

"No, but this could be easier and quicker.''

"Well, best of luck with it, Dorella. After all, too much concentration on the Karstrom story would tend to take you out of touch with everyday life.''

She yawned, eyes closed, hand screening her mouth. Then she laughed. "Sorry, Lance. Been wanting to do that for hours.''

"I'll run you up to where you're staying.''

"Thanks.''

While they were heading back to the Octagon, she said, "Why did you follow us out there after we left the airport?"

"I wanted to know exactly where you were, in case you ran into any kind of trouble."

She put her hand on his knee. "That was nice of you. But the girls will look after me. They really know their way around here."

For a while they traveled in silence. Then her hand gently caressed his thigh. "I was worried, listening to you and that man Segal on the radio. Especially when that thing flew alongside your roto! I began to wonder if I'd ever see you again. That flying thing seemed to upset you."

"It did. Anything else we've seen—except for the thing with the three-toed feet—could have been manmade. But that little automatic aircraft—no! Different technology. Instead of jets driving it . . . Well, how it actually worked isn't the point. The hard fact is that it was built by someone with a lot more expertise than we have."

"I wonder if we should ask the girls about it when you drop me there. They know a lot about many things."

"No! The fewer people who know about this, the better, for the moment. The idea of an invasion from another star system could set off a panic, and there can't be enough of the invaders here yet to pose a real threat. At this stage, any threat is better handled by experts."

"And you're the best expert we have?" Her voice sounded slightly tart.

"I wouldn't say that. But releasing the news generally could cause a stampede, and that'd achieve nothing." He looked at her set face. "So—can you resist the temptation to tell your girlfriends, just for a time?"

"If they're not listening to all this. We're getting close to their houses now."

"Hell, I forgot that. All right. No more of this until I drop you. You can reach me again through Pango." He slowed, pulled to the curb, and began writing in his notebook. "Here's my room number at the Mangala." He tore the page out, and while he was handing it to her, a car went past them, and Dorella gave a little cry of recognition. "That's one of the girls' cars, I think."

"Who was driving it?"

"Couldn't tell. They look alike from a distance. They all drive, except young Elli, and Thyra, who has herself driven about by a little zeegee, as they call him. It could have been Kalli, Heidi, Joy—any of those."

"Do you think she was following us?"

"Might have been. They're a devious lot of ladies. Listen! When we get to the house, you'd better come to the door with me and say goodnight there. It'll fit in better with the story I'm going to tell them."

He looked at her for several seconds, then put his arm around her and kissed her. "I think I underestimated you," he said. "I'm sorry."

He drove the remaining length of the avenue to Lake Circle, then swung around the circuit until he neared the house called Ismenia.

"Not here," said Dorella. "This is where Thyra lives. I'm staying next door with the others now."

He parked in the driveway of the adjoining three-storied house and escorted her to the front door. As they neared it, the door opened, and a tall woman stood silhouetted against the light from the hallway beyond. For a moment, Lance thought it was Heidi, with her blond hair swept up in a different style.

"We wondered where you were, Dorella," said the woman in an unexpectedly deep voice.

"Kalli, this is my friend, Lance Garrith."

The woman gave a formal little bow and stepped aside. "Come in, both of you. I've heard of you, Lance. Even seen a taped telecast of yours. Come on in."

After a moment's hesitation, Lance followed Dorella into the softly lit hall, with its golden glow of indirect lighting flooding from recesses high on the walls. He caught the subtle scent of Kalli's perfume as he passed close to her.

"In there," she said, and as she spoke a yellow door slid silently open on one side of the hall, giving access to a bright room that at first glance appeared to have large windows opening in every direction. Closer inspection showed that they were moving murals, on every wall except the one in the direction of the street. There was a normal window there, closed now by an antique Venetian blind shutting off the view of the street and park.

Dorella, walking into the room, stopped in front of one of the murals. "You've changed it."

"Heidi brought this one from Earth." Kalli went to stand beside Dorella, hands in the pockets of her quilted yellow jacket. She was a little taller than Dorella, with the lifted shoulders and deep chest that seemed the norm among Mars-born people. "I see you're still wearing the brooch I gave you."

Dorella glanced down at her lapel, where an ornament sparkled. "Yes, I love it," she said.

Lance froze. Why hadn't he noticed the damned thing? It was probably the same kind of mini-TV camera worn by Heidi and Joy in their headbands.

"Show me that," he said, and moved closer. It looked like an intricately carved butterfly, with a central jewel like an emerald. He tried to see if there was a pinpoint lens in its center, but as he peered closer, Kalli put one hand on his shoulder and the other on Dorella's.

"Cafeno?" she asked.

"Love one," said Dorella. Lance hesitated, remembering that he had once been knocked unconscious for over an hour by something administered to him by one of these women. Then, recalling the implant they had given him, he decided there was no reason to dope him again, and he nodded. If Kalli noticed his hesitation, she gave no sign of it. She walked over to a recess in one wall of the living room. She touched a few controls, and steam hissed.

Lance and Dorella looked together at the video-mural brought from Earth by Heidi. It had evidently been recorded in the South Pacific. White-topped surf raced over a reef to a placid emerald lagoon fringed with palms, and occasionally a seabird skimmed by, white against the deep blue sky.

Another wall was dominated by what he had first taken to be a large aquarium tank, but was actually a view recorded under water on some tropical reef, with vivid fishes darting amid fantastic formations of coral. Another scene was obviously recorded neither on Earth nor on Mars.

"Where's that?" asked Dorella, as Kalli returned with the cafeno. "The red sky's got me lost."

"Titan," said Kalli promptly. "That's solid ammonia floating on methane. I was there, years ago. Safe enough with the right equipment." She sipped her cafeno.

Lance had first taken her to be about forty years old. He revised his estimate upward. Sixty? Seventy? Perhaps even more, yet her manner was young. She indicated Dorella with a movement of her hand. "She's putting together a very good study of our way of life here."

Dorella flashed her an apologetic smile. "I've told him you're all clones," she said.

Kalli's eyes widened slightly. "He'll think we're all monsters. Do you?" She turned suddenly to Lance.

"Of course not." He hesitated. "You mentioned you'd been on Titan. That's a long journey, isn't it?"

"Yes. We have a mining operation out there, almost fully automated, getting hydrocarbons, mainly. I was at an age when I needed to begin cybernetic replacement, if I wasn't to let physical degeneration set in."

"Show him," said Dorella.

Kalli unfastened her yellow jacket and held it open. The upper part of her body looked mature but fit, the breasts full but still firm. From the thickened waist down, she was metal, a deep metal bowl poised on metal legs. Leaving her jacket loose, she walked closer to Lance, smiling. "It takes time to learn to use a cybernetic lower half, and the Titan voyage gave me a good opportunity."

At this moment, a vehicle came into the driveway outside and stopped near the front door. They heard the front door open, then the sound of two voices—Joy's and Phil Gray's. Kalli's long fingers moved to a set of recessed keys in the metal bowl that formed the lower part of her torso, and she lifted her free hand to her mouth, speaking into what Lance had taken to be a large ornamental ring. "Get rid of him," she whispered. "Dorella and Lance Garrith are here."

Lance heard Joy's voice, fighting a yawn that may have been either real or contrived. "It's been lovely, Phil, but I'm dreadfully tired. We haven't the stamina of you Earth people."

Lance looked at the tiny keyboard on the metal body. It was placed so that Kalli could manipulate it, if necessary, through a slit in the pocket of her jacket. Her eyes looked dreamy. "He's kissing her," she said to Dorella, then turned to Lance. "You might give him some lessons there, sometime."

"What makes you think that?" asked Lance.

Kalli smiled, "You should be able to figure that out, Lance. If you can't, ask Dorella."

Lance looked at Dorella, who seemed embarrassed. She tilted her head back, and her eyes flashed. "I think she means you got to know Heidi very well, and that means all of them came to know you extremely intimately."

At this point, a bell sounded in a little alcove off the living room, and Joy, who had just come into the room, went to it, after a brief greeting to Dorella and Lance. She returned after a few seconds.

"It's a call from Solar News. Will you take it, Dorella?"

Dorella walked into the alcove, Lance following. Pango Mori's face looked at them from a screen. "Thought I'd find you there," he said. "Call from Mort Channing, Dorella."

Zigzag lines blasted the screen, and then the face of Channing appeared.

"Dorella," he said, "I got your message. Sounds as if you have a top-level human interest story there. Shelve the research on Karstrom, and concentrate on that family of cloned women. If it's true they could help you with the visuals, you could put together an entire session. Leave it a bit long, so we can sharpen it at this end. How's Lance Garrith going with his probes? Get back to me, both of you, soon as poss."

The screen blanked for a second, and Mori's face reappeared. "I can tape your reply from there, if you like, and transmit it."

Lance moved across in front of the camera, so that Mori could see him. "It's all right, Pango. We'll come there. I want to check some more data I left at the office."

"Right," said Mori, after a moment's hesitation.

When Lance looked around, he saw Kalli and Joy had been joined by Heidi. He looked from one to the other of the three blond, almost identical faces. "Hi, Joy, Heidi. Will you excuse us? I have to go down to our office."

Simultaneously, the trio glanced at Dorella.

"I'm not going, Lance," she said. "I'll send my message from here."

"Very wise," said Kalli, and she looked at Lance. "You're welcome to do the same."

"Thanks. But I'll have to ask you to excuse me." Lance looked at Dorella. "I'll see you soon."

"We'll all see you soon—back here," said Heidi.

"Yes, maybe."

"No maybe about it," broke in Kalli. "We can be persistent." And the three, standing shoulder to shoulder, smiled simultaneously, their expression almost seductive.

That smile in triplicate haunted him all the way back to the Solar News office.

Pango Mori seemed surprised when Lance walked in.

"Hi, Lance. Thought you were with Dorella. She called in a reply to the Chief's tape a while back, and I sent it off. Got a tape for you here. Shall I run it?"

"Fine."

Mort Channing's face appeared on the screen, and he began

talking straight away. "Lance, shelve the story about the probe. I checked it out with the top astronomer at the Hellas/Olympus complex—fellow called Bergsen. He thinks the things are old survey probes returning from the Oort Cloud, so for the time being we'd better drop it, or we'll look naive. By the way, Dorella's come up with a very good human interest series on the way some people live out there. Maybe you could collaborate with her on it."

The tape ended abruptly, and Lance exchanged glances with Mori, who shrugged. "This is the trouble with long-range contact. You don't get the feedback you have in a face-to-face interview. Nothing to show you how the other guy's taking it—until too late."

"It's a damn pity he contacted Bergsen. I had the feeling someone had told Bergsen to drop the whole story of the probes, and Segal felt the same way as I did."

"But who'd do that?"

"I don't know. Nor do I know why."

"You want to send a reply to the Chief?"

"Yes. I want to tell him what I think of Bergsen."

"Right. Whenever you're ready." Mori moved to the recorder.

Lance spent a few seconds sorting out his thoughts before he signalled to Mori to start the tape running. "Chief," he said, "I still think the biggest story of all time is tied up in these probes. I've met Bergsen, and I wasn't impressed. I think someone's told him to back down on this story. Another astronomer called Segal—Earthborn, but half his career on Mars—flew me out to where the second probe was landing. I saw it come down. On the way back, our aircraft was followed by an automated surveillance craft that I'm certain was of alien design. I can't drop the story now—it's too big to miss."

Mori ran the tape through to check it, then transmitted it through a scrambler. "Nothing to do but wait, now," he said. "The delay gets longer as the Earth moves ahead of us."

When Mort Channing's face reappeared about twenty minutes later, it looked harder, the narrowed eyes like steel. "Lance! I told you I'd contacted the top astronomer there, and he's not with you! Furthermore, he isn't impressed by Segal. Look, we've worked together well in the past, but I think this probe thing has become an obsession with you. Remember, I'm the top honcho in our outfit, and so far I've been right a big percentage of the time. You've been under a lot of pressure. We'll still pay for your return voyage, but I'm terminating your contract as of now. I'll reinstate you when you get back here, and I hope we can go on working in the future." Channing hesitated, then went on. "I'm moving Dorella up to the top slot for a while. Long time since we had a woman up there."

Abruptly, the tape finished. Lance looked across at Mori, who lifted his shoulders and spread out his hands.

"That's life, man. But I wouldn't worry about it. This office is autonomous, and I can employ anyone I like. What say you work for me until you head back home?"

"Are you sure that wouldn't put you on the wrong side of Channing?"

"Certain. I could learn a lot this way—you've got all the experience in broadcasting about the place."

"But not much experience in handling the Chief."

"Nobody has a monopoly on that. Me, I just take advantage of the distance between us and try not to make too many waves. Anyway, man—welcome aboard."

He put out his hand, and Lance gripped it. Suddenly, Mori grinned broadly. "And if you do come up with the biggest story since the beginning of the human race, I want to be part of the action." His expression, always subject to lightning changes, became more thoughtful. "Where do we go from here, though?"

Lance took his notepad from his pocket, read a number from it, and punched it out on the visiphone. A young face, either female or immature male, appeared on the screen.

"Is Dr. Segal there?"

"One moment."

He waited while taped music accompanied whirling geometric spirals. Then an older, square-jawed female face looked out at him.

"I understand Dr. Segal has left us for a time on indefinite leave. He said he could be contacted at the Star of the Outlands accommodation house, West Gallery. I have the number here." She read off the figures, and Lance jotted them down. When the woman nodded acknowledgment to his thanks and vanished, he looked across at Mori.

"Star of the Outlands! What the hell's he doing there?"

"That place keeps coming up, doesn't it? First Jack Darch, then that monster out of a dinosaur's nightmare. What goes on there?"

Lance looked at the number on his pad, then tapped it out. The same tired receptionist with the bored eyes and oil-streaks of hair came on view. "Star of the Outlands," he said, apparently not recognizing Lance.

"I understand you have a Dr. Segal staying there. Could I speak to him?"

The receptionist turned his head aside, then after a few seconds glanced up. "He doesn't answer. Not in his room at the moment."

"Did he leave any message?"

"No. They come and go, you know."

Lance hesitated. "Do you have any vacancies?"

"You want a single room? Ground floor or second?"

Lance had a sharp mental image of the forced window in the ground floor room which Darch had been abducted. "Second."

"Give you Room 205. When are you coming in?"

Lance consulted his watch. "Tomorrow morning?"

"Right."

Lance looked across to find Mori studying him intently. "You're sure that's wise, man?"

"I'll be okay. There was an old saying, forewarned is fore-armed."

"But armed against what?"

"So I'm taking a risk. I think the story could be worth it a thousand times over. Here's the number of the Star, Pango, and of my room—205."

Mori looked at him lugubriously. "If the worst happens, I'll give you a nice obituary. But for Maui's sake—"

"I know," finished Lance. "Be careful."

Lance walked around to the Mangala, went up to his room, and showered, thinking of the accumulated warnings that had been directed to him. "Be careful!" He muttered the words to himself as he lay down in the bed, but fatigue overwhelmed him, and almost instantly he was asleep.

chapter
16

LANCE'S ROOM AT the Star of the Outlands gave an impression of light and space, with windows at either end of it, one set looking down on to the internal courtyard and the other at the dome-covered park and airlocks behind the building. The windows facing the park were slightly open. Remembering the insect-like device that had flown into Magill's office to kill his suspect, he closed them. Paranoia? Or simply common sense? He'd ceased to analyze his motives, as long as they were directed toward his survival.

The room was plainly furnished, with a double bed of large size by Earth standards, a couple of chairs, a wardrobe, en suite toilet and bathroom. In some ways, he liked it better than the more expensive room from which he had checked out at the Mangala. It was less modern, less central, but quieter and more spacious.

There was an old-fashioned audio telephone on a table beside the bed—no vision screen—and he put a call through to the Solar News office. Fran answered, and he asked for Pango Mori.

"He's out."

"That's all right, Fran. Would you give him this number?" He read out the number and extension from the phone.

"Got it. By the way, a woman named Heidi called asking for you a while ago."

"Thanks, Fran. I know where to reach her."

Replacing the phone, he sat for a time staring out the window. He could see the unobtrusive olive-green runabout he had rented—he thought it better not to drive one of the Solar News cars now, partly because of Channing's suspension of his contract, and also because it might make him more easily identifiable to his shadowy enemies.

He remembered what Heidi had said to him just before he left the house at Lake Circle the previous night: "We'll see you soon—back here." And Kalli's reinforcement: "No maybe about it. We can be persistent." He had a mental picture of the three almost identical faces, like pictures of the same woman at different ages, each with its different-aged version of that same luring smile. He had a fleeting temptation to call their number, but resisted it.

Three women, four, five—how many altogether?—linked electronically and perhaps chemically into a single multiple organism. And there had been a time when he had slept with one of them. Now, the idea seemed as horrifying as if he had slept with the Ambon sisters.

He suddenly thought of the way their clique had absorbed Dorella, and he felt protective toward her. Yet was it necessary? By now, she probably knew more about the successive clones' multiple life than he did.

Was he glimpsing the future? Was he like some accidental reptilian survivor of the Cretaceous Age looking at the strange habits of early Cenozoic mammals? Evolution went remorselessly on, and neither he nor anyone else could halt its future ramifications.

He tried putting a call through to Segal's room, number 17, but receiving no answer, he rode the elevator down to the ground level and walked along to his room and knocked on the door.

"He's not there," called a voice from the garden behind him. Turning, he saw an inquisitive-looking old man sitting on a bench. He waved an arm toward the far rear corner of the courtyard. "He went down to eat."

"Thanks." Lance set off in the direction indicated. At the corner of the courtyard was a restaurant he had not noticed before, screened by a dense growth of acacias and grevilleas. The restaurant was almost empty, only three people scattered in its sea of tables. Des Segal was sitting alone, eating a Chinese-type meal with chopsticks. He looked up as Lance approached.

"Hi, Lance. How did you find me?"

"They gave me your address here. Mind if I join you?"

Lance went to the counter and ordered a meal similar to Segal's from the gray-faced, blue-haired girl who seemed to combine the functions of waitress and hostess.

"The food's good here," said the astronomer, when he rejoined him. "The cook's Hellas-born Chinese, they tell me."

"I've been trying to figure the racial mix of the lass with the blue hair."

Segal nodded. "The blue hair isn't true, of course. The gray skin is. Looks like the result of some bio experiment. You get a lot of that sort of thing here."

"Experiments by Karstrom's people?"

"Probably. Although he's had imitators."

When his meal arrived, Lance found it delicious. It was the first Chinese-style food he had eaten since he had left Earth. He ate in silence for a while, then looked up at the astronomer.

"What's happening next about the probes?"

Segal shook his head in frustration. "I can't get the Division's roto now. No other way I can get out there."

"Can you hire an aircraft?"

"They're more expensive than I'd thought now." The door of the restaurant opened, and Segal, who was facing it, looked up with an expression of surprise. Lance turned and saw the Ambon sisters coming down the aisle between the tables, gigantic in a lemon-yellow tunic and trousers.

"Lance Garrith!" Belle exclaimed, with what seemed like genuine pleasure at seeing him, her eyes shining behind their rimless glasses.

"Knew you'd come back to us," added Maya, her words almost coinciding with her sister's. Belle put out her hand, and Lance gripped it, while Maya placed her hand over their two clasped ones.

"Have you met Dr. Segal?" asked Lance.

Segal stood up, bowing. "We have met. You once donated money to our Astronomy Division for an interferometer." He grinned. "I'd just arrived from Earth, and when the presentation was made everyone was very formal, but you ladies arrived in a fluorescent red suit."

Maya laughed. "Bergsen obviously didn't like it, but money is money, so he had to be nice to us."

Segal looked at Belle. "I was very impressed by that speech you gave about cooperation and teamwork."

"We've had to become experts in that," said Belle, and then she looked sharply from Lance to Segal. "Was it you two who flew out into the Badlands last night?"

Lance felt a resurgence of the discomfort he had experienced when he first met these women, when they had fired alternating questions at him too quickly for him to adjust his answers from one line of interrogation to the other.

"Yes," he said at the same time as Segal.

"What did you find?" asked Maya.

It was the astronomer who answered: "Frankly, I don't know."

"Did you think you were looking at the arrival of another extra-solar lifeform like the first one?" asked Belle.

"I think it's highly likely."

"But as a professional, you'd rather not commit yourself, eh?" Maya switched her attention to Lance. "What was your impression?"

Lance looked sidelong at Segal. "Personally, I think we *are* dealing with something from outside the solar system."

"Why?" Belle's query was the crack of a whip.

"We were followed home by a flying device that didn't look to me as if it were of human manufacture. Couldn't get a decent photo of it."

"Could you draw it?" When Lance nodded, Belle plunged her hand into the capacious pocket of her tunic and brought out a notebook and ballpen, flicked the book open to a blank page and put it on the table in front of Lance. He sketched the device that had flown alongside their roto, emphasizing the thin, straight tubes that seemed to channel its unknown propelling and lifting forces.

"How big was it?" demanded Belle.

Lance held his hands about a meter apart. "Say that long, and the same in wingspan. No more."

The two women looked at the drawing for nearly a minute without speaking. Then Belle took the book and pen and slipped them back in her pocket, turning her attention back to Segal. "Do you intend looking around the Badlands again?"

"I'd like to. Trouble is, I can't get the Division's roto again, and I can't see any other way of getting there."

"There might be," said Belle. The two dark ponytails swung as the women tilted their heads to look in each other's faces.

"You mean Red?" Maya directed her question to her sister in a low, quick voice, and Belle nodded almost imperceptibly.

"We might be able to help you," she said to Segal. "We have a close friend who runs commercial roto flights."

"He's expensive," warned Maya, "but he's good."

"Interested?" asked Belle.

Segal, slightly confused by their rapid-fire communication, kept switching his gaze from one face to the other. "I could be."

"When you're finished here," said Belle, "come up to our apartment. Top floor, far corner." She looked at Lance. "You know where it is. Both of you come along."

* * *

On the way up to the fourth level in the slow-moving elevator, Segal looked depressed. "Doubt if they'll be able to arrange anything," he said gloomily.

"Wait and see. They seem to have a lot of clout around here."

The door of the Ambon sisters' apartment was open when they reached it. "Come in!" came Maya's deep voice in answer to Lance's call. They went in and saw the two sisters standing in front of a visiphone screen.

"Try him again," said Belle. "You're the one with the charm."

Maya stabbed her finger at the keys without having to look up the number. The face of a ginger, freckled man of about forty Earth years came on the screen, his thin mouth widening in a grin of recognition.

"Hi, girls. Feeling lonesome for Red?"

"This is business, Red. Have you a roto available tomorrow?"

"Could have, for my favorite twins. Just for you, I can make a special juggling of schedules. Where you wanna go?"

"The Badlands. You'd better come and see us."

The ginger man's expression hardened. "Maybe I had." He glanced at his watch. "Be there in twenty minutes." The screen blanked out.

For a few seconds, the twins conversed with each other in their high-speed verbal shorthand, then they turned to Lance and Segal. "He'll take you where you want to go," said Belle. "Will you excuse us for a minute?"

The pair went through a wide door to an adjoining room. Segal, watching them go, said, "Looks as if you were right, about these ladies having a lot of clout, as you put it. As long as they can wangle me a trip to have another look where the probe landed, I don't care how they arrange it. I think the aliens—wherever they came from—may be setting up a base out there."

"I'd be damn careful, Des. Remember the thing that chased us halfway back to Hellas? Get too close to their base, and they might kill you."

"That's a risk I have to take."

"How about the fellow who's flying you there? You'll have to tell him the risk he'll be running."

"I take it you're not coming along with me?"

"There are limits to the risks I'll run for a story. This seems to be going beyond common sense."

Segal gave a long sigh. "I don't mind admitting it scares the sweat out of me. But the rewards could be worth it. It could be our first alien contact.''

Lance hesitated before he answered. "Actually, the first man to make this contact was Jack Darch. And where is he now?"

For a long time, the astronomer did not speak. Then, "You're right about the element of danger, but this is a chance in a lifetime for me to achieve something that'll live throughout history."

Lance grunted noncommittally. He had expressed his opinion, and he had the feeling further discussion would be as rewarding as arguing with a concrete wall.

Abruptly, Segal turned to him. "When we were out in the Badlands, and you'd left your radio open, you said, 'What the hell am I doing here?' I know how you felt. It's hit me a few times—once, just after I'd moved to Hellas. I'd already made some mark as an astronomer in Hawaii, and I thought my expertise would put me in the front rank here." He shook his head.

"Why didn't it?"

"There's a very high intelligence level here. Process of selection, of course. It costs so much to bring a person here, they have to show a good track record, and they have to be able to adapt, so competition is fierce. You get cliques here. Groups. It's as if the human race is breaking into different sub-species, specially adapted to some function, some way of life, or another. I've seen the beginning of this process back on Earth, but I didn't recognize it. Here, I'm still an outsider."

"Still? After eleven years?"

Segal nodded. "I married a Martian woman, second generation, an astronomer. Perhaps two astronomers in one family is a disaster recipe, even without the complication of different planetary cultures. Anyway, we split after a couple of years."

At this moment, the Ambon sisters came back into the room. "Who split?" asked Maya, hearing Segal's closing words. "You and your wife?"

"Unfortunately, yes." Segal looked up in surprise.

The twins walked across to the front door, looked out, then returned to sit on a wide sofa facing the two chairs occupied by Lance and Segal, leaving the front door open. Lance had the impression they were much younger than he had thought, and on looking closely he saw that they had applied subtle makeup.

"Better?" asked Maya, indicating her face.

"You look very nice," said Lance.

"The man we're expecting is a lover," said Maya.

"Whose?" asked Segal, looking from one of the twins to the other.

"Both. We're a package." Maya's voice rose slightly. "You don't have to look incredulous. We have no trouble in attracting men. Do we?" She glanced at her sister.

"Only in holding them after the novelty of a double lady wears off," said Belle. "But Red's been a good friend for years." Pushing back with her arm, Belle swung their double torso forward, putting her hand on Lance's knee. "This is not Earth, Lance. Lifestyles here are different."

She was interrupted by a masculine voice calling from the doorway, "Anyone home?" The sisters rose and strode quickly to the door, while a freckled, red-haired man came into the room to meet them. Taller than him, they seemed to engulf him, flinging their arms around him. His head moved to and fro as they kissed him. They brought him back to introduce him to Lance and Segal, each holding him by an arm, and looking over his shoulders. Both women looked sexually aroused.

"Dr. Segal wants to go to the Badlands," said Belle.

"Geophysical survey?" asked Red in a harsh voice, looking keenly at Segal.

"No. I'm an astronomer, not a geologist."

"Haven't I seen you at the airfield, flying the Astronomy Division's roto?"

"Yes. It's not available to me at the moment."

"Must be something urgent."

"I think some object from space came down in the Badlands last night, and I'd like to investigate it."

Red turned his head to look over his shoulder at Belle. "I heard something about that. I wiped it off as a rumor."

"It was real enough," said Segal. "I saw it, from a distance. Too far away for details, but I saw where it went down."

"And you want to go out there to locate it? How many other people know about this thing?"

"Lance here was with me when we saw it. Otherwise, only these ladies know about it."

Red seemed to think for a while. "It'll come expensive," he said. For a minute or so he and Segal haggled over the cost of the journey, and suddenly Lance broke into the conversation.

"Des, I don't want to jack the price up, but I think you should tell him there's an element of risk here."

"I was coming to that," said Segal. "It's just possible the

object we saw landing might contain some form of extra-solar life.''

There was about a quarter of a minute of complete silence between them all. Maya's arm crept protectively around Red, and Belle held him by the shoulder.

"We don't want anything to happen to either of you," said Maya anxiously, although it was obvious to Lance that she was concerned for Red rather than for Segal.

"We'll be okay." Red patted the thick, smooth arm encircling him. "You know me—always careful. All the same," he added, looking at Segal, "this pushes the price up a bit."

The astronomer made a gesture of assent.

"Tomorrow morning, then?" asked Red. "You'll supply your own suit? Okay?"

Lance moved away while they concluded their arrangements, although the sisters stayed to listen to every word.

Crossing the room, Lance filled in time by looking at a number of photographic enlargements on a wall. They had been taken in a wide variety of places, several showing the Ambon sisters. In one, they stood on a platform at some ceremonial occasion, Belle speaking into a microphone. Another, which startled him, showed their twin figure in a grotesque three-legged spacesuit, with a background of jagged pinnacles snarling against a black, unearthly sky. Yet another, taken at some athletic meeting under a Martian dome, depicted the finish of a footrace, with an Earthwoman crossing the line ahead of a number of Martian girls. The Ambon sisters, looking slimmer and younger than at present, were finishing about third or fourth, heads thrown back, faces strained, running with an impressively long stride that must have cost relentless practice in synchronizing their movements.

Lance started at a touch on his shoulder, and found Segal beside him. "You want to come with us?" he asked. "He wants a hundred grand. That's a hell of a lot of money. If we could split it. . . ."

Lance looked across at the sisters. "Mind if I call my office?" Getting a nod of assent, he crossed to the visiphone and tapped out the Solar News number, bringing Pango Mori's face on the screen.

"Pango, I've been offered the chance to run out to the landing site again, but it'd set us back fifty thousand. Can we stand that?"

"Not out of Hellas funds, Lance. Sorry, man, I can't authorize an amount like that."

"Okay, Pango. It was just a thought. See you." He turned to Segal. "Sorry, Des. I can't swing it."

Segal spun around to Red. "Any chance of dropping that figure?"

"Not by much." Red shook his head. "There's an element of danger—you admitted that yourself."

"Just a minute," broke in Belle, and the women sidled closer to Segal. "We could lend you the money."

There was a moment of silence.

"That'd be okay with me," said Red.

"You mean that?" Segal looked from Belle to Maya, then back.

"We can afford it. You can pay us back after you announce your big discovery."

"And don't forget who helped finance it," added Maya.

"That's very generous of you." Segal looked slightly stunned.

Lance moved toward the front door. "I'll leave you for now. Best of luck, Des."

The four of them looked at him as though each sought something to say. He gave them a wave of his hand and went quickly out.

When Lance got back to the Solar News office, Pango Mori had gone out, and the only person there was young Fran. Lance went into Mori's office to wait.

After a few minutes, the outer door opened, but it was not Mori who appeared. It was Dorella. She exchanged a word or two with Fran, then walked straight through into the inner office, apparently expecting to find Mori there. She looked intensely excited.

"I'm building up a tremendous story," she said to Lance as soon as they had exchanged greetings. "I'm learning more and more about the way these successive clone families work. There are a lot of them about, like the one I'm researching, although you wouldn't recognize them unless you saw a number of the same group together."

"You're not a clone, are you, Fran?" Lance called to Mori's assistant.

"Unfortunately, no," she replied. "I have to get by on my own."

"Why unfortunately?" asked Lance softly, so that only Dorella could hear him.

"I think they have different role models here," she whispered. Then, speaking in her normal voice again, "It's a real evolutionary step forward—*upward,* I think, although I'm not sure of that. It's early yet to try to evaluate where it's leading.''

"Like any other new development," mused Lance. "No one can stop it now. You can't turn the clock back."

"Anyway, how are you getting on with your extra-solar invaders, or whatever?"

"Running into dead ends, so far. Segal's going out there tomorrow, but it's costing him a lot of money. I couldn't get Pango to authorize me to split it with him."

"Yes, I heard about that. Where's he getting the money?"

"The Ambon sisters are lending it to him."

"You mean those siamese twin women who run the place where you're staying?" Dorella looked thoughtful. "Why are they doing that?"

"I don't know, unless it was an impulse."

"I wouldn't have thought they'd be impulsive, always operating as a team of two."

"The pilot who's flying Segal out there used to be their lover—maybe still is."

"You're joking." When he shook his head, she smiled. "How?"

He shrugged. "Their problem. Anyway, I'm learning a lot about the way Martian society ticks."

"So am I. I can't make up my mind whether they're way ahead of us or running off the track." Dorella looked as if she was visualizing a future audience. "You know, a lot of new avenues of research have come together here. Their micro-miniaturization techniques have helped their bio-engineering developments. That's what made their successive cloning feasible. You know, that's even farther out than I thought."

"In what way?"

"The older members of a clone family can contact the younger ones *selectively.*"

"But it doesn't work both ways?"

"It operates like this. After they pass middle age, or when parts of their bodies start to deteriorate, they have them replaced by mechanical and electronic parts, until they're eventually mostly cybernetic. You've seen Kalli—she's partly along the way to that. At some point along the line, they have a sort of switchboard incorporated into them, so they can control their channels of communication. Get it?"

"Yes. Remember when we were in their house, and Joy arrived

with Phil Gray. Did you notice how Kalli touched some keys on the metal part of her body and spoke into the little microphone on her ring?"

Dorella nodded. "I remember exactly what she said when she found Phil was there. 'Dorella and Lance are here. Get rid of him.' And Joy did just that."

"They must run their whole lives like that."

"They do. And they're only one among many clone groups."

"What makes them want to live like that?"

"The lure of immortality. Most of us experience that. You try to do it by creating video programs that will be shown to millions of people indefinitely into the future, and so do I. It's a substitute immortality, but it's better than nothing, isn't it? Immortality is the draw-card in practically every religion that's ever been thought of. But these people have made the idea tangible. They can live, theoretically, forever, without cutting themselves off from the experience of normal human emotions and sensations."

Lance walked over to the window and stood looking down at the people moving along the sidewalk lining the Octagon. How many of those diverse individuals were members of clone families?

"They must lose out somewhere," he murmured.

"Maybe so. I haven't found out where yet. Anyway, why do you say that?"

"I don't know. Just gut feeling. Maybe jealousy."

"Jealousy! I've had to watch that ever since I started digging into lifestyles here. Not that you don't find it on Earth."

He looked down from the window again, then after a few seconds turned to face her. "Dorella, are we dinosaurs?"

"Dinosaurs?"

"Dinosaurs at the end of another Cretaceous?"

A few minutes later, Pango Mori came in. He checked briefly with Fran for messages, then came through to the inner office.

"Hi, Dorella. Hi, Lance." He looked at Lance quizzically. "Fifty thousand! Man, you sure think big."

"Don't worry about it, Pango. I'll get all the data from Segal when he comes back."

"*If* he comes back. The way I see it, they let you get away from them last night because they gave you the benefit of the doubt. Next time—*pow!*" He drove his fist into his palm.

"I think Dr. Segal's being foolhardy going out there in daylight," broke in Dorella. "So's the man who's flying him there."

"What are you going to do now, Lance?" asked Mori.

"Go back to the Star of the Outlands for the night, see Segal off in the morning. I'll try to get him to keep in touch with me."

"Hey, I might have something to help there." Mori pulled open a drawer of a cabinet and took out three two-way radios. "These are matched, with the signals automatically scrambled on a code controlled by these dials." He set the dials to the same figures on their backs. "Three, four, seven. Remember that, if the dials get moved. Give Segal one, keep another, and I'll keep the third here."

"Right." Lance took two of the sets. "I see. This plugs into his suit radio outlet. Okay, I'll get back to the Star, where a lot seems to be happening."

"Good luck," said Mori.

"I think it's the twins," teased Dorella. "He wants to try women in matched pairs, like the radios."

Lance gave a mock shudder. "I've seen them handle Segal's pilot. And maybe Segal." Waving goodbye, he went out, rode the elevator down, then drove off in his rented car toward the Star of the Outlands.

He went straight to Segal's room and knocked on his door. The door opened, and Segal gave a shout of welcome. "Changed your mind? Coming with me tomorrow?"

"Sorry, Des. Like to, but I can't talk my office into putting up the money. But here, would you take this radio? It's tuned through a built-in scrambler to mine. If you accidentally move the dials, come back to 347."

"I'll make a note of that. Good. I'll give you a running commentary on everything that happens. If there *is* a hostile force out here, or anything remotely suspicious, I'll contact you."

Lance looked at his watch. "Feel like something to eat?"

"Not now, thanks."

Leaving Segal, Lance walked along to the restaurant. It was early for the evening meal, and there were only two other people eating there, apparently engrossed in each other's company in a far corner. Lance looked through the menu, and ordered Japanese teriyaki, which maintained the unexpectedly high standard set by his meal of the previous night.

He had almost finished his meal when another person walked

in. Absorbed in his thoughts, he did not look up until the woman
stopped near his table.

"Hello, Lance. I thought I might find you here."

Looking down at him with an elfin smile was Heidi.

chapter
17

"How DID YOU know I was here?" asked Lance.

"I'm good at adding details together." Heidi slid down into the chair facing him. "Notice anything different?"

He looked at her. "Your hair? No. You're not wearing your headband—the one with the little TV camera."

Smiling, she leaned forward across the table. "I'm on holiday from my family. Every girl needs a break from our style of life now and then." She reached out, impulsively, it seemed, and rested smooth, cool fingers on his hand. She dropped her voice, although there was no one near. "It's the first time I've met a man I really want for myself, without sharing our intimacies with the rest of my family."

For a long time, he looked thoughtfully at her eyes. "Heidi, what do you really know about me?"

Her smile returned. "I know you were born on Earth—I forget where—and that you grew up there. I know you had a wife back here, but something went wrong with your marriage. Guessing from here, I'd say you put too much time and effort into your career, not enough with her."

"That's quite perceptive." He tried not to sound cynical.

"When you're part of a trans-generation team like ours, you learn a lot about people."

"Trans-generation, you call it?"

"Yes. The intervals in our ages are shorter than in your generations, so you don't have generation gaps with their problems. We communicate better, all the time, except when one of us wants to withdraw for a while, as I'm doing now."

"You do this with the agreement of the rest of your family?"

"Of course. Otherwise it could become like living in jail. We only do this after we've reached a certain age, though." Her perfume drifted across to him, subtle and provocative. "Are you remembering that time on the *Yttria*?"

He nodded silently, looking at her gravely. She smiled.

"You were very considerate," she went on. "I remember you warning me about the viruses and germs you might have picked up traveling about Earth. And when you made love, you were gentle with me, although your Terran muscles could have crushed me."

"And then I heard that voice in your skull."

"That spoiled everything. The sad thing was, I didn't need any advice. That's why I've wanted to be really alone with you."

Lance gave a wry smile. "I can't guarantee privacy here. These rooms could be wired for sound, possibly video."

"That's no problem. We have a small villa on the Outer Circle. No one there, now, and I have a car here. We could be there in a few minutes."

Lance hesitated. "Sounds very attractive. But I have a lot of things on my plate right at the moment, Heidi."

Sudden spots of color showed on her normally pale cheeks. "I you're not interested—" She thrust her lower lip forward. "It's only that the length of time I can steal from my family is limited I thought—" A suspicion of tears glistened in her eyes.

He put his hand on hers. "It's not that, Heidi. Now that I think of it, I've nothing definite on my program tonight. I had the feeling Dorella might want to contact me about a future session we could collaborate on."

"Dorella? She's spending the whole night with Kalli and Thyr going into the history of the clone system. They'll be tied up for hours."

She suddenly seemed to him vulnerable. He squeezed her hand "Why not? I have a car outside, too. I'll follow yours. Just give me time to hook up the recorder to the phone, and maybe a quick shower."

Her face was instantly suffused with radiant happiness. If unde conscious control, it was very well done. Somehow, he felt it was genuine, even though part of his mind seemed to stand back an wonder whether he was believing what he wanted to believe—o what Heidi wanted him to believe.

Back in his room, he linked up the answering system with his phone and quickly ran his compact little electric shaver over his cheeks and chin, then used the needle-spray shower.

Heidi was waiting for him outside the building in her red car

He followed her in his rented vehicle down the West Avenue until they came to the intersection with the Outer Circle, where she turned left. Barrel-vaulted like the main galleries, the Circle apparently linked the eight outer ends of the octopus tentacles of the sealed city. The houses on either side of the road were small but varied, attractively designed. He followed the red car until Heidi swung into a carport on the left side. He drove his car in alongside hers, parking it on a vacant set of recharging contacts.

Heidi had gone into the house, leaving the front door open. A luxuriant growth of spray-watered vegetation screened the front of the villa.

"In here, Lance."

The interior was suffused by soft, indirect lighting which kept changing in color through an apparently random succession of pastel shades: pink, lilac, apricot, lime. A curiously haunting music pervaded the room, and a heavy perfume reminded him of the scent of incense he had once encountered in an Asian temple. He walked through a carpeted anteroom into a lilac-walled bedroom dominated by a broad divan with deep purple covering. Heidi stood at a sideboard by one wall.

She held out a tall glass of a sparkling drink that may have had some kind of aphrodisiac in it, because, as he drank, it seemed to combine with the sensuous music and her perfume to bring him to a relaxed state of mind in which he felt astounded that he had not appreciated her exotic beauty before.

Where most Martian-born girls had plump faces and torsos, and limbs so slender that they looked like stick figures of a caricaturist, Heidi had retained some of the muscular development she had built up in preparation for her trip to Earth. She had a fluid suppleness that seemed to combine the best physical characteristics of women of both worlds.

Without the headband, her broad forehead looked abnormally high, and he ran his fingers across its smooth expanse and back over the loosely waved blond hair.

"Probably my skull's too big for your standards of perfection," she smiled.

"It suits you."

"This is something we evolved a couple of generations ago—stretching the way the cells of an embryo keep doubling."

He stroked her hair. "You mean you're the next step up, like the step from hominid to man?"

She nodded. "They're still working on taking it a step farther."

"You're far enough along that line. I think you're perfect."

Her slim arms were cool around him, but her lips burned like fire.

Heidi made love to him as no one had ever done before. She seemed to anticipate every flicker of his changing moods.

Much later, as he lay beside her staring happily up at the ceiling, an unpleasant thought intruded.

"I must seem primitive to you," he said. "Like something halfway back to an ape."

She rolled toward him with a soft, gurgling laugh, her fingers riffling through the hair on his chest. "I like that. I think sometimes we've evolved too far. You still have a spontaneity about you, a *drive*."

She lifted herself on her elbow to look down at his face, her fingers caressing the slightly stubbled roughness of his chin. "I'm probably just an average member of my level—my caste, if you like to think of it that way—but you must be in the top few per cent of yours. You have intelligence comparable with mine, but it has a different base. More drive, and as to what else you have, I want to find out."

Her expression suddenly mischievous, she kissed him, holding him with a fierce possessiveness. Using the leverage of his legs, he rolled both of them over so that he was above her, carefully using his elbows to stop his weight from crushing her. The tips of her nipples brushed his chest.

A long time later—how much later he neither knew nor cared—he was again lying beside her with only his fingers entwined with hers, looking up at the ceiling.

"Thank you, darling. That was lovely."

He was about to murmur a reply, when he realized that what he had heard was not Heidi's voice. His mind snapped into hard, bright wakefulness as he rolled on his side to look at her relaxed profile.

Chilled, his heart hammering, he sat up. She had not spoken—she was drifting into sleep, her face softened by a drowsy smile.

The voice had come from inside his head, by bone conduction from behind the right ear. He had the feeling the words had not been intended for him, but for Heidi.

"What's happening?" he shouted.

Heidi came quickly into a sitting position, her eyes wide and blinking away sleep. "What is it, darling? Were you dreaming?"

"Did you say anything?"

She looked suddenly pale. "I don't know. I might have."

"No. This was clear, and it came from—" he hesitated, "—from inside my head."

"Oh, my God," she muttered. She looked away from him. She slid her feet off the divan, and went through into the bathroom, closing the door behind her.

"Heidi!" he roared, but she didn't reply. Springing up, he tried to open the bathroom door, but it didn't yield. It seemed lightly built, of some substance like lilac fiberglass. He might easily have smashed it open, but he resisted the impulse to fall back on force.

"Heidi!" he called again, this time with carefully controlled calm. "I just want to talk to you. Come out."

"I'll be out in a minute," came her voice from behind the closed door. He sat on the edge of the divan, forcing himself to breathe slowly and evenly. After a few seconds, the voice against his skull came to him again.

"I'm sorry, darling. I didn't mean to communicate with you, but you're such a marvelous lover, I became confused. I used a wrong channel."

He looked up, staring wildly at the blank lilac wall in front of him. *"Who the hell are you?"*

"You've met me. Talked with me. Even played 3D chess with me."

The shock of recognition of the voice brought him to his feet. "Jocasta Borg!"

His shout brought Heidi back into the room. She stood in the now open doorway of the bathroom, still naked, her eyes wide.

"You had to find out sometime, Lance," went on Jocasta's voice. "Kalli, Thyra, Heidi, Joy, and little Elli are all clones of mine, generated at different times. They all carry implants so that I can feel what they feel, as well as hear what they hear, all radio-linked to the appropriate receptors connected to my brain. At the touch of a switch within me, I can experience the sensations of a young girl, middle-aged woman, young woman—see, hear and feel with them."

Heidi must have been hearing the same words, because she suddenly shouted, "You don't have to tell him all this! Remember what happened to Thyra with that fellow Sutt?"

"Calm down, Heidi," came the voice of Jocasta. "Lance is quite a different type of man from Sutt. He's mature. It's better he knows at this stage. Lance, I suppose this is new to you, but you've been making love to several women simultaneously. There's an advantage to you: You have the accumulated experience that you'd hardly find in one girl of Heidi's age, unless she'd been very promiscuous—and that would have had a blunting effect on her.''

Lance looked at Heidi. "You mean you've been talking to Heidi all the time I—" He felt the blood warm in his forehead.

"Not all the time. Just an occasional helpful word."

He kept looking at Heidi. "But this is horrible."

"Why?" came the cool voice in his head.

"Because—" He hesitated.

"Because it's new to you?" Jocasta's soft laughter was the most horrifying sound he had ever heard.

Lance seized his underbriefs, shirt and trousers from where he had flung them across a chair. As he dressed, Heidi watched him.

"Lance, darling," she began, but he chopped her words short.

"You knew about this all the time," he roared.

She retreated from his direct anger, backing against the door leading out to the anteroom.

"Help me, quickly!" she said, and it was obvious that she was not talking to Lance. Fear made her less attractive. The slight plumpness of her light-gravity face had been acceptable when she was happy, giving an effect of cheerfulness. Now, the impression was of a small, childish, terrified face framed in fat cheeks and a double chin.

"Lance!" The voice in his head had a hard urgency now. "Don't be angry with her! It's not her fault. Wait there! And promise not to hurt her."

Lance sighed. The energy seemed to have drained out of him. "I won't hurt her," he said.

"Thank you," came the voice in his head.

"Yes, thank you," added Heidi, relaxing a little. "You know my elder clone sister, Thyra? Someone once went berserk with her in a situation like this—blinded her."

"What happened to him?"

"Oh, he's dead."

"How did he die?"

"After what he did to Thyra, we thought he didn't deserve to live. I think Jocasta and Kalli spoke to him through his head implant and made him face up to what he'd done."

"But that wouldn't have killed him, surely?"

She nodded. "They recorded what they said and left it playing in his head day and night. After a few days he killed himself, although it didn't give Thyra back her sight. She'll still be blind until someone perfects eye transplants. Often says what she'll do when she has an eye. Not if. When.''

On an impulse, Lance went across to her and put his hand on her shoulder. ''I'm sorry if I shouted at you. I was in a kind of shock. Nothing like this ever happened to me before.''

She managed a tremulous smile. ''Only once before.''

''On the *Yttria*? Yes, but that time I didn't realize what was going on.''

''Let me get you something to drink,'' said Heidi so abruptly that he wondered whether the suggestion had come from one of her clone sisters.

''It's all right, Heidi. We both feel shaken up. I'll leave you for a while now.''

But as he moved toward the door, Jocasta's voice rang authoritatively in his skull: ''Wait there for a little while, Lance. I think we all owe you an explanation.''

''You've given it,'' he said, and made one stride, and then it happened. A replay of that incident on the *Yttria*, when a sensation like a violent electric shock had jolted him across the back of the neck. He staggered, clutched at the edge of the door to retain his balance, then sprawled headlong. He seemed to fall into roaring darkness.

He was still in the same room when he regained consciousness, but some time must have passed, because there were now four people in the room, standing looking down at him as he lay on the floor.

''He's coming awake,'' said a voice, possibly Heidi's.

''We'll take him up to the big house,'' said another. ''Joy can bring his car along.''

He managed to get his eyes focused. Heidi, Joy, Kalli, and Jocasta were standing above him, all dressed in similarly styled yellow leatheroid jackets that looked like a uniform. Rolling painfully on his side, he looked across at their legs. Two pairs in close-fitting black trousers, the other two pairs black metal stilts.

''Can you sit up?'' asked Kalli.

With an effort, he managed it. Jocasta moved around until she was standing on his left, then she retracted her telescopic legs until her bulky cybernetic trunk seemed to be sitting on the floor beside him.

"I'll help you up," she said. She slipped the hydraulic arm around his body, holding him against her, then simply extended her legs again, lifting him without effort until he was standing. He still felt unsteady, and only the clasp of the thick, flexible arm kept him upright.

They trooped out to a long, almost buslike car, Kalli sliding into the driving seat. Heidi went to her own vehicle, Joy to the rented car Lance had been driving. Jocasta maneuvered Lance into the second of the long car's three seats, sitting beside him with her arm still holding him against her barrel body. He tried to move the hydraulic arm, but the gloved metal hand at the end of it suddenly gripped both his hands, holding them together. The grip was unbreakable.

"Just rest until we're home," said Jocasta, her voice coming through the implant. "I'm sorry I had to stun you, but you understand why, don't you?"

"Yes. Heidi told me what happened to Thyra." He turned his head to look at Jocasta's profile. "By the way, do you have to leave this implant in me?"

"The one in your neck?" (God, were there others?). "It doesn't cause you any pain, does it?"

"Not unless it's activated."

"Then you needn't worry. The controls are inside my body, and I'm the only person who can activate it. You trust me, don't you?"

"It looks as if I have to, doesn't it? Any time I do something you don't like, you can shock me into unconsciousness."

"That's unlikely, now we know each other better. The implant isn't just for that, Lance. I can talk to you, advise you, without anyone overhearing." The hand and arm moved him around the front of her body until they faced each other. "I can do better than that, Lance. I could give you other implants that could make you superhuman. I could change your hormone flows—thyroid, adrenal, pituitary, testosterone, as you need it. I could make you like a god."

"But why do you want to do all this?"

She did not reply straight away, although her lips curved in a smile. The metal fingers squeezed his hands, not painfully, but firmly. "You could say it's because I love you."

"What do you really mean by that, Jocasta?"

Her eyes darkened, and her mouth became a straight line. "You mean, how can a head on a machine body experience emotion? Is that it?''

Lance said nothing.

"Answer me, damn you," she snapped.

Still, he made no reply. A second later, pain like a knife thrust stabbed the back of his neck, and a blinding light seemed to flash before his eyes, with a thunderous sound that quickly waned. He looked at the angry face before him in horror.

"Did you do that?"

"I did that. When I speak to you, I expect to be answered. Remember that, Lance." Unexpectedly, she smiled, the metal fingers still gripping his hands. "And remember this: I have a short fuse."

By now, Kalli was driving around Lake Circle. She drove the long car around to the house with the Ismenia nameplate and swung into a carport in front of the building.

"Let's go inside," said Kalli.

As Lance stepped out of the car, the after-effects of the stunning were still with him. He staggered awkwardly, the illusion of a thousand needles piercing his back and legs. Jocasta moved beside him, slipping the flexible arm around his body, drawing him against her.

"Walk in step with me." He tried, looking down. The straight, shining legs swung like stiff pendulums, stabbing down at the ground to take her weight. Their rhythm was different from his, and when he stumbled she simply lengthened her legs to bring his feet clear of the ground, carrying him into the house and setting him on his feet in the center of the large living room with the moving murals.

Heidi appeared in front of him with a tall glass of green liquid. "Drink this." She held it to his lips. He swallowed some, and almost at once his head felt clearer.

Kalli came into the room and stood beside Jocasta, facing Lance. Heidi moved to the other side of Jocasta, and a moment later Joy came in and joined her. Lance looked along the row of blond faces, all of them smiling at him. The smile was welcoming, but for Lance the scene had an undercurrent of horror.

He was aware of a movement to one side of the silent quartet, and he saw young Elli come in, followed by the blind woman, Thyra. They stood slightly behind the others.

Lance looked along the row of faces. "What happens now?"

Jocasta moved slightly forward from the others. "I think we

have what we want,'' she said. ''A very interesting man who appeals to all of us.''

A little murmur of assent came from some of the others. Lance looked from one face to the next along the row. ''I'm flattered, ladies—should I say, honored. But—'' he hesitated, ''how can I put this?''

Jocasta's short left arm reached forward, and its metal claw clamped around Lance's forearm like a handcuff. Simultaneously, her flexible hydraulic arm slid around his shoulders, pulling him forward so that his face was drawn against the plump, blond head on its annular plastic cushion.

She kissed him, her head and face warm and alive in a weird contrast to the metal and plastic body, which felt as lifeless as an oil drum. When she released him, her eyes were very bright.

''I've wanted to do that since I first saw you,'' she said, and all the others laughed.

Unexpectedly, the little girl piped up. ''Our clone momma always gets what she wants,'' she said smugly.

Lance looked down. ''You'd be Elli, wouldn't you? Hi!''

The eyes of a girl in her teens looked up at him from the five-year-old face. He switched his attention back to Jocasta.

''Perhaps we might get to know each other,'' he suggested, but Joy answered immediately.

''We all know you very well.''

He looked blankly from one pair of blue eyes to another.

''We share you,'' said Heidi.

''*What?*''

''Except for young Elli,'' said Kalli, ruffling the small girl's hair. ''She'll have to wait.''

''I can wait,'' said Elli in a voice that sounded childish and mature at the same time.

''Let me touch him.'' Lance had forgotten the blind woman, who had been standing behind the others. Now she moved forward between them, her face mostly hidden by her hood. Her butterfly-light fingers explored his face ''Yes,'' she said. ''I still want him.''

''Look,'' he said suddenly, ''I like you all, but this won't work.'' He felt as if he were in a trap—not wholly unpleasant, but still a trap.

''If I'm the one who bothers you, I'll withdraw,'' said Thyra.

''No!'' chorused Heidi and Joy together.

Thyra lifted her hood back from her face. Her hair was not blond like that of the others, but gray, and the damage done to her face by her ex-lover sent a chill of horror through Lance. It looked as if her face had been seared by something like a blow-torch. The eyes were gone, their scarred lids closed over vacant sockets, and most of her nose was missing. She seemed to sense him looking at her. "I'm ugly now. But you'll find me restful."

The others remained silent, watching him. As he looked at Thyra a feeling of compassion came to him. He put his hands on both her shoulders.

"I don't think you're ugly, Thyra. You have an attractive mouth. I always look at that. A woman makes her own mouth."

Her face became suffused with red, except for the scarred area. He leaned forward and brushed his lips against hers. As he stood back, her mouth curved in a tremulous smile. "Thank you for that, Lance," she said.

Jocasta suddenly laughed. "We've found ourselves a diplomat."

"No," objected Kalli. "He meant it."

The younger women agreed with her. They all crowded close to Lance, reaching to touch him. He had an odd sensation, akin to drowning.

chapter
18

DROWNING... THE THOUGHT kept coming back to him as the women escorted him through a doorway into an inner room, smaller and more intimate. There were foam chairs placed in a rough circle, and all of them except Jocasta sat down, including Lance. Although he was used to confronting studio audiences numbering into the hundreds, he found the close-range, concentrated scrutiny of these women unsettling.

"Now that we're all together," said Jocasta, "are we all willing that Lance Garrith should become our man?"

There was a chorus of agreement from the others, and Jocasta moved deliberately toward Lance.

"It's an important step for a clone family of women to choose a man," she said. "There are responsibilities on both sides. We feel we could develop a highly productive symbiosis between us."

"Symbiosis?" he repeated.

The telescopic legs shortened, and the yellow-coated barrel body came down in front of him until their faces were on a level. "Your past career suggests a high level of ability in public relations, and we have access to information channels that could help you in a thousand ways no outsider would suspect."

"I feel honored, but I'd like a little time to think. I'd still like to remain an individual."

"But it's because of your individual personality that we're attracted to you," said Jocasta, and the others joined in with supportive monosyllables. "You'll find your life enriched, lifted to heights you'd never have believed existed."

"I realize that. I appreciate it. But I have a career I've built up, operating from Pacific City."

"You could run your programs from Hellas."

"But the power center of our organization is in Pacific City."

Jocasta smiled. "Eventually, you could make it Hellas."

"But I don't make the major decisions at Solar News. They're made by Mort Channing."

"He won't live forever," murmured Kalli.

"Neither will I," Lance replied.

The women exchanged glances. "That may not be as true as you think," said Kalli.

"With us," said Jocasta quietly, "you could live practically forever."

He looked down at the smooth bulk of her mechanical body. "In a body like that?"

"Eventually, before age begins to attack your tissues." She brought her gloved hand up and unfastened her jacket, revealing the glossy, bulging cylinder balanced on the retracted legs, and slapped her hand against its unyielding surface. "This will last for century after century, because its parts are replaceable. We could take the hurry, the urgency out of your life—enable you to plan a long way into the future."

Kalli moved alongside him. "Look ahead, Lance. In a hundred years, Mars will be the controlling heart of the solar system, and Earth will be an overcrowded backwater, with its vital resources used up."

"But it's our original home," objected Lance.

"So we've outgrown it," responded Kalli. "After all, the life we all evolved from originated in the sea, but we outgrew that long ago."

"In the same way," added Jocasta, "we've outgrown the home planet, and someday we'll outgrow the solar system. And each time we expand from one environment to the next, we climb—" she gestured upward with the hydraulic arm, "—to a higher level of living. Fish to amphibian, reptile, mammal, man, us."

"You're certain the trend is upward?" interrupted Lance.

"The leading sub-species always advances, not the entire species. That's the way evolution has moved since the beginning of the universe—behind a narrow cutting edge."

The muted chime of a bell sounded from a visiphone booth in one corner, and Joy moved over to answer the call. No one spoke while she was away from the circle, as if they felt the absence of one member might weaken their influence on Lance.

In a few seconds, Joy called, "It's Dorella. She's been trying to reach you, Lance, and she thought you might be here."

"What gave her that idea?" He stood up, immensely relieved at the interruption. "Excuse me, ladies."

Dorella's face looked worried as she appeared on the screen. "Lance, Pango's been trying to reach you all over the city. I'll put you on to him."

Mori's dark face replaced Dorella's. "Sorry to butt in on your social life, man. Have you heard from Segal?"

"No. Why?"

"Something I don't like."

"What's happened?" Lance looked across the room to the women, who were waiting patiently for him to finish his conversation. There was something almost predatory in their concentrated gaze. He focused his attention on Mori.

"Segal kept calling me by radio every so often, so I could plot his course on a map with magnetic markers. Then something wild happened to his radio."

"Wild?"

"There was a sudden sound like rushing wind. It built up to a shrill whistle, then ended in a crack. After that, I got no sound, except an occasional whisper of wind."

"Nothing else from Segal?"

"Nothing. I had the feeling his radio had been dropped out of the aircraft. Fell into sand, I'd say. I figure the thing's lying on a dune somewhere broadcasting wind, and I've no idea where Segal is."

"Think he might have gone overboard with his radio?"

"No, he'd have made some sound on the way down, even if it was only a scream."

"What about Red?"

"No sign of him. He hasn't come back, as far as I can find out. I didn't like the sounds I heard. I can only assume Red threw Segal's radio overboard."

"Why the hell should he do that?"

"I can think of several reasons, man. None of them I like."

For a moment, Lance said nothing. Then, "I'd better head back to the Star of the Outlands. When Red and Segal come back, they'll go there."

"You mean *if* they come back? I figure they're in something way over their heads." Mori hesitated. "Take care, man."

Lance walked back to the group of women as soon as Mori finished speaking. It was obvious they had heard every word both he and Mori had said, and they made no attempt to conceal it.

"You feel stable enough to drive yet?" asked Kalli.

"I'll be okay," said Lance.

"I'll follow him in one of the other cars," said Heidi.

"That's right." Jocasta moved closer to Lance and rested her cold, gloved hand on his shoulder, looking into his face. "You're important to us now. We have to look after you."

They all went out to the carport with him and stood watching as he climbed aboard his rented car. He still felt a trifle shaky from the stunning he had received earlier but was determined not to show it.

"He needs more adrenal," said Kalli softly.

"And pituitary," added Jocasta. She moved close alongside the car and looked intently into Lance's face. "Sit still for a moment," she said.

Something happened to him that he couldn't have defined in words—a curiously complex set of physical changes. Momentarily, he felt colder, then a quick sensation of intense energy flowed through him.

"Better?" asked Jocasta.

He had to admit to himself that he felt better than he recalled feeling for years. All the spontaneous vigor of youth had come back to him.

"Thank you for that," he said to Jocasta, without being certain exactly what she had done. He started his car and drove out of the carport, followed by Heidi in the red machine. She followed him until he parked outside the Star of the Outlands, then she waved and drove past, swinging back along the avenue out of sight.

Lance went straight to Segal's room, knocked, but had no response. Feeling an abrupt onslaught of fatigue, he went to his own room on the second floor.

He had not been asleep long before the buzzer of his radio awakened him. Rolling over, he switched on the bedside lamp.

Pango Mori's face showed on the small screen. "Are you all together yet, man?" he asked as Lance yawned, and when given a half-coherent affirmative he went on: "Red's just come in through the small West Airlock. And get this: He came in alone!"

"What's happened to Segal?" Lance was at once fully awake.

"Don't know."

"Where's Red now?"

"Getting out of his spacesuit. My guess is he'll head for the

Star. In case he goes anywhere else, I'll notify Magill, and his people can watch for him.''

Lance dressed quickly and stepped out onto the balcony. The great volume of air inside the domed city shielded it from sudden heat or cold, and although the temperature outside the domes would have dropped now to about a hundred degrees below freezing, it was little cooler inside than in daytime.

He watched the front archway leading into the quadrangle, and a few minutes later Red's figure came in, moving with long, loping strides toward the elevator. Lance walked along to the elevator shaft, but when he reached it the car was already humming its way upward. He saw the indicator register 4, then pressed the call button.

Red had obviously gone straight to the Ambon sisters. Lance waited impatiently for the car to return to his floor, then sprang in and pressed 4. At the top floor, Red was still standing at the door of the Ambon sisters' apartment, and as he heard the elevator arrive he spun around, looking at Lance with an expression of shocked recognition. He opened his mouth as if to say something, but at that instant the door opened, and he whirled back to face the sisters.

''What happened?'' came Belle's voice from within.

''I just got back.'' Red turned. ''Lance Garrith's here.''

Lance moved forward. ''Mind if I join you? I want to find out what happened to Des Segal.''

The sisters, evidently awakened by Red's arrival, still appeared to be fighting off the effects of sleep. They were fastening about them a short, enormously wide garment like a toweling wrap, reaching only to their knees. Below it, their legs and feet were bare, the double foot grotesquely broad.

''You'd better both come in,'' said Belle, and they stepped aside. Lance followed Red into the apartment.

Maya stretched an arm above her head, yawning. ''I'm no good this early without coffee,'' she said. They lurched into the kitchen the physical coordination between them not yet fully integrated. Their dark hair, unbound, drifted in two loose clouds about their heads in the low gravity.

Red followed the women at once into the small kitchen, and Lance sensed that he was trying to say something to them without being overheard. He moved quickly forward where he could hear what passed between them.

''As I said before,'' said Belle over her shoulder, while she and her sister began preparing the coffee. "What happened?"

"I lost Segal," said Red.

"You *what*?" shouted Lance.

"What happened?" snapped Belle.

"We were flying over the Badlands. Segal saw something on the ground that he wanted to investigate. I landed the roto on the nearest solid-looking ground, and he walked over to a sinkhole."

"What happened then?"

"I lost sight of him. The sinkhole was a couple of hundred meters away from me, and the edges sloped down into a deep hole. He climbed down into it. I waited in the roto for a quarter of an hour, then went looking for him. The edges of the hole were funneled out by wind erosion, slippery as hell. There were tunnels running three ways from the bottom of the hole—it was a place where the roof of an old, underground watercourse had fallen in, where a tributary met the main stream. I climbed down, but I didn't know which tunnel he'd taken, and I couldn't reach him by radio—the tunnels twisted in every direction."

"He still had his radio?" asked Lance.

"I gave him one when he left the aircraft."

"Did he have another radio when he went aboard?"

"Come to think of it, he did. Don't know what he did with that. We were using mine. Anyway, I couldn't find him—I had no lights to go searching underground. I waited until after dark, then headed home. I left a marker so I could find the same sinkhole."

"How much oxygen did he have?" asked Lance.

"Full supply when we left, and a couple of spare high-pressure cartridges, so he'll be okay for a few hours yet." Red looked at his watch.

"So he's still wandering around in the dark, underground," said Belle. Maya put a steaming cup of coffee in her sister's hand, then passed two others to Red and Lance. At a gesture from Belle, they all went out into the living room.

"We'd better go and look for him," said Belle.

"My office has notified Magill's that he's missing," said Lance.

The women studied him sharply. They seemed about to speak then Red said: "I'm the only one who knows just where he disappeared."

"That's right," said Belle, "and he hasn't much oxygen. If we leave it to Magill's people, all they'll find will be a dead body." She turned her head to look sidelong at her sister. "We

have bright handlamps in the storeroom.'' Turning back to Red,
she added, ''While we're there, you can help us into our spacesuit.''

Lance looked at the sisters in surprise. ''You're coming with
us? Out to the Badlands?''

''Yes,'' replied Belle. ''This is too important for us to dele-
gate.''

Half an hour later, Lance found himself in a rented spacesuit
sitting alongside Red in the back of a six-seater runabout, waiting
in the WG3 airlock for the outer doors to open. The Ambon sisters
sat in the front seat, gigantic in their double spacesuit, Maya doing
the driving with their left hand and foot. She drove skillfully and
efficiently, apparently unhampered by the suit.

As she drove out of the airlock, the sun was low in the east,
and the bright spot of Phobos or Deimos glowed above it in the
copper sky. They traveled westward for several kilometers along
a wide, vitrified road, with a wilderness of shallow, stony slopes
to either side. When they reached the airport, Red, using his suit
radio, directed Maya to one of the rotojets that was apparently
his, parked under one of the huge, transparent hangars erected to
protect the aircraft from the periodic Martian dust storms.

''If we lift off now,'' said Red, ''we should get no turbulence
until we hit the Badlands. After that, it's anyone's guess.''

Maya swung the car close to the indicated roto, and they climbed
out. The cabin of the roto had six seats, and as the sisters climbed
in to occupy the back pair, the springs of the undercart compressed
under their weight. Red took the pilot's seat, snapping a number
of switches as Lance climbed in beside him. The hydrogen jet
fired, and the broad rotor blades spun into a flickering ring of fire.

The machine took off with its high-pitched, pulsating scream,
slowly gaining height. As Red headed westward, no one spoke.

The spacesuit helmet made it impossible for Lance to see directly behind him, but as the aircraft had been built for people in
spacesuits it was well supplied with rear mirrors. In one of these,
Lance was able to see that the Ambon sisters were talking together
without using their suit radio, apparently able to hear each other
within their suit.

There were several maps in a recess in front of Lance, and he
selected the relevant one and spread it across his knees, trying to
keep track of their position. As long as he could see the tops of
a couple of giant volcanoes away to the northwest, pallid cones

against the lurid sky, he was able to stay oriented, but after a time they passed over rising ground that gave the appearance of an ancient seacoast, and the thin air became unexpectedly violent.

"Keep your belts tight," warned Red.

Soon they were passing over a chaotic region of broken ridges and gullies, and Lance soon lost any idea of where they were. He returned the map to its recess. Red, however, seemed to know exactly where he was all the time. After they had flown over the tormented landscape for an hour or more, he touched Lance's knee and pointed ahead.

"One of Karstrom's old launching towers," he said.

It may have been one of the towers Allen had pointed out to Lance from orbit. Seen closer, it looked older, its steel girderwork brown and corroded, stripped of all salvageable fittings.

After they had passed the tower, Red changed the aircraft's direction by a few degrees, a change noticeable only by the variation in the angle of the sunlight coming into the cabin. It occurred to Lance that Red had used the tower as a landmark.

A little later, when he glanced across, he saw Red's lips moving, but he could hear nothing on his radio. Suspecting that Red had switched channels, he began turning the channel selector on his own radio, but Red saw what he was doing and fell silent. Lance returned to the original channel.

"Who were you talking to?" he asked.

"Just talking to myself. I like doing that. I get such bright answers."

The wasteland below had not always been devoid of life. After continuing for a while, they flew over a long, paved runway with windblown sand encroaching on it. Farther on, Red reduced speed and flew low over a long, deep trench in the ground, where an underground channel seemed to have collapsed.

"Let's have a closer look at that," he said.

Killing his forward speed, he let the machine hover for a time, sinking vertically into the trench. It seemed to Lance too straight over too great a length to be a natural formation, a cleft two hundred meters wide and a hundred deep, reaching at least a couple of kilometers. Red lowered the roto and began moving slowly forward, the shriek of the jets echoing frenziedly from the walls to either side.

The sound died as the wheels touched the ground and the blades swung slowly to a stop, the air shimmering above the exhaust of their jets.

"Doesn't that look like a door up there?" Red switched on his powerful landing lights, probing the dark cavern at the end of the cleft.

"It looks like metal," agreed Lance.

"Let's find out," said Red, and climbed down out of the roto. After a short hesitation, Lance joined him.

"Wait," he said. "It mightn't be safe."

"I've got this," said Red, drawing a pistol-like object from an outside pocket on his suit.

"What's that?"

"Solenoid gun. High-power battery, coil, iron slugs. Deadly."

Lance thought suddenly of the man who had tried to disrupt the "Specialists' Report" program in Pacific City. He had been carrying the same type of gun—the first of its kind Lance had heard of. Things began to fall into place, and a chill came to him.

"Walk forward toward the door," said Red, a crisp hardness in his voice.

"Do as he says, Lance," came Belle's voice over the radio. "There's really nowhere else for you to go."

"What's the other side of that door?"

"What's grown from the Karstrom Foundation," said Belle. "Isn't that what you came here to look for?"

Red's voice came with a chuckle. "You might say you've walked right into it."

Uncomfortably aware of Red's solenoid gun, even though it was not pointing at him, Lance began walking toward the huge metal door. It was even larger that he had thought at first, close to a hundred meters high and fully as wide, set well back within the mouth of the cavern.

As he walked into the shadow of the walls, Lance noticed that they were made of some kind of molded concrete, the outer parts left irregular and colored to match the rocks of the surrounding landscape. What he had taken to be a rocky ridge beyond the great cleft was in reality an immense building disguised as a natural formation. With red rocks of the region cemented to its outer surface, it would easily escape observation from above.

He turned after he had covered a few meters and found Red walking a dozen paces behind him, the compact gun still held in his hand, although it was not leveled. Behind him strode the Ambon sisters, their faces hidden in the shadow of their outer helmets. Red gestured to him to keep moving.

Belle, who had apparently altered the channel selector of her radio, spoke into the microphone in her helmet. Lance could hear the muffled sound of her voice, but his own radio did not pick up what she was saying.

Perhaps in answer, the great door began to open in two halves which slid aside from a widening vertical crack, showing a space within flooded with red light, ending in another pair of doors set a considerable distance beyond. Obviously, the red-lit region was a huge airlock, at least five hundred meters long.

They walked into the lock across a smooth floor of gray concrete, the daylight behind them waning and shutting off as the outer doors closed with a metallic crash, leaving them in the eerie red-lit gloom. As they neared the inner doors, Belle, who seemed to have taken charge, said, "Wait here for the green light."

Lance could hear the hollow roar of air blasting into the lock, and at last the red lighting was replaced by white, with a single green light glowing above the inner doors. They slid slowly open, revealing beyond a vast, brightly lit, cavernous space with a paved floor, benches, and machinery like that of a highly advanced engineering workshop.

"Right," said Belle. "Now we can take off our helmets." They gestured to Lance to walk ahead of them through the second doorway, stopping near a table in the middle of the floor. While Red stood aside, still holding the solenoid gun, the sisters removed their helmets, both the outer metal ones and the transparent bubble helmets, placing them on the table. They gestured to Lance to do the same, and after some hesitation he obeyed. The air in the great room was thin and oxygen rich, but fresher than the air in his suit.

"You'd better wait here," Belle said to Red, who had not removed his helmet. Apparently hearing her through his suit radio, he gave a gesture of assent.

"Walk ahead of us," said Maya to Lance. He noticed that Belle was now holding Red's gun. Both women's faces looked quite dispassionate.

Lance began to precede them into the cavern, between trestle tables and heavier benches littered with complex apparatus that had a hurried, experimental look about it. He pointed ahead.

"What are those?"

"Starships," said Belle. "They'll be the first manned ships to reach another star system."

"Which system?"

"No matter. *They* know." Maya gestured forward. "The heads of the Karstrom Foundation. We're taking you to them now."

"What happens if I refuse to go on?"

Belle made a silent movement with the gun. Lance managed to smile, although it cost him a considerable effort of self-control.

"You're not going to kill me after going to all this trouble to bring me here," he said.

"True. But if you don't cooperate, we can disable you and carry you the rest of the way," answered Belle.

"Does that thing fire explosive bullets?"

"Not in here. Solid iron slugs. You have the choice of obeying or taking one in an arm or leg. Whichever you prefer."

"I'll cooperate," he said, and continued walking forward, the women's footsteps coming behind him. The cavern-like building was dimly lit by a few fluorescent tubes high on its walls, and its far end receded into gloomy distance. "How is it no one from outside ever found this place?" he asked.

"Some did," said Belle.

"None went back to report it," added Maya.

He thought that over for the next couple of hundred paces. Now it was becoming evident that he had underestimated the size of the two starships. They looked as if they were made of unmarked titanium, or some such metal, needle-nosed, with swept-back wings and fins for atmospheric maneuvering. The nearer one, at least, must have been five hundred meters long, and the one behind it, hidden in almost complete darkness, seemed basically similar.

"When will they be finished?" Lance asked in an awed voice.

"They made their experimental flights years ago," answered Maya.

"Wait here," said Belle, and as Lance stopped walking she lifted her voice in a shout that sent echoes booming down the building. "*Zon!*"

An answering shout in a voice like a clap of thunder came from the distance ahead, and more fluorescent lights came on in the upper part of the building. Bright light shone from a doorway in the side wall a couple of hundred meters ahead, and two figures emerged and began walking toward them.

Even the initial glimpse of them showed that they were gigantic and strange. As they drew nearer, Lance felt an eerie sense of horror.

They were like the figure in the picture taken by Jack Darch. Probably by the *late* Jack Darch.

chapter
19

LANCE LEANED BACK against one of the benches as the two figures came steadily nearer him, his pulse thudding audibly in his ears, his mouth dry. He realized now that he had always had the shadow of a suspicion that the photograph taken by Jack Darch had been faked, even after he had seen those monstrous footprints near the Star of the Outlands.

He had felt all along that the six-limbed, humanoid figure in the photograph had belonged in a bad dream. Yet here, with the suddenness of a single stride, two of these unbelievable beings had stepped out of his nightmare onto the concrete floor in front of him.

Seen in reality, they had a fluid, animal movement that immediately negated any suggestion of fakery. The leading figure was nearly three meters tall, the other only slightly shorter. Their approach was swift and purposeful.

Lance wrenched his gaze away from the advancing giants just long enough to look quickly over his shoulder at the Ambon sisters.

"They're aliens!" he shouted. "Not human! They've established themselves here already!"

The sisters did not speak. They glanced casually at the approaching beings as though quite familiar with their appearance, then continued to watch Lance.

All Lance's attention was now held by the taller of the two giants, who continued to walk toward him with a long, powerful stride. He halted a few paces in front of Lance, looking down at him with bright, cold eyes set in a massive head. The four long arms swung from openings in a brown garment like a sleeveless tunic, the upper pair lean and supple, the lower ones immensely muscular. The legs were like those of an ancient, bird-footed dinosaur, but smooth-skinned, not scaly.

"Are you from another star system?" asked Lance, thinking even as he spoke that the being might not understand his language. As it stared impassively down at him, it was joined by its shorter companion, which had creamy rather than tan skin, darker eyes, and straight, blue-black hair. The taller figure's hair was lighter colored.

"Why do you say that?" he asked in a booming voice that seemed to Lance to reverberate in his own chest.

"I heard a ship had come into the solar system from outside," said Lance, keeping his voice steady only with difficulty.

The giant nodded. "Logical, but no. That was one of our automatic vehicles returning with extra-system data." He glanced over to the Ambon sisters. "Our friends tell us you've been investigating our foundation. Why?"

Lance found the proximity of the two towering figures overwhelming. It occurred to him that he might be in danger of being killed within minutes, brushed aside like an annoying insect. Remembering the weak gravity, he flexed his knees and sprang lightly to stand on the bench, bringing his eyes closer to the level of those confronting him.

"I'm Lance Garrith, of Solar News," he said. "I'm a commentator on an Earth-wide network TV program called 'Specialists' Report.'" He paused for effect, detected no response, and continued, impelled by the certainty that he had to take some kind of initiative quickly to have any chance of staying alive. "I've been looking for you because I feel I may have something to offer you."

At least his impulsive outburst was unexpected enough to seize their attention. The two pairs of eyes, one pair steel gray and the other almost black, stared at him unblinkingly as if they were looking right into his head. The taller giant pointed to his own chest, then to his companion.

"My name is Zon. This is Meiko. What is it you offer us? Or are you simply talking to gain time?"

This was exactly what Lance had done, but in the seconds since his statement, his mind, racing with the stimulus of panic, kept him talking. "My specialty is presenting scientific facts in a form easily assimilated by a mass audience. I know you've been carrying out advanced research here for many years, yet as far as I've been able to see, very few people in the general population realize what you're doing. . . ."

It was the shorter giant who broke in, and from the deep, smooth voice he realized for the first time that she was female—something her name should have told him, had he not been confused by the nearness of two beings that still seemed to him alien. "You mean you're a specialist in public relations," she said, "and you'd like to act as our liaison officer, let's say?"

"Wait!" thundered Zon, before Lance had a chance to reply. "We have no intention of interacting with the old population."

Meiko spoke to her companion in a rapid torrent of words that Lance completely missed, and Zon answered her in the same way, without taking his eyes off Lance's face.

Looking back at him, Lance felt some of his fear abating. The great head seemed quite human, even handsome, with an enormous skull. While they confronted each other in silence, Meiko turned and walked away to where the Ambon sisters were standing, fifty or sixty meters off. The three of them spoke together briefly, and then Meiko came back, while the sisters each raised an arm to wave to Lance.

"Goodbye," they called, and as he acknowledged with a wave they pivoted around and set off with their measured stride back to the airlock.

Zon was still keeping his concentrated gaze on Lance. "You have obviously arrived here recently," he said. "Did you learn about this place before you left Earth?"

Lance had the feeling it would be useless to attempt to lie. "No," he admitted. "I didn't know it existed until the Ambon sisters and Red brought me here."

"Red?"

Meiko explained, "Belle and Maya's boy," gesturing toward the airlock, and Zon gave a grunt. He spoke again, very rapidly, incomprehensibly to Lance's ears, and Meiko seemed to make a sound of agreement. Unexpectedly, Zon reached forward and clapped a hand on Lance's shoulder.

"Your specialized knowledge may indeed be of use to us," he said, "although perhaps not exactly in the way you anticipated. Come with us, and we'll explain."

His lower arms, gorilla-like, massive as roof beams, reached forward and picked Lance up by the ribcage, lifting him with effortless ease to the floor. A moment later, he found himself walking along between the two giants, each of whom held him by a hand. He had a mental image of small children he had seen walking between their parents as they led him down the building to the side doorway through which light streamed.

* * *

The brightly lit doorway led to a passageway that sloped downward into what appeared to be an elaborately equipped laboratory. They led Lance along an aisle lined on either side with apparatus too complex and strange for him to even begin to comprehend. At one point, Zon paused, picking up a small device from a bench.

To Lance, it looked like a compact cassette recorder. Zon continued holding Lance's hand with one of his lower hands, while the upper pair extracted a tiny cassette from the device he was holding and replaced it with another taken from a drawer in the bench. Then they moved onward, turning into a smaller room with soft green walls, dark red laminated tables and large, green foam sofas.

"Now," said Zon, sitting on one of the sofas and waving Lance to one of the others, "in a little while, we'll explain to you exactly what we're doing here."

Meiko went away for a minute or two, then returned with a glass filled with some colorless liquid that seemed to be effervescent.

"Drink this," she said. Lance sipped some of the liquid, then looked at her inquiringly, noticing a taste he couldn't identify. "What's this?"

"Drink it. It will have the effect of enabling you to recall things we tell you, clearly and accurately."

Zon handed Lance the recorder he had brought from the laboratory. "This will help you remember," he said, "but there will be less chance of misunderstanding later if you absorb the information we give you quite clearly from the beginning."

Lance drank the liquid. Its effervescent, citrus flavor no doubt masked the taste of whatever active substances it contained. Meiko took the glass from him as he finished it, as she sat on another of the green sofas. "It will take a few minutes to be effective," she said.

"We'll wait," said Zon.

Lance looked from one to the other of the giants as they sat motionless in front of him. Their most salient characteristic seemed to be an intense vitality, as if they were fired by a superhuman enthusiasm. Just now, they looked completely relaxed, although at one moment a faint beep made Zon take a small device from his pocket. He looked at it, and spoke with such rapidity that Lance could not follow what he said. A muted voice from the thing in his hand answered him, and he snapped out some kind of command, then put the communicator back in his pocket, to all appearances as relaxed as before. Lance had the uncomfortable feeling that the passivity of these people was a surface illusion, like that of an apparently sleeping crocodile that could instantly flash into explosive ferocity.

"Controlled evolution," he said musingly.

"Nothing new in that," answered Zon. "Horse breeders and other animal breeders have used it for hundreds of years."

"But all mammals have four limbs. How is it that you have six?" A chill crept into his blood. "Are you really descended from human stock?"

"We came from here." Zon pointed to the floor, as if he had originated on that very spot. "Our foundation—an offshoot of the Karstrom Foundation—has been carrying on work in the fields of recombinant DNA and synthetic gene manipulation for a long time. We have traveled a long way."

Meiko took up the explanation. "The Martian settlements skimmed the cream from the top levels of the population of Earth. Now, we've skimmed the best from the Martian population. Someday, the same process will go onward, selecting the best from our descendants."

"It's a process that's gone on naturally since the beginning of life," added Zon. "All we've done is accelerate it, control it." He looked at what appeared to be a wristwatch.

"Why haven't you carried out your work openly?" asked Lance. "Published its results to be appraised by the whole Martian population?"

"In the earlier stages, our organization made mistakes," admitted Zon. "They had a number of failures which they thought it best to eliminate. That was an attitude unacceptable to the Martian people, and one that would have been utterly horrifying to Earth governments. That's why we moved our operations out here."

"I could help you here," said Lance. "I could publicize your work so that it's accepted by a large proportion of the people."

"Not large enough, yet," countered Zon. "It would need to be practically a hundred per cent before we released our data, and I can't see that happening this century. However, there may be a use for what you propose, although not in the way you suggest." He glanced again at his wristwatch.

"In what way, then?" asked Lance.

"In the interest of future historical accuracy," said Zon, "we can show you what we are achieving, not to release immediately on one of your evanescent programs, but to clear the record after we've left the solar system."

"Did you say you're leaving the solar system?" Lance leaned forward, wondering if they were aware of his carefully suppressed eagerness. This would make the greatest story ever to be aired on Earth-wide TV.

"You've seen our starships out there," said Zon.

"But can you actually reach another star system?"

"Our automatic vehicles have already made the journey a number of times and returned."

"But—how long will the voyage last?"

"Many years. We have a thoroughly tested system of suspended animation—but Meiko is the expert on that."

"We've perfected an entirely new method making use of molecular stabilization," said Meiko. "I can show you some of our capsules in use."

"But why go to another system?"

"Our earliest major achievements were two," explained Zon. "Prolonged lifetime and increased brain capacity. Once our type had been stabilized—as you see exemplified in Meiko and myself—the other developments followed easily: starship design, our suspended animation techniques that will make the voyage possible."

"But why go?"

"If we stayed in the solar system, we would eventually clash with the old population, which is not yet ready to interact with a life-form with approximately four times its brain capacity. You can easily foresee a war between us, extrapolating from mankind's earlier history. We would win, but at a terrible cost."

"And yet you'll sacrifice all the existing civilization built up over millennia?"

"No. We'll take with us micro-recorded copies of all the old human cultures—our base to build on."

"Even selected animals and plants in suspended animation," added Meiko. "But come. We'll show you some of the capsules already in use."

She led the way out of the room by a different door than the one through which they had entered it, Lance following her, Zon striding behind him. They passed through an airlock into a long gallery, dark when they first entered, but brilliantly lit when one of them threw a switch.

Lance felt his pulse quickening. God, if he could get even a recording of these people and their creations on "Specialists' Report," the program would be immortal!

Meiko led him to a long, transparent chamber, one of several hundred vanishing down a vast perspective along the gallery. Only a few hundred meters of the gallery were lighted, but he could see that it extended far beyond that.

Inside the chamber slept a naked figure like Zon, with wires running from little sensors attached to various parts of its body. A small green light glowed above one of the capsules farther down the line, and Meiko said, "Come and look at this."

Another six-limbed figure lay within this capsule, this time a female. Where the man in the first capsule had been completely inert, she showed twitching facial movements.

"She's waking up!" said Lance.

"No," answered Meiko. "We don't keep them in molecular stable condition all the time. At intervals, they're brought up to the level of REM sleep—you know?—but not to full consciousness. We've found that's better for the sleeper."

"You must have wondered what had happened to your friend," broke in Zon. "Come over here."

He led Lance across to one of a row of the capsules set aside from the main lines. In it was a figure much smaller than the six-limbed occupants of the others. Moving quickly forward, Lance gave a shout.

"Segal! What have you done to him?"

There were a number of other men in capsules. Lance tried to recall what he'd heard of the description of Jack Darch.

"You're taking them with you?" he asked, whirling to face Zon.

"No. Their physique would not be suitable for our new home."

"Where is it? A planet of Alpha Centauri? Of Barnard's Star? Tau Ceti?"

"You don't need to know that," said Zon sharply. "Neither does anyone else. Anyway, you wouldn't even have a name for it."

"What happens to the people you leave behind?" Lance indicated the capsule containing Segal.

"We'll bring them out of stasis before we leave. Then we'll turn them loose near a geological station or mining camp, somewhere they'll be found."

"And what happens to me?"

"Valuable individual as you are," said Meiko, smiling, "we can't take you to our new home. Your physique would not be suitable."

"Now," said Zon, "let's work out the body of data you'll pass on to the population we'll be leaving behind."

They began explaining their systems with a rapidity that left his mind numbed with the inflow of information, despite the clarity of the presentation. The life-support systems of the capsules, monitoring blood and oxygen supply, heartbeat and respiration, were all in triplicate. The pulse and breathing seemed frighteningly slow to Lance, and the temperature of the capsules felt so low that he couldn't understand why it did not kill the occupants. Yet Zon and Meiko assured him that their systems had been thoroughly tested.

"Who puts the last one to sleep?" he asked.

"In practice, it's all pre-programmed, computer monitored," said Meiko. They had stopped in front of a capsule that was empty, a sealable door open at one end. Meiko picked up a case of instruments from a nearby bench.

Zon, who had moved behind Lance, suddenly took hold of his wrists and ankles with his four hands, lifting him easily. Meiko turned quickly, her larger pair of hands stripping off his left glove and pushing up his sleeve, holding his arm as if in a vise. Simultaneously, her slimmer, upper hands held an old-style hypodermic syringe vertically, expelling air until a drop of fluid appeared at the tip of the needle. A hand—he did not know whose—swabbed his arm with a chilling liquid.

"Here—" began Lance. The needle stung his arm muscle lightly. "What are you doing?"

A rushing sound built up in his ears. Meiko looked at him with a vivid smile that made her seem suddenly very young.

"You'll be our living time capsule," she said.

Lance was still trying to work out what she meant when the darkness came. . . .

chapter
20

IT WAS DIFFERENT from ordinary sleep. He was left with the impression of the passage of an enormous period of darkness and silence in which fleeting fragments of dreams, or memories of dreams, flitted like shadows.

Consciousness first began to creep back with light glowing redly through his closed eyelids. He tried to open his eyes, but the lids seemed to be stuck tightly shut. Dimly, he felt something being placed over his eyes, shutting out the red glow like a piece of dark felt resting on his face.

There were sounds somewhere in his vicinity—the murmur of voices, and much farther away an uneven, hollow roaring and clanking, like the noises made by large earth-moving machines. He lay still, letting awareness gradually seep back into his mind.

He tried to concentrate on one voice that seemed clearer than the others—a woman's voice, deep and smooth. The words meant nothing to him at first, and then he became aware of a phrase or two, repeated over and over.

". . . inject two cc's of fluid from the green hypodermic syringe, as shown in the diagram . . . two cc's of fluid from the green hypodermic syringe, as shown . . . fluid from the green hypodermic . . ."

Slowly, the words wore their way into his consciousness with the persistence of running water. He began to recognize the voice. It was the voice of Meiko, but speaking with an unaccustomed slowness, like a woman talking patiently to a retarded child. The repetition bothered him, especially as the words were being repeated with exactly the same inflection, and sometimes broken in the middle of a word.

Then the truth filtered through the haze that was still engulfing his mind. He was listening to a recording of Meiko's voice played by someone who was following her instructions step by step. He felt the sting of a needle in his arm, the slight localized pressure of the fluid until it dispersed along his veins.

"That's it," came a somewhat raucous masculine voice. "What now?"

The recorded voice continued: ". . . green hypodermic syringe, as shown in the diagram. Next, bathe the eyes with cold water, with three drops from the violet phial dropped into one hundred milliliters of the water . . . Next—" The instruction was repeated several times, as someone ran the recorder back, then Lance started slightly as the piece of dark material was lifted away from his closed eyes.

"There!" said a second masculine voice. "He moved a bit! D'ja see it?"

"I saw it," came a reply from the first man who had spoken. "We're getting him back! Better step away a bit, mate—you, too—he might need all the air he can get."

There was a mumble of voices. Lance felt cold water on the upper part of his face, some of it running into his eyes, and a piece of cloth mopping the surplus away. The stickiness lessened between his eyelids, and he experimentally opened them slightly.

He was lying in an enormous room, its arched roof high above him, with weak sunlight streaming in from one side. There were four men standing near him, and it took him a few seconds to focus his eyes on them. He had vaguely expected white-clad doctors or medical aides, but these men looked like construction workers. They wore tough-looking bright yellow coveralls and hard, shockproof hats of what looked like yellow fiberglass, except for the man closest to him, who wore a white hat of similar type with a red cross enamelled on the front of it.

This was evidently the man who had injected the fluid into him. He had a square, ordinary-looking face, unexpectedly suntanned.

"Hyar, mate," he said as he saw Lance's eyes open. "We gotcha back!"

Lance tried to say "Thanks," but as yet he couldn't get his vocal apparatus under control.

"Don't try to talk yet, mate," advised the square-faced man. "I'm Harry Green. I'm the doc on this project." He swept his arm around to indicate his surroundings.

Lance managed to whisper his name. "I'm Lance Garrith. Lance Garrith, of Solar News."

"Sole what?" asked Green.

"Solar News."

Green looked around at the other men. "Anyone know it?"

"Never heard of it," said one, and the others shook their heads.

Lance closed his eyes for a moment, then reopened them, trying without success to lift his head. "Where are we?"

Green gave a cheerful grin. "Place hasn't got an official name yet. We're putting in a landing strip. We cut into this hillside, found all this. Looks as if it's been forgotten for a hundred years. You're the only bloke left here—but they must have meant you to be found. They put notices up, arrows, left instructions for getting you awake." He put out his hand. "Don't try to get up yet. Plenty of time for that."

"What year is this?" croaked Lance.

"Two oh nine."

"What's that in A.D.?"

Green spun around and looked at the youngest of his three companions. "You were the last at school, Gino. How you work out A.D.?"

"I forget."

Green turned back to Lance and shrugged. "Anyway, wassit matter? You're alive."

"Yes," said Lance. "Yes. Thanks for that."

"Thank the lady who left the instruction disk. She was good. Thought of everything. We couldn't go wrong."

"Yes," murmured Lance. "She was good."

"What was she like?"

"Oh—different."

"Yah. She sounded different." Green backed away slightly. "You get some rest for a while. No hurry."

Lance closed his eyes as the four moved away from him. He noticed they had left a container of water beside him. The hollow, metallic sounds like those of earthmoving machines continued. Experimentally, he began moving his neck, then his fingers, arms, feet. Some of his joints made sounds like rusty hinges. Innumerable needles seemed to stab him all over his body, but by slow degrees the sensation wore away. At last, he was able to observe his surroundings more clearly.

He was in the same vast room where he had first met Zon and Meiko, but it had changed almost beyond recognition. The two great starships were gone, and so was much of the machinery and the complex apparatus that had littered the benches. The floor was covered with dust so thick that it showed the footprints of his rescuers. But the major change was that a hundred meters of one of the walls had been knocked down, leaving long mounds of rubble through which a pathway had been cleared by something like a bulldozer.

It was through the break in the wall that the sunlight was entering. Outside the opening, huge, lemon-yellow machines lumbered about in clouds of reddish dust. But there was something different about the very sky.

The pink and coppery shades had gone, and the area of sky he could see from here was of a deep violet color, shading to a greenish tint near the horizon. For the first time, he realized the significance of the fact that Harry Green and his associates were not wearing spacesuits, not even respiratory masks. They were breathing the Martian air without any respiratory equipment—and so was Lance himself.

He raised his head and looked down the length of his body, which was naked, with a few wires running from sensors stuck to his skin at various points. He was lying on a pallet that had apparently been slid out of the cylindrical capsule in which he had been in stasis.

Stasis—for how long?

After the first joyful surprise at finding himself alive, a paralyzing horror crept over him. How long had he been in the capsule? Green and the other men had never heard of Solar News, the greatest information network in the solar system. Enough time had passed for Mars to have been terraformed to the point where men could breathe in the open. As to Zon, Meiko and their companions, they must have gone so long ago that these men, discovering their base of operations by accident, were unaware of what they had found.

He must have slept for a while, because when Harry Green returned to him with a steaming mug of some beverage in his hand, the angle of light through the gap in the wall had changed markedly.

"Sip this," said Green. "I've put something in it to get you more with it."

Gratefully, with Green supporting him with a hand behind his head, Lance drank the soup-like liquid. It was true that he began to feel better almost immediately, so that after a minute or two he swung his legs off the pallet and began to stand up.

"Take it easy," cautioned Green, an arm around his shoulders.

"Thanks for all this," said Lance.

"Us Earthies have got to stick together."

For the first time, Lance realized something that had been nagging at his mind since his awakening. Green and his companions were not Martians. They had the physique of Earthmen.

"Yes," said Lance. "You're all Earthies, aren't you?"

"Course. All our gang. You wouldn't get Martians sweating around in dust like this. They pay well enough to bring us all the way from Earth to do the hard work. Crazy, right? Still, it's worth it to us."

"How long d'you stay here?"

"Contract's two Martian years, but we can renew it if we want to at the end of our spell. Think I will. The money's damn good by our standards. And employment-wise, there's nothing happening back home."

With Green still partly supporting him, Lance took a few tentative steps, shivering a little in the cool air.

"You'd better get something on," said Green, and he picked up a pair of yellow coveralls of the type worn by the other construction workers. "I picked out these for you—they look about your size. There are some clothes in a locker over there that we figured were yours, but they look like something for a masquerade."

Lance found the coveralls fitted him reasonably well. He looked at his wrist. "I had a watch."

"Yah. It's over there with your gear. Battery's shot. We couldn't start it for you—it doesn't take a standard battery."

"I used to feel lost without it." Lance gave a sour smile. "But time doesn't matter much now. Looks as if I've lost contact with everyone I used to know."

"Hey," said Green suddenly. "You'd be able to settle an argument we've been having ever since we smashed our way in here. Who built this place? The Pilgrims?"

Lance looked at him blankly. "The Pilgrims?"

"Yah. The Star Pilgrims. Whoever put you in stasis must have been them."

"I never heard them call themselves pilgrims."

"S'pose they wouldn't. Star Pilgrims was the name that stuck to them, after they went. Like the Pilgrim Fathers that sailed from one side of the Atlantic Ocean to the other—only these went from Mars to some other star system. I never met anyone who'd seen one. Djou see any of them?" Suddenly excited, Green looked expectantly at Lance.

"I saw a couple of them."

"Hey! We could make a lot of money out of this! Look, there's a crowd got a TV station in Argyre that run odd-ball interviews. I could get you on the air."

"Let me get my bearings first."

"Sure. We've got all the time in the world. Say, I'm flying over to Argyre on the weekend. I could take you. That's two sols from now." Apparently, the suggested name "sol" for the Martian "day" of 24 hours, 37 minutes and 23 seconds had gone permanently into the language.

When they reached the opening in the wall, Lance was astounded at the change wrought in the landscape of jumbled ridges and gullies he remembered from the time Red and the Ambon sisters had brought him here. A vast, level runway seemed to extend for several kilometers, the cleared ground bordering it coming close against the wrecked wall of the concealed workshop.

"What's the runway for, out here in the Badlands?"

"Emergency strip for spacecraft." Green pointed. "The boss was lucky here. Much nearer this way, and we'd have had to reposition the runway, or else get into an unholy tamarsha with the archaeologists."

"What's that?" Lance pointed to a tall, mushroom-shaped tower on a ridge a few kilometers away, with a shimmer of moving air above it.

"That? One of the atmogens. They're scattered all over the planet."

"Atmogen?"

"Atmosphere generator. Gets oxygen out of the rocks, releases it as a gas. That's how we can breathe out here, mate." Green gave a sudden grin. "Not too well, yet, but we're getting there."

The great yellow excavating machines had all fallen silent, and the men who had been operating them were converging on the break in the wall. Green looked at his watch.

"Time to eat. Will you join us?"

As the men who had been driving the excavators and leveling machines came in, each of them gave Lance a curious glance, and some volunteered a perfunctory greeting. Two or three of them were women, which Lance noticed only as they came closer to him, for all of them wore the same yellow coveralls and boots.

A few of the long tables near the break in the wall had been swept clear of their century-long accumulation of dust, and it became evident that the construction people had fallen into the habit of using one as a dinner table. On a shorter table nearby, also swept clean, they had set up a large metal urn like a Russian samovar, and alongside it what appeared to be a microwave oven. Following the electric leads, Lance saw that the power source of both of these units and a number of nearby standard lamps was a single rounded metal object about the size of a football. It hummed softly, as if its bomb-like shell contained a powerful generator.

The food, prepacked, was like a Japanese *bento*, each man or woman supplied with a plastic lunchbox. Green gave one to Lance. It was warm, having been put in the microwave oven.

"Better not eat too much at the start. The woman warned us about that on the disk she left for us to thaw you out."

The food was warm and tasty, but Lance found he was unable to identify most of its components. Some of it looked like lasagna, and there were small vegetables that might have been unusually flavored potatoes, but the meal seemed balanced enough, and was satisfying.

"I'll take you over to Argyre with me the sol after tomorrow," said Green as they sat eating. "By the way, you'll need credit for food, things like that. I can get you fixed up with a credit card. I can back it up for a reasonable amount—should help you get by until you can make a deal with the TV station. After that, you can pay me back."

"That's very kind of you."

"No worries. I think we could be on to something good."

Lance rested and recuperated during most of the next day—or sol, to use the local idiom—and the following morning Green took him out to a private aircraft for the journey to Argyre.

The Argyre Depression was an area somewhat like the larger Hellas, well below the Datum Level of the Martian surface, which had been surveyed where the original atmosphere had a pressure of 6.1 millibars, the limit at which exposed water could remain liquid. The generation of extra atmosphere by the atmogens had altered the landscape dramatically. As they skimmed over it in Green's flier, Lance was astounded at the changes wrought during his century in stasis.

The thickening of the atmosphere had enabled transport to be carried out with relatively conventional aircraft. The whirling rotor blades with small jets near their tips had fallen out of use, and the new machines had long, fixed wings of gossamer lightness, usually translucent. The power source, however, seemed to be one of the bomb-like generators connected to long tubes running across the wings parallel to the axis of the aircraft. Green called these electrojets, and as he noticed the shimmer of St. Elmo's fire behind them, Lance recalled where he had first seen something like them—on the menacing little automatic craft that had pursued him and Segal through the desert night so long ago.

As they flew farther into the depression, he found himself looking down on an almost Earthlike scene of plowed fields, strips of forest and irrigation canals, their silvery water open to the air—something that would have been impossible in the Mars he had known before his period of stasis.

"How long did it take to terraform all this?" he asked Green.

"Oh, they put the first of the atmogens in about a hundred years ago. You can pick a few of the old ones out by their style of construction: sort of square, rolled iron girders, bolted and riveted together. Clumsy looking, but they've let them stay in among the newer type—the more the better. Now you can breathe anywhere in Argyre."

"It must have taken an enormous amount of work to put these machines all over the planet."

"The newer type—the ones that look like giant mushrooms— were designed by the tetrabrachs, before they left the planet. Not that they needed them for themselves, just as a gesture of goodwill to the other local Martians. They use them, keep building more to the same design, but I don't think they feel grateful. Funny, isn't it? The tetras gave them a livable world, but they don't appreciate it, don't even admit it. It's obvious to us Earthies when we come here from outside, but the local types don't see it."

"Why?"

"I think they feel there was so much else that the tetras could have given them, like starships. Maybe the tetras thought they couldn't trust 'em with some of their more advanced things."

"No one likes to feel they're completely outclassed by someone else, Harry."

"Suppose that's right. Although, come to think of it, these Martians outclass us in technology, but we don't get uptight about it. Like the jets driving this aircraft—we don't have these back on Earth."

"That's a tetra invention," said Lance thoughtfully.

"Don't think so . . . Is it?"

"It is. I'd seen it on a surveillance machine before I was put into stasis."

"A hundred years ago? Yeah?"

"That's right."

"I'll be damned. They never told us those things had been given to them." Green laughed. "Wait until you're ready to go on TV! Anyway, as I was saying, we don't get uptight about feeling outclassed by the Martians. We come here, work for a while at rates of pay that'd be astronomical back on Earth, then go home and enjoy it. Take everything as it comes—I reckon that's the best attitude, wherever you go."

Green landed his aircraft at an airfield close to the center of the main city of the Argyre Depression. Named simply Argyre, it had a number of focal points dominated by tall, frail-looking buildings that looked as if they were made of metal and tinted glass.

From the airport, they rode a moving walkway into the heart of the city, a mode of transport Lance expected to be slow until Green pointed out to him that there were a number of differently colored adjacent belts in the system, each traveling about one walking speed faster than the one beside it. Green took him by the hand and led him on swiftly accelerating, sidestepping leaps from one belt to the next, until they were leaning forward into the wind, eyes slitted, skimming at the speed of a fast car. Lance had the uncomfortable foreboding of what might happen if the belt suddenly jammed, allowing their momentum to hurl them forward, but no such idea seemed to enter Green's head.

Pointing forward, he said "Now!" and drew Lance sideways again onto successively slower belts until they stepped off onto ground that to Lance seemed for several seconds to be moving backward.

"First," said Green, "we'll get you that credit card."

He took Lance along a broad sidewalk with tinted glass and metal buildings along one side of it. On the other side was a wide road where extraordinary vehicles streamed along, a few moving on wheels, but most skimming clear of the surface, like hovercraft.

Yet there was a vital difference between them and hovercraft. There was no roaring downward blast of air or gases supporting them. Lance would have thought them lifted by magnetic repulsion, had the road surface been of metal, but it was not. The surface looked like ceramic, or perhaps vitrified sand. The machines seemed to generate some force that acted like a reverse of gravity, controllable and limited to a short range. It was something completely new to him.

Oddly dressed people walked past along the sidewalk, some of them glancing curiously at the two Earthmen. Almost all the passersby were tall, with the long, slim, low-gravity legs and deep chests that gave them a slightly congested appearance. Some of the women wore bizarre hairstyles and outlandish makeup.

Green took Lance into a credit office where he was photographed and had a minute particle clipped from a fingernail for analysis. After a short interval he was supplied with a credit card on which a magnetic pattern had been imprinted, together with a photograph of his head and shoulders, and a thumbprint. Green guaranteed him for a certain amount of credit.

"I'll get it back," he said confidently, "as soon as you make your hit with the media. Now, let's find you a place to sleep."

Lance, still shaken and confused from the after-effects of the prolonged stasis, was happy to let Harry Green make all his arrangements. The differences between the Mars in which he had entered stasis and this century-later world were overwhelming. Although the pink and copper sky of the old Mars had gone, the deep violet sky that had replaced it was just as alien to his terrestrial eyes, and its sheer unexpectedness added to his sense of unreality.

After all, when he had first come to Mars, he had been prepared for most of the things he had found by what he had read of the place, and the pictures he had seen. But this new world made a thousand assaults on his expectations.

Green booked him into a kind of motel evidently used mostly by farmers staying the night in Argyre after driving their produce in from outlying parts of the surrounding plains. Green gave him a drink of something that promised to "steady him down a bit," and when he left, Lance stretched out on the bed and was almost instantly asleep.

He must have slept right through the evening and night, waking with the windows of his room filled with the light of a weirdly colored sunrise.

He used the needle shower attached to his room, then went out to explore the shopping center adjoining the motel, still wearing his yellow construction worker's coveralls, which did not seem to arouse much interest among the other people he saw, all of whom were native-born Martians obviously accustomed to seeing an occasional Earthborn worker.

He found a fast-food shop and used his credit card to obtain a meal, which he chose almost at random from a number behind transparent doors in a form of automat.

The meal was tasty, although he could not identify its components. Finishing it, he strolled through the shopping center until he came to a store selling clothing—men's and women's, as if there was little distinction between them. Using his credit card, he was able to change his coveralls for a suit of smooth, beige material of the type worn by most of the men he saw about. He had to take the largest size available in stock, to enable him to fit his muscular thighs, hips, chest and shoulders into it. The legs were too long, but an assistant at the store shortened them for him.

As he looked at the final result in a mirror, he saw that his beard was beginning to grow visible. On the direction of the assistant, he was able to find a general store where he bought a compact electric razor with a tiny battery that gave its little motor surprising power.

Returning to his motel room, he shaved. He found he was feeling relaxed—more relaxed than he remembered being for years. The world of the year 209 began to take on the look of an interesting place to explore.

Then the visiphone bell tinkled.

Lance walked over to the control and pressed the key that opened the channel. A woman's face looked out at him from a large 3D screen.

"Lance Garrith?" she asked.

He had never seen her before, nor anyone like her. Her hair, drawn straight back from a large forehead, was in alternating stripes of yellow and deep blue, and there was something strange about her eye makeup, although the total effect had an off-key attractiveness. One eyebrow was blue, the other yellow, with the colors reversed in the shading below them.

"Yes?" he said, wondering how she had known he was here.

"I'm calling for Karu Vorl. Will you be at your motel thirty minutes from now?" Her accent was odd, unplaceable.

"Sure. Why?"

"Okay if Karu Vorl calls on you?"

"Fine. But I don't know anyone of that name. What's it about?" Lance thought it unwise at this stage to point out that he knew absolutely no one in this city.

"I'm speaking from Argyre Instant Update Newscasts. I understand you just came out of stasis."

"That's right."

"Good. Karu Vorl's a historian. Wants to interview you about the period you came from."

"I'll be here."

As the screen blanked out, Lance crossed the room and surveyed his reflection in a wall mirror. The little electric shaver had done an excellent job, and it occurred to him that he was fortunate that Meiko's molecular stabilization chamber had temporarily stopped such physical processes as the growth of hair. The new clothes he had bought looked odd to him, like gear thrown together for a masquerade, but their style did not clash with the apparel worn by other people he had seen on the street.

He kept looking at his new watch. As the time neared thirty minutes after he had received the visiphone call, he went out onto the porch in front of his unit and looked up and down the street. A media interview! His life was beginning again!

Argyre Instant Update Newscasts was probably located in the center of the city, where he could see high, delicately colored towers hazy with distance, like pictures on a stained glass window. A few translucent-winged aircraft gleamed against the violet sky, and lower down he could see vehicles streaming on elevated roads among the towers.

He kept watching the traffic coming from the direction of the shimmering towers, glancing repeatedly at the watch Green had given him. It felt good to have the dimension of time added to his life again, as if it conferred structure to an otherwise meaningless flow.

At last, one of the skimming, ground-effect cars slowed as it approached him and sidled off the street onto a strip of moss lawn in front of the motel units. It was open-topped, sleek with unnecessary streamlining. Sitting within it was a fat woman with white hair swept back from a high, broad forehead, a single blueblack lock beginning at the hairline and waving back in striking contrast to the white.

The car came quite close to him, silent except for a muted hum hovering half a meter above the lawn.

"Lance Garrith?" asked the fat woman in a deep, smooth voice. When he nodded, she added: "I'm Karu Vorl." The door on the right side of her car, the side near him, slid open. "Come in," she said.

Lance slid into the seat beside her, and she turned to face him. Her eyes were vividly blue, reminding him of Heidi's eyes as the surveyed every part of his body with candid curiosity. He didn' mind that, as it gave him a license to study her the same way. He suppressed a shudder.

Her age was hard for him to determine—perhaps forty-five Earth years. She had the typical Martian characteristics of a broad, plump, pallid face between hunched-up shoulders, as if her neck had been pushed down into her rounded torso. The torso was huge, with a wrap-around turquoise dress stretched over heavy shoulders and high-set, bulging breasts above an enormous stomach. She held out a large hand, her vivid cyclamen lips curved in a smile that made her smooth cheeks seem even plumper.

"Welcome to our century." Her hand was soft yet strong as she gripped his.

Facing forward, she set the car in motion. The controls seemed concentrated on a single lever with a small wheel on top of it. She steered with her hand covering the wheel, pushing it forward and pulling it back to brake or increase speed.

"I've checked up on your earlier career," she said. "I understand you ran a TV program on Earth with a worldwide linkup. Right?"

"True. 'Specialists' Report,' we called it."

"And you came to Mars to investigate an unexplained object coming into the solar system. Yes?"

"That's right. Apparently it was a probe returning—"

"Sent out by the tetrabrachs, yes. I understand they placed you in stasis."

"They explained—" He hesitated. "I've just remembered something: They gave me a little recorder to keep an explanation of everything they showed me—every project they'd worked on! That could be invaluable—but I've lost it!"

The woman raised her free hand and shook it from side to side, a gesture evidently equivalent to a head-shake. "It's all right. It's not lost. I have it. But I'd like to hear your impressions of the tetrabrachs when we get to my office."

He looked at her profile—the massive forehead, short nose, plump cheeks, and double chin, the large, rounded shoulders lifted almost to her ears, so that her head was apparently unable to move independently of her torso. He wondered how she could see traffic at the sides of her vehicle at intersections, and then he noticed, just below the windshield, three little TV screens that enabled her to see what was beside and behind her car. She drove quickly and confidently, one plump hand doing all the work. At one moment she lifted the other hand and looked at a tiny watch set on a finger-ring. Her sight must have been unbelievably sharp, because Lance, sitting beside her, could not see whether the watch was digital or of dial format.

Satisfied that she could not turn to look at him while driving, Lance glanced downward. Beneath the smooth bulge of her body, a pair of small, childish legs were bowed inward, their neat, bare, prehensile feet resting on a keyboard. The toes looked lean and supple on the almost infantile feet.

"Here we are," she said suddenly, and swung the car off the road into a parking lot adjoining a group of buildings of strange geometrical complexity. The door slid open beside Lance, and he stepped out. Karu Vorl emerged from the other side of the car, but she didn't *step* out. Her seat came out with her, hovering above the ground like the car, without visible support. She glided swiftly and noiselessly around the car to join Lance, rising higher above the ground until her face was level with his. He saw now that her seat was like a floating saddle, its movements controlled by her toes on the keyboard. Her large arms hung down at her sides, her hands swinging below the level of the saddle.

"Come inside, Lance," she said. She leaned forward and glided to the door of the nearest building, the door sliding open at her approach. Inside, blue and green light filtered through translucent walls. She led the way into a circular room that seemed to have no ceiling, forming the bottom of a round shaft that extended up fifty or sixty meters. She reached out and took hold of Lance's arm, thrusting her other hand into a luminous pattern of light-streaks like an unfocused hologram.

Suddenly, Lance found himself lifted off the ground, as if he were in free fall. His solar plexus seemed to contract into a knot as he looked downward at the receding floor. When they were perhaps fifty meters above its level, the upward movement stopped, and a horizontal force swept them through a doorway onto a solid floor. Lance felt sweat running down his back. The woman led the way to another door, which again opened at her approach, and into a large room with windows overlooking a luxuriant park. Looking down at the trees, Lance realized that water was no longer a problem on Mars, and the irrelevant thought seemed to calm him.

Karu Vorl glided across beside him, putting a thick arm around his shoulders. "Sit down here," she said, and guided him to a molded sofa that seemed to float unsupported in the air. He was reminded of the magnetic seats in Mort Channing's office so long ago in Pacific City—something excitingly new then, but taken for granted a century or more later.

He sat, and she moved around facing him. "Now," she said, "tell me about the tetrabrachs. I know they were six-limbed. Were they four-handed the way I am?"

"No. Their lower arms were developed from legs, but they were very strong. The legs below seemed to have been added."

"Yes," she said, "by recombining synthetic DNA. What else about them do you remember?"

"They had enormous brains."

"Bigger than mine?"

"Much bigger. But they were very big people."

"Any formation like this?" She spun around, her hand indicating the back of her shoulders, where a broad, smooth hump seemed to extend across behind her shoulderblades.

"Now that I think of it, yes."

She turned to face him again, her eyes thoughtful. "That houses brain tissue for augmented memory storage. They must have used the technique, too, long before us." A vertical crease deepened between her brows. "They seem to have evolved farther and faster than we thought. It's so hard to get reliable data."

"I think they had some way of controlling people by a form of hypnosis. Someone made a man try to shoot me while I was on air in a TV station."

"Ah, I remember seeing records of that."

"You seem to have an extraordinary memory for detail."

"I *am* a historian. And I have augmented memory." Her eyes darkened. "Although the tetras seem to have been ahead of us in that. It looks as if they incorporated extra brain tissue within the skull, not just down the spine."

"Would that make any difference?"

"Of course. Closer connections. Faster retrieval. Never mind. Let's get on with what we're doing. . . ."

Karu Vorl was a skilled interviewer, something Lance was able to appreciate. They worked steadily for about four hours, digging up all kinds of miscellaneous details of life in his own century, building the total picture unhurriedly, like a jigsaw puzzle. Immersed in his description of life on Earth more than a hundred years ago, Lance was frequently surprised to find that things he considered banal needed explanation now, a measure of the gigantic strides human culture had made during his period in stasis.

At last, when he found momentary difficulty in recalling some detail, Karu Vorl switched off her recording apparatus.

"You're getting tired. I'd forgotten fatigue would catch up with you quicker than with us." She glided toward him, her blue eyes alight with enthusiasm. "We have material for a major series here: Earth life at the period just at the end of Earth's dominance of the solar system. The series will make you famous, bring more money that you've ever seen. Rani will arrange all that, of course."

"Rani?"

"You met her on the screen—the girl with the blue and yellow striped hair. She's a perfectionist. She'll want to arrange your contract before we begin work again."

"When's that?"

"Come back here in three hours. Explore some of the little shopping arcades and parks down below."

"Do I have to go down that elevator shaft without an elevator?"

"The grav shaft?" She laughed. "I'll take you down."

She rode down with him in the shaft. Stepping into it with a gulf of fifty meters below him, supported only by the absence of normal gravity—whether it was canceled or opposed within the shaft, he didn't know yet—he controlled his vertigo by keeping his attention focused on the woman beside him.

"We never had these," he said. "We used cars hung on cables."

"That sounds unsafe."

"What happens here if the power fails?"

"It can't. There's a triple backup."

A term he'd heard used by the tetras. Had they presented these people with the grav shaft, too?

At the main floor of the building, Karu showed him how to operate the pattern of colored hologram streaks for the return journey. As she explained it, something in her expression reminded him of Heidi.

Heidi, now lost to him a century in the past. Or was she still living? He wasn't sure he wanted to see Heidi at a hundred and thirty Martian years of age. He was suddenly aware that Karu Vorl was looking at him intently.

"What happened?" she asked. "You seemed to think of something."

"Nothing, really. Just for a moment, you reminded me of someone I knew before I was put into stasis."

"On Earth?"

"No. Here on Mars."

She looked thoughtful. "It's possible. There were some clones of ours around in that period. Blond, tall. We modified the body-pattern later. One you might remember, a woman with one eye. Thyra. Eyepatch."

"Thyra, yes. I remember her, but she was blind."

Karu hesitated. "Then you knew her before she had her eye transplant."

"There was another clone of hers, younger, called Heidi."

"There have been many of us. Scattered, now, all over the solar system."

He wondered what had happened to Heidi. Karu had not volunteered to tell him. He was torn by an inner conflict—the desire to know what had happened to Heidi, and the fear of what he might hear if he persisted.

The woman seemed trapped in her own thoughts, too. "Scattered," she repeated, as if speaking to herself. "Once, we could all keep in contact with each other." A shadow of anger passed over her face. "But I'm getting lost in the past. You might say that's an occupational hazard for a historian, right?"

He carefully controlled his voice. "What happened to Heidi?"

The woman gave a vague gesture with her hand. "I don't know. Some of the older women in our group went out to a new settlement on Titan. They were all the old body type, before we developed this pattern." With an almost smug pride, she indicated her own body, apparently unaware that it seemed grotesque to Lance. "They all had cybernetic replacement done, fifty or sixty years ago." She looked at the ring watch on her left middle finger. "Well, I'll see you in three hours, up in my office."

She turned and glided into the grav shaft.

Lance turned and strolled out through the foyer of the building, looking up at the high, luminous walls that swept into structures like the arches of a Gothic cathedral. As he walked along, he heard his name called.

"Hey, Lance! How the hell did you find your way here without me?"

He turned and found himself looking into the square, now aggressive face of Harry Green.

"Hi, Harry. Good to see you again."

"Never mind about that, mate. Looks as if I've been cut out of our deal. Let's talk. Over here'll do."

Green took him by the arm and drew him across to an alcove at the side of the foyer that seemed to give access to what appeared to be a combined restaurant and bar.

"Now," snarled Green. "Who the bloody hell brought you here?"

chapter
21

LANCE SAID NOTHING for a few seconds, while Green stood with his feet apart, his hot eyes widened like those of an angry dog, a tic pulsing in one tanned cheek.

"What difference does it make?" asked Lance. "*You* put them in touch with me. Who did you contact?"

"Don't give me that crap. I've only just found out where the bastards are located. I came here to set up an interview for you, and I find you already here. Look! We both know there could be a big deal in this, and you find your own way along. Thought you'd cut mug Harry out of the deal as soon as you had the smell of big money, did you?"

"Don't be a bloody idiot, Harry. Nothing like that. Listen, I still remember it was you who found me, brought me out of stasis. I won't forget that in a hurry."

"Yeah? Bullshit! You could make billions out of this. I can see the way you're thinking. Stuff Harry! If he kicks up too much, they'll deport him back to Earth, and you can forget him!"

"Listen, damn it! I told you *they* found *me*. Naturally, I assumed it was through you."

Green's eyes seemed to smolder. "Billions, this could be worth! We could both go home and never have to work again, unless we wanted to for kicks. You owe me something, mate. In fact, you owe me everything!" He slammed his fist against a wall.

Lance felt his own anger beginning to flare. "God damn it, man, use your head. It *must* have been you who told Karu Vorl about me."

"Karen who?"

"The historian woman."

"Not me, mate."

"Then it must have been one of your team."

Green hesitated. "Nah. They haven't been on Mars long enough to know their way around. They couldn't pull a stunt like that on me." He seemed to be reviewing the possibility. "Don't think so. Dunno."

"Listen," said Lance. "I think we could both do with a drink. We can get drinks from that automatic gizmo over there."

Green stood for a few seconds numbed by indecision. "Okay," he said at length. As they moved over to the dispenser, looking at pictures of filled glasses and inserting their cards into slots, Green said, "Trouble is, you can't get anything with a real kick in it around here. This mob think alcohol's what farmers use for tractor fuel."

They took their drinks over to a table, and Lance touched his glass against Green's. "Here's to our future billions," he said, and for the first time Green's face relaxed a little.

Lance's drink was horrible, stinging his tongue and leaving a taste like powdered chalk. It reminded him of the kava that Pang Mori had given him, so long ago.

"Look, Harry," he said suddenly, "I've already got enough clout here to get you on a program, if you want that. The man who found the tetrabrach hideaway. The man who rescued the guy from the past! I can take you to Karu Vorl." He glanced at his watch. "I'll be seeing her in a couple of hours."

Green hesitated, then shook his head. "I'll have to take a rain check on that. I've got to get back and stand over my team. If I'm not there, they stop work at the first problem."

"Well, perhaps we should wait until I'm better known in the organization," said Lance. "After a few sols."

The stinging in his mouth made him thirsty, and he raised his glass. "Mates again?" he asked.

"Guess so. Sorry if I blew my stack." Green looked at his watch. "I better get back. I'll keep in touch with you at your motel."

"Or here. I'll be at one place or the other, mostly."

"You know," said Green as they stood up. "I nearly didn't know you, cleaned up and in modern gear." He grinned unexpectedly. "See you, Lance. Damned if I know how they got on to you. Anyway, what the hell? It's working out all right."

After Green had hurried off, Lance went out of the foyer and began exploring the shopping arcades radiating from the building into verdant gardens. Some of the shops he passed carried eletronic equipment of bewildering variety and unfathomable purpose.

Ahead of him, as he strolled along a sidewalk with multicolored paving, a tall, dark young woman in metallic green strode out of one of the stores fifty meters off. She looked in Lance's direction once, then walked away.

A pulse thundered in his ears. He began to run, a sudden, irrational joy surging within him.

"Dorella!" he shouted.

Some of the people in the area turned to look at him, but not the dark-haired girl, who strode on with the same free, long-limbed movements.

"Dorella!" he called again as he ran. "It's me! Lance!"

Finally, when he was within a few paces of her, she turned. She looked no different from when he had last seen her, although she held her shoulders slightly higher, perhaps in unconscious imitation of the Martian girls. The magnificent hazel eyes had some makeup around them that made them appear even larger than he had remembered them, but they looked straight at him without a flicker of recognition.

"Dorella! You must remember me! Lance Garrith!"

She gave a little, puzzled shake of her head, her dark hair swinging about her shoulders. "My clone mother was called Dorella," she said, "but you couldn't possibly have known her. She's nearly a hundred and twenty years old. I'm Nerissa."

A great emptiness came to him. "How is she?"

"She's well, like all totally cybe people. She goes on forever."

"Cybe people?"

"Cybernetic." Her look of puzzlement abated as she seemed to find a possible solution. "You must be thinking of one of my clone sisters. I know we've never met. I'd remember."

She smiled with Dorella's smile, then went on her way, leaving him standing open-mouthed on the multi-colored sidewalk.

He walked slowly down the arcade to a spacious garden opening from the end of it. There were trees and bushes in it descended from Earth species, and other, unfamiliar plants that must have been the result of experiments in gene manipulation. A purple bird with a golden crest fluttered among the trees, trailing long tail plumes. So they manipulated birds, too, as well as plants and people.

With a sudden, immense weariness, he sat down on a bench

facing a small, ornamental lake with plants like strangely modified
willows drooping feathery blue foliage over its banks. There were
black waterlilies floating on the surface of the water, *black*, with
vivid red stamens. Bright insects darted above the water. Lance
looked at them with narrowed eyes, thinking of the miniature
surveillance machines that had once haunted him, but these were
simply dragonflies whose ancestors must have been brought from
Earth.

He was chilled by an abysmal loneliness. He was apparently
the only person in Argyre who had come here, via the suspended
animation techniques of Zon and Meiko, from a hundred Martian
years in the past. No one here knew him. Once, his name had
been well known all over the Earth. Here, it meant nothing. It
was understandable that the one person who showed any interest
in him now was a historian.

Someone—*not* Harry Green—had put them in touch with one
another. And the historian had turned out to be a clone of Heidi!

He held his hands against his throbbing temples. The coincidence was too bizarre to be believable.

"Must be going mad," he muttered aloud.

Although there was no one near him in the peaceful park, a
voice seemed to answer him. A faint, clear, slightly metallic voice
came from inside his head, against the back of his skull behind
the right ear.

It had been so unexpected that he didn't absorb what it actually
said. He looked wide-eyed across the small lake, at the drooping
blue trees that were not quite willows, at the widening ripples of
hidden fish, at the dragonflies zigzagging above the black and red
waterlilies. The lingering fear of miniature surveillance instruments was dispelled when two of the dragonflies mated on a lily
pad in front of him.

There was no one within hundreds of meters of him. Then the
voice came again.

"Welcome back, Lance. It's been a very long time."

He continued to stare across the lake and the garden, with the
sensation that icy water had been injected into his veins to replace
his blood.

"Jocasta!" he shouted. "You never give up, do you? Never in
a hundred years."

The unit against his skull transmitted her dry laughter.

"If you play it my way, Lance—*never in a thousand years.*"